The Lady's Guard

OTHER TITLES BY CHRISTI CALDWELL

Sinful Brides

The Rogue's Wager
The Scoundrel's Honor

The Theodosia Sword

Only for His Lady

Heart of a Scandal

In Need of a Knight
Schooling the Duke

Heart of a Duke

In Need of a Knight
For Love of the Duke
More Than a Duke
The Love of a Rogue
Loved by a Duke
To Love a Lord
The Heart of a Scoundrel
To Wed His Christmas Lady
To Trust a Rogue
The Lure of a Rake
To Woo a Widow

To Redeem a Rake
One Winter with a Baron
To Enchant a Wicked Duke

Lords of Honor

Seduced by a Lady's Heart
Captivated by a Lady's Charm
Rescued by a Lady's Love
Tempted by a Lady's Smile

Scandalous Seasons

Forever Betrothed, Never the Bride
Never Courted, Suddenly Wed
Always Proper, Suddenly Scandalous
Always a Rogue, Forever Her Love
A Marquess for Christmas
Once a Wallflower, at Last His Love

Danby

A Season of Hope
Winning a Lady's Heart

Brethren of the Lords

My Lady of Deception

Nonfiction

Uninterrupted Joy

The Lady's Guard

Christi CALDWELL

Montlake Romance

Text copyright © 2017 Christi Caldwell
All rights reserved.

Published by Montlake Romance, Seattle

www.apub.com

Amazon, the Amazon logo, and Montlake Romance are trademarks of Amazon.com, Inc., or its affiliates.

ISBN-13: 9781477848920
ISBN-10: 1477848924

Cover design by Michael Rehder

Cover photography by PeriodImages.com

Printed in the United States of America

To Rory
Every day I stand in awe of your resilience, courage,
and strength in the face of adversity. I am so very lucky
to be your mama.

Prologue

London, England
Spring 1822

Biting the inside of her cheek, Lady Diana Verney kept her gaze trained forward and continued walking.

She didn't want to be here.

It was not the stench of decay and death that hung heavy in the air that repelled her, but rather—fear.

As a pockmarked attendant led her through the wide corridors of Bedlam, silence reigned. Their footsteps echoed eerily off the white-washed walls.

There is nothing to be afraid of. It is not as though there are souls streaking these halls, wailing with their own madness . . .

An endless scream sounded from deep within the old hospital, kicking her heart into a frenzied rhythm. Diana quickened her steps, those rapid strides setting her skirts dancing wildly about her ankles. It spoke to the hell of this place that she'd take her chances with the burly guard against the distant sounds of agony pealing around the halls.

After a long, winding journey, the man stopped alongside a non-descript wood door, nicked and marked, showing its age. It was just a wood panel, and yet Diana stared at it, transfixed. How very different this slab of oak was from the ornate, carved doorways in her family's many residences.

"Ya've ten minutes, my lady," he ordered, bringing her back to the moment.

Ten minutes. Coward that she was, Diana didn't even want one minute.

And it did not have anything to do with the fact that if she was discovered in this very place, she would be ruined. Diana had been ruined long before this moment.

Nor was it fear for her reputation that kept Diana frozen.

It was an altogether different fear. One that could come only from catching a glimpse into your future. Given the one awaiting Diana, she wanted to flee. She wanted to run as far and as fast as her legs could carry her until the building, the woman inside, and all of it just faded to a distant memory that belonged to someone else.

Fingers shaking, Diana stuffed the handkerchief inside her cloak and pressed her palms against her skirts.

It is time.

Battling back her panic, Diana managed to nod once.

The servant pushed the door open, and immediately the scent of feces and urine slapped at her face, burning her nose. She gagged and yanked out a kerchief, pressing it to her nose.

The old guard chuckled.

She'll end up locked away . . . just like her mother . . . just like her mother.

Diana's fingers twitched with the need to clamp her hands over her ears and blot out those whispered words from gossips all over London.

It took a moment for Diana's eyes to adjust to the darkened space. Not a sconce or otherwise strategically placed candle lit the window-less cell.

"What do you want?"

That harsh voice, familiar and yet not, rasped around the cramped chambers. Diana searched for the owner of it. Her heart lurched.

Her mother, the once regal, proud duchess, sat in a corner of the small cell. With her knees drawn tight to her chest and hair hanging greasy and unkempt around her back, she bore no hint of the woman she'd once been.

The all-powerful, leading hostess of London had been reduced to this animalistic creature curled in the corner.

With fingers that shook, Diana pushed her hood back.

"Diana?" The duchess struggled to her feet and took a lurching step forward. She stumbled and then crawled over like a wounded dog.

Emotion clogged Diana's throat at seeing the shell she'd become. "M-Mother," she greeted, taking a hesitant step forward.

"Diana," the duchess whispered. The stench of sweat and her unwashed body filled Diana's nostrils. She choked on it, hating herself for noticing, hating herself for caring. In the safety of Diana's sheltered existence, it had been so very easy to hate her mother for her crimes. Only to find herself humbled and hurt by her mother's suffering.

"She came."

"Yes, Mother." Guilt and regret made those words come out hoarsened. She'd spent days working up the courage to come to this place. In the end she'd come because this was the woman who'd given her life and she'd owed her a visit. Now, seeing her again, sadness weighted that sense of obligation. Diana stretched a hand out, and her mother immediately slipped dirt-stained fingers into her own. She stared down at her mother's jagged nails. Her skin was coarse and callused against Diana's previously immaculate glove. The juxtaposition of hand and glove filled her with another wave of sorrow. How quickly a person went from living to . . . *this*.

"She is here," the duchess whispered. "She's returned."

Is this what a life of solitariness did to a person? Where one carried on as though speaking to oneself?

"I am here." Diana gave her hand a slight squeeze. "I'm sorry I did not come soon—"

"Are you a duchess?" her mother entreated, releasing Diana's hands. She grabbed her daughter. "Tell me you're a duchess." Ragged nails bit painfully through the fabric and into Diana's arms.

This is what she'd said?

The note smuggled from Bedlam into Diana's hands had not been a need to see her only daughter or to express regret or shame for what she'd done, but to probe Diana on her married state? A vicious pain stabbed at her breast. "Mother?" she asked cautiously. For the whole of Diana's life, her mother had hung to a hope that Diana would wed the Duke of Somerset's son and heir, Lord Westfield. She'd been so determined to see that match made, she'd tried to orchestrate the murder of Lord Westfield's true love—Diana's half sister. It had driven her outside these walls and by her questioning consumed her even within them.

"Lord Westfield," her mother said, with an eerie normality to her tone at odds with her vacant eyes.

"Mother," Diana said slowly. "Remember, Lord Westfield married Helena." *Please show remorse. Please demonstrate shame and horror and guilt for what you attempted to do.*

Her mother went as motionless as those macabre statues that lined the steps of the hospital. "Helena?" she parroted, as though she'd never before heard the name. The name of a woman she'd sold to a brute in the street and then tried to have killed by that same man years later. Her mother cocked her head at an unnatural angle. Then a mad glimmer lit her eyes. "But is she not dead?" the duchess whispered. She shot dirt-stained fingers out and gripped Diana hard by her cloak. Dragging her close with a surprising strength, Mother shook her. "Tell me she is dead. Tell me it was not for naught and that you are to be the future duchess. Then it will be all right. A debt paid."

Her stomach roiling with nausea, Diana wrenched away from the madwoman who'd given birth to her. She stumbled back, knocking against the thin metal bed with stained white sheets. "I am no duchess," she said on a breathless exhale. "Helena and Lord Westfield are married."

Her mother grabbed strands of hair and pulled. "No. No. No," she moaned and began to pace the cramped quarters. Then she whipped her head up. The seeds of her hatred and madness glimmered in her eyes. "Payment is due. Must pay. Must pay. Must pay." While the mad duchess muttered and mumbled to herself, Diana slinked slowly away.

She'd come here desperately hoping to see a scrap of good in her mother. Needing to see it. For both selfish and unselfish reasons. But there was no goodness left in her. Mayhap there never had been.

As she rambled on, Diana inched closer to the door, taking a step away. Away from this woman who'd given her life . . . and who'd also attempted to take away life. Two of them. Diana's half brother and half sister.

Diana gave a quick rap, welcoming the uncertainty posed by the guard who stood in wait over the madwoman now prattling and giggling to herself.

The door opened.

"Diana?" her mother cried, as Diana stepped out into the hall. She quickened her steps, not allowing herself to look back. Not allowing herself to look in the other cells that had been stirred to life.

Diana stumbled, tripping over herself in her bid for escape. Her body shook. *This is my future.* The pleading patients' screams rose, bloodcurdling and desperate. Diana's breath came in ragged little pants as she hurried onward to freedom.

Heart pounding in her ears, she sprinted down the steps. Holding her hood in place, she bolted across the street, her eyes fixed on the hackney that marked her path to freedom. She staggered to a stop.

Out of breath from her exertions, she drew great, heaping gasps of air into her lungs. Moments later her driver handed her up into the carriage, drawing her away from Bedlam and the horrors someday awaiting her there.

Diana let her head fall back on the squabs.

I am safe.

Chapter 1

Niall Marksman, the most lethal fighter in the Dials, hadn't come into his ruthless surname by coincidence.

A former guttersnipe turned proprietor, and head guard at the Hell and Sin Club, he had picked his name with the same methodical precision he had picked the pockets of fancy lords and ladies.

When one was the baseborn brat of a cheap London whore, whelped in the streets and turned over to a thug, one was afforded certain rights and responsibilities.

Picking one's name fell into the first category.

Shaping oneself into the merciless, unapologetic fighter of the underbelly fell into the latter.

Kill or be killed. These words, etched in his flesh and in his mind, had served as the basis of his rotted existence. That mark burned through the fabric of his Dupioni silk shirt.

Seated in the far corner of the Devil's Den, Niall made a show of drinking from his full tankard of ale. All the while he surveyed the enemy's surroundings. Niall was many things: a bastard. A former pickpocket and murderer. But he wasn't a fool. He knew better than to step inside the enemy's lair and sip his spirits. The pungent hint of vinegar burned his nose, speaking to the dregs who ran this hell. It also spoke to how vastly differently Niall and his brothers ruled their gaming empire at the Hell and Sin.

Niall scraped his gaze over the crowded hell, inventorying floors. His eyes missed nothing, from the lax guards, busy eyeing the prostitutes, to the deft-handed dealers skimming from the bottom of the decks. The lords who'd recently begun to frequent these hells were too in their cups and too arrogant to see they were being fleeced by the man whose establishment they frequented. And the guards were too damned stupid to see they'd allowed the enemy within their midst.

Even through the din of the club, a loud buzz went up.

Niall's every muscle thrummed to life. He worked his gaze over the floor. Searching, seeking. And then finding—*Broderick Killoran*. The ruthless enemy who'd nearly killed the wife of his brother, Ryker Black, and who'd infiltrated the Hell and Sin. A golden-haired devil, Killoran, in his vibrant green attire better suited to a fancy lord, strolled through his club, lifting his hand in greeting to his noble patrons, while bypassing the sailors and street toughs who'd built up his fortune.

A stinging hatred iced Niall's veins, and the fighter who lived inside him screamed to be set free. To storm the floors and tear the bastard apart. But as a street tough, Niall had been schooled on the valuable lesson of patience. So, he remained frozen, the brim of his hat pulled low over his face, as he watched Killoran's every move. The bastard's lazy steps were so full of cocksure arrogance, Niall grinned around the rim of his tankard.

He lay in wait until the moment Killoran started for the back entrance of his club. As soon as he'd passed, Niall set his drink down and came stealthily to his feet. "Lovely evening, is it not, Killoran?"

The proprietor spun around with a lack of finesse that would have earned him a caning at Diggory's savage hands. He felt a rush of satisfaction at the man's ashen hue.

Donning the same lethal smile he'd worn when he'd killed to survive, Niall touched his brim in greeting. "Killoran."

The owner of the Devil's Den briefly flicked his gaze about. Indecision raged in his eyes. Another baseborn brat reared by Mac Diggory, Killoran would appreciate how damaging this moment was. To have one's enemy slip inside so easily, for a confrontation, was a mark of a person's weakness. In a world where people looked to you for protection, one had to be above reproach.

Which I haven't been . . . First there had been the infiltration of the private suites, and then Penelope's almost murder. That tattoo on Niall's chest throbbed with the life lesson handed down.

Killoran quickly regained control of his emotions. The other man's lips formed a grim line. "Marksman." To falter only weakened one. It was a lesson this man would know. "Are things so dire at your own club that you'd seek out work here?"

Niall chuckled.

"What do you want?" Killoran demanded.

"I don't intend to have this conversation in the middle of your gaming floor with your henchmen about." Niall slipped his jacket open, revealing the gun at his fingertips.

Two street toughs born to darkness and mentored by the king of evil, they now wrestled for supremacy, and Niall would sell his already blackened soul to the Devil ten times over before he allowed this man to defeat him.

Kill or be killed . . .

It thundered around his mind as real now as when his mentor had first placed a dagger in Niall's hand and ordered him to murder. His insides knotted as he fought the pull of memories.

"Brodie! Where in blazes are you? I told you, you were needed abovestairs. Ophelia and Gert—oh, excuse me."

Both men looked to the bespectacled girl. The child couldn't be more than fourteen years. Slender as every last waif in the streets, the only thing that set her apart from St. Giles was the fine fabric of her satin gown. A gown that spoke to her elevated station inside this hell.

"Go abovestairs now, Cleo," Killoran said with a succinctness that roused a scowl from the girl.

Niall watched on as he was dealt the trump card.

Killoran noted Niall's focus and swiftly moved himself between Niall and the girl. Murder raged in his eyes. Of course, he wanted to end Niall. It was in their blood. It was part of the fabric of who they were and could not be divorced from their worthless lives.

But everyone had a vulnerability. The girl and the Devil's Den indicated *two* for Killoran.

Tension snapped off the proprietor's tall frame. "I'll join you shortly," he pledged.

"You said that before," she snapped. The odd girl jerked her chin at Niall. "Who is this?"

"Not now, Cleo."

An unspoken battle waged between the pair. In all her days, not even Helena had gone toe-to-toe with Ryker the way this girl silently dueled Killoran.

"Fine," she muttered. "But do hurry." With a final derisive glance for Niall, she marched off.

"You have five minutes." The rival owner started forward.

Did he believe Niall had been born yesterday? Slipping his pistol out, Niall closed the slight distance between him and Killoran and placed the head of the pistol against Killoran's back.

Killoran stiffened.

"No guards."

"I have better form than to kill you in my club," Killoran said tightly as he led them down a narrow hall lit by a handful of sconces. "It would be bad for my business."

They reached the office, and Killoran pressed the handle. Niall blinked to adjust to the darkened space and did a quick search for enemies. Shoving the proprietor between the shoulder blades, Niall propelled him forward.

Killoran cursed and turned back. The words withered on his lips at the gun Niall trained on his chest. With the heel of his boot, he kicked the door closed.

"I heard tales of your evil, Marksman," Killoran said as Niall locked them inside the room, "but I never heard mention of madness." Of course the man named Diggory's heir, the final apprentice he'd taken under his wing and made his second, would have been fed both truths and stories about Niall and his brothers.

Not taking his pistol from Killoran, Niall resumed his search of the room.

"You must have a death wish entering my club."

"Your men stabbed Penelope Black like a dog in the street," Niall spat. It was Niall who'd failed her, and for that, Ryker's wife had nearly paid with her life. A red blanket of rage descended over his eyes once more, momentarily blinding him.

Killoran flicked a speck of imagined dust from his sleeve. "I didn't touch Black's wife. None of my people did."

Kill or be killed . . . Kill or be killed.

Niall stalked over, and Killoran hastily backed away.

Niall felled him with a single blow to the nose.

The cur crumpled to the floor.

"That was for Black's wife." A move that was long overdue. Revenge should have been sought weeks earlier when Killoran's men had nearly ended Penny.

Rubbing his jaw, Killoran climbed to his feet with the ease of a gentleman greeting visitors in a fancy parlor. Yanking a pale-yellow kerchief from his jacket, he pressed it to his nose. The fabric immediately went crimson from the flow of blood.

The man before him threatened the hard-won security Niall and his siblings had scratched, clawed and, in Niall's case, murdered for. "If you come near my people again, I will find you," Niall pledged, jabbing his gun at him. "I will hunt you down and rip your entrails through your throat and then choke you with them."

To Killoran's credit, he gave no outward show to Niall's threat. The elegantly clad owner stuck a foot out. "If I'd intended to do the lady harm, she would have been slain that day in the streets." He spoke as casually as a gent discussing the weather or a wager.

Any other person would have felt a modicum of horror at that admission, but this ruthlessness was all Niall had ever dealt in. "Do you think I'm fool enough to believe a lie coated in sugared shite from your mouth?" he jeered.

The right corner of Killoran's lips quirked, but he said nothing.

Niall lowered his pistol. "Your men have entered our club."

"That I will take credit for," he said, touching an imagined brim.

A seething rage took root and grew. Niall fought to suppress his emotions.

Killoran smirked. "Yes, that was entirely me," he went on, sketching a mocking bow. "You see, your gang ended Diggory, and with the rules you play by, you'd expect . . . what? I should kill you, hmm? Black's wife?" He flicked a gaze over to Niall. "Your brothers? But I rule differently." He put his face in Niall's. "You'll pay for ending Diggory." The lethal threat was reflected in his brown eyes. "There are other ways to destroy a man. Ruin his marriage. His business. But murder?" He scoffed. "Why, that would allow a man an easy out for the crimes he's guilty of."

The crimes he was guilty of? Killoran's warped loyalty for a sadistic villain like Mac Diggory defied nature's logic. "Diggory was a dog," he spat.

White lines formed at the corners of Killoran's tense lips.

Exploiting that weakness, Niall continued to taunt. "If you didn't order Penelope Black's attack, the men you've inherited are less loyal than you credit." Niall pressed the mouth of his pistol to Killoran's head. Killoran swallowed loudly, and Niall took pleasure in that display of cowardice. "Let this serve as your warning, Killoran." He thumped a hand over his heart. "An eye for an eye." The mark etched in Niall's flesh by Diggory burned with the memory of a long-ago agony. They were words Killoran had beaten into every boy and girl to serve in his gang.

Killoran faltered and then his nostrils flared. "Get out."

Having once had his every movement dictated by another, Niall now reveled in control. "Remember what I said this night," Niall warned. Since Niall had escaped Diggory's clutches, he'd both beaten and threatened men over the years. However, every single act had been to protect and defend. It was a detail neither Killoran, nor any other man in St. Giles, could know. Not if Niall wished to retain his power. With a jeering grin, Niall backed away, keeping his gaze trained on the proprietor. One never presented one's back to the enemy.

Not if one hoped to live.

He had reached the door when Killoran called out. "Does Black know you've come?"

Niall stiffened. Ryker's softness of late came from his roots as a duke's illegitimate son. Niall, however, had nothing more than the blood of a whore and a nameless stranger running in his veins, and he wasn't subject to the norms that drove *civilized* society.

"I do not believe so." The other man stank of his own self-confidence.

But for the boys who'd wrestled him for supremacy when he'd been a boy, Niall wouldn't hurt a child. Nor did he intend to begin. Niall was not, however, above the threat of it. He held his pistol up, and Killoran went motionless. "I believe Cleo is waiting for you?"

Killoran turned white, and all further cocksure gibes were silenced. Holding his weapon close, Niall yanked open the door. He ducked his head out and searched. Finding it silent, he slipped from the room and then, with purposeful strides, rushed deeper into the hell.

Killoran's guards, standing sentry at the door, sprang to attention. Niall shot both elbows out simultaneously, crumpling the men. They landed in a noisy heap. Not breaking stride, Niall stepped around their prone frames and slipped into the empty kitchens. Picking up his pace, he rushed for the back door and then stepped outside.

Blood pumped through his veins the same as it had when he'd picked his first pocket, with the thrill of capture at war, and the thrill of surviving. He padded silently through the alley.

A boy stood in wait with the reins of his mount.

Sticking his weapon back in his waistband, Niall handed over a fat purse and then climbed astride Chance. He nudged the mount into a quick canter.

No honorable man would have entered a gaming hell and threatened another man at pistol point.

Kill or be killed . . .

It was the merciless way of their world. Ryker had forgotten. It was, however, a lesson ingrained into Niall by the gang leader who'd bought him and had him thieve and murder to grow his street power and wealth. Niall had sold his soul to survive long ago. He'd battle the Devil himself to protect his club and the employees and family dependent upon him. Even if that meant defying Ryker's new, misguided sense of honor.

Niall leaned over his mount, giving him room to stretch his legs.

He drew hard on the reins as he reached the front of the Hell and Sin. The facade was awash in candles' glow as patrons streamed through the front doors, a testament of the club's prosperity.

A servant clothed in black came forward to collect his reins.

"Marksman," the younger man greeted. His gaze touched on Niall's sweaty brow and bruised knuckles, but the man was wise enough to say nothing more.

Niall stalked up the front steps and stepped through the double doors that were thrown open by a liveried guard.

The smells, sounds, and sights of the Hell and Sin were familiar and welcoming. Home. And Niall would be damned if Killoran or anyone else shattered that. Moving into position on the sidelines of the gaming hell floor, Niall surveyed the club.

A tall figure stepped into his line of vision. His brother from the streets, one of the four proprietors of the hell, Adair Thorne eyed him suspiciously. "You're late." It was spoken as an observation more than anything.

"My meeting with the liquor distributor went long," he lied. Niall sharpened his gaze on a garishly clothed dandy in purple breeches, striding close to a faro table filled with drunken lords. "Has there been any trouble tonight?"

"None."

"It is coming," Niall said from the side of his mouth.

"You're worrying needlessly," Adair insisted. "Attendance is nearly back to the previous numbers," he pointed out.

Niall grunted noncommittally. Following Ryker Black's marriage to a lady of the *ton*, the number of their patrons *had* climbed. But numbers had nothing to do with danger. Two gentlemen now snared his attention. Hooding his lashes, he studied their exchange. They nodded periodically and gestured to a table.

Dandies were slurring fools and staggering drunkards. They were not, however, the coolly unaffected figures now sizing up the club.

"What is it?" Adair's hushed question reached through the din of the raucous activity at the hell.

Years of living on the streets had elevated Niall's senses. Just one mark of his skill as a fighter.

The two gents previously conversing scurried off. *There it is.* "Trouble," he said in a gravelly whisper.

A shout went up at the back of the club. "Cheat!"

Niall was already moving. "Be sure the private suites are secure," he ordered, and Adair sprinted off. Too many times in the past year, the private suites had been infiltrated. He'd not see them make the same mistake again. Niall surged forward, as the guests at the faro table erupted into a volatile explosion.

"Dishonorable to be angling for a man's cards," a young lord with greased blond curls shouted to the man seated at his left.

The other noble jumped to his feet. "By God, I'll face you at dawn." He knocked his opponent in the temple with a sloppy blow.

Even had the gent been armed with a knife and pistol, he wouldn't have survived a day in the Dials. Niall quickened his step. Not taking his gaze off the instigator in purple breeches, he lifted his left fist in a signal to Calum, another club owner, who was closest to the fray. Calum had long been the calm to Niall's ferocious temperament. From the corner of his eye, he detected the other man separating the nobles.

Fury pumped through Niall's veins. Even the inebriated patrons had sense enough to step out of his path. He made for the man who'd wrought chaos at the table. Niall, Ryker, Calum, Adair, and every employee here had sacrificed too much to see the dregs set upon them by a dead Mac Diggory destroy their empire. Gritting his teeth, Niall surged forward.

The shifty-eyed gentleman spied Niall and stumbled.

"Ya bloody whoreson," Niall hissed. Arms out, Niall launched himself at the new *patron.*

The man cried out, staggering back, but Niall's fist easily connected with his nose, felling him with a single blow.

Frenzied shouts sounded through the club, and with the thrum of the fight raging through him, Niall grabbed the dandy's neck. He hauled him up by his lapels. "Who sent you?" he demanded.

"R-release me," the blubbering lord cried.

"I asked who sent ya." He gave him a violent shake.

"By God, unhand me. I am an earl and a patron, and Lord Chatham will not take to your—" The man's warning ended on a swift exhale as Niall punched him hard in the belly.

"That is enough." The sharp command cut across Niall's haze of fury as Ryker Black captured his wrist, preventing another blow from landing.

A primal growl rumbled from Niall's chest, and he fought off the other man's hold. "This ivory turner was—"

"I said enough," Ryker uttered quietly, fury glinting in his eyes.

Niall's chest moved fast with the force of his exertions. Married not even two months ago, Ryker had once been the most ironfisted leader in St. Giles. Until he'd gone and married—a fancy miss, high on the instep. Niall liked Lady Penelope. Respected her. But Ryker's marriage to her had left the man weak in ways that put them all in peril. Niall wrenched his arm free.

"This man accosted me," the earl said, with a bolder confidence than before. He pressed a purple kerchief to his bloodied nose and glared over the scrap. "I took membership here only because I believed reports that your club was safe once more." *Once more.* And that was only after Diggory's men had wrought havoc here, orchestrating brawls that had sent their daily attendance into a decline.

Just as Diggory man had intended. Niall gnashed his teeth. Not deigning to look at the ugly blighter, he directed his words to Ryker. "He knocked into a toff at the faro tables." Niall motioned to the other fop responsible. "They attempted to start a brawl." And Niall would be goddamned if he allowed a cracksman from the Dials or a lord from the London ballrooms to enter this hallowed place and destroy it from within.

Ryker narrowed his gaze but otherwise gave no outward reaction to that reveal.

"Marksman, in my office," Ryker ordered, sending Niall's hackles up.

The other man might be majority owner of the hell, and a friend turned brother from the streets, but long ago Niall had bristled at directives. It was a resentment that had come from being beaten down like a dog by the man who'd reared him.

Ya answer to me, boy . . . Unless ya want a bullet in your belly, do it.

The loud report of a pistol echoed in his mind, and he flinched, coming swiftly back to the moment.

They locked in a silent battle, and, swallowing back a curse, Niall jerked his shoulder in a dismissive gesture and stalked off, leaving a trail of loud whispers in his wake.

A muscle jumped at the corner of his eye. Aye, to the bloody toffs who entered the Hell and Sin, their comfort mattered most.

But then, that self-centeredness should not astonish him. After all, he'd been an emaciated boy, starving in the streets, invisible to these same people. That truth had made him celebrate every pocket he'd nicked as a hateful, snarling lad. And it made it all the sweeter to collect the fortunes they now lost at his table, as a man.

Niall reached the back of the club, and the guard Oswyn inclined his head. "Mr. Marksman," the big, bald man greeted.

Niall lifted his head in slight acknowledgment. He stole a final glance over his shoulder in time to see Ryker ushering the dandy with a bloodied nose over to a table, setting him up with a bottle of brandy. A sound of disgust escaped him, and, shaking his head, Niall climbed the stairs to the private apartments and stomped down the hall. Ryker would cater to a man whose services could be bought. Free of scrutiny, Niall let loose a string of black curses. When had the other man become so bloody weak that he'd allow anyone seeking to ruin them a place at their tables?

He reached his brother's office and pressed the door handle, stepping inside the nauseatingly cheerful room. Niall flexed and relaxed his bruised knuckles as he took in the changes made to the once cluttered, now austere space. He gave his head another disgusted shake. Isn't that what had inevitably become of Ryker? After he'd killed Mac Diggory and saved a duke in the process, he'd become a hero to the Prince Regent and earned himself one of those hated titles.

As though summoned by the mere thought, footsteps sounded in the hall, and Niall stiffened. He turned, just as the door opened and his brother stepped inside. Again, the other man's slightly scarred face was set in a hard mask that revealed nothing, as he sought out his desk. "Sit."

Niall jutted his chin out. "Oi—"

"I said sit," Ryker bit out, claiming the chair behind the broad mahogany piece. Once sloppy and littered with ledgers and reports, the room had been put to rights by his brother's new wife. Not a book out of place, not a speck of dust on the furniture. The lady had exacted change not only on the objects in this hell but on the owner of it, as well.

Niall let his arms fall to his sides and, with stiff movements, claimed a seat. It was one thing to change your office. Quite another to shape yourself into someone altogether different.

Ryker propped his elbows on the surface and leaned forward. "I've already spoken to you. You cannot go about bloodying every single club member."

"He was working for Diggory's men." Niall answered with a confidence that came from knowing just how those vile thugs thought. People of the streets would pledge their loyalty to Satan himself, if it meant safety. That loyalty was honored in living and in death.

Ryker gave a slight shrug. "Mayhap."

That was all he'd say? Niall gritted his teeth. "Oi saw the exchange." Fury had made him slip back into his Cockney.

"I don't doubt it." The other man, impossibly cool, leaned back in his seat. He layered his palms on the arms of his chair. "But they are noblemen. By their birthright and their place in this club, they are afforded protections." It was the way of their world. As a boy that truth had grated. It had kindled a burning hatred for those pompous lords and ladies who cared for nothing and no one but their own pleasures, until his loathing had spread through him.

"Oi won't have a man at me tables who's out to ruin us."

"We don't have a choice," Ryker said with a blunt matter-of-factness that set Niall's teeth on edge. Equally driven and ruthless, they'd never see eye to eye over leniency with the nobles who visited their hell. "The Earl of Dunwithy is in deep." Ryker pushed back. "He's a man in need of coin. Those men can be bought." All men could be bought. "Those men also spend at our tables, and we cannot afford to beat down a nobleman for the message that sends." Ryker leaned forward. "Are we clear?"

Silence stretched on, punctuated by the ticking clock. Since he'd been a boy of four or five battling an older, bigger lad for the scraps in the street, Niall had never backed down. And yet, not only was Ryker majority proprietor, he was also the man who'd saved Niall's worthless skin. "We are clear," he bit out. "I'm returning to the floor." Niall shoved back his chair, and it scraped noisily along the wood floor.

"You are relieved for the night." His brother climbed to his feet.

"I'm not tired." He forced those words out in the perfectly cultured tones he'd practiced. The ones he dragged out when he was demonstrating his calm. Those and the fancy garments he donned were the concessions he'd made to the peerage.

Ryker folded his arms at his chest and studied him through black lashes. "This isn't about whether you're tired. Where were you earlier?"

At that abrupt shift, Niall remained unblinking. Christ. He couldn't know. "I paid a surprise visit to our liquor supplier." Their latest one, who'd also begun sending them broken bottles.

Ryker eyed him for a long while and then nodded slowly. "You're relieved for the night."

A protest sprang to Niall's lips.

Ryker leaned forward. "Nor am I asking you to quit your post for the evening. I'm telling you. Your head isn't clear."

It hadn't been clear since Ryker's wife had nearly died under Niall's watch. At that remembered failing, he clenched his jaw. Still, he'd make no apologies for his volatile temper. Not against a fancy toff who'd deserved more than a bloodied nose. "Is that all, *my lord?*" he asked tauntingly, dragging out the courtesy title that had been bestowed upon the other man for saving the now Duke of Somerset from Diggory.

Except Ryker, unflappable as he always was, even with marriage, didn't rise to the bait. He merely inclined his head. "No, that isn't all. Your temper is creating problems here, Niall. The moment we four entered this hell, we made a pact that this club came before all else," Ryker continued somberly.

Niall's entire body coiled tight, as tension thrummed through him. His brother would call into question his actions at the club?

"I put this club before all else," he gritted out. Nothing mattered more than the Hell and Sin. It had become the only home he'd known and the security he'd once thought impossible to attain.

"No," Ryker said calmly. "You put our reputation *above all else.* So much so that you'd defend it, jeopardizing our success."

Niall met that quiet pronouncement with a stony silence. His brother may have forgotten key codes of the street, but Niall had not. A man's word and honor came before everything else. Allowing a person to call that honor into question cut the legs out from under a man with greater lethality than the sharpest blade.

Tamping down a curse, Niall sketched a mocking bow and started for the door.

"Niall?"

He paused and glanced back.

"You don't have anything to prove. Mistakes happen."

Not in their world. There was no place for mistakes. Nor was Niall's inability to ferret out who'd infiltrated their club for the better part of a year a mistake. It was a failing. Penelope's near murder while under his watch was a failing.

Forcing his head to move in a tight nod, he left the room and made his way through the halls. Niall reached the back of the club and waved off the guard at the exit. Fishing out a cheroot, he touched the tip to a sconce. Niall pushed the door open with his spare hand and stepped outside.

Setting his back to the building wall, he folded one arm across his chest and proceeded to smoke. He allowed it to fill his lungs and exhaled. The smoke hung in the darkened space.

Distant shouting and the occasional rumble of carriage wheels—familiar sounds—drove back some of the tension boiling under the surface of his taut frame. *This* was his world. *This* was where he was safe. Where he belonged. These streets he'd been born to, where whores, rapists, and murderers ruled and where the weak perished.

As boys, when Calum and Adair had spoken of a life outside St. Giles, Niall had allowed them that foolish musing. Eventually, however, he'd come to believe it. His lips turned up in a sneer. What a bloody fool he'd been. That veneer of civility may have earned them a successful hell, but it had also marked them as weak to the lords of London's underbelly. The threats on their club and Ryker's wife had proven the folly in that facade. You could dress a man in fancy garb and teach him to speak like a gent, but you could never erase whom a man truly was. As such, Niall had dropped his false smile and presented instead the merciless man who'd once killed for coin.

Men like Calum, Adair, and him didn't belong anywhere but here. For the danger that dwelled and lurked, these streets were safer because of Niall's understanding and mastery of them.

Niall took another pull from his cheroot, and with his gaze did a sweep of the always dangerous alleys. Ultimately, Niall Marksman was a bastard born of the streets and destined to die here.

And he'd have it no other way.

Chapter 2

They said Diana was mad.

They said evil flowed through her veins, and the only future awaiting her was the halls of Bedlam.

Never were those whisperings of insanity truer than they were in this moment.

The carriage door opened, and Diana jumped as the wiry-thin driver jammed his head inside. "Oi said this is your stop."

Seated on the torn, threadbare squabs of the hired hack, Diana nervously darted her tongue over her lips. *Already?* With shaking fingers, she tugged the curtains aside.

The moon splashed a white glow on the streets of St. Giles. Unpredictable streets. Dangerous ones that no person, especially not a duke's daughter such as herself, should ever know. And yet, a year ago, she'd witnessed the hellish peril that came in walking these pavements. She lowered the tattered fabric back into place.

"This isn't my stop," she said, deepening her voice. Hers was across the street and three buildings away. Such a distance would not mean much in Mayfair. But this was certainly not Mayfair.

The driver waved his hand. "Oi said it is, boy." *Boy.* Diana dropped her gaze, and heat flooded her cheeks. Apparently her disguise, borrowed from one of the stable lads, had proven far less flimsy than she'd feared. How very different a *boy* in threadbare garments was treated from a lady in a velvet cloak and deep hood. Giving silent thanks for the cover of darkness, she pulled her cap lower.

Drawing on the limited—very limited—exposure she'd had, she mimicked the driver's coarse speech pattern. "Oi ain't getting out. Ya said ya'd bring me to the Hell and Sin Club." She stole another look outside and squinted. "And this ain't it." On most occasions, she'd have sooner sliced off her fingers than take a jaunt through St. Giles. This, however, was not most occasions. As such, she'd step out into these streets, but on her own terms.

With a growl, the driver ducked farther inside the carriage. "Ya already paid."

First streetwise mistake. Diana cursed her too-late error. Her brother and sister born in the Dials would never commit that folly.

Diana dug her heels in. "I'm not getting out until you do what you were paid to do." Society might see her as a pampered duke's daughter on her way to madness, but she was no coward.

He reached inside. "Oi said out, or Oi'll do it for ya. Oi've more customers to collect."

Diana caught the inside of her cheek between her teeth. The weight of the coin in the pocket of her breeches fairly burned her. To brandish the small fortune before this man would be as wise as taking tea with the Devil.

"Something wrong with your hearing, boy? Oi said out."

"Only thing wrong with either of us is your manners," she spat. Tamping down a curse, she glared. "Out of me way," she growled, shoving past him.

She leapt to the ground and staggered, then quickly righted herself. The driver scrambled back onto his perch and then sprang his conveyance forward.

Gasping, she stumbled away from the hack and stepped out into the street. Into the path of a fast-galloping horse.

Stomach lurching, she jolted sideways and came down hard on the cobblestones. Pain radiated up her hip, and Diana winced. She searched about for another hack, but alas the time for abandoning her plans had passed. She could not have risked putting down onto paper the words that she needed to relay. Yes, she'd crafted this plan, and she'd see it through. Shifting her cap back into place, Diana hopped to her feet. She found the beacon across the street. Awash in candles' glow, the most notorious gaming hell in London beckoned.

Her brother's establishment.

Or, if one wished to be precise, her half brother.

Diana, however, had long believed blood was blood, and regardless of how much was shared, the key was that it was shared. He was kin.

Even if he does despise you . . . even if he wants nothing to do with you.

That truth had been evidenced in his failure to come 'round, invite her to his wedding, and . . . well, all host of indicators. But she needed him.

What would her father have done had she gone to him again with fears that someone, intending Diana harm, had entered their home? The same thing he'd done when she'd expressed her worries over the twice-broken axles. He'd have seen those worries as a mark of her madness. A daughter seeing ghosts in the shadows, as he'd said that first and final time they'd spoken of it.

"Hello, lad. Wanta earn some coinnn." That slurred offering slashed across her inopportune musings, and she swiveled her head sideways. A gentleman in a sapphire cloak stumbled closer. A feral grin split his face, and his pearl-white teeth gleamed bright.

Surprise slammed into her. The Earl of Stone? Of course, she knew lords frequented these streets and visited these hells, and yet there was something astounding in his presence here. He was a gentleman who'd once danced attendance on her, but who'd abandoned all pursuits, like so many others, when the truth of her family's madness came to light. He was . . .

"Come on, boyyy," he cajoled, coming closer. He fiddled with the front of his breeches.

By God, he was attempting to . . . seduce a *boy*? Fear turned in her belly. Fingers shaking, she pulled the fish knife she'd pilfered from the evening meal out of her boot. With the small but reassuring weight of it in her hand, she neatly sidestepped the earl. Heart crashing against her rib cage, Diana bolted across the street.

She sprinted over the cobbles, avoiding the throngs of gentlemen making for the club. St. Giles was a place where humanity ceased to exist. That mocking truth echoing around her mind, she made a beeline for the narrow alley between the Hell and Sin Club and a neighboring establishment.

Was this world any less ruthless than the one she belonged to? Chest heaving, she staggered to a stop. She darted a last look about for a hint of the loathsome Lord Stone. Preferring the unknown demons that lurked down the dark aisle, she ducked between the adjacent buildings.

With the inky black of the night an eerie shroud, Diana pressed her back against the building and allowed her heart to slow its frantic rhythm. *You have done this before . . . visited these streets. And you're intending to leave London on your own at the end of the Season.* Six weeks, to be precise. *This should be nothing.* Those silent reminders proved futile. After all, she'd once visited this end of London in the very light of day and witnessed firsthand the dangers of it. What greater evil lurked at night? Fueled by that reminder, she crept farther along. The leather soles of her boots muted her footfalls as she continued her trek. Her foot sank in a deep puddle, and the icy chill rang a gasp from her.

Lifting her foot from the ankle-deep water, she picked her way over the sludge and pressed ahead. *This is madness.* Of course, that evidential truth merely proved every last whispered word about her true. Whispered words and oftentimes not so quietly spoken tales told of her and her family. Then, it was not every day a duchess ordered the death of her husband's illegitimate children.

As such, there was hardly any escape to the claims and worries of Diana's own sanity. Nonetheless, madness was sometimes merited. This was one of those times.

From somewhere in the distance, a faint cry went up, followed by the retort of a pistol, and her heart kicked up a frantic rhythm. Diana tightened her grip on the knife in her hand. *I am going to die here.* Which was rather ironic given that the sole reason for being in these dank streets of St. Giles was to prevent the whole dying business.

Diana had never been a dramatic sort. She'd had accomplished governesses and nursemaids, all of whom had schooled her on deportment.

Those lessons had been further ingrained into her by her mother, the Duchess of Wilkinson, when she'd been near. Which hadn't truly been until Diana was reaching her Come Out and of use in the marriage-making department.

It was why it took not one, not two, but three attempts before she came to the realization—someone was trying to kill her.

"You're going to see the task done for them," she muttered under her breath. Pressing herself closer to the hard building, she crept farther down the alley. Her foot sank into another puddle, and she winced.

A shout went up, followed by the rumble of ribald laughter and a slurred exchange between strangers out on the street. Diana bit her lower lip.

Think of painting and the island of St. George's and . . . living. Think of living.

Something scurried across her feet. Gasping, she jumped away from the wall. A faint, raspy breathing filled the alley, and Diana whipped her gaze about just as something jammed against the back of her leg. Terror skittered along her spine, and, wielding her knife before her, she slashed a path forward.

An immense figure stepped out of the shadows into Diana's path, tearing a cry from her lips. *For all my efforts, I'm going to die here, anyway.* The thick shroud of darkness shielded his features. He reached for her, and she cried out. Bringing her arm back, she thrust her knife at him. He swatted her hand. Diana's blade grazed the side of his leg.

She may as well have stabbed him with a feather. The massive giant grunted, yanked the knife from her fingers, and tossed it to the ground. Fear held her petrified as that weapon clattered in the empty alley.

Run.

Diana turned on her heel, but a powerful arm immediately wrapped around her waist. Had the hulking beast shouted threats and brandished his own weapon, it couldn't be more terrifying than his absolute silence. "P-please," she rasped out. Merciless, he drove her stomach against the wall of the building. The force of that movement pushed all the air from her lungs.

"Who are ya?" he demanded in a guttural Cockney, and through the haze of terror there was a faint familiarity.

She angled her head back over her shoulder. It had been more than a year since she'd heard that voice, but through her fear, she caught the crooked nose, broken far too many times to ever mark the man as handsome. But it was his eyes that held her motionless. A shade of deep sapphire, so dark they were nearly black. Niall Marksman. The man whose arms she'd run into a year earlier, when she'd sought help for her sister, Helena. In those immediate days and months after his intervention, she'd wondered after the fierce, laconic guard who'd plucked her from harm, until, with the passage of time, it was as though she'd merely dreamt of him and his heroic intervention that day. Surely he remembered—

He spun her around to face him. Relief assailed her. *He recognizes me.* She slid her eyes closed. Her relief died a quick death. Niall jammed his forearm against her throat, cutting off airflow. Panic spiraled in her belly. There could be no mistaking he was very much real and very close to ending her.

The harsh, angular planes of his heavily scarred face set in an unforgiving mask while the vicious scar at the corner of his mouth that ran down to his neck proved him wholly unlike any of the gentlemen who'd once sought to court her.

The jagged white scar throbbed at the corner of his lips. "Oi asked who ya are, boy," he seethed.

Diana fought to push words out, but his ruthless hold squeezed off all airflow. She scrabbled with an arm that may as well have been carved of granite. Her efforts proved futile. Stars dotted her vision, and he shifted his arm slightly. She sucked in great, gasping breaths.

"I'll not ask ya a third time." His voice emerged as a low growl, better fitting a primitive beast than a mere man. He caught her by the forearms, giving a slight shake, and the pins holding her cap in place loosened, tipping sideways.

The long, tightly wound braid tumbled down past her shoulders in a damning testament. "L-Lady Diana Verney," she managed to get out through her ravaged throat, and collapsed against the wall. She sucked air into her aching lungs.

Incredulity registered in the dark depths of his cobalt eyes.

A gentleman of the *ton* would be ashen-faced with horror at nearly ending a duke's daughter in a St. Giles alley. Then, Niall

Marksman was not most men. In one fluid movement, he bent, retrieved her hat, and then straightened. "By God, ya didn't learn your lesson the first time ya were here?" he growled, jamming the article back on her head.

Nearly witnessing her sister's death? Running into a crowded gaming hell and having her reputation then shredded? Yes, she well knew what came in visiting St. Giles. Limbs still shaking with her latest brush with death, she forced her head to move in a semblance of a shake. "I need—"

"Drop your goddamned voice. Why were ya running?" He was already searching over her shoulder.

As her terror receded, embarrassment trickled in to take its place. She'd imagined monsters in the shadows. Diana massaged the sore muscles at her throat, loath to admit that mortifying fact. He singed her with a look that demanded answers. "Something startled me."

Just then, a faint whine punctuated the end of that admission, and as one, they looked down. She flared her eyebrows.

A dog?

The mangy pup with a coat covered in grime growled back.

That is what had pressed against her leg. Certainly not a monster. Not even a blasted rodent.

Feeling Niall Marksman's mocking gaze on her, Diana dropped her arm back to her side. So, she'd been startled by a dog—this time. That in mind, she searched around for her knife and stooped to retrieve it from a muddied puddle. Her gaze went to the emaciated wolflike creature eyeing her. Poor thing. To calm her frayed nerves, she reached out a hand to stroke his greasy coat.

"Are ya mad, princess?" Niall hissed, jerking her hand back, loosening her grip on the knife. At that sudden movement, the dog slunk off, leaving Diana alone with the equally snarling man. Gathering her by the wrist, he proceeded to drag her down the alley.

She dug her boots in, forcing him to stop or pull her to the ground. He stitched his dark eyebrows into a line.

"My knife," she blurted.

He peered at her.

Diana gestured to the instrument.

Mr. Marksman muttered something under his breath that sounded a good deal like "Madder than a Bedlamite streaking the halls of the hospital."

"That isn't a knife," he said.

He'd called her mad not once but twice. That charge was tossed out casually. It was grating, a reminder of her blood. "Then you're a lackwit if you don't realize it is a knife."

The guard thinned his eyes into narrow slits; those sapphire irises darkened to a near obsidian. Diana wet her lips as unease skittered along her spine. What did she really know about the man, after all? The head guard at the entrance of her brother's gaming hell, who, by his forceful grip, could snap a person's neck with a mere flick of his hand. And none would be any wiser.

With a mocking chuckle, he turned her weapon back over. Had he followed the path her thoughts had wandered? *Do not be a coward. He sees you as an impulsive child visiting a place you have no place visiting and as scared of a dog.* She jutted her chin up a notch, and this time when she spoke, she took care to adopt the hushed tones he'd used earlier. "I'm here to see my brother."

"Your brother?" he asked with a sardonic twist of his lips that made a mockery of those two words. She was nothing to the recently titled Viscount Chatham. *I am nothing to anyone.* A pawn for her now imprisoned mother. An afterthought for a father who'd never cared for or loved her mother.

She thrust aside the useless self-pitying. All these men and their twisted sense of family could go sup with Satan. "Yes. Mr. Black," she said, sticking out her leg and planting her hands upon her hips. "Your employer."

"Ya think he's my employer?" No person could ever mistake the humor lacing those words as anything of real amusement. Harsh. Mocking. Disdainful. All rolled together to rattle her once more.

She tugged at the fabric of her breeches. An unsettling thought slid forward, and she inched sideways. "Has he sacked you?"

"Oi'm one of the proprietors."

She opened her mouth and closed it. "Indeed?" Odd, she'd not known Ryker Black had partners. It just highlighted even more how little she knew of the man who shared her blood. Why *should* he help her?

Mr. Marksman raked a condescending stare over her person. The kind of stare belonging to a man who'd assessed her and found her wanting, in a look that had become all too familiar in Society. "Ya think only a duke's by-blow capable of running an establishment?"

Given the fact she stood in the middle of an alley, in a boy's attire, it was farcical to be discussing social snobbery with this man. And yet his icy derision struck painfully. Diana curled her hands. The *ton . . . all* of Society had only ever seen a duke's daughter. Now, they saw a duke's mad daughter. As such, this man's ill opinion should not matter, but the lowly thoughts stung still. He could go to the Devil alongside the lot of them. Ignoring his question, she started past him.

She made it two steps.

Mr. Marksman planted himself before her, and she gasped, her mouth going dry. The gentlemen she'd had the misfortune of seeing in Polite Society were pathetic, pale shadows of this life-hardened warrior. Broadly muscled, more than a foot taller than her own five-feet-three-inch frame, and yet he moved with the speed and stealth of a chimney sweep she'd once seen darting over the roofs of Mayfair town houses late one evening. He did a quick sweep of her, his eyes lingering on her breech-encased thighs.

Diana warmed under that scrutiny, but when he met her gaze, not a hint of emotion shone from within those nearly obsidian irises. He shot out an arm, and she recoiled. His lips formed another contemptuous grin. "After you, *princess.*"

She fisted her hands. God, how she despised that moniker. That jeering taunt of a man who'd condemn her for her birthright. Just as other men had condemned her, for altogether different reasons. Well, if she'd had other options, she'd certainly not be here now. But she had none but to humble herself before Ryker Black.

Holding her head high, she marched forward.

Chapter 3

Of all people to be caught sneaking outside his club, it was Ryker's damned half sister. The privileged chit, born with a silver spoon in her mouth.

Following close behind Lady Diana, Niall gave his head a disgusted shake. The woman carefully picked her way over refuse and muddied puddles as though performing the intricate steps of those silly ballroom dances.

The bloody nobility and their sense of privilege.

The lords who lost their fortunes at the tables of the Hell and Sin, and the ladies in those posh Mayfair residences left behind while they pursued their pleasures, all believed the world was their due.

His gaze involuntarily dipped to the back-and-forth sway of her generously curved buttocks encased in tight-fitting breeches. He lingered on her rounded hips and shapely legs befitting a woman accustomed to riding.

He grunted. Mayhap, not precisely like all the other ladies of the *ton*, in their fancy gowns. After all, how many of them would don a pair of tight-fitting breeches, brandish a fish knife, and sneak through the alleys of St. Giles?

He clenched his jaw. This was the second time that this same impulsive creature had come. Granted, the first she'd been accompanying her sister, Helena, but now she had taken to donning boys' garments and prancing around St. Giles alone.

The bloody twit would get herself killed.

Lady Diana faltered and then quickly righted herself. Neck heating, Niall ripped his gaze away from her lush form. He'd be damned if he lusted after, appreciated, or had any dealings with a bloody lady.

They reached the doorway all deliveries came through. Reaching past her, he pressed the handle.

The lady hesitated, peered inside a long moment, and then looked up. Wariness seeped from her expressive blue eyes. Eyes that revealed all and concealed nothing. She was afraid. A boy, born of the streets, who'd sold his soul to simply exist, recognized that emotion better than he did any other. He'd too often used such fear to make himself stronger. "A little late now for reservations, princess," he taunted.

"I do not have r-reservations." That slight tremor made a liar of her. Then, with the regality befitting the princess he named her, she stepped inside.

The distant din on the club floor filled the corridor, a mark of the evening's success. Yes, patrons had returned. He steeled his jaw and glanced down at the golden hair of the braid hanging down her back. The last time a lady had been caught with one of their ilk, the hell had almost been brought to its knees. What would members think of a duke's daughter, dressed like a boy, in Niall's *less worthy* presence?

"Follow me," he ordered crisply and, not bothering to glance back, started up the stairs ahead of her. He registered the quick scurry of her booted footfalls as she climbed behind him.

"I—"

"Not a word," he bit out.

"Because I'm a woman," she snapped, bringing him to a quick stop. With several steps between them, he towered over her. Squarely meeting his gaze with a directness even he would be hard-pressed not to admire, Lady Diana scrambled to keep up. She paused at the step below his.

"Oi don't have a problem with women," he said curtly, giving her more explanation than her accusation merited. Lady Diana's eyes softened, and he swallowed a curse. "Wot Oi do have a problem with is ladies." He fixed a glower on her. "Particularly with bored ones who'd come in here and threaten my club." Jerking his attention forward, he finished the climb, waiting for her to reach the main landing.

Lady Diana clasped and unclasped her long, unblemished fingers before her. "It is not my intention to threaten . . ." At his pointed look, her words trailed off.

Niall ducked his head into the hallway of the main suites. He motioned her forward. The lady hesitated and then fell into step beside him. They moved along the corridor at a brisk clip, with Lady Diana stretching her smaller strides to match his. As Niall and Ryker's half sister walked, he skimmed his gaze over the floors.

Whether or not Ryker wished to deal with the truth, Killoran intended to topple their empire. The Duke of Wilkinson's daughter strolling the halls of the Hell and Sin was just the morsel of gossip that a wolf like Killoran would devour and then spit out and feed to the *ton*.

Niall suppressed a growl.

If the lady were discovered here, the club would never recover. Not again. The nobility had no qualms about tossing coins down at their tables and wagering away their fortunes. Those same lords, however, would never countenance four orphans, raised in the streets, brushing shoulders with their women.

Ryker had earned himself the title of viscount for saving his brother-in-law, the Duke of Somerset's, life. As such, a titled lord, even a by-blow, could be forgiven certain affronts.

Men like Niall, Adair, and Calum would be sent to Hell over even a hint of a dalliance with a lady.

They reached Ryker's office. Niall thumped on the door.

At his side, Lady Diana shifted back and forth on her feet. Her nervousness radiated from her slender frame.

He knocked again. Empty. Niall dug out his watch fob and squinted in the dark to bring the numbers into focus. At this hour his brother often sought out his office, but with the crush of patrons and the earlier fight, he'd likely remained on the floors. Niall stuffed the piece back in his pocket.

"He'll see me, won't he?" the lady blurted.

Something had brought the reckless miss here. Most men might feel curiosity, or seek to calm the girl. Niall, however, had been born with an edge of roughness and felt nothing—for anyone.

Ignoring her panicked query, he pushed open the door and jammed his finger at the upholstered seat recently brought in by Penelope when she'd decorated Ryker's office. "Sit."

She remained fixed to the floor, brow furrowed, while she studied that chair. Footsteps sounded down the hall, and, swallowing a curse, Niall shoved her between the shoulder blades, propelling her forward. He quickly yanked the door closed and looked up.

Calum stood several feet away. The second in command at the hell, Calum possessed self-control Niall had striven the whole of his life to master. Suspicion glinted in the other man's eyes. "What happened to your leg?"

His leg?

Niall followed the other man's gaze downward and creased his brow. A wet stain marred the sapphire breeches, that crimson hue turning the fabric black. By God, she'd stabbed him. The bloody chit had actually drawn blood with that pathetic weapon. His neck heated. He whipped out a kerchief from his jacket and pressed the white fabric against his thigh. "Oi'm fine," he muttered. He'd sooner lose the leg to infection than admit he'd been maimed by a lady with a fish knife.

"Get Ryker." He nudged his chin at the door. "He's got company."

The other man's shoulders grew taut. "Company?"

"Lurking in the alley." The last time that had happened, Ryker had ended up married.

Calum cast another glance at the office. "Ryker doesn't like surprises."

Glowering, Niall put pressure to the crimson-stained fabric at his leg. "And Oi don't like being sent from the floors like a child."

Calum snorted. Then, turning on his heel, he stalked off. Calum gone, Niall returned his attention to the rapidly spreading stain.

The lady had better have a damned good reason for infiltrating his club—again. Regardless of her connection to Ryker and Helena, Lady Diana was a duke's daughter, a step shy of royalty. Niall turned a glare on the wood panel between him and that flawless English princess. Those self-absorbed peers could never be trusted.

Ever.

She'd been instructed to sit.

She'd been ordered not to touch anything and to remain in the indicated chair like an obedient pup. Or a well-mannered English lady. In this stilted society to which she belonged, it was really all the same.

At one time, she'd have followed those very directives issued by the menacing guard, who, with his tousled, too-long, midnight hair, had the look of a dark angel, cast out the gates of paradise. Her heart pounded hard. A man more ruggedly beautiful than any gentleman of London Society.

"Do not be silly," she muttered under her breath and gave her head a clearing shake. A year ago, saved from peril by that same man, she'd briefly lifted him upon the pedestal where young girls exalted brave, fearless men who plucked them from danger.

But she was no longer that romantic, demure daughter all English lords and ladies aspired to raise.

Disregarding that plush, upholstered chair, Diana attended the whole of the tidy, elaborate space. Welcoming the distraction, she tipped her head. How very . . . peculiar. When she'd rushed inside the club, the crimson carpets and heavy, dark gaming tables had exuded sin and wickedness. Yet Ryker Black's office, with its broad mahogany desk and floral paintings, was better suited to an elegant Mayfair residence than the most perilous streets in London.

Restless, Diana wandered over to a rose-inlaid table and set her knife down beside a delicate vase with white-and-pink peonies. Mesmerized, she picked up the porcelain piece. She ran the tip of her finger over the couple painted upon the creamy white porcelain; that enrapt loving pair, twined in each other's embrace. She briefly closed her eyes and raised the blooms to her nose, inhaling deeply their fortifying scent. With her eyes shut, she could almost imagine she was any young lady other than the whispered-about, maybe more than half-mad woman.

Mr. Marksman stepped into the room, his broad, powerful frame filling the doorway. "Wot are ya doing?" That raspy baritone rumbled over her shoulder, startling a gasp from her.

The vase slipped from her fingers, sailed to the floor, and exploded in a spray of glass and pink-and-white peonies. She'd not even heard him. How did a man of his sheer size and strength move with such stealth?

He scowled.

Diana swiveled her gaze between the shards of glass littering the wood floor and the sad array of flowers. She dropped to her knees and made to start cleaning the mess. It wouldn't do to begin a meeting with Mr. Black after destroying his property.

"Leave it," Mr. Marksman barked, and she faltered, nearly stumbling backward.

Diana hurriedly righted herself. "I—"

"Oi ordered ya not to touch anything," he snapped.

She drew in a steadying breath. *Don't be intimidated by him. Just because he's the head guard in this London underworld and nearly killed you, he . . .* Oh, blast, she'd be a lackwit not to fear him. Nonetheless, for all his condescension, she'd braved these streets once before, and she'd not be threatened by Niall Marksman. "No, Mr. Marksman," she said carefully, in the crisp, polished tones her nursemaids and governesses had ingrained in her since she'd been a babe in the cradle. "You advised me to sit." Diana paused. "Like a dog." His slashing black eyebrows dipped, and the menacing glint in his dark eyes momentarily knocked her off-kilter. Before her courage deserted her, she continued on in a rush. "And I assure you, I'll not be ordered about by you or a-anyone." That faint tremble ruined her bold retort. A man who'd wrestle an unknown someone against the alley walls outside would take umbrage with being challenged. Particularly by a lady.

Yet, Mr. Marksman angled his body in a coolly dismissive manner, flummoxing her.

Diana squinted in the dimly lit room and then crept forward. Her eyes remained riveted on his leg. Then she stopped abruptly and slammed a palm against her mouth. "My God."

He wheeled to face her.

"I stabbed you," she whispered. Nausea churned in her belly. "You're bleeding." Previously preoccupied with an alternating fear of the laconic guard and a silent appreciation for his chiseled features, she now took in the details that had escaped her a short while ago.

A hard grin lifted his lips. "Queasy, princess?"

Ignoring his question, Diana looked frantically about. She couldn't very well go ripping up any of Mr. Black's fabrics. She'd already destroyed his vase. Hurriedly shrugging out of her jacket, she raced forward.

He shot his dark eyebrows to his hairline. "Wot in bloody hell—"

Blasted gentlemen and their unwillingness to take help. "You're hurt." And she'd been the one responsible. *Blood will tell.* Her gut clenched, and Diana dropped to her knees. Ignoring his furious growl, she wrapped the arms of her jacket around his leg . . .

And registered absolute silence.

Picking up her head, she froze.

Ryker Black stood in the doorway, with Mr. Calum Dabney at his back. Both men moved their gazes from the shattered vase littered about the floor to Diana's hands. She followed their stares. Hands unpardonably close to the front-fall of Mr. Marksman's sapphire breeches. She gasped and quickly lowered her arms.

The surly guard backed away from Diana as though she'd caught fire and he feared being singed by the blaze. Cheeks burning, she shoved to her feet. *If I was ruined for running inside this establishment for assistance, what would the* ton *say to see me now, with my fingers on Mr. Marksman's person?*

Focus on the reason for your being here. Or, in this case, the person accounting for her visit. "I . . ." Her voice trailed off.

Several inches past six feet, dark, silent, and assessing, Ryker Black was the manner of man who filled a person with unease.

And he was her brother.

Whether he wished it or not.

How did one go about greeting a man who shared one's blood and yet wanted nothing to do with you? She nibbled at her lower lip. No doubt such an exchange required formality. "M-Mr. Black," she said quietly, stumbling over that name. She hurried to pull her now blood-stained jacket back on.

His eyes revealed nothing. Instead, he fixed that inscrutable stare on Mr. Marksman and then lifted a single dark eyebrow.

"Don't be an arse," Mr. Marksman growled, shattering the silence. "It ain't how it looks."

Widening her eyes, Diana looked between the two men studying each other. Granted, she'd been kneeling at Mr. Marksman's feet, with her jacket wrapped about his leg, but really, how *did* it look?

"It looked damning," Mr. Dabney said, with a bored amusement. "And we should have all learned with"—he jerked his chin at Diana's brother—"Black's circumstances what happens to those caught in an 'It isn't how it looks' moment."

Mr. Marksman moved quickly around her. Diana gasped and hurriedly stepped into his path, blocking his forward movement. "There was nothing damning," she said frantically. "I'm certain it appeared damning because . . ." She was destined to exist in a perpetual state of blushing. "Well, because." She settled for that vagueness. "However, I merely sought to help Mr. Marksman." Whether he wished it or not. Which he'd decidedly not. "Given I . . ." Ryker's steely eyes encouraged her to continue. "Given I . . ." Diana gestured to Mr. Marksman's bloodstained breeches and then let her arm drop to her side. "Stabbed him." That admission came, dragged from her, and her insides twisted.

She's just like her mother.

Silence thundered around the room, thick and tense. If Ryker Black had despised her before, he'd now be more inclined to hurl her from the club into the streets without a backward glance, and he'd certainly not be offering any assistance with the needs that had driven her here.

"She *stabbed* you." Mr. Black looked beyond her shoulder to the man who stood at her back. What happened to a young lady who stabbed the head guard at a wicked gaming hell? Her heart thudded loudly in her ears, and she braced for his fury.

Mr. Dabney emitted a snorting laugh. "She stabbed you."

Diana should be fixed on the crucial business that had brought her here, and yet . . . "It was not his fault," she said defensively. No person, man or woman, regardless of station, cared to have their capabilities questioned. "I surprised him."

Another pall of silence rang.

Mr. Dabney and Mr. Black dissolved into harsh laughter, until both men wiped moisture from their eyes.

"Go to 'ell," Mr. Marksman barked, and the vocal amusement from the pair at the front of the room only doubled.

Some of the fear left her. She didn't wish for the surly guard to be the source of their amusement, but she also didn't wish to be hurled into the streets for injuring one of their own.

Abruptly, Mr. Black's amusement faded. "Out," he ordered. "And Niall, see your leg is tended to. I'll not have you kicking your toes up because you were stabbed with a—" Ryker Black turned to Diana expectantly.

Her skin pricked with the glare Mr. Marksman leveled on her. "Fish knife," she supplied.

Another bark of laughter left Mr. Dabney. He dropped a quick bow in Diana's direction and then swiftly exited. Without so much as looking at her, Mr. Marksman strolled from the room and then closed the door hard behind him.

Diana's heart pounded. She'd gone from being surrounded by one scowling and two laughing strangers to a brother who'd never acknowledged her.

But surely he'd not wish me dead?

"My lady," he said in a brusque, businesslike tone so very similar to the one her father used when speaking to his man-of-affairs. Mr. Black motioned her to the chair opposite his desk. As he took a spot behind that broad piece of furniture, she hastily claimed the seat he'd motioned to.

"Diana," she corrected swiftly. Why could he not say something? Manage a smile? Anything, other than the unreadable lines of his face. When still he said nothing, she continued. "Please, if you'll call me Diana," she finished lamely.

"Diana," he said solemnly.

She clasped her fingers on her lap. Surely that admission on his part was an encouraging sign? Mayhap he'd not turn her away, after all.

He leaned back, and the folds of his aged leather chair groaned, shattering the quiet. Most would pepper her with questions as to her presence here—at this hour, no less. Ryker, however, simply sat in wait.

"I would not have come, if there had been another option," she forced herself to say when he remained silent.

"A note is safer than wandering the streets of St. Giles in the dead of night," her brother said dryly.

"Yes," she concurred. She'd briefly entertained sending a note, but had swiftly discarded the idea of putting such sordid details to paper. Not with the risk of it being intercepted. "Under most circumstances." In this, Helena could not have helped. Bound for the country, she'd already helped Diana the only way she could have: by introducing Diana to her seafaring relatives, who represented a dream of freedom.

But not even proud, spirited Helena could help her in this. Their father, doting as he'd been toward his daughters and wife, did not see a woman in the same light he did a gentleman. Then, that was the way of their society.

Oi don't have a problem with women.

Well, it would seem with the exception of Mr. Niall Marksman. Thrusting aside thoughts of the rugged, scowling guard, she returned to her request. "I have no place asking you for any favors given my . . .

given my . . ." At the emotionless glitter in his eyes, she dropped her focus to her clenched hands, white from the tight grip that had drained the blood from them. She knew not the details of her father's relationship with Ryker Black's mother, but had gleaned enough at keyholes and from servants to know he'd loved the woman. And Diana's mother had robbed him of that happiness. A vise squeezed at her heart.

"What do you require, Diana?"

The gentleness in that query brought her head flying up. Ryker would never be a warm or tender brother, but in this instance, there was a quiet encouragement that erased all the terror and tension that had weighted her since she'd boarded the hack.

"I'm looking for protection," she said softly and then drew in a deep breath.

His expression grew shuttered. "Protection."

Diana hesitated. When she'd spoken to their father, he'd merely patted her hand and waved off her fears. "Someone is trying to kill me," she said, studying Ryker closely for his reaction.

He went still.

Did he think her as mad as her mother? Her rib cage tightened around her lungs, squeezing hard. Her gaze wavered, and she looked to the gold-framed portrait behind him, a floral country landscape at odds with this ruthless world. She forced her eyes back to his. "I know it is silly to think anyone would wish me dead, and yet . . ." Despite the first and final time she'd raised that concern to her father, she knew it with an irrational understanding deep in her gut.

"And yet?" he prodded, in a commanding, perfunctory manner.

Diana lifted her palms up. "I believe it to be true."

Ryker steepled his fingertips together and drummed them. "What does your father believe?" *Your father.* The man who'd sired them. How odd to speak of him as a stranger, but then, isn't that what the Duke of Wilkinson was to Ryker? A boy snatched from the arms of his mother and turned over to a street thug in a merciless act orchestrated by

Diana's mother. How *could* he feel anything but, at best, removed, and at worst, hatred for the duke?

She spoke in halting tones. "My father said no one could possibly wish me harm." If one wanted to be truly precise, he'd patted her on the head and laughed in his usual jolly fashion, in the first real amusement she'd seen from him since his wife had been carted off to Bedlam.

Ryker stopped that distracting tap of his fingertips. "You are of a differing opinion."

She'd told him, and even though he questioned her still, he hadn't laughed, or patted her on the head, or sent her on her merry, innocent way. "Oh, yes," she said with a matter-of-factness that raised a frown. "There was a broken axle on the hackney I hired in the winter."

"You rented a hackney?" His eyebrows melded into a line. "For what purpose?"

She cursed her loose tongue. Diana required his assistance, but she'd not share her visit to Bedlam with him. "To travel," she said with a deliberate vagueness.

He frowned, but did not press her for details.

"Axles break." With that casual reminder, he proved more like their father than different.

"Twice?"

That effectively silenced him, and Diana proceeded to tick off on her fingers. "I've discovered my chamber doors opened, with my window thrown wide. On three occasions." The remembered terror of ducking her head inside the wind-chilled room sent ice racing along her spine. "My saddle broken." When he continued scrutinizing her with that piercing assessment, she rested her palms on her lap. "And sometimes you just *know*."

All earlier calm had been replaced, and Ryker sat opposite her with a tense alertness. "You've told your father all of that and he still hasn't provided you a guard?"

Ladies had powerful footmen assigned them. Not surly guards who'd cut off a person's airflow. She gave her head a slight shake and hedged her words. "The last I spoke to my father of it"—the first broken axle—"he . . ." She thought of the vague, empty shadow of a man who occasionally exited his chambers. "He had nothing to say on it."

Given her family's history of madness, the last thing Diana could afford to do was go about seeing monsters in the shadows and have anyone believe her sane. Particularly the man who'd sent his wife off to Bedlam and then descended into his own state of lunacy.

"When did the attempts begin?"

That was it. The pressure in her chest eased. There were no doubts or further questions. Just this calm acceptance of her words as fact. For the first time in the past two months, the fear receded. "Just after Helena's ball," she stumbled. All of Society had been abuzz when Ryker had been caught in a compromising position with Lady Penelope. Diana, however, had been forced to learn anything and everything about her sister-in-law and Ryker in the scandal sheets. Diana hadn't even received an invitation to his wedding—of which there had, curiously, been *two* to the same lady.

Something flickered in her brother's eyes and then was gone. His expression grew shuttered once more. "Tell me what you require."

He will help. Relief washed over her. Even if he despised the connection between them, he'd aid her anyway. "Will you speak to my father?" The man had stopped seeing her long ago. "You can make him listen."

Ryker nodded once. "It is done."

She cocked her head. That was it? She'd toiled over coordinating this meeting and slipping off in the dead of night, fearing she'd ultimately be met with derision, only to have him so readily believe and pledge his assistance? Diana searched his face. "Why should you believe me on nothing more than what I've told you?"

"Sometimes you just know," he said, tossing her words back at her. The ghost of a smile hovered on his lips and then faded. His features fell into their usual somber mask. "I survived the streets of St. Giles by trusting the very intuition you speak of, Diana." He cast a look over her shoulder in the direction of the ticking longcase clock. "You should not be here. *Ever.*" He punctuated that reminder. "If you need me, send a note. Ya aren't to come here," he said, slipping into Cockney. "I'm seeing you home now." He shoved to his feet. "Tomorrow I'll come and speak with the duke."

Diana hopped to her feet. As she allowed her brother to escort her from his office and the Hell and Sin, for the first time since her mother had been carted off to Bedlam and her father became a deadened shell of a man, she felt . . . not so very much alone, after all.

Chapter 4

The four proprietors at the Hell and Sin were never collectively called away from their responsibilities unless there was trouble.

As Niall stood in Ryker's office with Adair and Calum, the heavy tension filling the room portended only one thing—trouble.

Ryker stood at the front of his desk, hands clasped at his back. There could be no doubt that the trouble was directly connected to the breeches-wearing lady Niall had discovered prancing around the alley an hour earlier.

Ryker opened his mouth to speak when the door opened. As one, they immediately faced the door.

Niall relaxed.

Penelope stood in the doorway in a nightshift and wrapper. Burying a yawn behind her fingertips, she looked around and then, uninvited, strolled inside. "Well," she prodded after she'd closed the door.

The harsh set to Ryker's features relaxed. "You should be—"

Penny planted her hands on her hips. "If you're going to say sleeping, asleep, or any other variation, I'd substitute it with 'here,' Ryker." There was a faint accusatory edge there. "You were gone." Husband and wife engaged in some silent dialogue.

Theirs was a closeness Niall hadn't known with a single soul. Not with his siblings from the streets. Not even with the woman who'd given him life. Uncomfortable with that intimacy, Niall averted his gaze.

Ryker released a sigh. "Lady Diana arrived earlier this evening."

Surprise stamped Penelope's features. "Your sister?" she asked, coming forward.

When she stopped before him, Ryker captured her hand in his and raised it to his lips.

A blush stained her cheeks. "Do not try to distract me, Ryker Black."

The once ruthlessly hard gaming-hell owner grinned. "I wouldn't dare." He indicated the chair beside him. His wife ignored it, proving herself the same stubborn creature who'd run to aid Niall in Lambeth Street.

When everyone again fell silent, Penelope shifted her gaze between them and then at last settled her probing stare on Ryker. "Well?" she demanded, arching a dark eyebrow.

From the corner of his eye, Niall detected Calum's and Adair's matching grins, and if he were one of those fellows capable of amusement, watching Ryker Black be challenged by this slip of a lady would certainly be grounds for it. Of late, however, life had given Niall little reason to smile and every reason to be silent and guarded.

"Diggory's men are at work," Ryker said, his gravelly tones conveying the severity of that admission.

How easily Ryker now handed information over to his wife. The rules of keeping all nobility out had been shattered the day he'd wed Lady Penelope. Niall would never let a person in the way Ryker had.

Penelope cocked her head. "But Killoran assured us that he'd rein in all of his men."

"They were once loyal to Diggory," Adair quietly reminded her.

It had been a good day when that sod had drawn his last breath. However, it had unleashed a war within the streets that even Diggory's heir apparent, and owner of the Devil's Den, could not quash. In the underbelly of London, you didn't end a man without revenge being handed out. Niall would have paid that price if Penelope hadn't intervened.

Penelope whipped her gaze to Ryker.

He gave a slight nod. "He's infiltrated the Duke of Wilkinson's Mayfair residence."

That is what had brought Lady Diana here, then? Niall scratched at his brow. Why would the fancy miss, and not the bloody duke, brave the streets of London to come here?

Ryker proceeded to convey his exchange with Diana.

After he'd concluded, Adair marched over to the sideboard and helped himself to a glass of brandy. "When did it begin?" he asked, turning back to face them.

Ryker twined his fingers with Penelope's and raised her knuckles to his lips in a tender exchange. "Shortly after Helena's ball." The chance meeting that had seen Ryker wed to a societal lady.

Niall shifted back and forth. Feelings were something he didn't deal in. He'd been born an unwanted child to a whore in the street and used as a fighter to grow a ruthless gang leader's empire. Since his marriage, Ryker had gone soft in many ways, but surely he didn't believe Lady Diana Verney had become the focus of Diggory's henchmen?

Calum rolled his shoulders. "And you believe they've turned their sights on her, as a means of exacting revenge," he said, vocalizing Niall's unspoken thoughts.

Ryker shook his head slightly. "I don't know," he confessed, releasing his wife's hand.

Adair cursed and then tossed back his drink. He set the glass down on the sideboard. "Given Killoran's inability to bring all of Diggory's men to heel, it's no surprise."

Niall scoffed. "Killoran, nor Diggory when he was living, would have bothered with Wilkinson's daughter." The whole of London well knew Ryker Black despised the Verneys.

Penelope folded her arms and met his gaze squarely. "Because Lady Diana is only Ryker's half sister?" she challenged.

"No, because he's no dealings with the girl or her father," he shot back. He'd not be lectured on familial loyalty. Not even by Ryker's wife, who'd saved his own miserable arse.

Ryker's mouth tightened. "Enough," he bit out tersely.

"We're discussing Diggory's attempts on the girl's life," Calum interjected, bringing them back to the reason for the meeting. "Do you believe they're after the lady?"

Ryker rolled his shoulders. "I don't know," he said with the same blunt honesty he'd shown since he and Niall had tussled in the streets as boys from warring gangs.

"Would you question her because she is a woman?" Penelope challenged.

Her devoted husband perched his hip on the edge of his desk. "I'd question anyone until I'd thoroughly investigated the circumstances," he countered, and some of the fight left his wife. "But I can't afford to ignore the lady's worries." This time, he looked out to the trio. "The lady requires a guard."

That was the reason for the meeting, then. To discuss who'd oversee the lady's well-being. This was safe. This was something Niall *did* deal in. As head of security inside the hell, he knew every last detail about every man who served the club. Ryker settled his gaze on Niall. "I summoned you here so that you're aware. So that you're listening and alert. I'd speak to Niall, alone."

Avoiding his eyes, Calum and Adair filed out of the room. Niall waited while husband and wife exchanged hushed words. Periodically, Penelope nodded and then spoke, raising a frown from Ryker. He gave her hand a squeeze, and then a moment later, she marched to the front of the room. She paused beside Niall. "You once hated me," she pointed out. "Wanted me gone from the hell."

At the unexpectedness of that unneeded reminder, he eyed her, confused.

"Diggory was a terrible monster," she said softly. "As are the men determined to avenge his death." She held his gaze. "But not all people born of the streets are evil." The lady was a bloody fool if she believed that. In the streets, boys like him wielded knives and slayed others at the command of their overlord. "Just as one shouldn't judge all ladies of the peerage." Penelope cast one last look over her shoulder at Ryker and then took her leave.

As soon as the door closed, Ryker motioned to a chair. "Sit."

You advised me to sit . . . like a dog.

He scowled and thrust back that unwanted thought of the bold chit who'd stabbed him in the alley. Mayhap another man would feel guilt at ordering her about. Niall's very job was to do so. The welfare of every member of this establishment fell to him. Reluctantly, Niall pulled out the chair and sat.

Ryker moved behind his desk and reclaimed his seat. "The lady requires a guard." He rested his forearms on the surface of his desk. "Niall, it has to be you."

What was he on about?

The other man nodded slowly, and Niall thinned his eyes into narrow slits. Mayhap he'd lost more blood from the wound inflicted on him by that little termagant, but he sought to muddle through that blasted nod. Surely Ryker wasn't saying—

"Wot 'as to be me?" Niall repeated, gritting that question out.

"Niall, I'm sending you to be Lady Diana's guard."

That pronouncement sucked the air from the room. The residual silence was punctuated by the steady ticking of the longcase clock.

Abandoning his seat, Niall unfurled to his full height. Pressing his palms to Ryker's desk, he leaned forward. "You are bloody mad," he seethed, taking care to stretch out the words in practiced tones. The cultured tones he hated, that he'd perfected to grow their empire. "You want to send me out into Polite Society as a nursemaid for your *sister*. The bloody sister you don't want any dealings with?" he spat. Fury pumped through his veins, and his muscles twitched with the vicious need for a fight.

With an infuriating calm, Ryker leaned back. "She is my sister. As such, she's deserving of the same protection that Helena is."

Niall scoffed. "You'd remember that now?"

Ryker turned his palms up. "There wasn't a need before."

Nor was there likely a need now. "Then send Calum or Adair," he insisted with unwavering logic. The other two partners were far glibber and in possession of their tempers around the nobility. Niall had abandoned all pretense after Diggory had reemerged and shaken their ordered universe. "They fit in that world more than Oi ever would."

"I know," Ryker concurred. "Which is one of the reasons I'm sending you."

Sending him. In the streets of London, a person honored the man who ranked above him. This was Ryker. His brother. He'd do anything for him. And yet . . . "Oi'm in charge of all the guards. Responsible for the safety of all, and you'd send me away to care for one noblewoman?" A lady in every sense but for the full crimson lips made for kissing and even darker, wicked acts. He started. Where in bloody 'ell had that lustful urging for the English princess come from?

"I've known you nearly my entire life," Ryker said solemnly. "I call you brother. I know your loyalty. I trust it."

He studied Ryker a long while, taking in the set lines of his scarred face. When Ryker Black set his mind to something, one had better hope of moving the earth from its axis than altering him from the course he'd set. Nonetheless, Niall made one last attempt at swaying him. "Diggory's men will strike, and ya want me here when that happens. Do ya truly believe anyone would 'arm your half sister?"

The other man held his gaze. "We both survived by seeing danger everywhere, Niall. I'll not abandon that instinct now. Not to keep you here and happy."

Keep him happy? Is this what the other man thought this was about? It was about being cast out like an aged member of a gang who no longer served a purpose. It was a mark of failure and weakness. "How long?"

Ryker layered his palms along the arms of his chair. "Niall—"

"Oi said how long?" he snapped.

"Until you confirm the state of her safety." The blasted traitor may as well have been speaking of forever.

Niall curled his hands into fists. "That is all, my lord?" he jeered.

Ryker waved a hand, like the king granting a benediction. "It is settled."

Panic spiraled, and he fought to conceal it as he turned on his heel and stomped across the room.

"Niall?" Ryker barked, staying his movements, and for the fledgling of a moment, hope stirred.

He glanced back.

"You're the only one who doubts yourself. We depart for Wilkinson's at nine o'clock." Niall tamped down another string of epithets. "Lady Diana's suspicions will remain between us and the young lady herself." So they'd keep the foolish girl's equally foolish imaginings from the bloody duke.

"Perfectly clear," he spat, and, yanking the door handle, Niall took his leave. He slammed the door hard behind him, and the loud boom thundered in the quiet corridors. Niall stalked down the halls, making his way to the stairs.

Niall in a goddamned Mayfair town house, with his only responsibility a duke's pampered daughter? With a growl, he quickened his stride down the stairs. With every step the raucous din of revelry and coins clinking with coins grew louder. The sounds safe. Comfortable. This is where he belonged, and Ryker Black would send him away to care for a spoiled child.

Niall reached the entrance to the gaming-hell floors and stopped. Pain radiated in his leg from where the bloody chit's knife had grazed him. Another growl worked up his chest.

The old, burly guard Oswyn glanced at him. Niall flexed his jaw. Let him say one word. Let him say one bloody word about being sent away, because there was no doubt word had already begun making its way among the guards. Guards who'd now answer to Adair. Instead, something glinted in the laconic man's eyes—pity.

I've seen that glimmer before. It had been there when Helena was cast out.

Only now it was him. *Over my damned body.* Niall took two steps around Adair. The blond-haired proprietor blocked him. Near in height to Niall, the other man easily met his gaze. "That will be all, Oswyn," Adair said quietly. Without hesitation, Oswyn stalked off.

How easily he'd stepped into Niall's role here. Ignoring his brother's piercing stare, Niall flicked his gaze over the crowded hell. The tables were overflowing with drunken dandies and garrulous lords, while other gentlemen weaved between the crush of bodies to find an empty place at a gaming table. He curled his hands into tight fists, leaving crescent marks on his palms. This was where he belonged. Nowhere else. And certainly not rubbing shoulders with the bloody nobs. He'd rather lop off his thigh with that dull fish knife.

Adair positioned himself at Niall's side. "It is not permanent," Adair reasoned.

"Go to 'ell." Niall continued searching the room. Since he'd been old enough to walk through the streets of St. Giles, he'd always been searching—for threats, for danger. Because ultimately it was there, waiting for a person to make a misstep.

At Adair's silence, he looked over. The ghost of a smile hovered on the other man's lips. But then, that had always been Adair. Where Niall couldn't move those muscles in any rendition of mirth, Adair had always been more sparing with those useless expressions. "One never knows. You may find yourself wishing to remain, like Helena."

Niall stuck up his finger in a crude gesture that earned a laugh from Adair. Then the other man stopped and patted Niall on the back once. "Go. I have it."

He had it. Adair had control of the security inside the hell.

A battle warred inside Niall. An urge to stay and fight for his place here. And a bloody sense of acceptance.

But to play damned nursemaid to a duke's daughter?

He'd always known the fate awaiting him—Hell.

Being sent to Mayfair to watch over a duke's pampered daughter, it would seem the Devil had come to collect.

Chapter 5

The following morning, standing silent before the Duke of Wilkinson's desk with his hands clasped behind his back, Niall trained his gaze over the top of the portly, foolishly grinning nobleman.

"My boy, how very good it is to see you." The Duke of Wilkinson's weak voice barely reached Niall's ears. "To what do I owe the pleasure of your visit?"

My boy?

Niall stared on incredulously. Mayhap the Duke of Wilkinson had a touch of the madness that afflicted his wife. The duke's lowborn son hadn't visited in the whole of his lifetime. In fact, the only time he'd had any specific dealings with him had been when Ryker had sent Helena here for hiding. And even then, the duke had been summoned to Ryker's territory. Yet he'd greet him as though this was a special social visit between a beloved father and son?

Ryker didn't bother with pleasantries. "I'm here about your daughter."

Worry chased away the duke's earlier smile as he alternated his stare between Ryker and Niall. "Helena?"

Interesting. Niall scrutinized the older nobleman through hooded lashes. The duke didn't worry after the child with pure blue blood, but rather his bastard. It spoke volumes about just how cherished the girl sprinting down the St. Giles alley, in fact, was. Who'd have believed a highborn lord would worry after his illegitimate whelps more than the princess with her pure blood?

Laying claim to the duke's space, Ryker motioned for his father to sit.

His Grace dropped his rotund frame into the seat, settling himself on the edge. "Have those men come for her again?" he blurted. "I believed after that vile monster was killed—"

"Helena is fine." Ryker's emotionless interruption bore no hint of a man seeking to provide reassurance. He settled into one of the vacant wing chairs across from the desk.

Niall kept his hands clasped at his back and remained standing. He was not here on a social call and knew better than to lower his defenses in any way during any meeting.

"You are certain?" the duke pressed, ringing his hands together.

"Your other daughter," Niall snapped. He didn't like the princess who'd stolen into the alley last night and resulted in his being ousted from his position as guard, but he liked even less a man disloyal to his kin. "We're 'ere because of your other daughter," he said, deliberately slipping back into his coarse street tones.

"Diana?" The incredulity in the duke's voice rang as clear as the bells in St. Giles.

"You have more bastards running about, then?" Niall drawled, rolling his shoulders. He pointedly ignored the frosty glare trained on him by Ryker.

Confused lines marred the man's wrinkled brow. "What? No . . . I . . ."

Ryker's harsh baritone cut across the man's muddled reply. "I have reason to believe that someone intends to harm Lady Diana."

"Diana?" the duke parroted like one of those bold-colored birds Niall had once spied in a street show in the Dials. Then the old nobleman dissolved into a rumbling laugh.

"I assure you. There is no reason to worry after *Diana*."

Niall and Ryker exchanged a look.

Niall didn't like admitting he was wrong.

He'd suffered through too many broken noses and fists to the belly before he'd dared breathed those words or any variation of them aloud.

But in this instance, he admitted, at least to himself, he'd been wrong. Very wrong. Lady Diana had far more sense than he'd credited, trusting her welfare to Ryker, a stranger who hadn't acknowledged her existence over this pompous duke. How differently these lords and ladies moved through life. They feared nothing. Saw danger nowhere . . . and invariably they were right to those simplistic thoughts. Their lives mattered in ways no person reared on the streets ever would.

Dazedly, the duke shook his head. "S-surely not. Why . . . what . . . who would want my girl harmed?"

Surely not.

Niall schooled his features, concealing his disgust. Even though it was unlikely Diggory's men, or any person, would wish to harm Lady Diana Verney, as Ryker had pointed out, one would be a fool to ignore a possible threat.

Even the reckless, innocent Lady Diana Verney saw it. Saw it when her own father didn't.

"Wilkinson," Ryker went on gravely, "there's reason to worry after your daughter's well-being."

"But *here*?" the duke whispered. "This is Mayfair, Ryker. Those kind of people do not live here—"

"Tell me, where do they live, then, Your Grace?" Niall put in before Ryker could speak. "The streets of St. Giles?" He leveled the powerful lord with a hard, taunting glare. "The halls of Bedlam?"

At the thinly veiled reference to his wife, the older man paled. His throat worked hard, and he dropped his eyes to the surface of his desk.

Ryker broke into the quiet. "Niall will remain on here as a guard for the young lady." His tone brooked little room for argument. But then this was a man who commanded and controlled both the streets of St. Giles and powerful peers such as the Duke of Wilkinson.

"Ryker," the duke said in a faintly pleading tone, "you do not have many dealings with Diana." *Any dealings.* "After she entered your club," the man went on, clasping his hands together, "she was . . ."

Niall attended the duke. "She was what?" he snapped when it became apparent no additional words were forthcoming.

Wilkinson jumped. *"Ruined,"* he said on a rough whisper. "How would it now appear if . . . if . . . one of your men—"

"Brothers," Ryker interjected crisply.

An involuntary sneer peeled at Niall's lips. Of course, a stiff-necked lord would never recognize the bond between his bastard son and the proprietors of the Hell and Sin as more powerful that a blood one.

His Grace hastily averted his gaze. "Brothers," he conceded. "How would it appear if one of your *brothers* was following her about?"

Niall rocked on his heels. So this is what that polite refusal was about, then. Appearances and social standing. God, how repulsive this world was. Niall might be a merciless thug to the streets, but the men and women he'd made his family would lay down their lives for one another and send Society on to the Devil if one but asked it. Whereas these peers would sacrifice their daughters to appease Society's sensibilities. "Ya'd risk your daughter's life?" Niall snapped.

The duke lifted his palms beseechingly. "Please, you must understand." There was nothing to understand. One placed the safety and well-being of their kin above all else and all others. "How do you expect me to have her make a match with . . ." His eyes strayed over to Niall, and then he swallowed audibly. "A *guard* following her about?"

Niall made a sound of disgust. Scurrilous blighters, they were, these fancy toffs who ruled Society. Ryker shot him a hard look. Ignoring it, Niall hooked his fingers into the top of his breeches.

"Regardless of her birthright, Lady Diana shares my blood, and that marks her unsafe," Ryker continued.

"Unsafe?" the duke repeated, his voice hollow.

At last, Ryker had penetrated the naive nobleman's misplaced concerns.

His son nodded once.

His Grace wiped tired hands over his face. Those digits trembled in a mark of his weakness. A man didn't shake and shiver unless he was prepared to have that frailty laid out before the whole of the world. Ultimately, those fragile souls perished. "You are certain?" the older man asked gruffly when he'd dropped his hands to his lap.

Both men remained silent. Your word in the Dials was your bond. Neither could speak with an absolute certainty or fact born of any definitive truth about the young lady's well-being. That, however, did not mark her safe. The duke could never, nor would ever, make the distinction that both were invariably the same.

"Come." He struggled to his feet. "You must meet Diana."

Together, Niall and Ryker stood.

Yet the duke lingered.

"What is it?" Ryker asked with his usual impatience.

"It is just . . . I'll not have Diana worry."

The lackwit lord didn't even recall his daughter speaking to him with concerns about the broken axles. But then, men, regardless of station, failed to hear a woman's words. It was the way of most Society. Not in Niall's world, however. He'd learned firsthand from the streets the treachery and skill a person was capable of regardless of age or gender. "I do not know how to explain . . ." His pudgy fingers fluttered in the air as he gestured to Niall.

Niall curled up his mouth in the corners in a faint, mocking grin. He'd long ago ceased to care about Society's deservedly ill opinion of him. He was a thief turned gaming-hell owner and made no apologies for who he was. He did, however, take an unholy delight in the discomfort of those pompous lords.

"You'll tell her the truth," Ryker said bluntly. "You'll tell her there is reason to suspect someone might wish her harm, so that she is prepared." It was a familiar lesson in the Dials. But one anathema to the fabricated existence manufactured by these nobles.

The wrinkles around the duke's eyes deepened, but then he gave a reluctant nod. "I will explain it to the girl. Shall we?" he asked, and then with his slower, methodical steps, he started for the doorway.

Ryker set out behind him, and Niall kept a distance, trailing after the father and son. Eager to be on with this assignment, so he could prove the girl was seeing ghosts in shadows and be free of this stifled, stilted world.

From where she stood at her easel, Diana squinted, trying to bring the numbers on the ormolu clock into focus.

Ryker had not yet arrived.

Just past nine o'clock, it was early by Polite Society's standards. Men such as Ryker Black, and the scowling guard who'd pinned Diana against an alley wall, however, seemed to exist without sleep.

She'd didn't know what to expect of Ryker and Father's meeting.

Given her brother's aura of strength and power, she'd convinced herself that Father would at last leave his rooms and step out into the living—and listen.

She tightened her grip on her paintbrush. Men always invariably trusted other men. Where were women? Well, women like her were secreted away for their own good and doted on like cherished porcelain, not sturdy people capable of knowing their own minds.

Giving her head a shake, she returned her attentions to her painting.

Since her mother's treachery had been revealed, Diana had existed in a peculiar state. She was disdained by the peerage and yet exalted by the servants in the Duke of Wilkinson's employ. The members of her father's household staff treated her with reverence, but never anything more.

It was, at best, a lonely world.

At worst, a miserable one.

Even the flood of invitations and visits from the peerage had come to an abrupt stop.

Only a handful of invitations had been issued for the once respected family. Beyond that, there was not a single friend, caller, or suitor.

The irony was not lost on her. When her mother had been around, she'd scrutinized Diana's every movement and decision with such intensity, Diana had secretly longed for privacy to simply exist without fear of reproach.

Never before would she have been able to sneak out, hire a hack, and avoid detection. Not as long as her mother had been present.

Now, with her mother gone, there wasn't a single person to care about her painting, or embroidering, or . . . *her*. Her sister, Helena, spent more time in the country than she did in London. Her brother, Ryker, though he'd pledged to help her, hadn't uttered a single word to her in the whole of her life before that.

She scrunched up her mouth. Nor had her mother truly cared about Diana. She hadn't. At all. If one wished to be truly specific. Diana had listened in at too many keyholes to know that she'd served only one purpose—to make a great, advantageous match that would grow their family's wealth, power, and prestige.

Then there was Diana's father. The always smiling, benevolent papa, who since his wife's sins had come to light looked through Diana but never at her. Instead, he closeted himself away in his rooms, rarely coming out but for meals. Her stomach muscles clenched. He'd been bereft since he'd discovered the hand Diana's mother had played in getting rid of his beloved mistress and his illegitimate children. *Mad . . . just like the duchess.*

Those whispered words she'd overheard between two serving maids reverberated around her mind.

Her fingers curled reflexively around her brush, and she forced herself to ease that grip. Diana made another several strokes upon the canvas.

A slow-simmering resentment boiled to the surface once more. There was surely a darkness in her soul that she should hate her father. She did not hate him for having loved a woman other than his wife and giving that woman two children. She did not hate him for publicly declaring those children his own, as he should have done years earlier. She did not even hate him for his collapse this past year.

What she could never understand, or forgive, was the ease with which he'd sent his wife to Bedlam, a prison more than a hospital. As a duke he'd the power and influence to at least see her in an establishment where she was not abused.

As such, she had no doubt that when she did indeed board a ship bound for St. George's, he'd never give Diana another thought.

Abandoning all futile efforts at creating anything of her own, Diana tossed the brush down onto the palette. It landed with a hard, satisfying thwack, splattering paint on the table. Loosening the strings of her apron, Diana pulled it off and rested it on a nearby shell-backed chair. Restless, she snagged the large leather book lying open.

Some of the tension left her frame.

Resting one palm on the table, with the other she flipped through William Gilpin's collection of landscapes, her gaze skimming the pages. She stopped on a familiar, dog-eared page. Diana froze. A pair of men marching a path down a long road toward the impressive keep. She

trailed her fingertips over the turbulent sky. The thick clouds, portend-
ing night's approach. Had the artist captured his own desolate thoughts
of *home*? Or did he, with the two figures shoulder to shoulder, hint at
a closeness of two who would weather the darkness on the horizon?
Darkness. Danger—

Meredith stumbled into the room. "Murderers," the girl panted,
clutching at her side. "We were wrong for doubting you."

"I . . . what?" she blurted. They'd doubted her? It was a silly detail
to fix on given the servant's warnings. And yet . . .

"My lady," Meredith implored. "We have to hide. Please. Demanded
to see His Grace and are in his office now."

Then Meredith's earlier words slipped forward.

Tall. Dark. Scarred. With weapons.

"Did one of the men have a scar that ran from here"—she motioned
to her lip—"down to here?" she asked breathlessly, dragging her fingertips from her jaw just under her neck. A man with the face and body of
a battle-hardened warrior. How had he come by those vicious wounds?
Sadness and curiosity pulled that thought around her mind.

Meredith nodded frantically. "An ugly monster, my lady," she whispered, clutching at her throat.

Diana blinked. "Ugly?" Niall Marksman would never fit with society's standards of beauty, but there was a rugged masculinity to him that
made him real in ways gentlemen of the *ton* were not.

"His eyes are black like Satan's, and the man with him?" Meredith
gulped. "Equally scarred. Evil."

Diana registered a thick, charged silence. Her stomach sank.

Ryker, Father, and the very *devil* Meredith had come to warn her
of all stared back.

Bloody hell.

By the harsh glint in Niall's piercing blue eyes, he'd taken Diana for
one of those gossiping sorts.

Her lady's maid shrieked and rushed behind Diana. *So much for loyal servants,* she thought dryly as the girl cowered at her back. "Meredith, my brother, Ryker, and . . ." What to call Niall Marksman? *Nor have you felt a thing sisterly toward him since the day he folded you in his arms at the Hell and Sin.* Cheeks warming, Diana cleared her throat. "Mr. Marksman and my brother are here to visit. Will you see to refreshments?"

Meredith paled as the three men stepped inside. With a hasty curtsy, she rushed past the men at the front of the room.

Her glassy-eyed father looked at Diana as though he puzzled through a familiar stranger's identity. Not even a greeting was issued.

Then, when was the last time her father had paid her a visit? Their exchanges were nonexistent since Mother had been moved to Bedlam and he into his chambers.

Ryker sketched a bow, and she went through the motions of greeting her brother. Niall Marksman hung back, not joining the group.

Her heart knocked wildly against her rib cage.

Danger.

Everything about him, from the soot-black lashes and glacial eyes to the tightly coiled muscles straining the fabric of his loud, splendidly tailored garments, exuded the very essence of that menacing word.

She gave thanks as her father performed useless introductions, and took the opportunity to settle her racing heart. Surely this was not the man Ryker would assign to stand as guard?

By the jeering glimmer in those near-obsidian eyes, Niall Marksman had neatly interpreted her very thoughts.

"Please, please, let us sit," her father said in vacant tones.

Stealing an occasional sideways peek at Mr. Marksman, Diana took the curved, gilt wood bergère chair—farthest away from the menacing guard.

While Ryker and her father settled into their respective seats, she set out to calm her panicky nerves.

It was silly fearing Niall Marksman. Just because he'd had her pressed hard against the brick wall abutting his gaming hell. Just because he'd put his hands all over her, everywhere. Including her throat, when he'd nearly choked the life from her.

Niall moved into position alongside Ryker's chair, giving him the look of one of those ruthless warriors defending his liege. She swallowed hard. Yes, well, mayhap it was prudent to fear him. If even just a little. She'd not, however, dwell in a constant state of it—for him, or any person. It was why she'd see him as no one more than Niall, Ryker's brother.

Well, mayhap not his brother, per se. Not given the wicked ponderings she'd carried for the man a year earlier, when she'd been a pathetic, romantic miss. She—

Registered the peculiar silence.

Heat rushed to her cheeks, and she folded her hands primly on her lap in that demure acquiescence drilled into her by a stern-faced nursemaid and then equally stern-faced governess.

"Ryker came to see us today," her father supplied needlessly, grinning the first real expression of mirth, one that reached his eyes, for the first time in more than a year. The aging duke leaned over and patted his son on the knee.

A pang struck her heart. Regret, guilt, and pain, all neatly rolled together. Of course, why shouldn't her father be restored to the living? He had before him a son he loved, given him by a woman he'd also loved. A woman Diana's mother had ultimately seen destroyed. "Ryker," Diana greeted softly. How many times as a small girl had she yearned for a brother or sister to call friend? Only to end up with this aloof stranger who wanted nothing to do with her?

He inclined his head, saying nothing, revealing even less.

But regardless of how he felt, or didn't feel, about her, he was here. And that said something about his honor and character.

Their father rotated his gaze between his two children. By the emotion glittering in his eyes, they were assembled for an intimate family gathering and not a previously arranged meeting Diana had single-handedly orchestrated.

"Shall we take refreshments?" their sire suggested.

"I am not here on a social call." Was Ryker's reminder intended for Diana or their delusional sire?

That statement, however, had little impact on the duke. "No," he concurred, and then turned to Diana. "Your brother is here—"

Niall snorted, and she favored him with a razor-sharp glare. "I'm sorry, Mr. Marksman. Are you unwell? Mayhap you require tea, after all, to clear whatever is in your throat?"

His jaw dropped, and she delighted in that momentary lack of control. *Good.* Served him right. He might belittle Ryker's relationship to a duke's daughter, but their blood was the same.

"Foine," he said, touching the brim of an imagined hat.

How easily he slipped in and out those throaty, guttural tones. Was it a bid to disconcert? Shock? Or was it simply what came from living between two worlds? Shoving aside her piqued curiosity, Diana returned her attention to her father.

"As I was saying," he went on. "Your brother is here because he cares about you."

It was Diana's turn to choke, and her skin burned with the feel of Niall's hard, mocking gaze turned on her.

"I always knew the bond between my children would be strong, if he—"

"Perhaps we might discuss the reasons for Ryker's concern?" she suggested in a rush, in a desperate attempt to cut off that humiliating delusion he waxed on about.

"—cared about you."

Feeling much like an owl startled from its perch, she blinked wildly at Niall Marksman.

"Your father didn't say Ryker was concerned but rather he cared about you."

A vast difference and also a noticeable slip on her part. One that Niall exploited, earning a glower from his brother from the street. *Oh, blast.* She was not made for this subterfuge business, but he did not need to needle and mock her. Diana adopted a serene expression her mother had insisted she master in front of a mirror at the age of eight. "I'm certain you did. Did you not, Papa?" She laced that question in feigned confusion, meant to distract. Of course, no one had truly listened to Diana all these years. Her father was content to see the surface and nothing more.

He blinked his befuddlement. "Concern. Care for. All the same, is it not?"

No, it was not. Caring came from a place of affection, if not love. Concern could come from a place of guilt or remorse. She, however, knew better than to debate her father's point. "Indeed," she murmured.

Niall's blue-black eyes nearly disappeared behind his thick, sooty eyelashes. She forced herself to remain still through his derisory study.

Ryker took command of the discussion. "I have reason to believe there are men who might wish you harm."

Three pairs of eyes fixed on her. Why could she not have been one of those cleverly prevaricating ladies? And why had she not considered just how she'd let that surprise play out? Or was it terror? They expected something. Oh, drat. Which was it they expected?

Ryker took heart. "I see you are shocked."

Belatedly, she let her mouth fall agape.

And then wonder of all wonders, a grin, not at all mocking and very much real, curled Niall's mouth in the corners, momentarily transforming his scarred, hardened visage into something wholly beautiful. Which was odd to think of a man as beautiful, and yet his square, noble jaw and chiseled cheeks were better suited to stone masterpieces than a mere mortal.

He caught her regard, and all hint of softness dissolved behind the rugged exterior. Heat exploded in her cheeks at being caught staring. "Wh-who would wish me ill?" she blurted, embarrassment lending credence to that stammer. It was also a question that had dogged her sleepless nights and worry-filled days since that first broken axle.

"I don't know specifically who," Ryker replied. "But I have enemies. Many of them. The same men who stabbed my wife on the street." That reminder threw a somber blanket of silence over the room.

It didn't matter which station a person was born to. Either one lived on the streets and battled foes or one danced in a ballroom, the recipient of snide whispers and ruthless barbs.

"I don't know what to say." And mayhap it was the very truth to that admission that allowed it to tumble forward so easily.

"Ryker's friend—"

"Brother," Ryker corrected the duke, a harsh edge to that single utterance.

"Brother," their father reiterated, bobbing his head. "Mr. Marksman will be a guest here. Looking after your . . . your . . ."

"Safety," Ryker supplied.

"He'll be keeping you company." The duke dabbed at his eyes. "Like a friend. Until the threat has passed. It will be good for you to have a friend here." Niall Marksman emitted a strangled, choking sound, and Diana shot him a sideways look. "With your lack of—"

"Thank you," she hurriedly interrupted, jerking her attention to her father. It was one thing to be friendless. It was another for two strangers to know that pathetic detail. Diana stood, and after her father and brother rose, she held her fingers out to Ryker, and he hesitated a moment before taking them. "Thank you for your concern." Not caring.

She gave his hand a slight shake in a bold gesture that her mother would have lamented and then released his callused hand.

She turned her attention to Niall and offered him her hand. "Thank you, Mr. Marksman, for offering your services on my behalf." A muscle leapt at the corner of his eye.

He did not wish to be here.

Does that surprise you? Did you think he, the owner of a gaming hell and man responsible for that club's security, would welcome living with you, in this household? Diana herself despised these stifling walls.

Then, with all the enthusiasm of one grabbing the edge of a burning blade, he placed his gloveless hand in hers. The air lodged in her lungs as a searing charge radiated from his touch. It tingled a path up her arm and set her heart pounding.

All from a touch. *It's because you've never felt a man's naked hand on your own before.* Even so . . . Diana swiftly yanked her hand back. She lowered her shaking fingers to her side and retreated a step. Taking care to avoid his gaze, she stood silent while her father and Ryker concluded their meeting.

A short while later, Ryker departed and, in his wake, left behind his ruthless guard—Mr. Marksman.

Diana glanced about for the maid, who'd already gone.

"Scared, princess?" he taunted, earning a gasp.

She pressed a hand to her chest. Niall Marksman wore that cool mockery with the same ease he owned his icy ruthlessness. *This* was the man Ryker had left behind to ensure her safety. "We've gotten off to a rather ignominious beginning."

"Ya like to use fancy words, do you, princess?"

She'd not let him shake her. Not any more than he already had. "You're not, you know," she said softly.

He nudged his chin, commanding her without words to finish that thought.

"Ugly, evil, or d-dangerous." She stumbled over that last word. "As my maid earlier suggested. You're none of those things."

Mr. Marksman laughed, the sound as ragged as a graveled road. "You're a bloody twit if ya believe that."

With that he spun on his heel and marched out into the hall, closing the door hard behind him. The broad oak shook in its frame.

Diana's knees gave out, and she sank into the nearest seat.

Mayhap, dangerous. Yes, mayhap that.

Chapter 6

Niall should be breaking up a fight.

He should be deterring foul play in the Hell and Sin.

There were any number of other things he *should* be doing.

Instead, here he was playing nursemaid to a spoiled English princess.

An English princess now humming happily some unfamiliar tune as she strolled down the carpeted halls of the Duke of Wilkinson's lavish town house.

He'd been here three damned days, and there had been not a single cause or call for alarm. Not an unlocked window. Not a door left agape. Nothing. Even so, here Niall was to remain, until the spoiled chit wed.

Following behind Lady Diana, the lady now in his care, he scowled at her sashaying frame.

How long until Ryker was assured of the girl's well-being? One month? Two? At most, three? God help him. Then he made the mistake of dipping his gaze ever so slightly. Just a fragment . . . and yet enough that his stare landed on the generous swell of the lady's flared hips sashaying as she walked. Hips that fair begged a man to sink his fingers into and—he groaned. Mad. After three days in this goddamned household, he'd gone and lost his bloody mind. He'd be for Bedlam before this assignment was done.

The lady paused and angled her head back. The wide smile on her crimson bow-shaped lips was at odds with the calculated grins worn by all the women Niall had dealings with in bed and in business. "Are you all—?"

"Fine," he snapped. He lied. He'd not been fine, good, or any variation of the sort since he'd been yanked from his role as head guard at the only home he'd ever known.

Undeterred, Lady Diana gave a pleased nod, another smile, and resumed her forward march. *"Believe me, if all those endearing young charms which I gaze on so fondly to-day, Were to change by to-morrow, and fleet in my arms, Like fairy-gifts, fading away,"* she sang.

He dusted a palm over his forehead as she continued singing. Adair and Calum would be having a bloody laugh at the sight of it. Niall, trailing along like a dutiful pup after a singing miss, who couldn't be more than seventeen or eighteen years old. The lyrical, whimsical quality of her voice was not flawless as one might expect of a duke's daughter. Instead, she sang with gusto and abandon that made mockery of the title affixed her name.

"Here we are," she said, coming to a stop outside a closed door framed by a stone archway. Here they were, just as they were every damned day since he'd arrived.

The lady shifted the burden in her arms and made to grasp the handle.

She'd still not learned. "Get out of the way," he said bluntly, and a breathy gasp exploded from her lips as he shot a hand out, reaching past her. Every day, she visited the same room first. And every day, she made to open her own damned door.

"I've told you at least ten"—thirty-two—"times, I can open my own doors." Yes, every single room they approached, she always sought to see to that task herself. He opened his mouth to at last deliver a stinging lecture on the perils of a lady, by her own fears and worries, hunted, who'd see to that dangerous task herself, but she gave him a benevolent smile, and he froze.

He'd done an admirable job of looking at Ryker's blue-blood sister, but never truly seeing her—until now.

Her creamy white skin was smooth and unblemished. Her eyes were wide aquamarine pools that put him in mind of a pirate's tale of the Caribbean waters that Niall had struggled through when he'd first been learning to read. Endless blue depths that a man could happily lose himself in.

A small, delicate hand settled on his arm, and he blinked slowly, following those long, graceful digits up to the face of the person who'd dared touch him. Worry marred Lady Diana's features. "Are you certain you are all right? Mayhap you need to rest?"

Rest?

He recoiled and wrenched his arm back.

He'd wager he found the single pampered peer, outside his sister-in-law, who didn't insist a servant or her social inferior see to that task for her.

"Have you ever walked into a room and had a man pull a blade on you?" he asked harshly.

Her mouth worked, but no words were forthcoming.

"Or stepped inside a darkened space to find the butt of a pistol jammed against your back?"

She shook her head wildly, and a golden curl slipped free of her chignon and cascaded down her back. "N-no." A deserved wariness settled into the delicate planes of her face, and, clutching her throat, Lady Diana pressed herself against the wall.

Of course she hadn't. He'd already known the answer.

Most men would feel some compunction in the terror that lit her innocent eyes. Niall, however, wasn't here to coddle or pacify Lady Diana Verney. Ryker might be fairly confident there was no threat, and Niall was of like opinion, but he was here to look after her. He'd learned as a boy, when a small girl had begged him for a scrap of food and rewarded his kindness with a knife to his side, the perils that came in not being sufficiently wary—of everyone.

Hand on his hip, his fingers close to the heavy pistol that had saved his life more times than he deserved, Niall pressed the crystal door handle.

Sunlight streamed into the hallway, momentarily blinding, and he blinked several times to accustom his eyes to the brightness. Withdrawing the blade he kept in his boot, he entered the cluttered parlor. Every last corner contained an easel, table, or chair littered with art and books.

Hardly the tidy, impeccable room he'd expect in a duke's household. It had taken but his brief stay here for Niall to determine this was the girl's sanctuary. It was a place she'd laid claim to, that her father had allowed. Every day she worked like a woman possessed, sketching and painting, filling every spare corner with art.

As he slipped farther into the parlor and verified there were no enemies lurking, his gaze snagged on a solitary figure sketched upon an easel, and he briefly halted his search of the room. A faint curiosity stirred. A curiosity that went against everything and anything Niall was, and he battled it back, attending to the only task at hand that mattered. Cursing himself for that momentary distraction, he searched under the sofas and behind the carved walnut lounge chairs.

Moving with a methodical precision, he combed every corner of the sloppy parlor. Reaching the final, uninspected full-length window, he held his blade close and dragged back the gold velvet curtain. Surprising flecks of dust, his only company, danced in the morning sunlight.

Empty.

As he let the rich fabric go, it fluttered heavily back into place.

He turned to give the call for Lady Diana to enter, but his gaze snagged once more upon that figure roughly sketched on the otherwise stark white page. A lone woman in a cheerless brown dress. She stood at the edge of an ocean, with the waves lapping at her skirts. Even in the still imposed by art, Lady Diana had expertly captured the faint tug of the faceless subject's curls, giving movement in an imagined breeze. He moved closer, peering at it. Pink sands and crystal-blue waters? He scoffed. *Pink sand and blue—*

"Can I come in?" Diana's too-loud whisper slashed across the quiet. He hastily backed away from that unfinished painting. "Aye."

Ryker's sister entered. Her gaze went from him to the canvas.

His neck heated. He'd not been studying the painting. He'd been . . . He'd been . . . Well, bloody hell, he'd just happened to note it in his search.

Wordlessly, the young lady came forward and deposited her arm-load onto an already overflowing table. The books tumbled noisily onto the surface, knocking other volumes strewn haphazardly about. She fetched an immaculate white apron that hung from a gold hook in the corner of the room. Niall stared on, momentarily transfixed, as she pulled the garment over her head and concealed her slender frame . . . but not before he detected the stretch of her pink satin dress as it clung to her curves. The lady paused, midtie, and looked to him. "Perhaps you would—?"

Not allowing her to finish that question, or formulate another, he stalked from the room and took up position in the hallway. Prior to his forced stay, Niall had believed the only thing a lady of the peerage gave a jot about were shopping trips and baubles. Diana Verney, however, didn't attend a single *ton* event or venture out onto Bond Street.

Regardless, he'd not come here to make friendly with a lady. He'd come to do a job. And as soon as he verified there was no threat, Niall would be free of this place and at last be able to return to the only place he'd ever been at ease—the Hell and Sin Club.

———⁂———

Standing at her canvas, Diana contemplated her painting. Determined not to be bothered with Niall's brusqueness. Determined not to give a jot whether or not he liked her. Which he decidedly did not.

She committed another stroke to the scene taking shape. Leaning closer, she squinted at the waters of St. George's. Something was off in the painting. The books and all the accounts she'd heard of the far-off island had the sands as pink and the waters as cerulean blue. Diana released a sigh.

For eighteen years of her life she'd never ventured outside her family's properties. Her mother had so restricted Diana's movements, she'd not permitted her to set foot outside in the rain without a servant and an umbrella. *I am no longer that same restricted girl, under my mother's oppressive thumb.*

Giving up on her attempts at capturing that paradise an ocean away, she tossed aside her brush and contemplated Niall Marksman once more.

For all her earlier silent protestations of the contrary, she *did* care that he didn't like her. Despite his tangible antipathy toward her, she felt an inextricable bond with him.

He'd been cast out of the Hell and Sin to see after Diana's well-being. And she had been turned out of Society for the crimes of her mother. In that, they were more alike than different. As such, even though servants scurried in fear whenever he came down the hall, it was hard to remain afraid of someone one shared something in common with.

She sighed.

Alas, there still remained the problem that Niall was always working and at some point decided that meant he stood in wait outside the rooms she visited. Only after he'd done a search of the space, of course.

The floorboards outside groaned, and she quickly looked up.

Her heart sank with disappointment as her maid appeared. Just as she always did. At the same precise time. With the same tray of pastries.

"I've brought pastries, my lady," Meredith announced, with a deferential curtsy. "Shall I place them over"—*here*—"here, my lady. Next to your"—latest painting—"current painting?" Diana sighed. *Close enough.* The maid moved with rote steps that came from following the same dreary routine over and over. The kind of routine of puff pastries and powdered tarts that made a lady want to stamp her foot and scream until she gave in to the madness that surely awaited.

Fighting back the maelstrom of frustration swirling in her breast, she mustered a smile. "Thank you, Meredith."

The young servant waited patiently. "Is there anything you require, my lady?"

Freedom. Fresh air. Friendship. "No. That will be all." No sooner had the words left her, Meredith was starting for the door. She disappeared a moment later, leaving Diana alone. She glanced over at the silver tray. Two dozen pastries. An amount better suited to a lady expecting callers. Other than when Helena came to visit, the staff had not admitted a single guest in these walls in a year. Untying her apron, she shrugged out of the garment and then carefully draped it over the back of the sapphire-blue Louis XIV settee.

She considered the tray and then alternated her stare to the doorway. How very quiet he was out there.

Not Mr. Marksman, as Diana's father had referred to him. Not Marksman, as Ryker had. Rather . . . Niall.

This being his third day in the household, Diana had taken to calling the guard assigned her—*Niall.*

"Niall." She silently mouthed the two-syllable word that was his name.

It had been a very winding process, in coming to her determination to abandon his surname. After all, ladies did not call men by their Christian names. Most of the starchy matrons referred to their husbands by their surnames, Mr. This-or-That.

In the end, it hadn't been propriety or fear of impropriety that had ultimately led to her decision, but rather—his surname. Or, if one wished to be *truly* precise, it hadn't been propriety or familial connections that resulted in her silent address of Niall, but rather—a painting. A painting that had evoked dark thoughts.

Sunlight streamed through the floor-length windows and bathed the room in a soft light.

Settling into the chair nearest the bronze-mounted side table, Diana ignored the pastries in favor of the single book, forgotten until now, resting on the corner. She snatched the book and flipped quickly through, searching for that dog-eared page . . . and then paused. *A Battle on Horseback* by Gerrit Claesz Bleker. Diana worked her eyes over the page. It was not the crimson-uniformed soldier, arched back, shield up, in his moment of death that intrigued her. Diana dusted her fingertips over the soldiers sketched in the distance. Rather, it was the marksman, so wholly unfazed by the tumult around him. Looking past the man being felled into the eyes of a victim who'd share that same fate. Some distant figure who existed as nothing more than an imagined person, for the viewer and the marksman there to end him.

Diana quickly snapped the leather tome closed and shoved it aside.

Niall he would only be.

Which was a good deal better than the hint of death and murder attached to that surname. In thinking of him as Niall, she'd stripped away some of the automatic fear that came from an aloof stranger who waited outside one's room and who trailed along in one's wake.

She chewed at the tip of her index finger. Mayhap he was one of those men bound by proprieties. After all, how many men, women, and children, regardless of station, treated Diana differently simply because she was born a duke's daughter? Mayhap Niall simply awaited an invitation.

Diana sprang to her feet. Collecting the tray, she started for the entrance of the room and then stopped in the arch. With a smile, she ducked her head into the hallway. And her offering went straight out of her head.

Having made her Come Out more than two years ago, she'd had the opportunity to observe many gentlemen. Not a single man had ever looked like Niall Marksman.

He stood sentry, like one of the king's guards, hands clasped behind him and his back just a hairbreadth away from the wall. His solidly muscled frame, poised like a serpent ready to strike, hinted at a man who neither wanted, needed, nor would ever take a break from work until the day he drew his last breath. And even then, he'd likely battle the Devil for a post.

That ruthless focus trained forward, and then he slid his gaze sideways, taking her in from the corners of his eyes. Not allowing his icy exterior to shatter her calm, Diana placed herself directly in front of him. The aromatic hint of cheroot and bergamot wafted about. It was an odd blend, both masculine and sweet, that filled her senses, momentarily distracting—

"Wot?"

Startled from her reverie, Diana curled her toes into the soles of her slippers. "I have refreshments."

I have refreshments?

"I see that."

Ignoring the sardonic humor lacing that reply, she tried again. "I thought you might join me—"

"No."

"For pastries," she said, speaking over him.

"I said no." His blunt rejection froze the smile on her lips.

The tray faltered in her hands. She eyed the confectionary offering she held out and tightened her grip on the silver handles. She might wish for company, but Diana had far too much pride to beg this man, or anyone, to join her.

After a year of confronting that same derisiveness in the world around her, Diana's patience snapped. She lowered the tray. "You don't like me much, Niall." When he made no immediate attempt to refute the charge but just looked at her through those veiled eyes, she took solace in her safe, comfortable indignation. "You, however, do not even know me. What do you see when you look at me? A pampered princess." Bearing the burden of her tray, Diana stepped out into the hall. The silver platter shook, and she quickly righted it. That jerky movement shattered all attempt at grace and control. "A precious duke's daughter?" she continued. How far he'd be from the truth on that one.

He frowned, the slight downturned corners of his mouth a surprising hint of what—his displeasure? Annoyance? What was it? "It doesn't matter if Oi like ya," he muttered.

No, it didn't. Or it shouldn't. But, blast it all . . . it did matter.

"Listen here, Niall." She took a step closer, turning the unwarranted frustration on this man. "I'm sure you'd rather be at your club . . . guarding." Did she imagine the ghost of a grin on his hard lips? "And I'd rather not need anyone assigned to me at all. But I do." In this instance, and any instance, she'd put her desire to live over any other wants or desires. "So the least we can do is be friendly while we're stuck with each other . . . *sir*."

"I'm no sir, lord, or even a partly fancy gentleman," he retorted in gravelly tones.

It was a bloody good thing she had a blasted tray in hand, because by God she ached to throw up her palms. The stubborn dunderhead.

"Being born into a station does not determine your worth, Niall. How you treat others and how you conduct yourself, however, do." Her chest rose and fell quickly, and she struggled to rein in her rapidly spiraling, out-of-control-emotions. It wasn't his fault that her life was . . . well, her life. She did not, however, have to suffer through his miserable company while he was here.

He flexed his jaw several times but remained silent, as he'd been since their first meeting. "I shall leave you to your company," she said evenly, and then, dropping an automatic curtsy, she returned to the room.

Diana deposited the tray back on its respective position, and, plopping onto the shell-back chair, she plucked a sugar-dusted cherry tart. She polished it off in several bites and then reached for another.

All these years she'd believed diffidence to be a trait reserved for the nobility, only to find that men and women, regardless of station, were very much alike in that regard.

Dropping one elbow onto the tabletop, she nabbed a bite-size powdered pastry and popped it in her mouth.

Although Ryker had assigned Niall as her guard, Diana had been so long-starved for companionship, she'd allowed herself to foolishly imagine a friendship of sorts with Niall.

Given their exchange these past three days, the last thing Niall Marksman wanted was friendship with her.

It was fine. She'd gone most of her life without companionship or friendship. She could go another bloody nineteen years if need be.

Chapter 7

For the first time in Niall's thirty-some-odd years of life, the unimaginable had happened.

He'd been taken to task.

And by a slip of a lady, no less.

Diana had given him a damned dressing-down, if one wished to be truly precise.

An unwanted wave of desire for the spirited, generously curved lady heated his veins. Diana Verney was not the pampered girl he'd taken her for. Niall stole a quick sideways glance at the doorway she'd stormed within mere moments ago. In this instance she was a *furious* woman . . . and a desirable one at that. People did not challenge Niall; men, women, lord or lady, or strangers in the street. Until this one.

Only—his gaze slid unwittingly over to the parlor doorway—it wasn't solely her indignant fury that occupied his thoughts now.

It was guilt. An unwanted, useless sentiment he'd indulged in just once in his life—when his failure to guard Ryker's wife had nearly gotten the lady killed. No good, however, came from that emotion. A man scratched and clawed to survive. To make apologies for that was a rejection of the very breath one drew. Along the way people were hurt, and if one built adequate walls to protect oneself, then one felt nothing. Which was the way it should be.

He gritted his teeth. Standing sentry, with Lady Diana Verney ensconced in the room, Niall reminded himself once more he wasn't here to be the lady's friend.

He was not here to join her for pastries. Or talk to her about the weather, or whatever mundane topics a duke's daughter spoke of.

So why did the memory of her fading smile dance around his mind?

What do you see when you look at me?

It had taken little on his part to deduce Lady Diana Verney was unlike the image he'd crafted for one of her status.

Who was this woman who'd not only speak to Niall, merciless bastard from the streets, but also invite him to sit with her?

Enough . . . Niall dug the heels of his palms against his eyes and rubbed to force the image away, but it remained anyway. *It is only because she's Ryker's sister.* Given her relationship to Ryker and Helena, by all accounts, Niall's siblings from the streets would consider that connection extended from Niall to the young woman.

The young woman with alabaster white skin that begged to be explored with his mouth. He forcibly tamped down those wicked musings for the lady. Nay, she wasn't a sister . . . or any relation.

She was just a woman. *One you bullied.*

Mayhap he was more human than he'd credited over the years, because by God, the memory of her diminishing happiness twisted his stomach muscles in vicious knots.

Bloody hell.

Niall was many things: the son of a whore, a violent street urchin trained to kill and thieve, and now a gaming-hell owner.

But he was not a bully. Not after being kicked and spit on by the man who'd taken him in.

He'd join her while she finished her pastries and then he could leave, without guilt for being a bully like the gang leaders who'd laid claim to Niall as a child. Quietly cursing, he ducked his head inside.

His gaze immediately locked with Lady Diana's. Round-eyed as she'd been since he'd discovered her lurking outside his alley, she stared back, a pastry halfway to her sugar-dusted mouth, and there was something so very . . . endearing about her in this instant.

She had the look of a child caught with her hand in the biscuit jar. His lips twitched at the corners. "May I?"

Lady Diana cocked her head, and she looked at the pastry in her fingers.

He motioned to the parlor.

"You may enter," she blurted. She jumped to her feet with such alacrity, her chair toppled backward, even as the pastry slipped from her fingers. The small treat fell onto the tray. "Of course you may," she encouraged, rushing around the fallen seat.

Niall came forward and rescued her seat, setting it upright.

Once more Lady Diana held the tray aloft. "Pastries?"

An immediate protest sprang to his lips.

She raised it higher. "I insist."

The determined glimmer in her aquamarine eyes earned his full attention. What was she saying? The pastries. Disgusted with his musings, Niall gave his head a slight shake. "I don't—"

"I said, I insist," she said, wagging the tray under his nose.

This lady bore the determination of ten of the toughest street fighters he'd faced, and Niall had survived three decades of life by knowing when to concede and when to advance. This was the time to concede. "Fine," he said brusquely.

Resetting the tray on the marble tea table alongside the pot of tea brought earlier by the maid, Ryker's sister slid into a seat. He furrowed his brow.

In Niall's world the fewer words spoken, the better. Such had been a necessity, more than anything. What was expected of him here?

She smiled up at him.

"Won't you sit?"

Niall tugged at his collar. "Oi don't—"

"I insist," she repeated once more. He hesitated, and then with stiff, jerky movements, he claimed the chair farthest from her own floral-painted one.

The lady had been correct in one regard. As they were to share each other's company, even with the station divide between them, they could at the very least strike a peaceful accord.

Undeterred by his glacial silence, Diana reached for a painted porcelain teapot. The soft flow of liquid filling the delicate cup thundered in the quiet. "How do you take your tea, Niall?" she asked, not taking her attention away from her task.

Niall. It had been the name given him by the street thug who'd purchased Niall from the woman who'd given him life. Two syllables he'd never given much thought about—until Lady Diana wrapped them in her husky, lyrical timbre. Desire pumped through him.

She paused midpour and glanced up. "Do you take cream and sugars?" Those perfectly cultured tones doused his lust like a bucket of muddied shop water being hurled at him. "Most say it's un-English to do so," she said casually, prattling on. Lady Diana lifted the lid, revealing perfectly formed cubes of sugar. "But I often prefer it."

And then it hit him with all the weight of a fast-moving carriage. By God, he, Niall Marksman, trained killer from the Dials, was sitting down to *tea*—with a duke's daughter. He choked on his swallow. One day, when he was a boy nicking purses in the streets, Diggory had ordered him to return with no fewer than five purses. Niall had stumbled upon a street performance with Punch and Judy. This exchange with Ryker's sister felt remarkably like that farce from long ago.

It also drew forth images of those powerful peers who'd been so consumed in their frivolous pursuits that they'd not seen a scrawny child with greased hair and a too-thin belly. "Oi don't drink tea," he said bitingly. Most women would be deterred by the chilly frost of that harsh Cockney. It kept him strong, and sane, and content. It was just one reason why he hated the arrangement thrust upon him. In fact, he'd rather sup with Satan than suffer through pastries and tea with a lady. It had taken but two run-ins and three days in her family's household to determine—Lady Diana was not most women.

Lady Diana gave him a bemused look. "Surely you must. It is unpatriotic to not drink it."

"I don't have any allegiance to king or country."

On a gasp, she stole a surreptitious glance around the room. "You'd be disloyal to your own country?" she pressed him, on a scandalized whisper.

Most men would feel some shame, particularly given the horror wreathing her delicate features. Niall dropped his elbows atop the gold arms of his chair. "I don't have loyalty to a country. I have loyalty to my siblings and the people who work for me." He nudged his chin toward her. "Close your mouth, love, or you're going to catch flies."

Ignoring that jeering command, Lady Diana scrambled forward onto the edge of her seat. "But that is treason." She spoke as one attempting to puzzle through a complex riddle.

He'd not stand on ceremony or pretend to be someone other than he, in fact, was. He leaned forward, shrinking some of the space between them. It was best she knew precisely the kind of monster she'd invited into her midst. "Do you know what treason is, princess?"

She gave a faint shake of her head.

"Treason is a king living in a palace lined with gold"—he flicked his hand at the gilt frames hanging neatly about the parlor—"while boys and girls starve on the streets, begging for scraps. *That* is treason."

A boy starving in the streets.

He'd tossed those words like sharp daggers that found their mark.

Is that whom he'd once been? The cynical glint in his world-weary eyes and scarred visage said yes. And not for the first time since she'd learned of Helena's existence, Diana was filled with shame at her own self-absorption for failing to see how those outside the nobility lived.

He went on, ruthless. "Treason is hanging a boy for stealing a loaf of bread to feed his kin. So do not talk to me about king and country. Are we clear, princess?" he demanded scathingly.

Was he clear? He couldn't have been clearer if he'd taken her charcoals and sketched a picture of it on one of the empty easels. "We are clear," she whispered.

She'd had lessons drilled into her by governesses in conversing. Not a single one, however, prepared her for how to respond to such gut-wrenching admissions. He spoke with a brutal honesty that shamed her. *I am my mother in so many ways.*

What she'd intended to be a friendly, casual conversation had traveled to a dark place. Mayhap there was nothing else where Niall Marksman was concerned.

Nor did she regret his speaking with her in such harshly real terms. It was how she'd longed to speak with someone for the whole of her adult life. Unnerved just the same, she proceeded to pour two cups of tea with tremulous fingers. She added two lumps of sugar to each, and the crystal thumped loudly in the otherwise still of the room. Diana held out one of the delicate porcelain cups.

"What is that?"

She glanced about in search of what had wrought that horror-filled demand. Furrowing her brow, she followed his stare to the porcelain cup in her fingers. "Tea?"

"I told you I don't drink tea."

Diana wagged a single digit. "No. You said you'd never tried it. Therefore, how will you ever know if you enjoy it or not, *unless* you try it?"

Even a stubborn man like Niall Marksman would be hard-pressed to argue with that logic. Nonetheless, he glared daggers at the teacup like she held out poison for him to consume. Diana set it down on the table between them—part offering, part challenge.

And waited.

The champlevé enamel clock ticked away the passing minutes.

When she was a small girl, Diana had taken in a mangy pup she'd found outside her family's town house. She'd snuck in the emaciated, snarling creature and given him sanctuary in her room, even a place in her bed. The yelping dog had fought every time she'd lifted him onto those white sheets. Until one day she'd entered her room and found him burrowed in her pillow. The moment he'd spied her, he'd jumped down from the bed. It had been as though he'd not wanted to reveal that he wanted or needed any comfort. How very much Niall Marksman reminded her of that beloved pup.

A pang of sadness struck her in the chest. For both the man opposite her and Prince. Over the years she'd not allowed herself to think of the dog her mother had found and tossed out into the streets. Until now.

With a curse, Niall grabbed the teacup, sending liquid droplets splashing over the side, onto the table. He downed the tepid brew in one quick swallow.

Welcoming the diversion from the solitary childhood her mother had imposed, Diana hid a real smile behind her glass. "It is meant to be sipped."

Niall wiped the back of his hand over his mouth. "Why?"

"Why?" she parroted.

"What's the point of it?" he asked, abandoning his empty cup on the table beside him.

"I don't . . ."

"To quench your thirst," he supplied. "Then why all this"—he slashed his hand at the delicate china set—"pretense of anything else?"

Diana cocked her head. She'd not given much thought to those set rules on drinking tea. Pinkie finger out. Sips small and silent. How . . . odd, to only just now question those social norms, when until now she'd not truly questioned a single one. She eyed the cup in her fingertips and thought of it from his perspective, as a man wholly unfamiliar with the trivialities imposed on ladies of the *ton*. "Sipping tea is not about quenching one's thirst," she began slowly.

He snorted and stretched his legs out before him, looping one ankle over the other. "Because the stuff is rot." At his faint smile, she relaxed in her chair. She preferred him this way. Teasing, rather than mocking. Grinning, rather than scowling. "One would do better with a glass of brandy." He glanced around the room, as though searching for one of those nasty bottles.

"Like brandy, I expect tea is an acquired taste." Now *that* was rotted stuff.

Niall arced a black eyebrow. "And you've much experience with French spirits?"

Her cheeks warmed. She knew enough about it after she'd made off with one of her father's bottles years earlier and downed enough glasses so that the following morning she was abed simultaneously praying for death and casting up the contents of her stomach. Her parents would have been horrified had they discovered that secret. What would this man have said of it?

He winged up an eyebrow.

Diana cleared her throat. "We were speaking about tea."

"Ah, yes. Of course, princess," he drawled, and for the first time that hated moniker didn't feel as though a slap upon her character. "Enlighten me."

"What is the purpose of your club?" That scandalous place in which her sister had worked and her brother still lived. Diana had entered that establishment twice now. The first time to beg for help. The second, when this man had dragged her to Ryker's private offices. Never, however, had she truly gone there and been permitted to look in on that wholly foreign world of sin and debauchery.

Niall said nothing.

Did he wish to shield her from the truth of what unfolded inside those establishments? She'd gone through her existence, until just a year ago, protected and shielded from all aspects of life. Not for the first time, she wished she'd gone somewhere . . . known *something* more in her sheltered existence. *At the Season's end, you will . . .*

At his protracted silence, she went on. "Gentlemen attend your club and sit down for games of whist and faro. No doubt, they sip brandies and other spirits and converse. There is no point to those ventures, other than the companionship of friends and acquaintances."

He folded his arms. "Is that why you believe lords visit my club?" Laughter underscored his question. "To spend time with friends?"

Diana wrinkled her nose. Yes, she rather did. "Didn't I just say as much?"

His lips pulled again at the corners in another surprising show that added a realness to Niall Marksman that hadn't otherwise been there, dulling her fear of him and transforming him into someone quite human. "It was a rhetorical question, princess."

Humph. A *mocking* human. "Oh."

Niall dropped his voice to a conspiratorial whisper. "I'll not tell you the real reason they visit."

Her heart skittered at the tantalizing lure he dangled. "You may, you know," she said quickly. "Tell me. That is . . . I will not—"

"We were speaking about the correct way to sip tea." He winked.

Her pulse accelerated. Not a single man, of any station, had ever done something as simple as wink at her. And more . . . it softened him in ways she'd not believed an oft-scowling, usually laconic man like him could be. "Yes, tea," she said, forcing herself back to the original matter of their debate. "Ladies do not visit clubs. Unless we're wed, we're not permitted to so much as attend the gaming tables set up inside the homes of members of the *ton*." She set down her suddenly hated cup of the drink that spoke to the limitations placed on women. "With so many restrictions imposed on women, when do we talk and where?" Diana jabbed her index finger at the teacup.

Niall followed her point.

"Over tea," she explained. If one had a friend or companion to speak to.

She braced for his condescension or mockery. Instead he pushed to his feet with a languid grace. Silently, he strolled the perimeter of the room, pausing periodically alongside the easels containing her works. Unnerved by his silent examination of those intimate drawings, she curled her hands into tight fists.

Her mother had forbidden Diana from sketching any animate subjects. Her father, Diana wagered, didn't even know she found joy in sketching and painting. But there was this man. Even with their shared connection to Ryker and Helena, a stranger, more than anything, who now saw and knew about the subjects that she'd paid homage to on those once-blank canvases. As he stopped at the same incomplete piece he'd examined earlier that morn, she felt exposed in ways she'd never been.

"Did you paint all these?" he asked, not glancing back.

She acknowledged his words with a nod and then remembered he could not see her. "I did," she ventured cautiously. What would he say if he knew what they really were for? Or rather, whom?

Niall rolled his broad shoulders, and his muscles strained the black brocade tailcoat. It was a surprisingly bold garment for a man given to silence. As though he dared others to venture close, so he could cut them with his steely edge.

Diana wet her lips. After her mother was sent away, Diana sought to bury herself in art. Anything other than the depth of her mother's evil and the future awaiting Diana inside that bleak institution. One day she'd visited the Royal Arcade and found a book that contained painting after painting of men, resplendent in their nudity. For endless minutes she'd flipped through those pages, riveted by the strength and power captured in each still. In this instance, a shamefully wicked part of her wished to peel back those garments and memorialize Niall Marksman's warriorlike frame upon the pages of her sketch pad.

He shot a quick glance over his shoulder, and she burned hot from the tips of her toes to the roots of her hairline. Niall jerked his chin. "Have you been to these places?"

She'd been nowhere, and sadness at the wholly empty life she'd lived kept her silent. It was that cage her parents had confined her to that she'd sought out Helena's assistance to escape. What would a man such as Niall Marksman think of Diana's plans to leave this world behind? Would he be one of those who believed a lady shouldn't have freedoms and instead be locked away in a gilded cage?

He cast a questioning look back.

Diana shook her head. "No," she replied, belatedly answering his query. "I haven't." *But I will.*

Clasping his hands at his back, Niall rocked on his heels. "I should return to my post."

Did she, in her desperate need for company, imagine the regret there? "Of course," she said, coming to her feet.

The scarred planes of his chiseled face set, and his gaze again wintry, he bore no hint of the winking man from moments ago. Staring after his retreating form, she mourned that loss. "Diana," she said.

He froze in his tracks.

"My name isn't princess or 'my lady.' My name is Diana."

Giving no indication he'd either heard or intended to honor that request, Niall took his leave, and she was left alone.

Just as she'd always been.

Chapter 8

In the following days, Diana and Niall settled into an easy truce.

There were no more deep talks of tea and treason, but he didn't refer to her as "princess," and so Diana took that as a testament of that truce.

And for the first time since the attempt on her life two months earlier, Diana didn't feel fear. It was hard *to* feel fear with a man like Niall always close. With his strength, size, and ability for silence, she'd wager he could sneak a blade on the Devil himself.

Strolling at a brisk clip through the empty grounds of Hyde Park, her maid trailing at a distance behind, Diana stopped and perused the landscape. Thick gray clouds rolled across the early morn horizon. She lifted her hands over her eyes, narrowing her scope.

Niall moved into position beside her, so close their bodies brushed. Through her thin muslin cloak, little shivers of heated awareness raced through her. Her heart knocked within its cage, and she glanced over at Niall. He briefly dusted one hand over his squared jaw. The artist in her clung to that slight movement. There was even strength in Niall Marksman's bone structure. Unlike the pasty lords with their padded chests and soft cheeks, he exuded a raw, primal strength better suited to warriors of old. "It's going to rain," he observed, shattering the spell cast by his body's nearness.

Recalling the purpose of her visit to Hyde Park, Diana looked out. Her visit here today had been with that hope in mind. "It's not going to rain. It's a perfectly lovely day."

Thunder rumbled in the distance, making a mockery of her assurance.

He snorted, the casual sound at odds with the tension pouring from his broad frame. His hand remained in a familiar position at his waist, his fingers never far from his pistol. "I swear you are the only duke's daughter who'd prefer to stroll in the rain," he muttered, as she resumed her search.

Helena had married the Duke of Somerset a year earlier. Ryker was titled the Viscount Chatham shortly after by the king for saving the Duke of Somerset's life. Even with his connections to the nobility, Diana hadn't spied him at a single event hosted by Helena. "Do you know a good many duke's daughters?" she asked. Her curiosity with the enigmatic Niall Marksman grew.

"You're the only one." By the dry edge there, he was glad for it.

Diana frowned. "Helena," she reminded him. When he turned his questioning gaze on her, she clarified. "Helena is also a duke's daughter." A beloved one, at that. Helena and Ryker would forever hold a special place in their father's heart because they'd been born to the only woman the Duke of Wilkinson had ever loved. Nor did Diana resent her siblings for their father's regard. After the misery and hardship they'd endured, they were both deserving of a lifetime of love and happiness.

"Helena is not a duke's daughter."

Another deep rumble shook the ground, almost as if nature punctuated Niall's angrily spoken denial.

Forgetting her search for the ideal spot to sketch, Diana folded her arms and met Niall's gaze squarely.

Meredith reached them. She took one glance at their mutinous positions, swallowed hard, and then turned on her heel, fleeing.

"Do you believe just because Helena and Ryker share only some of my father's blood that they are not, in fact, my siblings?" Diana asked, after the girl had gone.

"I'm saying that blood doesn't make a bond." He pounded his right fist against his chest like a primitive warrior laying down law. "Loyalty does."

His meaning rang clear: the Duke of Wilkinson had been a disloyal cur to his illegitimate offspring. She jutted her chin. Damn him for being correct in this instance. "It might not make"—*us*—"him family." Not to Niall. "But it can't be erased from who they are." Niall had it only partially accurate. Blood made for *some* bond. Just as Diana would be forever marred and linked to her own mother's evil, Diana and Ryker were connected, too. "No matter how much they might wish it," she added softly, to herself.

Feeling his piercing gaze on her, Diana called over her maid. She'd not come here to lament her past or present, or the future that awaited her. "Meredith?" Her maid came rushing over. "I will take those," she said, relieving the servant of the supplies. "You may return to the carriage."

Meredith hesitated. "My lady?" Swallowing loudly, her gaze flitted over to Niall.

The irony of that was not lost on Diana. "He is Lord Chatham's brother," she said gently, dimly registering Niall's body coiling tight. "And he is here for my benefit. No harm will befall me." Still, Meredith hesitated. "Go," she insisted. "Before the rains come."

"His Grace—"

"Would not want you sitting about in the rain." That fabrication came out easily. The truth being the duke would care little for either Meredith or Diana. That hadn't always been the case. He'd once been a devoted, doting papa. The muscles of her chest tightened. "Go," she repeated. This time her voice emerged harsher than she intended.

Meredith dropped a stiff curtsy, skirted a wide path around Niall, and bolted back down the graveled walking path.

A gust of wind stretched through the park. The cool gale sent the branches overhead swaying, and the green leaves danced in an uneven rhythm to that movement. Feeling Niall's gaze on her, Diana started forward.

"I thought you said it wasn't going to rain," he reminded. With his every forceful step, his black leather Wellington boots kicked up rock and gravel. Where most men had a lace-up and a slight heel, Niall's footwear spoke of a functionality and power, with little regard to fashion dictates. They perfectly suited him.

"I lied," she said, clutching her books close. She stepped off the neatly paved walking trail and started for the edge of the lake.

"You also lied to that girl about your father."

She drew herself up tight.

"The duke wouldn't want you in public without a maid about to guard your virtue."

Diana scoffed. For that to be true, one required a father who'd care and a gentleman *interested* in claiming her virtue. "I require a guard, Niall, but not one to protect my virtue." As soon as the bitter admission escaped her lips, she wanted to call it back. Humiliation streaked a blazing hot path over her cheeks. *Please, say nothing more. Please, let the matter rest.*

And mayhap he was more of a gentleman than he'd credited, for Niall didn't probe. Coming to a stop at the shore, Diana sank onto the ground so close to the lake, her hem nearly brushed the softly lapping water.

With her charcoal pencil in one hand, she opened her sketch pad, turning to a blank page. Then she focused on the rippling water. Or she attempted to.

Frowning, she tipped her neck back. Niall loomed over her. It was nigh impossible to clear one's mind when there was a ferocious bear of a man blocking out the light. "Would you care to sit?"

"No." He continued to pass his gaze over the empty grounds. He was always working. What must it be to go through life in that perpetual state of preparedness? How did he not go mad from searching for danger in every crevice and corner?

She sighed. "I cannot concentrate when you're hovering."

Niall paused in his search to glare at her. "I'm not hovering. I'm guarding you."

Diana smiled. "It is just past seven in the morning. It is nearly raining. Lords and ladies do not visit Hyde Park at this hour, and in the rain, no less." It was sound logic.

"It's not lords and ladies who'd wish you dead," he said with such brutal realness a shiver iced her spine, and her smile melted.

With the lack of suspicious events in her household, and the absence of danger, she'd allowed herself to forget the threat that had sent her to Ryker. But there could be no divorcing herself from that reality. This man who stood close at her heels at all times was proof of that. She'd simply allowed herself to pretend he was a friend, and not the guard, he, in fact, was. "Fair enough," she concurred.

His midnight eyebrows shot up.

Did he expect she was an unreasonable lady who'd not see the merit of his reminder?

"But perhaps you might back away, just a bit." Diana held her index finger and thumb apart a smidgen.

Niall placed several paces between them. Close, but not looming, and enough that she might be able to now attend her latest project.

Looking out once again, Diana took in the surroundings. The air bereft of the kestrel's song hinted at the storm that hung heavy in the air.

A lady must not be caught in the rain, Diana . . . Rain leads to chills. Chills lead to red noses. Red noses lead to disinterested gentlemen.

Yes, Mama.

Diana curled her fingers tight around the pencil. All those wasted years on lessons that hadn't mattered. Lessons in securing a husband and being prim and polite. Back then when she'd kept a list tucked away detailing all the traits and characteristics of the man she'd one day wed. Until life had proven just how honorable men were.

Even her mother, on the surface, had evinced those very traits she'd sought to drill into Diana. All she'd earned for it was an empty marriage. One that had twisted her into a heartless woman who'd draw her final breath inside the halls of Bedlam.

I did it for you, Diana, and I would do it all, again . . . You are my daughter. We are the same . . . Someday you will understand that.

Crack. The pencil splintered in half. She stared blankly down at the remaining piece of charcoal in her fingertips. Yes, she was very much the Duchess of Wilkinson's daughter, for she felt no regret or love for the woman who'd given her life. All Diana felt was a vicious, terrifying hatred.

Feeling Niall's gaze on her, Diana set aside the pencil and reached for another. A single raindrop hit her nose, and she brushed it back.

"Wouldn't it be better to come back when it is sunny?" Niall muttered under his breath.

That would defeat the purpose in her being here. "We live in England, Niall," she reminded him, as she put her pencil to paper. "It is *never* sunny."

He chuckled. That sound, rusty and full, brought her head flying up so quickly her bonnet slid backward. In the week since he'd moved into her household, she'd never heard his laugh laced with anything other than cool mockery.

"It's been sunny two of the last three days," he pointed out, adjusting his hat and then swiftly returning his hands to their battle-ready position.

Diana resumed her sketching. "I never took you for one who'd be afraid of a little rain," she teased.

Another distant rumble shook the ground.

"Oi'm not afraid of anything." His eyes flashed dangerously.

Had he never been teased? Ryker and his siblings from the streets did not strike her as the joking sort. Just like that the icy wall between them was thrown back up. The glint in his eyes would be enough to silence most grown men, but perhaps Diana's madness had already taken root, for she no longer felt a jot of fear where Niall Marksman was concerned. "Everyone fears something, Niall," she said softly, not backing down from the challenge in his unforgiving gaze.

Fire flashed in his eyes. "Only people who are weak know fear." Is that how he saw her? As a weak, pathetic creature who'd humbled herself before Ryker Black? Niall's tone signaled the discussion was over, and a year earlier, dutiful and obedient in every regard, she'd have let the matter die. Would never have even raised a challenge to begin with. But she was no longer that girl . . . and she was certainly not weak.

"When the axle of my carriage broke, I was tossed around inside," she said softly. "I landed on the floor, knocking my head here." She touched her fingertips to the edge of her temple, drawing his hooded gaze to the place she'd once worn a vicious lump. His eyes darkened like a storm-tossed sea. "The lead windows exploded, spraying me with glass." Diana turned over her left palm to study the arrow-shaped scar made by a jagged shard of glass on that day. The slightly puckered flesh marked the accident, transporting her back as the terror of that day trickled in. Her cries had blended with the driver's shouts as the carriage had careened out of control, with moments stretching on into eternity. Diana concentrated on breathing evenly. She forced her eyes away from the scar and met his gaze square on. "Asking Ryker for help does not make me weak. It makes me smart for choosing life over my own pride."

Before she descended into the same state of madness that afflicted her mother and father, Diana intended to live life to the fullest. And because she knew how faithless gentlemen in fact were, that life most certainly did *not*, nor ever *would*, include a husband.

Chapter 9

Niall would hand it to the lady.

Clever and brave, she was far more intelligent than he'd credited a week earlier when he'd discovered her creeping around his alley. Then, Diana did, as she'd reminded him on numerous scores, share Ryker and Helena's blood. She might not be born to the streets, or able to survive for a day in them, but there was some strength to her, and his grudging respect for the lady grew.

Another blast of wind battered about them, and he quickly righted his hat, tugging the brim down.

"What is it like?" she asked, turning the page in her sketch pad. "Life in St. Giles," she clarified.

Vile. It stank like heated shite on a summer day. Ruthless. Why did she care to know, anyway? "Ya've been there," he said gruffly, not wanting to talk about home. Not when it only reminded him that he'd been banished for his failures. For failing to protect and defend the people dependent on him.

"Twice," she conceded. "The first time I saw barely anything after . . ." Diggory's attack. Her cheeks went ashen, a marked reminder of her frailty. "And the other when I paid a visit to Ryker."

Paid a visit. If that wasn't taking liberties with her clandestine sneaking in disguise through his alley, he was King George's mad da back from the dead. "If I tell ya, will ya hurry up so we can leave, princess?" That request came not solely from the rising storm, but also a disquiet at visiting a park where peers freely strolled.

"Diana," she reminded him.

He growled. "Oi'm not calling ya Diana." The chit was a step below royalty, but that wasn't all. To remove that proper form of address only took down another layer between them.

"But you are Ryker's brother . . ." She left that thought unfinished.

"And?" he snapped.

She sighed, and another breeze carried that soft exhalation to his ears. "And I am Ryker's sister." He stitched his eyebrows into a single line. "So that nearly makes us"—surely she was not going to say—"siblings." She'd said it.

"Ya aren't a sister to me," he clipped out. Not when he'd appreciated the curve of her hips and trimness of her waist.

He may as well have kicked her pup for the hurt in her gaze. Bloody hell, and here he'd thought himself immune to a lady's wounded eyes. "Dirty. St. Giles is dirty," he volunteered, abruptly shifting the discourse back to the question that had preceded all her you're-like-a-brother-to-me talk. There, he'd given her that. Except she made no move to stand.

She wrinkled her pert nose. "That is hardly descriptive."

Battling the urge to toss her over his shoulder and carry her from the damned freezing park, he growled. "Ya didn't say Oi had to be descriptive."

"Obviously it is implied, if I ask you to tell me what St. Giles is like."

"It's not implied." A person was wise to not make assumptions, unless one was prepared for an outcome alternative to the one desired. By the square set to her narrow shoulders, she'd about as much intention of abandoning her post at the lakeside than he did of giving up his club to Killoran's care. She wanted a glimpse of his world; he'd give her the details unsparingly. "The streets are crowded with whores and beggars at every corner. Shop doors and windows hang open to rid the hovels of the stench inside." For even the rancid smells of the rookeries were better than the noxious scents of those homes inhabited by unwashed thieves and whores.

Her cheeks paled, and she thankfully resumed her sketching in silence. Had he horrified her with his frank talk? That had been in part his intention. To both shock her into quiet and hurry her up so they could leave this bloody—

"What of the buildings?" What of the . . . ? She froze midstroke and lifted her head. "What are they made of?"

She was relentless. "Oi don't have a bloody clue." He scratched at his brow. Nor had he ever given it any thought. It didn't matter what walls or ceilings were made of, as long as they provided shelter from the elements. "I . . ." He glanced down and over her shoulder, caught sight of her work.

The very streets he'd described had begun to artfully materialize on the page under her masterful strokes. That was why she'd asked about the rookeries. So she could sketch it. Niall knew as much about art as he did courtly manners, but he could still appreciate her deft hand.

She angled her head, blocking his view of her work.

Then it began to rain.

The wind battered his garments, soaking the fabric and chilling him from the inside out. It was a misery he'd not suffered through since he'd poured his stolen fortunes into the ownership of the Hell and Sin. Ironically, he'd be forced back out into the elements by one of those peers he'd spent his entire life hating. "It is raining," he reminded her snappishly.

"It is drizzling," she said, not taking her gaze from her sketch pad. "Entirely diff—" A gust of wind stole those words, drowning them out.

Niall had known all number of odd types in the streets. But a noblewoman who'd sit and draw during a bloody squall? He rubbed his hands together to force warmth back into the freezing digits. How could she even move her fingers to sketch in this bloody cold? He clenched his teeth hard to keep them from chattering. God, he did not miss the brutal agony of living outside in the elements as he had for more than eleven years of his life. He'd never forget the hell of it. He did, however, relish the warmth and security that came in living at his club. A club he'd not see until Ryker's sister found a husband to look after her.

"You should try gloves, Niall," Diana suggested, making another mark on that page. She paused and ran her eyes over his frame. "At the very least, a cloak."

"Gloves and cloaks slow your movements." A lady born to high society, she'd never needed the dexterity to draw a blade and slash a man to save herself. Even if she saw danger in broken axles, she'd not had to battle a person for the right to draw another breath.

How smug the nobility was. They might have the advantage in wealth, power, and prestige, but they didn't know shite about survival. The wind kicked up. He scraped his gaze over the gray horizon.

Lady Diana made no move to quit her sketching. She bent over that book. If the rain marred her works or that page, she gave no indication, just continued merrily on in her task. For all intents and purposes, she may as well have been picnicking in the damned park, but she wasn't. They were here indulging her damned frivolities. Suffering through the rain for her pleasures.

All his age-old resentments boiled to the surface, as they so often did when presented with those lords and ladies who put their own interests before those of anyone else. He opened his mouth, set to blister her ears, when she stopped suddenly and turned the book around.

The rain had begun to mar the pencil on the pages, but it did little to detract from the brilliance of her work. She'd brought the rookeries blazing to life; he could almost hear the raucous din as whores hawked their services to drunken sailors.

"Of course, it's not perfect." She was wrong. She'd portrayed everything from the uneven cobbled roads to the dilapidated buildings. "Someday, when I visit, I'll be able to better capture it."

She spoke the way a lady might speak of a future voyage to the Continent and not some of the most perilous streets in England. He pulled back his lip in a cynical grin. The dandified fops who'd one day marry her themselves only visited those threatening streets to wager their fortunes and bed their whores. Not a single sane one of them would risk their highborn wife. "No husband will ever let you step inside St. Giles." A husband who'd claim her body and crush her spirit and—

Diana snapped her book shut and began to gather her belongings. "There are no worries on that score. I've no intention of marrying," she mumbled.

Niall sank to his haunches and quickly overtook the task, eager to be done with this place. "Here." He stood and helped her up. Sketch pads and pencils cradled close, Diana waited as he gathered the blanket. Hastily folding it, Niall tucked it under his arm, and then they started at a quick pace down the path.

Then her words registered.

He came to an abrupt stop, his heel sinking into a thick patch of mud.

The skies opened up in a violent deluge that matched the tempest raging inside. Water streamed in rivulets down his cheeks, blinding him, and he blinked back the moisture. Tossing aside the blanket, he stalked forward and circled his hand around her delicate forearm.

A gasp exploded from her lips on a loud exhalation. The books toppled to the ground between them. "N-Niall." That tremor hinted at her fear.

Good. The silly chit should fear him just then. He tightened his grip on her arm. "Wot in 'ell did you say?" he shouted into the wind.

The lady's limp, wet curls hung about her, highlighting those lush, crimson lips made for sinning, now stark red against her pale cheeks. Strawberries. They put him in mind of that summer fruit and the first time he'd sampled such joys.

Do not look at her bloody mouth. Or think about how badly he wished to claim her lips and learn whether they tasted like berries and goodness.

Except . . . Diana spoke, not allowing him to look away. "Which part?"

The bewilderment in her question effectively doused his ardor. "About marrying," he raged.

"Uh . . ."

Fury descended over his eyes, momentarily blinding him with his rage. *That was what she'd say?*

With a surprising show of strength, Diana used his distraction to her advantage and tugged her arm free. She hastily gathered her drenched books. "P-perhaps w-we should have this d-discussion in the carriage." With the regality of a queen, even in a raging storm, she proudly stood.

Raindrops struck his cheeks, burning his skin. Ignoring the discomfort, he stared after her retreating frame.

Now she wished to escape the bloody rain? Now, when it was convenient to her?

She broke out into an all-out sprint. Who'd have believed a lady, hampered by skirts, could race off with the speed of a deft London street thief?

He had suffered through this past week with the ever-present reminder that his role here was temporary. This daft lady's marital state was inextricably linked to his freedom. As soon as she married, she'd become some other man's concern and Niall would be free to return to his home and hell. Only to find out she'd no intention of marrying, leaving him effectively trapped—unless his brothers relented and voted on his return. In five long strides, he easily overtook her, blocking her escape.

She shrieked, hugging those books close to her soaked garments. "You startled—"

"Why did ya say ya have no intention of marrying?" He interrogated her with the same biting fury he did traitors inside his club. Except . . . His gaze dipped lower. The green muslin cloak was plastered against her generously curved frame, highlighting her lush femininity. He briefly closed his eyes. He'd been too long without a woman. There was no other accounting for the lust she roused. Disgusted with himself, he gave his head a hard shake. "Oi asked ya a question," he compelled.

To the lady's credit, this time she did not back down. Rather, she stood, a veritable rain goddess wholly unfazed by the storm raging about them. "Because I do not," she said with the same matter-of-factness as when she'd probed him on his damned preference for tea. And just like that, she marched off again.

He flared his nostrils. If she thought that flippant four-word reply ended the matter, then she was dicked in the nob. "Diana Verney, Oi'm not through with this discussion."

Diana sighed, grateful for the volatile wind that concealed that troubled exhalation. Niall already took her for a weak, brainless twit. She'd not feed those unflattering assumptions.

Again, he gripped her by the arm.

Of course, he'd not let the matter rest. It had been a dratted slip of information. Information she'd intended to keep secret from the whole of the world. And just like that, she'd breathed the truth aloud—to this man. Fury burned from the sapphire orbs of Niall's eyes.

Fiddling with the sopping strings of her hopelessly ruined bonnet, she conceded he was a good deal more than that. A vein throbbed at his temple. He was livid, and yet what business was her marital state to him? "By your response, one would think you were a disappointed papa."

It proved the wrong thing to say. "Is this a game to you?"

Diana winced as he tightened his hold, and the fear she'd known in the alley at St. Giles stirred to life once more. For, in this instance, she was brutally reminded that this man, who so easily and harshly handled her, was not like the affable gentlemen of the *ton*, who'd never dare put their hands on a lady. Not unless they wished to marry, or face a duel at sunrise. "Release me," she countered, not allowing herself to give in to the fear he roused.

Surprisingly, he did.

"Well?"

Goodness, he was unrelenting. And because Diana knew he'd keep her here until she either expired from the frigid, rainy weather or gave him an answer, she explained. "I have no intention of marrying."

His eyes formed round, horrified circles. "All ladies want to wed."

"Most do." Only the naive, hopeful ones. "Some do not." The practical ones who knew the peril in trusting your life and future over to a man.

"And you fall into the category of some."

At last he understood. She would not, however, explain the pain that had brought her to the decision. Or the fear for what she ultimately faced. Those were pieces of herself she'd share with no one. "I do."

Suddenly he released her. Unleashing a vitriolic stream of inventive curses, he began to pace a frantic path. Despite the icy rain penetrating her cloak, Diana's cheeks went warm at the words spewing from his lips. Words no man, woman, or child should ever hear. "It matters so much to you whether I marry?" she puzzled aloud. Her own father didn't give much consideration anymore to Diana's unmarried state. Then, he didn't give much thought to anything, since he'd discovered his wife's treachery against his beloved, now dead mistress.

Niall stopped abruptly, midstride. He dragged off his wet hat and slapped it furiously against his leg. "Do you know why Ryker sent me here?"

They spoke in unison.

"To protect me."

"To protect you."

Niall jammed his hat back atop his drenched black curls. Moisture sluiced down his rugged cheeks. It was on the tip of her tongue to point out that he was better off without that soggy article, but she took in the vein bulging at the corner of his eye and thought better of it.

"It was a bloody rhetorical question."

Diana stamped her boot, damning the muddied earth that robbed her of a satisfying tap. Him and his dratted rhetorical questions. "Don't ask a question, then, if you don't expect an answer."

"I'm here, forced out of my club, to protect you from an imagined foe."

Diana stopped beating her foot on the ground. A wave of shock went through her. It shouldn't surprise her, given how little her parents had regarded her intelligence, that this man should also doubt her. "Why would you trust the word of a woman?" Uttering those words left a bitterness in her mouth.

He gave his head a shake, spraying her face with droplets of water. "That ain't it. I know plenty of women and trust their judgment."

That revelation held her momentarily frozen. In a world where not a single man of her acquaintance or relation trusted a woman's judgment, this man did. He . . . He . . . Then the weight of his meaning sank into her slow-moving brain. Diana buried a gasp in her nearly frozen fingers. "You don't believe *me*," she whispered. She didn't know why it mattered that, as he'd said, he knew plenty of women—women whose judgment he trusted—but it did. Damn him.

Niall caught her around the wrist, halting her, this time with a gentleness she'd not believed a man of his size and power was capable of.

But then he spoke, shattering that illusion. "It doesn't matter whether or not I believe you." Letting her go, Niall growled, a guttural sound better suited to an incensed beast than a man. "It matters what your brother believes. And as long as you are unwed, then I am stuck"—he slashed a hand back and forth between them—"here."

She recoiled and curled her fingers to keep from slapping his insufferable face. And from crying. She wanted to give in to that pathetic emotion, too. It was only because she was wet and miserable. It was foolish to feel the sting of pain at those angrily spoken words, and yet they gutted her still. For ultimately, that is what she was . . . to Society. Her father. Her brother. Niall. A burden everyone could do without. Diana angled her quivering chin up a notch. "You can go to hell." With that remarkably cool deliverance, she stalked off.

Lightning lit up the dark sky with an eerie blue. "I'm not done with you, princess," he bellowed.

Princess. Her teeth set. "I am done with you, sir." Dismissing him, she lengthened her stride.

"I already told ya, I'm not a damned gentleman—"

She spun about so quickly, Niall nearly collided with her. He skidded to an abrupt stop.

"And I'm not a bloody princess." Her heart raced. She'd not even heard or felt his approach. The fabric of his sopping, midnight-black coat clung to his thick chest and corded arms. And she damned herself for responding still to that raw, powerful masculinity. Rain soaked her head and ran in rivulets down her cheeks, blurring her vision. Through her lashes, she squinted up at him. "My name is Diana," she yelled into the storm, "and I have no intention of marrying. Nor do I owe you answers or an explanation. And furthermore—"

Niall caught her about the nape and brought his mouth down hard on hers.

Frozen, Diana clung to her sketch pads as he devoured her lips. Devoured her as though he wished to consume. With a moan she released her books, and they tumbled to the ground. As a young girl, not even a village boy had dared to steal a kiss from the duke's daughter. As a young woman, she'd arrived in London craving a hint of passion and a gentleman's embrace. Nothing in all her waiting, wondering, or dreaming could have prepared her for this hedonic exchange. His breath came fast against her lips, in time to the frantic rise and fall of his chest.

She twisted her fingers through his long, damp locks, turning herself over to his violent possession.

Groaning, Niall parted her lips and laid claim to her. A shock like walking barefoot on a carpeted floor burned her at the satiny soft flesh plundering her mouth. She tentatively touched the tip of her tongue to his. An animalistic groan filled her mouth as he cupped her buttocks, dragging her close.

Through the damp fabric of her skirts, his shaft thrust hard and insistent against her belly. She should feel shame. She stood in the middle of Hyde Park in a raging thunderstorm hungrily kissing a man who, but for a brief encounter a year earlier, she'd otherwise known a week. In this instance she cared about nothing but this burning heat pooling between her thighs. And this need to be closer to him. To—

Thunder ripped across the horizon, and Niall tore himself away so quickly Diana stumbled. She shot out her hands to balance herself, as that connection was shattered.

"That was a mistake."

His words sucked the breath from Diana. Another chill gripped her. One that had nothing to do with the rain and everything to do with the icy diffidence of his gaze. He'd bestowed her first kiss, reduced her to a puddle of aching sensation, and that is how he'd refer to it? As a mistake? *Then, what do you expect of a man outraged that he's stuck here with you?* That taunting voice whispered around her mind.

He gathered her books and held them over.

With fingers trembling, she reached for the wet offering.

"It will not happen again," he said, freezing her midmovement.

It will not happen again. His words turned a beautifully passionate exchange into nothing more than a regret and a mistake. Teeth chattering, Diana remained stonily silent.

For the world's ill opinion of her, Diana had too much pride to force a man who wanted nothing to do with her into the role of guard. She steeled her jaw. A man who didn't even trust that someone, in fact, wished her ill.

Niall Marksman didn't want the role of guard. At all. That was fine. He could be on his way, and Diana would continue as she'd been for the past year—alone, with only herself to rely on.

She was better off with him gone.

So why, as they reached the carriage, drenched from the steady rain, did it feel as though she lied to herself? *Because he kissed me. Because he is the first man who'd never given a jot about my status as duke's daughter and treated me instead as a woman to be desired.* It was heady stuff, indeed.

Or it had been.

The driver hopped down from his box and hurriedly pulled the door open. He held a hand out to assist her, but Niall reached past him and, clasping Diana about the waist, hefted her inside like he handled a sack of potatoes from the market. Grunting, Diana rubbed at her lower back, glaring at Niall.

Meredith cried out, "My lady, you'll catch your death." The plump servant scrambled against the side of the carriage, making room for Diana.

Without a backward glance, Niall slammed the door closed.

A moment later, the barouche dipped as he climbed up beside the driver.

He'd rather face the fury of the storm than keep company with me inside the carriage. Yanking off her sopping bonnet, she hurled it onto the wet floor. Good, let him be miserable. As soon as the uncharitable thought slid in, she sank her teeth into her lower lip, damning that black part of her soul that would wish him discomfort. *Just like my blasted mother.*

Diana's teeth chattered. With numbed fingers, she fiddled with the grommets at her throat.

"Oh, my lady," Meredith fretted. She hurried to help Diana out of the sodden cloak. They slid the offending garment off Diana's trembling frame. It landed atop the flower-rimmed bonnet. "I knew I shouldn't have left you." Tears welled in the servant's eyes, and despite Niall's callous treatment, Diana was warmed by that show of concern from her maid.

She hurried to reassure her. "I am—"

"Your father is going to sack me, my lady," Meredith wailed, and then promptly burst out sobbing.

Shivering, Diana huddled inside her wet gown. This was the truth of her existence. She lived in a world where no one truly saw her. She was an obligation. A chore. And otherwise meaningless to anyone. Including Niall. Especially Niall, the eager-to-be-free-of-you guard assigned her by Ryker.

Moisture flooded her eyes, and a single drop slid down her cheek. Diana swatted at it. *I'm merely miserable from a jaunt during a rainstorm.*

"Oh, my lady," Meredith hiccupped. "Are you . . . crying?" With that, she dissolved into another noisy round of tears. And that was how the remainder of the long ride through London went: Diana seeking to reassure her blubbering maid, and Meredith begging forgiveness.

At long last they arrived in front of her pink stucco town house. As soon as the carriage rocked to a stop, Diana shoved the door open and leapt down.

She gasped at the force of her landing. Pain shot from her heel up to her leg.

Niall jumped down from the box. Heart quickening, Diana rushed ahead.

The butler, God love him, stood in wait and pulled the door open.

She sailed inside and, trailing water in her wake, took the stairs two at a time. Determination fueled her steps. As soon as she'd reached her room, Diana pushed the door shut behind her. Ignoring the gooseflesh dotting her body, she made for the small secretaire situated in front of the window.

Diana tugged out her chair, grabbed a pen and paper . . . and proceeded to write.

Chapter 10

The following morning, stationed outside her chambers as he'd been for the better part of an hour, Niall consulted his timepiece—again.

Diana was late.

One hour and fifteen minutes. He snapped the lid closed and stuffed his watch back inside his jacket.

Which should not surprise him. Since they'd returned yesterday from the storm, soaking wet and unbendingly silent, not another word had passed between them. She'd sought out her rooms, and he'd gone to change, grateful for the space between them.

When he'd made for the lady's rooms, her maid had informed him that Diana would be resting for the remainder of the day.

Other than his nightly check of her windows and locks the previous evening, he'd not caught a glimpse of her since.

For the tenth time, Niall dragged his watch fob out and consulted the time. One hour and eighteen minutes. Tucking it away once more, he folded his arms and leaned against the blue satin wallpaper.

He should be grateful that the lady wasn't pestering him with talks of tea and pastries or the streets of St. Giles. He'd not come here to be her friend, but to do a job. An assignment that, given her revelation yesterday, had no proverbial end in sight. So why had he awakened eager to go toe-to-toe again with the spitfire?

It was because people didn't challenge him, and there was something enlivening in being with a slip of a lady, bold and unafraid.

Or she *had* been unafraid.

He stole a sideways glance at her paneled door. Two serenely smiling cherubs carved onto that white panel met his gaze mockingly. Niall scowled at the insolent, albeit inanimate, angels.

For the first time since she'd gone into hiding, he forced himself to think about their embrace. He'd kissed her with a violent intensity better reserved for the whores he'd coupled with. And by Diana's hesitation and then eventual abandon, she'd never known a man's embrace.

That should horrify him. He, Niall Marksman, a man with a made-up name and no definitive birth date, had kissed an innocent noblewoman. There had been a primal sense of masculine pride that he'd been the first to take her lush mouth under his and awaken her to the passion that could be found in lovemaking.

The lady, however, had apparently been of a differing opinion.

With a sound of disgust, he propped the heel of his boot against the wall. *What did you expect?* That she should take pride and pleasure in being kissed by a guttersnipe? It was an embrace that should never have happened and, as he'd pledged, never again would happen. She was off-limits not only because she was a lady but also because she was in his care . . . and because she was Ryker's sister. In the fury of the lightning storm, he'd let down his defenses and given in to the violent hungering he'd felt for her since he'd noticed the flare of her hips more than a week earlier. Restless, he unsheathed his knife, finding a comforting weight in the heavy blade. This is what Ryker had spoken to. The reason it had been Niall who'd been sent away.

He passed the gilded handle back and forth between his palms. Since Diggory's men had infiltrated the club and turned patrons against them, Niall had been shaken. He'd sooner take this blade to his own throat than admit to Ryker he'd been right on that score. With every ill word spoken against the employees of the Hell and Sin, and infiltration from those thugs who sought to avenge Diggory, Niall was proven powerless. And in a world where you had no power, you perished . . . as did the people in your care.

Niall stretched the knife out, pointing the edge of the dagger at Diana's door. He closed one eye and looked over the weapon at the oak barrier between them. Whether either of them wished it, Diana was now the person in his care. She might despise him for his momentary loss of control, one that had seen her thoroughly kissed. She might hate him for doubting the realness of the threat against her, but he'd a task to do. And she was that task.

Niall lowered his arm to his side.

For her shows of strength and courage, the fact that she hid away from him even now was hint of her fear of him. He recalled her fiery eyes, flashing with outrage, when he'd questioned the threat on her life. Yes, there was no doubt the lady was equally outraged over that, too.

He stole another impatient glance at the door. He'd no idea how to handle a displeased lady. The women he dealt with were raw, real creatures who'd sooner punch a person in the face than hide behind a door, sulking. Not his sister, Helena. Not the former prostitutes turned servants and dealers. Not a single one of them at the Hell and Sin would lock themselves away.

He frowned. Except . . . who would have believed Diana Verney was capable of such prolonged silence? It didn't fit with the humming, singing, and always smiling lady he'd guarded this past week.

He stilled.

It didn't fit with her at all.

Warning bells clamored at the back of his mind.

Don't be stupid. You checked her windows and doors before turning in and were stationed outside her room at the customary six o'clock hour.

Nonetheless, Niall edged closer to the door. Pressing his ear against the wood panel, he strained for a hint of sound. "Diana?" Sliding his knife back in his boot, he knocked once.

Silence.

An irrational, unfamiliar sentiment squeezed his chest—fear. It soured his mouth and seared his veins, leaving him motionless.

The distant groan of a floorboard snapped him from his paralysis. He shook his head hard. *Don't be a bloody lackwit.* The lady had been clear in her displeasure; her silence now was only further proof of it. Childish games. "Princess?" he challenged, in a bid to startle her from her stubborn silence.

The loud hum of quiet served as his only answer.

Blood pumped quickly through his veins, as it did during every street battle. With slow, careful movements he drew out his pistol. Frowning, he pressed the door handle. It easily turned, allowing him entry. Niall did a swift search of the room, bypassing the neatly made floral coverlet and gold-framed vanity. Gun close, he moved deeper into the delicate, ladylike space. His eyes took in every empty corner and crevice of the immaculate chambers as he struggled for control of his spiraling thoughts. She couldn't have just . . . vanished. Stopping at the floor-length windows, he tested each lock. Equal parts relief, fury, and frustration warred in a vicious blend.

Bloody hell.

The soft tread of steps in the hall brought him around. Leveling his pistol at the doorway, he drew back the hammer.

Diana's maid stopped abruptly, her wide-eyed gaze on the barrel pointed at her chest. All the color leeched from her rounded cheeks. She swallowed loudly.

"Where is your mistress?" he demanded, startling a cry from the girl.

"Sh-she is painting, Mr. Marksman." Tears flooded her eyes.

Unmoved by those crystalline drops that could be turned on at will by a skilled deceiver, he searched for a lie there. "When?" he pressed, taking a step forward.

The servant stumbled, tripping over her skirts in her haste to be away. "This morning," she cried. "Five o'clock, I believe. It was early. Dark, still," she rambled, her words running together.

Niall assessed her and then lowered his pistol. "Why didn't I see her?"

The girl collapsed against the doorway, taking support from the frame. "It was before you awakened, M-Mr. Marksman."

"Impossible." The shocked denial burst from his lips. He'd learned to subsist and thrive on nothing more than three hours' sleep, and what he did take was so light, the distant creak of a floorboard could stir him. Eyeing the woman with a renewed suspicion, Niall advanced. "What are ya doing here?"

Diana's maid dropped her eyes. "H-His Grace requests your p-presence in his office." Her voice emerged as a breathless squeak.

The duke. Diana's father. His neck went hot. Had she told the rotund, witless noble Niall had put his scarred, lowly hands on her? It was the kind of offense that would earn the rage and promise of retribution from any nobleman. Hadn't the Hell and Sin nearly collapsed after Ryker had been discovered in a compromising position with his now wife? And Ryker was a duke's son and now titled lord.

It mattered not that Ryker, Niall, and Helena had forged a bond deeper than blood. Such a connection would be insignificant to a high-in-the-instep toff. To whom Niall would never exist as anything more than a dreg of the underbelly. With a curse that sent the girl scampering back several steps, Niall returned his pistol to the waist of his breeches.

He stalked from the room. Mayhap she hadn't said anything to the duke. Mayhap the man wished to review Niall's observations and findings in the week he'd been here. Marching down the halls, Niall scoffed. And mayhap he'd been lauded a prince and placed on the throne.

He descended the stairs and started along the corridors leading to Wilkinson's office. Every step took him past portraits of Diana's distinguished ancestors. Even memorialized in time, they peered down their hawkish, noble noses at him. The lady's powerful kin, dead and alive, were not who Niall worried after. Rather, one relative: Ryker Black. The man who'd tasked him with the responsibility of looking after Diana. Not mauling her or lusting after her the way he might a Covent Street doxy.

Reaching the duke's office, Niall flexed his hands and knocked once. The loud rap thundered around the otherwise silent halls. Then, Niall had never been one of those subservient bastards who scratched at doors like a desperate animal.

"Enter."

That jovial greeting didn't fit with a man who wanted Niall's blood for breakfast. Warily, he pressed the handle. He stepped inside and quickly closed the door behind him.

A wide smile on his fleshy cheeks, Diana's father struggled to his feet. "Come in. Come in, Mr. Marksman," he encouraged, tossing his arms wide, drawing Niall's attention inadvertently to the corner of the room.

He froze.

Ryker and Calum stood shoulder to shoulder in the corner of the room.

And Niall, who was never thrown off-kilter, rocked on his heels. They wouldn't be here unless either harm had come to one of their own . . . or the club was suffering. "Wot are ya doing here?" he rasped, stalking over.

"Mr. Marksman, please. Sit. Sit," the duke cajoled, the way those wastrel dandies did their acquaintances at the gaming tables.

Niall opened his mouth to order the grinning lackwit into silence, but one hard look from Ryker and he let the dire threat wither.

"Sit," Ryker advised.

Sliding into one of the leather wing chairs, Niall sat on the edge.

His Grace claimed the chair beside him. Folding his hands, he trained his focus on Niall. "I appreciate your work this past week, looking after Diana."

Stiffening, Niall searched the old lord and then the other two men present for a hint of knowing. For a hint that Niall had, in fact, claimed Diana's mouth, in public, where any passersby might have witnessed her ruin. "I'm not looking for gratitude," he said gruffly. "It's work." Only, it hadn't been solely that. He'd enjoyed Diana's chattering and singing and sketching. Those were secrets he'd take to his grave when he kicked up his heels and went on to meet the Devil.

Ryker rested a hand on the high back of Niall's seat, and he briefly glanced up at his brother.

The duke inched his chair closer, and the wood legs scraped noisily along the floor, reclaiming his attention. "And you've admirably overseen your task." Niall would have to be deafer than a post to fail to hear that exaggerated platitude. "I would not, however, ask you to stay, if it is . . ." His Grace scrunched his brow and rubbed his hand contemplatively over his mouth. Then his eyes lit. "Difficult for you."

Nothing from ending a man's life to filching a fancy lord's purse had proven difficult for him. "Difficult for me?" he parroted, a player upon a stage without the benefit of his lines.

Ryker's father patted Niall's hand in an awkward gesture that sent his hackles up.

People didn't touch him. Not unless they were prepared to swallow their teeth for supper.

He made to grab that offending unblemished palm when Ryker's father went on, in gentling tones better suited a fearful child than a ruthless killer. "Diana explained all, Niall."

Uncaring that this pompous lord had commandeered his name, Niall honed in on those three words preceding it. "Oh?" He stretched that single syllable out in an icy steel that had earned him his ruthless reputation. "Just what did she explain?"

Silent until now, Ryker held out a folded note.

"It happens to all of us, Niall," the duke assured. "Why, I was sad to be away from Eton when I was a boy."

With her father rambling on about strange places and strange sounds and missing loved ones, Niall unfolded the crisp ivory vellum. He skimmed the page.

Dear Ryker,
Please, let me begin by thanking you. I am incredibly grateful to you for worrying after my safety.

Worrying after her safety. It had been Niall who'd seen to her well-being. It hardly mattered that he'd been forced into the damned Mayfair residence and the lady's employ. Not that he wanted her gratitude or appreciation, but he didn't want her crediting Ryker for doing anything. He hadn't. Tamping down a growl, he resumed reading.

I am also appreciative that you would provide me with Mr. Marksman's services . . .

He crushed the pages as a black rage momentarily blinded him to those graceful strokes made in Diana's hand. Not Niall, as she'd insisted on calling him a few days after his arrival. But Mr. Marksman. What should he expect, given their violent clash in the park?

"Something the matter?" Calum asked, a curious trace of amusement lighting his eyes.

Yes. The lady spoke of him the way she might a damned pack mare. "No," he muttered. His fury swelling, Niall forced himself to continue reading . . . and then stopped.

Mr. Marksman, however, is . . .

Niall read the handful of sentences several times and then blinked. Surely he'd imagined those words there. He blinked again. But no matter how many times he did, the mocking note in Diana's hand remained. His hand tightened reflexively on the page, crushing it in his palm. *"Homesick?"* he choked out.

From behind him, Calum emitted a strangled laugh, and Niall swiveled his head around and locked a dark glare on him. The faithless bastard gained control of his vocal amusement, but the mocking grin on his lips remained firmly in place.

"There is nothing to be ashamed of, Niall," the duke comforted, bringing Niall's attention forward.

Feeling burned by that damnable sheet, Niall hurriedly set the page on the edge of Wilkinson's desk. "I'm not homesick," he gritted out, shoving quickly to his feet. Then the duke's words registered. "Or ashamed." He felt any number of things: Livid. Enraged. Murderous. Ashamed was the least of his damned feelings just then. The vexing chit. By God, she was lucky she wasn't here. Not only had she sacked him, but she had also shredded his male pride and dignity, and with nothing more than three paragraphs. Niall let fly a black curse.

Red splotches bloomed in Wilkinson's fleshy cheeks. He glanced desperately in Ryker's direction.

By the ghost of a smile on his scarred lips, Ryker shared Calum's amusement. Faithless bastards. The pair of them.

Always the lord over all, Niall's fate included, Ryker laid siege to the duke's office. "Wilkinson, will you allow us a moment?"

The duke struggled to heave his rotund frame out of his seat. Tugging out an embroidered kerchief, he mopped at his damp brow. "Of course. Of course." With his spare hand, he thumped Niall between the shoulder blades. "Remember, there is nothing to be ashamed of, son."

Son.

Niall glared at Calum, which reduced him to another round of amusement.

Apparently, with one humiliatingly penned note, Diana had also peeled away the duke's cautiousness around Niall. God help him, she'd made him . . . *human*. Niall blanched and moved hastily away from Wilkinson. "Oi'm not scared of a goddamned thing."

"Of course. Of course."

At Wilkinson's placating assurances, Niall took a furious step forward. If the old nobleman uttered that false profession one more time, he'd personally show him—

Ryker's knowing eyes froze him in his tracks. This was the lack of control that had resulted in Niall's ouster from the club. Niall took a breath. Forcing his shoulders to relax, he hooked his hip on the edge of the desk in a feigned nonchalance and waited.

As soon as the door closed behind the duke, Ryker spoke. "Homesick?" he drawled, lifting an eyebrow.

The duke gone, Calum freely gave in to his laughter. Doubling over, he caught his sides until tears streamed down his cheeks, and he snorted like a pig caught by Cook. And though Ryker's insufferable command over their group had always grated, he gave thanks for the other man's presence. Because one thing his brother did not tolerate was laugh—

Ryker's cool facade crumpled and he joined in, his booming hilarity thundering around the cavernous office.

Apparently the fearless street leader had found his amusement. At Niall's expense.

Niall flipped up a middle finger. "Go to 'ell," he snarled. "Both of you."

They only laughed all the harder.

When they'd regained control, Ryker motioned to the sheet. "My sister wrote on your behalf."

Ryker hadn't acknowledged Diana in more than a year. All of a sudden he'd claim her as kin? The lady who crept along alleys and visited parks alone in rainstorms deserved more loyalty than that. He blanched. Since when had he given a rot about what a noblewoman needed or deserved? *Since she invited you to sit for pastries and stripped away the divide between you.* That was the only reason for his loyalty in this instance. An undeserved one for the traitor who was happy to be rid of him. "So, she's your sister now?" Niall taunted.

Anger turned Ryker's blue eyes a shade of midnight. He rushed forward, and, welcoming the fight, Niall brought his fists up.

Calum swiftly inserted himself between them and placed a staying hand on each of their chests. "Enough," he ordered, ever the peacemaker of their ragbag group.

Tension seeped from Ryker, and then he quickly regained control of his emotions. Briefly smoothing his palms down the front of his black jacket, he stopped and pointed to the note. "You did not want the assignment."

No. He hadn't. He *didn't*.

"Diana's missive indicated you're miserable here."

I was. Yesterday, in Hyde Park, when she'd revealed her intentions—or, rather, her lack of intentions—where finding a husband was concerned, he'd been so caught up with the implications on his future, he'd made no attempt to conceal his horror. Nor had he given thought that she would even care about his reaction.

He'd hurt a lot of people. Maimed others. Killed some. Those ruthless crimes of his past had made him immune to feeling.

Or that is what he'd believed.

I hurt her.

That truth hit him like a kick to the gut.

Feeling Calum's and Ryker's stares on him, he wandered over to the window and stared out at the streets below. Niall gripped the edge of the sill and leaned forward, surveying the cobbled roads with an absent stare. Since he'd discovered her outside the alley, he'd proven himself to be everything he'd ever hated—a vicious bully.

Just a few days ago, he wouldn't have given a bloody damn if he'd hurt or harmed a lord or lady. But Diana was wholly unlike the satin-clad ladies who'd peered down their noses at the grubby-faced beggar boy he'd been.

From within the crystal windowpane, Ryker moved into focus. He stood just beyond Niall's shoulder. "It was unfair of me to ask you to enter this world you so hate," Ryker began quietly. "For you and Diana." Yes, it had been. "You are relieved. Calum will serve as Diana's guard."

It was precisely what he'd wanted since Ryker had announced his plans for Niall—freedom from the unwanted role and the ability to return to his club.

Niall pivoted on his heel. "Calum?" His heart thundered in its cage. "You'd have *Calum* watch after her?"

Ryker's second-in-command cracked his knuckles. "What in hell is that supposed to mean?" he challenged, taking a menacing step closer.

Inspecting the tall, chestnut-haired man he'd known since they were lads fighting for the same scraps of food, he saw glimpses of that irascible boy. That thinly controlled fury at odds with the man who ruled with reason. "It means you can't be her guard."

Calum swept his brown lashes low, veiling his eyes, but not before Niall detected the savage glimmer there. After all, it didn't matter how much a man mastered his emotions. When a person questioned his capabilities, he had an obligation to prove his strength and worth. "Oh?" And Calum was spoiling for a fight.

Niall balled his hands, eager to unleash his frustrations somewhere, even if it was his brother's mocking face. He took a step.

"Enough," Ryker said, in a tone that brooked no room for challenge. "I've a meeting with Mrs. Smith." The new bookkeeper. A strait-laced, severe-looking creature who'd taken on the accounting after a string of unsuccessful hires. "You"—he pointed to Calum—"will see to Diana. Niall"—he jerked his head toward the door—"you are free to leave with me."

Ryker stalked over to the door.

Go. He's letting you return to the world you belong to. His brother grabbed the handle.

Niall's panic swelled. "I've never failed at an assignment," he blasted. This resistance was born from his need of mastery of himself and his emotions and the responsibilities charged to him. Nothing else.

Turning back, Ryker leveled him with a probing stare. Then looked to Calum. Calum lifted his shoulders in a shrug conveying his befuddlement.

Ryker caught his chin between his thumb and forefinger and rubbed. "You've given Diana reason to believe you don't want to be here."

No, he hadn't. Niall said nothing. Nor did he want to, nor would he ever, call Mayfair home. "I don't give up my responsibilities."

"Is that what this is about? Your responsibilities?" Calum delved into a question Niall's own mind shied away from.

He gave an uneasy nod, feeling the lie in that slight, silent gesture.

Ryker let his arm hang to his side. "Very well. This is not forever. Either until you verify Diana's well-being or until she weds."

There are no worries on that score. I've no intention of marrying.

It was a detail as a brother, Ryker was deserving of. But something held the words back. The sense that Niall would be betraying a secret Diana was entitled to . . . even if it kept him trapped in her world. "Do you believe me a toff fit to care for her?" he snapped.

Casual as you please, Ryker rolled his shoulders. "I believe I want your assurance that there is no threat. I've also hired runners to look into the lady's concerns, as well." *Runners. As though those respectable investigators knew a bloody thing about the underworld.* "Their efforts have turned up nothing." He consulted the longcase clock in the corner of the room. "*Have* you found cause for Diana's concerns?"

This was a safe topic. One that kept Niall from wondering why he wanted to remain on as guard to Diana, instead of returning to his club. "I haven't." He proceeded to run through a cataloging of his searches of the duke's town house and Diana's daily routines.

At no point had there been a hint or threat of danger.

Ryker nodded. "How long, then?"

Niall started. "How long?"

"Until you make a determination about the lady's safety," Calum clarified for Ryker.

His mind stalled. If Killoran's or Diggory's henchmen intended Diana harm, surely there would have been some hint of it in the week Niall had been here. Yet there had been nothing. Not a curtain out of place. Not a suspiciously gaping window or door. Not an unfamiliar servant. A threatening note. Nothing.

"Niall?" Ryker pressed.

"It's too soon to know," he settled for, evading an answer that would mark his time here done. "I'll not leave prematurely only to have harm befall Di—" Both Ryker's and Calum's eyebrows went up. "Your sister," he belatedly substituted. He grimaced.

Ryker nodded slowly. "Very well. When . . . *if* you determine there is no threat, then you may return."

With that decree befitting a king, Ryker stalked off. Calum followed after him.

As soon as they'd taken their leave, Niall made for the doorway.

Now there was the matter of finding the fiery chit who'd attempted to have him sacked.

Chapter 11

Niall was leaving, and Diana knew so because she'd orchestrated his departure. *It is my fault.*

Standing at the window, she shielded her gaze from the bright sun hanging in the early-morning sky. She forced her gaze down to the street, to the black lacquer carriage below bearing her brother's ominous crest.

Two lions locked in battle. It conjured death and power and darkness—a perfect symbol for the men who ruled the underbelly of London. Diana absently traced a lone raindrop left from the violent thunderstorm.

What must Niall's life have been like as a boy, and then as a man, that he'd become filled with so much hatred? His loathing for the nobility contained a palpable life force. He saw Diana as one of them and hated her for it, not knowing she'd been cast out of their fold. And she never wished to rejoin it. There was no point in thinking of him or wondering about him, because he was not long for here.

Ryker and Calum had arrived a short while ago and been ushered into Father's office.

She'd been expecting it. Having sent her brother a missive last evening, Ryker would be here to free Niall of his responsibilities. There would be no goodbyes or teasing smiles or those hated rhetorical questions. She sighed and let the gold curtain go. It fluttered back into place, shielding her view of the streets.

Better to not think about it.

Niall would leave, and just as servants moved in and out of this household, so, too, would the man assigned to her by Ryker. She'd spied Calum entering and knew he would take Niall's place.

The floorboards groaned, and Diana turned, colliding with a towering, muscular frame. A cry sprang to her lips, and she shot a fist out.

Niall easy caught the blow before it could find its mark. *He is here.* "Niall?" she breathed. Had he come to make his goodbyes?

"Expecting someone else, princess?"

Princess. It was that scornful address that hinted at his displeasure. He released her quickly. A muscle jumped at the corner of his left eye.

What reason did he have to be displeased? Surely Ryker had not denied Niall the right to return to his club? She darted her tongue out, trailing it over the seam of her lips, and his hooded eyes settled on her mouth. His irises turned dark and volatile like a thunderstorm. Diana immediately ceased that distracted movement. "Did you come to say goodbye?" she ventured. He didn't strike her as one of those who cared much with making goodbyes.

"Do I strike you as the manner of fellow who worries much with goodbyes?" he asked on a silken whisper.

"Uh . . . no." He struck her as a man who didn't worry much about anything. Society said the same thing of Diana, too, and she knew the lie there.

"No," he confirmed. With languid, menacing steps better suited to a tiger about to pounce, Niall started forward.

Oh, dear. "You are angry," she observed, moving hurriedly around the mahogany side table and putting the upholstered sofa between them. It wasn't that she feared Niall, per se, but she had witnessed firsthand the power of his fury and would rather not be burned by that volatility.

"I am angry."

That silken whisper ratcheted up her nervousness. Gulping, Diana continued her hurried retreat.

"Do you know why that is, princess?"

"Diana," she hurriedly corrected, backing up. "Uh . . . no." His eyebrows dipped. "Yes?" Actually, she had no blasted idea. She could only begin to venture.

He stopped coming, leaving five paces between them. "Which is it, princess?" Niall crossed his arms at his chest and waited.

And then his fury made sense.

"Ryker would not agree to your reassignment."

It was the wrong thing to say. The wrong conjecture, to be precise. Another gasp burst from her lips as he pounced. Diana stumbled over herself in her haste to keep some space.

"Oh, he agreed," he purred, and her heart lurched.

He'd agreed. Which meant Niall was no longer for this place. "This is you coming to say goodbye, then." A pang struck her heart. It was silly. Their parting had been inevitable. If it wasn't when he caught the person who wished her harm, then it would have been in five weeks' time when she boarded a clipper bound across the Atlantic. But blast it all . . . she'd enjoyed his being here. He'd been the only person—lord, lady, servant, or family member—who treated her as more than a fragile, brainless miss. Fighting back the twin waves of sadness and regret, Diana extended her shaking hand.

Niall slapped something in her palm.

Blinking wildly at the crumpled ball, she slowly unwrinkled it, revealing a letter. She lifted her gaze to Niall's sardonic one.

Her letter, to be exact.

Ah, this was the reason for his anger. Diana set down the creased page on a nearby rose-inlaid table. "Oh."

His life-hardened eyes glinted. "That is what you'd say?"

Diana wet her lips. Apparently the wrong utterance, yet again. "You wrote my brother—"

"My brother, too," she reminded him.

His mouth opened and closed like a trout plucked from the Thames. He sputtered. "You are *not* my sister."

"I didn't say I was." A man whose kiss set her body afire, and who occupied her waking and sleeping thoughts, was certainly not one she held brotherly sentiments for. "I was merely pointing out that Ryker is my brother, and you and Ryker are also—"

"I said I am *not* your brother."

"Brothers who do not share blood."

He pressed his palms over his eyes. His mouth moved as if in silent prayer. Then he dropped his arms to his sides. The stoic, always-in-control lord of St. Giles was back firmly in place. "You told him I miss home."

Apparently they were done on the debate about the sibling business. Diana sighed. "I believe we're both aware of the contents of my note." Except . . . "Furthermore"—she raised a finger—"you *do* miss home," she felt compelled to point out. It wasn't as though she'd penned a lie. Did he find shame in that?

Niall's arm jerked reflexively into the easel. Diana shot her hands out, catching the frame. She righted it and favored Niall with a frown . . . and registered the wintry frost in his eyes. She swallowed hard. Oh, dear. Diana took a small step and then another. "You should be relieved." The back of her leg caught the edge of the sofa, and she winced, but continued her retreat. "You are free to leave."

"You're right. I should."

Pleased that she'd finally broken through his usual stubbornness, she smiled and bumped into an easel. The wood frame shook, toppling sideways. Hurriedly, Diana moved behind it, catching it before it fell, while placing the small piece between them.

Niall arched an eyebrow.

She gulped. Who knew even an eyebrow could be menacing? Everyone had them. Then, anything and everything about this man exuded danger. "You do miss your club, do you not?" That black eyebrow slowly fell back into place. "So it was not *really* a lie."

He strolled closer, springing her back into movement. Diana collided with the door, effectively halting her escape.

Niall shot out a hand, and her breath caught on a gasp. But he only reached around her and turned the lock.

He'd locked them in here. Alone. Waiting. Watching.

Oh, dear.

He'd stay here until the crows came home. "You don't want to be here," she tried, reasoning with him.

"No."

Diana frowned. She should appreciate that candor. "You don't like me," she reminded him. Though he certainly didn't require a reminder on that score. Bitterness tasted acrid in her mouth, and she slid her gaze past his shoulder.

He brushed his coarse, scarred knuckles over her jaw, forcing her stare back to his. That gesture was surprisingly tender. The aromatic hint of cheroot and bergamot that always clung to him flooded her senses, and her lashes fluttered wildly. It was an odd blend, both masculine and sweet, and it conjured images of him taking a blade to those rigid cheekbones and scraping away the dark growth that covered his jaw in the late evening hours.

"Oi don't loike anyone, Diana."

Diana. At last he laid possession to her name, his street-roughened tones primal and raw and so very beautiful for it. So different from the dandies and gentlemen who'd once courted and called. Men who'd proven themselves spineless, seeing nothing more in her than her rank as duke's daughter. And now seeing a woman with tainted blood. Whereas *this* man knew precisely what evil her mother had worked with her hands and treated Diana as he did anyone else. Concentrating on drawing air into her lungs, Diana sank against the door. She angled her head back to meet his piercing eyes. "That isn't true, Niall." Her reminder emerged breathless. "There is Helena and Ryker and Calum and Adair. And no doubt the employees in your club. You care about them."

He continued his tender caress, the back-and-forth movement a distracted afterthought that elicited delicious shivers. "They are kin."

Her heart twisted. *Kin.* And she was nothing to him. Diana angled her head, breaking that contact. She made to slip out of his reach, but he brought his elbows up, blocking her escape.

Her breath hitched. She'd scaled oaks in Somerset narrower than Niall Marksman's powerful frame.

"Afraid?" The whisper of cheroot on his lips fanned her skin.

"I'm not afraid of you, Niall." The airy quality of that denial weakened her words.

He chuckled, and that slight movement brought their chests together. Surely he felt her heart pounding against his? "No, I do not believe you are afraid of anything, princess." That moniker, once used to taunt, now rang like a gruff endearment. "I don't dislike you, Diana."

Her lips curled up in a smile. "I believe those are two compliments from a man such as you." To steady her trembling hands, she rested her palms on his midnight jacket, the kerseymere wool soft under her fingers.

He dropped his brow to hers. "Oi like you enough." That admission, as graveled as an old Roman road, was dragged from him. A concession she'd venture Niall Marksman had never made to a person of her station.

"Is that why you're staying on as my guard?"

He placed his lips close to her ear, his breath a wicked caress that stirred a yearning to know his embrace more. "Who said I was staying on?"

Diana turned her head slightly, so their mouths nearly brushed. "You do not say goodbye," she whispered against his mouth. "Unless you've come to dress me down before you go."

He'd sought Diana out for one singular purpose. To lay out the terms that would drive and dictate their remaining time together. Not an unspoken truce. Rather, a real one. One where Niall treated Diana with a deserved civility. It was a feat he had managed toward the nobility for almost ten years at the Hell and Sin, in his role as head of security at the club.

He was capable of practiced smiles and casual banter. But all of that skill had faded when presented with the danger and treachery that infiltrated their empire.

Now, three words had thrown him off-kilter.

Dress me down.

They were just three words. But breathed to life in Diana's husky contralto, there was a lusty wantonness to them. Words that conjured Niall releasing the row of pearl buttons along the back of her dress and sliding down the soft satin gown, exposing her naked skin for his appreciation. Moving that mint-green fabric lower, over her breasts, her hips, and then letting it pool about them.

Niall briefly closed his eyes. The hint of jasmine clung to her skin, intoxicating.

"Niall?" she whispered, forcing his eyes open.

It was a mistake.

Her plump crimson lips quivered, bringing his focus to that generous flesh. His throat moved painfully. What had begun as an intention to lay down a new groundwork for their relationship had shifted to something dangerous and volatile.

She darted her tongue out, and that pink tip trailed over the plump contours. "What is—?"

I am lost. With a groan of supplication, Niall crushed her mouth under his in a savage meeting. Her back thumped noisily against the door as he slanted his lips over hers again and again. It spoke to the blackness in his soul that he'd lust after and put his scarred hands on Ryker's sister. But Niall had never presumed to be or presented himself as anything other than a man who took what he needed, and in this instance, she was what he needed. Never breaking contact with her lips, he roved his hands down her body, learning the curve of her hips, memorizing them. Through the smooth fabric of her silk gown, he cupped her breasts, bringing those large orbs together.

Diana whimpered, and he swept the inside of her mouth with his tongue. She tasted of peaches and honey, the sweet taste of her more intoxicating than any dangerous opiate. Abandoning her mouth, he trailed kisses along the corner of her jaw, and lower, finding the place where her pulse pounded wildly in time to his own.

"You're so goddamned soft," he rasped against her throat. "Like satin." And where he'd always sneered at that fine and fancy fabric, he wanted to spread her down upon it and lay her open for his invasion.

"Niall," she moaned, clenching and unclenching her fingers in his hair.

That ragged sound wrapped around his name sent a primal sense of satisfaction through him. She, a golden-haired lady of the *ton* in her purity and innocence, hungered for him, Niall, a baseborn blighter without even a simple surname as his own. That truth heated his veins and fueled his lust.

He filled his hands with her hips and pressed himself against her belly. She went limp in his arms, and he caught her against the door, anchoring her close. His shaft swelled painfully in his breeches. He ached to free himself, yank her skirts up, and bury himself inside her.

He dragged his mouth along her décolletage, pressing kisses to the soft flesh. Breathing deep the floral scent that clung to her skin. Subtle, and containing the suggestive hint of summer, and so very different from every other woman he'd made love to before whose pungent perfume had stung the senses.

The tread of footsteps beyond the parlor penetrated this momentary lapse into madness. His pulse pounding loudly in Niall's ears, he quickly broke the embrace and hurried to right her gown.

Her eyes heavy with passion, Diana blinked slowly. "What—?"

He touched a fingertip to her lips, silencing the question there. Tucking a lone golden curl behind her ear, he unlocked the door and moved swiftly into position across the room.

The door opened, and Diana's father stepped inside. He failed to either notice or care about Niall's presence at the far back corner of the parlor. A smile wreathed the man's rounded cheeks. "Diana," he greeted, entering the room.

"F-Father," she stammered.

Any man need take but one look at her crimson-kissed cheeks and swollen lips to know just what she'd been doing. Except, it would seem, this man. The duke drew a thick sheet of vellum from his pocket and waved it merrily around. "You will not believe what I have here." He did a small little jig.

Arms clasped behind him and gaze trained forward in the ready position he'd adopted at the Hell and Sin, fury wound through Niall. The duke should toss Niall's arse out on the immaculate Mayfair stoop and only after he'd bloodied him senseless. Guilt sluiced away at his insides. What madness had possessed him? Not once, but twice he'd put his scarred hands upon Diana. A lady off-limits not only for her station, but also because of the blood she shared—she was Helena and Ryker's sister.

She snuck a furtive glance in Niall's direction. With her pathetic attempt at subterfuge, the lady wouldn't have lasted a day in the Dials. It was a sobering reminder of just who she was and what Niall had done.

And in this moment, Diana had proven correct more than a week ago when she'd slipped into the alley outside the Hell and Sin for protection. Only, the protection she required wasn't necessarily from the foe she'd imagined in the shadows, but rather an oblivious, and for it, neglectful, papa. The duke was unfit to care for her.

"You haven't asked me what I have," the duke chided, waving that page under his daughter's nose.

"What—?"

"An invitation."

An invitation? As a duke, the man surely had endless invites to those infernal affairs hosted by the peerage. *Yet, in the week you've been here, the lady and her father hadn't attended a single one.* It was a detail he'd given only a sparing thought. He'd just been grateful for not being forced to attend those *ton* events. Now he paid attention to those details he'd only fleetingly considered.

Diana gathered that page with shaking fingers. "An invitation?" That query came as though dragged from her. From the corner of his eye, he detected another stolen peek in his direction from the lady.

"Lord and Lady Milford are hosting a ball." He patted Diana's hand. "I told you the invitations would again come. And then there will be suitors and a courtship and marriage." As he prattled on, Diana attended that sheet of vellum.

So that was the reason for her solitariness. It wasn't arrogance or conceit, but rather a lack of invitations from the people who shared her station. And he, who'd prided himself on feeling nothing, felt a slight tug in his chest at the idea of Diana—the humming, singing, winsome lady who sketched in the rain—cast out of Society's fold. Fools, all of them.

While the duke prattled on, Niall gave his head a disgusted shake. That was the way of the peerage. Self-indulgent. Unfeeling. Heartless. They had no loyalty to kin or members of their lot. Not unlike a boy born to the streets, who put his survival before anything and anyone, so, too, did the *ton* with their prized reputations and power. And yet a guttersnipe from St. Giles also gave his allegiance to the gang he called family. The peers knew nothing about family.

"As you were, gel." Her father patted the top of Diana's golden curls like she was a child of nine and not a woman of nineteen. "I'll let you see to your embroidering."

Embroidering? Niall creased his brow. He'd been here a week and a day, and even Niall knew Diana Verney didn't touch one of those useless wood frames.

"Mr. Marksman." The duke called out his greeting as an afterthought. "I'm pleased you've chosen to remain on and look after my Diana."

He met that with stony silence. The duke's happiness and desires had been the last thing Niall had considered when he'd fought for his position here. It had been Niall's stubbornness, an unwillingness to admit failure. *And you despised the idea of Calum serving her in your stead.*

Thrusting aside that unwelcome truth slithering around his mind, Niall crossed his arms before him.

Finally Wilkinson ambled his portly frame out of the room, leaving Niall and Diana—alone.

She attended the page in her hand, as though she'd not already skimmed it three times. As though she didn't, in fact, know what was contained upon that expensive cream vellum. She laid it down atop one of her many leather sketch pads.

Had Niall not been studying her so closely, he'd have missed the faint tremble of her long, graceful fingers. But he had been, and he abhorred that show of weakness. It hinted at her fear and unease, and mayhap a week ago, it wouldn't have mattered what this woman felt. That, however, had been before he'd known her as a woman. Now he did. And whether he liked it or not, her damned quivering frown mattered. "You don't want to attend?"

Diana didn't pretend to misunderstand. She gave her head a slight shake and then dusted her fingertips along the ruffled edge of the inlaid table. "Do you know my father has not smiled in over a year?" she asked wistfully.

Arms still crossed at his chest, Niall propped a shoulder against the wall. "Every time Oi see 'im, he's wearing a grin."

"There is a difference between smiling and *smiling*, Niall."

A lock tumbled over his wrinkled brow. He'd never understand a lady's logic.

Diana drifted over. She stopped so close a mere handbreadth divided them. So close the summer scent of flowers wafted about him. What fragrance did she dab behind her ears? A lord born of her station would know the names of blooms and mayhap even their smells. But for the beggars hawking their wilting buds and the arrangements scattered about Ryker's office since he'd been married, Niall wouldn't know a rose from a weed.

She curled her lips in the corners, dimpling her cheeks in a smile that did not reach her sad eyes. "*That* is a false smile, Niall," she said softly, letting the mask fall. "That is what my father has worn since . . ." Since her mother had tried to have Helena killed.

"That is why ya don't attend your fancy events," he mused, as the pieces of the proverbial puzzle finally fell into place. It was why there were no callers or suitors or jaunts through town. Diana had shut herself away.

"Do you believe the nobility so heartless they'd be forgiving of a woman who sold off her husband's illegitimate children and then tried to have one of them killed?"

There was such a stark pain in her eyes, the muscles of his belly contracted.

"Your mother's crimes aren't yours," he said gruffly. That was a street truth she wouldn't know, but true all the same. The merciless duchess who'd made herself an accomplice to Mac Diggory and attempted murder bore no resemblance to Diana, the spirited woman who'd sketch in the rain.

Diana wandered over to a nearby easel. "No," she agreed. "But I share her blood." Those softly whispered words barely reached his ears, but he'd been trained from the cradle to detect a person's subtle movements and sounds. Sometimes to steal. Other times to pounce on an unsuspecting enemy. And hear Diana, he had.

Over the years, Niall had served as guard. He'd fought for his siblings and fellow gang members in St. Giles and continued that fight inside the Hell and Sin Club. Never once, in all his thirty or thirty-one or however many years he'd attained, had he sought to provide comfort.

Nor had anyone looked to him or expected it . . . because they'd been wise enough to know Niall Marksman incapable of anything other than brute force and strength.

Diana, with her slumped shoulders and distant voice, was new territory. Unfamiliar. Similar to the talk of tea and treason they'd had his third day here, only deeper, for it had moved into the uncharted territory of her emotions.

Niall yanked at his stiff cravat. He'd rather draw a blade and fight a man to the death than muddle through this. And with any other person, his siblings included, he wouldn't have bothered to try.

"Do ya know you're the only person who doesn't fear me," he conceded, his words bringing Diana slowly back around. "Not moi brothers or Helena," he clarified, slashing his hand at the air. "Moi employees. The patrons at moi club. Strangers in the streets." Regardless of rank or station, they all skirted his path on the pavement, and he preferred it that way.

"You haven't given me reason to fear you," she pointed out.

Then she was a lackwit if she believed that. "Oi almost snuffed ya in the alley." How easily he could have crushed her windpipe. The faintest bit of pressure incorrectly applied, and he'd have snuffed out her effervescent light. A wintry chill stole through him.

"That hardly counts," she objected, snapping him from torturous musings. "You believed I intended you harm."

The corners of her plump lips twitched, and the air lodged in his lungs. This was the look she'd spoken of. That glimmering warmth that softened her heart-shaped features and danced in her eyes like the handful of stars that managed to peek out through the murk of the London night sky. This was the difference she'd spoken of.

Since the day he'd drawn his first breath, he'd never been capable of such purity. It was an unnecessary reminder of how vastly different they were in every way.

"The man who raised me . . . Diggory," he began, giving that monster's name life. The same man her mother, the duchess, had worked in collusion with. Diana went still and her smile faded, ushering in a somber darkness. How peculiar to find Niall and Diana had been linked early on in the unlikeliest of ways. "He was a killer. A murderer." Like Niall.

Kill him . . . or be killed, Niall.

That mordant command, clear in his mind's eye. The bite of a dagger against his threadbare garments still fresh. Moisture beaded his forehead. He'd not allowed thoughts of those days in. Had kept them carefully and deliberately at bay. Until now. *Do not listen to him—'e's gone now.* Dead and in Hell, burning with Satan himself. He forced out the remaining words. "Diggory was a thief. A rapist."

The color bled from Diana's cheeks, but she remained motionless, not weeping or fainting as any other lady would surely be doing had he spoken to them about such evil.

"Am Oi the same as Diggory?" he asked. A part of his soul had been tainted by Mac Diggory. It mattered not whom Niall had become, but rather what he'd once done.

"Of course not." She spoke with such vehemence, his numb-until-now heart swelled.

"He raised me since Oi was a babe." Though in truth, no person born to the streets was ever innocent. They entered the world on a blanket of hard stone and dirt, and grew into evil. "Do ya see my bond with Ryker as an empty one? Oi don't share 'is blood but have called him brother."

"Of course not." As soon as the denial left her lips, she froze.

He winked at her.

"It is not the same thing, Niall," she said tightly.

Niall rolled his shoulders. "It's exactly the same thing, love." He touched an imagined brim. "That is, by your thoughts on being responsible for the crimes of another man . . . or woman." He'd not fill her ears with the truth. He was very much Diggory's spawn. He'd killed, thieved, and beaten people within an inch of death. Whereas Diana? There wasn't a mark or crime against her pure soul. That was the distinction even he, a rotted, jaded bastard, couldn't bring himself to utter.

He stuck out his hand, and Diana eyed it with a healthy dose of suspicion. "A truce," he said gruffly. "A real one for as long as I'm here. You won't write letters to have me sacked, and I'll . . ." She cocked her head. Niall coughed. "And I'll not be a miserable bastard every time we're together."

A little laugh spilled past her lips as she trustingly laid her long, elegant fingers in his palm. "A truce," she said softly.

He folded her hand in his grip.

Chapter 12

The fortnight passed in a blur.

It was that truth that gave Diana some slight comfort as she sat on the fringe of the Marquess and Marchioness of Milford's ballroom. For if those fourteen days could pass so very quickly, then an evening inside the home of a leading societal hostess should, too.

That was the assurance she'd given herself as her maid helped her through her preparations, and then through the never-ending carriage ride, and then through the equally never-ending receiving line.

Only, time crept by at an interminable crawl.

Swallowing back a sigh, Diana assessed the crush of guests present.

Though in fairness, the plump hostess who'd braved Society's scorn to issue Diana an invitation had been nothing but kind. The marchioness and her devoted husband had warmly greeted Diana like she was any other lady, and not the daughter of a madwoman complicit in a murder scheme.

No, it was not the host and hostess responsible for Diana's misery, but rather the sea of gossiping guests. The same guests who'd stared at Diana since the moment she was announced. Stared at her as though she were an oddity escaped from the Piccadilly Circus. Which, in fairness, she wasn't much different from.

With a Bedlamite for a mother and a faithless father who'd sired and then lost his illegitimate issue, Diana, by association, could never be anything but odd.

And now there was a fierce guard stationed in the corner of the ballroom, intently watching Diana's every movement, who only added to the whispers that went with her name.

Though, seated on a neat shell-back chair alongside the handful of other partnerless ladies, Diana admitted there was something comforting in Niall being here. Something that made her feel less alone.

He stood with his hands at his back and his chiseled face set into a hard mask daring a person to venture near. Diana unabashedly studied him. Her mother had often stated that lords of London held the power, but seeing how Niall inspired fear in an entire ballroom of those same ostentatious peers, there was no refuting that he was very much master of any room he entered.

Lady Milford's guests cut a wide berth around him, and Diana stared on, bemused.

Not even three weeks ago, she'd felt that same panicky fear in Niall's presence. Even as the primal rawness of him had set her heart racing, it had done so with a blend of her body's awareness of him as a man . . . and an equal part terror.

Peering around the dancers who performed the intricate steps of a quadrille, she continued her study of him. Four or five inches taller than the majority of guests present, he stood out among the crowded ballroom not for that great height or the crimson neck cloth expertly folded at his throat, but for the powerful aura he exuded. He was a living, breathing reason men had been made subjects of sculptors.

Just then, a colorful dandy passed too close, and Niall scraped a gaze over him. The young man tripped over himself, scurrying off in the opposite direction, and Niall promptly resumed his watch of the ballroom.

There could be no doubt that the man at the edge of the room was no guest, but in every way a guard. The thickly corded muscles of his arms and shoulders strained the fabric of his elegantly cut garments, hinting at a man braced for battle. Occasionally his lip peeled back in a visible testament of his derisiveness to the frivolity he was forced to observe. He wanted no part of the *haute ton* . . . and in that, Diana felt a kindred connection to him. He no more wanted to be here than Diana herself. Despite all his statements of the contrary, he'd proven to be more like Diana than he'd surely ever credit or like.

From across the dance floor, their gazes clashed. It was a bold, unapologetic locking of their eyes that sent heat unfurling in her belly. Niall subtly angled his head, breaking the connection. Diana let her shoulders sag against the miserably stiff shell-back chair.

No man should possess that dangerous smolder. A glimmer that had the power to set her ablaze with the mere promise of what had come before.

Diana's heart kicked up a wild beat as the floodgates of her memory opened with the remembrance of his kiss. His touch. An embrace that had not been the one stolen, regretful exchange in the park, but another with her framed between his thickly muscled arms. In Niall's arms, Diana didn't think about the bleak future awaiting her or the misery of this past year. Instead, she relished in simply being alive. While Niall's intent gaze continued its sweep of the ballroom, Diana continued to devour him with her eyes. *I want to know more with him.* She ached for the coarse drag of his callused palms over her skin. For in his gloriously splendorous embrace, Diana was not "Diana the Mad" or the "Lady of Madness," but rather a woman who was very much alive and free.

A young lady stepped between them, and Diana gasped. She glanced up and started. The vaguely familiar woman, Lady Penelope

Chatham, who'd found herself embroiled in scandal earlier in the Season and then married Diana's half brother, stared back.

Registering the patient smile on Lady Penelope Chatham's lips, Diana sprang to her feet. "My lady," she greeted quickly, sinking into an automatic curtsy. She searched that smile for a hint of malice, but nothing but gentle warmth reflected back in the tilt of her lips that reached her kind blue eyes.

Her skin burned with the attention now trained their way. After all, it wasn't every day two estranged sisters-in-law met amid a crowded ballroom.

"Shall we give them something to truly talk about?" Lady Chatham suggested with a waggle of her eyebrows, and extended her elbow.

Diana eyed that offering cautiously. Unlike the friendship Diana had struck with Helena, Ryker had been plainly clear in his feelings about the Duke of Wilkinson's legitimate daughter, Diana—he wished nothing to do with her. It was why reaching out to him and asking for his assistance had been humbling and humiliating. Diana hadn't even been invited to his wedding, of which there had been two. What use did his wife have of her, daughter of the woman who'd orchestrated Ryker's disappearance years earlier?

Lady Chatham's smile slipped. "I certainly understand why you would be hesitant."

Diana stiffened and braced for that onslaught of deservedly vile charges against the Verney line.

"I haven't been the most loyal of sisters-in-law."

"Beg pardon, my lady?" Diana blurted.

"Please?" Lady Chatham said this time, lifting her elbow once more.

Having been rebuffed and rejected by family and Society alike, Diana would never be one of those ladies who deliberately saw a person humiliated in like fashion. She looped her arm through the other woman's.

A loud buzz, like a thousand swarming bees, filled the soaring ballroom.

"As I told you," Lady Chatham said on a mischievous whisper as she leaned close. "Something to really talk about."

Despite the misery of suffering through Lord and Lady Milford's ball, Diana managed a smile.

"That is better." The viscountess winked. "Confuse them with a smile. Now we should laugh and really watch their mouths hang agape."

As they strolled the perimeter, Diana carefully studied Ryker's wife out of the corner of her eye. Near Diana in age, there was a surprising openness to the lady at odds with the mask worn by the stone-faced viscount. Diana searched the crowd and easily found her brother. He stood shoulder to shoulder beside Niall on the fringe. Both looked to be equal in their misery at being forced to suffer through Lady Milford's ball. Niall, however, followed Diana's every movement, like a hunter guarding its prey. She shivered, pitying the man foolish enough to defy Niall Marksman.

"Do not be fooled by his scowl. He's really quite warm and loving." Lady Chatham cut across her musings and brought Diana's gaze whipping back.

"M-my lady?" she squeaked.

"My husband," the viscountess clarified.

Relief flooded Diana. For a horrifying moment, she'd believed the other woman had noted Diana's interest in Niall. Then the viscountess's words registered. Warm and loving? Diana flared her eyebrows. She was certain there had been ruthless soldiers in the King's Army who'd bore more warmth than Ryker Black.

The viscountess patted her hand. "You mustn't let him know I've said as much. He does value that gruff reputation."

With their every step, whispers followed in their wake, and yet through each one, Lady Chatham gave no indication that she either heard or cared about those gossips. Since the scandal that had rocked society, Diana believed herself immune to that chatter, but walking arm in arm with Ryker's wife, smiling and wholly unaffected, Diana acknowledged the lie she'd also lived. As the viscountess steered them past gaping couples, onward to the corner of the ballroom, Diana's discomfort grew. Mayhap this is where she wished to take Diana to task for daring to put a favor to Ryker. After all, what right did Diana have to ask him for anything?

As soon as they stopped, Diana spoke quickly. "Is there a reason you wished to speak to me, my lady?" she asked with a straightforwardness that her sour-faced governesses had managed to drum out of Diana for nineteen years of her life.

Lady Chatham looked at her. A flash of regret lit her pretty blue eyes. "I'd ask, given we are sisters-in-law, that you please call me Penelope."

Diana chewed at her lower lip, searching for the trap.

Ryker's wife stared back. "I've been remiss," the young viscountess murmured. "I've made little attempt"—no attempt—"to seek you out for an introduction, and you are Ryker's sister."

The orchestra concluded the lively reel, and as they plucked the strains of the next set, Diana picked her way around her thoughts. "Why should you have?" she countered, stripping away any inflection from her query. Glancing about to verify there were no observers about, Diana went on. "My mother wronged Ryker and Helena, and I wouldn't expect you to strike up a friendship with me." Too much had come to pass between their families. Where Helena had forgiven, Ryker never had, and as such, Diana and her eldest sibling never would know peace.

A spasm contorted Lady Chatham's face, and she gathered Diana's hands, giving them a firm squeeze. "It was wrong of Ryker or me to cut you from the family because of . . ." She grimaced. "Things that came to pass because of your parents."

Diana made a small sound of protest and made to pull away.

Lady Chatham, however, retained her hold. "This is not the place for wrongs to be put to right, but I would ask we begin again, as sisters-in-law."

Diana nodded. "I would like that very much," she said softly, and Lady Chatham's smile was restored.

Her sister-in-law cleared her throat. "Ryker and I would like to have you join us for a small dinner party." A dinner party? "Ryker believed you might—" Lady Penelope immediately closed her lips. Color flooded her cheeks.

What did Ryker believe? "I would be honored," Diana said cautiously. There was more to that offer.

Penelope smiled. "Splendid." Her sister-in-law again offered her arm.

Diana automatically looped hers through and allowed the other woman to guide her around the ballroom. The viscountess wrinkled her nose. "Dreadful affairs," she muttered. "I used to look forward to them," she confessed.

"As did I," Diana revealed. Yes, there had been a time when she'd been hopelessly romantic, dreaming of love and marriage and a happily-ever-after found only in books. Though . . . she again glanced at Ryker's wife. That wasn't altogether true. Ryker and his wife appeared very much in love, as did Helena and her husband. They, however, were deserving of it.

They shared a look, and Lady Penelope applied gentle pressure to Diana's arm, commiserating, and just then Diana felt very much un-alone. Humming a discordant tune that rivaled that of the orchestra's Scotch Reel, the viscountess glanced around the ballroom. "You are doing well, I trust, with Mr. Marksman?"

Diana missed a step, and then, cheeks warming, quickly righted herself. "My lady?" she asked at that abrupt shift in discourse.

Looking around, Lady Penelope found Niall with her gaze and gave a discreet wave in his general direction. His scowl deepened.

"I understand you wrote my husband, and I wanted to be sure that you are not uncomfortable with Mr. Marksman's presence." Ah, so in addition to an attempted peace between their families, this was another reason why the lady had sought her out.

"Is that why you believe I wrote Ryker, my lady?" she asked carefully. "That I wished to have him remove Mr. Marksman because I feared him?" Mr. Marksman, who existed in her house and mind only as Niall.

"Is it not?" Lady Penelope pressed. With that directness, this unflinching woman was the only one who would have ever been a match for Ryker Black.

"It is not," she returned, shaking her head. Diana feared death and her descent into madness. She did not, however, fear a person, man or woman . . . including the ruthless Niall Marksman. "I am not afraid of Mr. Marksman."

"Truly?" Lady Chatham looked at her with a new appreciation glimmering in her expressive eyes.

"Truly, my lady," she confirmed. Diana cast a glance over to where Niall and Ryker quietly conversed. Nodding at something the other man said, Niall's gaze found hers. Her heart fluttered.

"I like you all the more, Lady Diana." The viscountess beamed. Taking her by the hand, she coaxed Diana onward. "Come, allow me to introduce you to some of the few friendly members of the peerage. I promise there are a few."

With Niall's gaze piercing her retreating frame, Diana allowed herself to be pulled along.

Through narrowed eyes, Niall stared on as Penelope introduced Diana to the Earl of Maxwell. The blighter who, with his roguish grin and unscarred skin, had tossed down coin at Niall's tables and now Killoran's.

That same blighter collected her hand and raised it to his mouth, placing a kiss on the inside of her wrist.

He growled.

This need to cut through the silly prancing partners on the floor and rip Maxwell's hand from its bloody socket filled Niall with a bloodlust only previously born of street battles.

"And our liquor suppliers have been fleecing us . . ."

The earl scribbled his name on her goddamned dance card, which meant for the first time in more than two hours, Diana, who'd been partnerless on those lonely chairs at the back of the ballroom, would have a partner. Nay, not just any partner. The grinning, affable Lord Maxwell.

"Membership is down . . ."

Goddamned interfering Penelope Black. What was she on about, introducing Diana to a lord who drank too much, wagered even more, and often did it with a whore or two on his lap?

"Calum is taken up as head guard at Devil's Den . . ."

Niall blinked slowly.

Ryker snorted. "I see I have your attention."

"Go fuck yourself," he muttered under his breath, earning a deep chuckle from Ryker. Laughing, teasing, lighthearted—what in blazes had Penelope Black done to the ruthless Lord of the Underbelly?

"You aren't listening to a damned word I've said," Ryker observed, casually folding his arms at his chest. The tension pouring from his frame made a contradiction of that outwardly show of indifference. Ryker Black might be capable of jesting and laughing, but he was not one who took to being ignored.

"I'm seeing to my responsibilities," Niall snapped, and a servant walking within earshot fumbled the tray in his hands. The liveried footman swallowed loudly and managed to right his load, and then made off in the opposite direction.

"Diana," Ryker said needlessly.

Yes, Diana. The young lady he'd struck a truce with, whose cheeks even now blazed crimson at something Lord Maxwell said. "Unless there are other responsibilities Oi don't know about?"

"Walk with me," Ryker commanded.

The earl led Diana onto the dance floor and put his hand on her waist—Niall narrowed his eyes—too low. The bastard's bold fingertips brushed just over the generous swell of her buttocks. This is the manner of gentleman Penelope and Ryker would turn Diana over to? "Oi'm on duty," he seethed. It mattered not that the lady had disavowed marrying any gentleman. It mattered that in this instance, her cheeks were blooming red like those crimson flowers Penelope filled the damned club with, while that fancy toff led her through the steps of a waltz.

"Calum is present," Ryker reminded him.

"As a guest," he muttered. Unlike Niall, who was employed here as a guard, strictly to look after Diana's well-being.

"It's not for you," Ryker persisted.

And Niall registered the raspy quality of Ryker's graveled baritone. The faint panic glimmering in his hard eyes. They all carried their own demons. Ryker's fear of crowds was his. Niall paused a moment more, looking out at the sea of fancy lords and ladies, those men he'd spent his whole life despising, ultimately finding Diana at the center of them.

With the ease of the London pickpockets they'd once been, Niall and Ryker found their way outside to Lady Milford's gardens.

Once outside, Ryker sucked in a deep, jagged breath. Reaching inside his jacket, Niall fished out two cheroots and handed one over. Sometimes a man needed the fortification that came from a healthy pull of a smoke.

Ryker hesitated.

"She won't know," Niall encouraged, lighting the tip of his cheroot to one of the lighted posts lining the graveled path. It was no secret that Ryker had sworn off cheroots for his wife. Just as she'd led to changes with the decor and redefining the role of the prostitutes, Ryker Black was very much second-in-command now.

"She knows everything," Ryker muttered. Though the little glimmer in his eyes disproved that gruff annoyance.

A rusty chuckle rumbled deep in Niall's chest, and he took another pull from his cheroot, smoke filling his lungs. They settled into a companionable silence as Ryker regained control of his panic.

Niall flicked his ashes and stared out at the handful of stars that managed to peek through the thick grime coating of the London night sky.

Where do you wish to go? Diana's question whispered around his mind. He'd only ever slept under the London sky. He'd not allowed himself to think of a life outside it. Whereas she, with her every painting and word, spoke of any world but here.

"There was another fight inside the club," Ryker said suddenly, unexpectedly.

Niall whipped his head sideways. The same rage and panic that always came with mention of a threat to their security flooded him now.

"One of Killoran's guards," Ryker went on. "Carried a warning that if any one of our men threaten their own again, it will be worse. Do you know anything about that?"

So, this was the reason for Ryker's request. To interrogate. Fucking Killoran. A dull heat climbed up Niall's neck, and with a curse he tossed his cheroot down and ground it under the heel of his boot. "He has a sister. It was useful information to obtain." The owner of the Devil's Den, in entering their hell to get forth a message and wreak more havoc on the club, had proven more courageous than Niall had credited. Or bloody stupid. It was all the same.

His brother went motionless. "Ya threatened the man's sister?"

Niall jutted his chin and held mutinously silent. He'd make no apologies. He'd acted when the others should have.

Ryker let loose a stream of curses in an uncharacteristic lack of control. "Goddamn it, Niall. We do not threaten women. We aren't Diggory and his henchmen." He slashed the air with his cheroot, the slender lit scrap flickering in the dark.

"He is threatening everything we've built." Their security. Their safety. Peace. All of it could be gone, and then what became of them? Black, with his viscountcy and lands, would live on in wealth and relative peace. Niall, Calum, Adair, and everyone else dependent upon them faced destruction.

His brother said nothing for a long while, and then: "His threat is against our club. He wants our members," Ryker concurred. "But we do not descend into the level of evil they do. We do not threaten women and children." Fury frosted his eyes as he took another pull from his cheroot. He exhaled a round ring. "Am I clear?" As clear as a moonlit night. He'd not have his orders on this gainsaid.

Since he'd been beaten like a dog into submission, Niall had chafed at being made to obey. It had taken a brotherhood of men and women who'd suffered those same hells to break him free from the snarling, snapping boy always spoiling for a fight. With a man's logic, however, he saw the necessity of obeying commands that were for the good of the group. Niall nodded tightly.

His brother finished his cheroot and crushed it under his boot. "They found Penelope's assailants."

At that again abrupt shift, Niall jerked erect.

Ryker glanced away, but not before Niall detected the spasm that contorted his face. The recent attack that had nearly seen his wife dead. After he'd been cornered in the streets, Penelope had paid the price of a blade to her side. In the end, both blighters had escaped. "Who?" he demanded. He'd had one on the ground underneath him, and the useless constable had lost his hold on the man. Or, more likely, he'd been in the pocket of the gang leader.

"They weren't Killoran's men," Ryker explained. "After Diggory's murder there was a split. Some challenged Killoran as the replacement. Sought to carry out revenge for Diggory."

Niall put those pieces together. Living in the streets, there was always a struggle for power when one's leader went down. "How do you—?"

"Killoran paid a visit."

They were the wrong words. They were gentlemanly ones that conjured an image of polite lords meeting over brandies and cigarillos. Killoran entering their home hinted at darkness and danger.

Niall curled his hand into a tight fist.

That spawn of Satan had entered the Hell and Sin, and Niall had been in the Mayfair District playing chaperone to Diana, kissing her crimson-stained lips, following her through the parks, sitting down to tea and pastries. And worse, he'd enjoyed every single damned moment in her presence. A ball of shame lodged in his throat, and he forced words past it. "Wot did 'e want?"

"A blood truce." Ryker held his gaze. "A pledge that the feud will continue between the clubs, but that our families and employees will be safe through it."

Niall's mouth moved. One would have to be dicked in the nob to trust a pledge made by Broderick Killoran. "And you believe that?" His incredulity rang loud in the nighttime quiet.

Ryker gave a brusque nod. "I do."

Fueled by his fury, Niall stalked away from that hard stare. "And yet he'll continue to bring fights and instability to our club," he seethed.

Ryker leveled him with a glacial stare. "Killoran said that was a token of your visit, and any further such visits will be paid in kind." There was a wealth of weight behind that barely veiled charge.

Niall whistled through his teeth. He'd underestimated the miserable sod. Bold as you please, not only had Killoran entered the Hell and Sin, but he'd also used Niall's words and actions to paint him black before his brothers and employees. Restless, he withdrew another cheroot and lit it against a nearby lamp. Taking a long, deep pull, he allowed it to flood his lungs. He exhaled slowly.

The gravel crunched under Ryker's heavy boot, indicating he'd moved.

"Take some consolation." Still thrumming with a restless fury, Niall inhaled from his cheroot once more. "You return tomorrow." And he choked on the mouthful of smoke. His shoulders shook at the sudden paroxysm, and tears stung his eyes. Leave? Of course, the obvious course. The assailants caught and a pledge reached with Killoran, there would no longer be a need for Diana to traipse about London with Niall's scarred self for company, and yet the oddest panic pounded away at his chest.

Ryker eyed him peculiarly. "Are you all right?"

"Inhaled wrong," he muttered, when he could coherently string a reply together. Which was rot. He hadn't choked over a cheroot since he'd taken his first pull as an orphan in the streets. "Ya don't think it's a risk for her to be without a guard?"

His brother proceeded to tick off on his fingers the very details Niall had already silently cataloged. "Killoran vowed a truce. Your and Penelope's assaulters have been apprehended, and the men working with them, as well." It was, of course, sufficient reason to abandon his post inside Diana Verney's household.

So why did the prospect of returning to the hell leave an odd, aching hollow inside his chest? It was because she was the only person who'd treated Niall as anything other than a ruthless thug from the street. Even his brothers saw him as a crass, merciless bastard to guard and protect, but not much more than that. Which is how Niall should want it. He'd spent a lifetime building himself into that pitiless Lord of the Underbelly.

Didn't he?

"You're certain?" he demanded gruffly, attempting to set his thoughts to right.

Ryker rolled his shoulders. "Has there been an attack or hint of one since you've been assigned her?" It was a methodical inquiry from a man who'd tasked Niall with an assignment more than a concerned question posed by a brother. Niall's teeth set painfully in his mouth. Not a soul was loyal to Diana Verney.

He shook his head once.

"Then there is your answer." Ryker pulled out his watch fob and consulted the time. "Penelope will be looking for me." He tucked the metal chain back in his pocket, but lingered.

For a fraction of a moment, Niall thought Ryker might put a request for more time assigned to Diana. But then . . . "We'll be hosting a dinner party."

At the abrupt shift in discourse, Niall cocked his head. "A dinner party?" Ryker Black avoided *ton* events at all costs.

"Penelope is of a mind that Diana should be introduced to prospective suitors," his brother explained. Those casually spoken words hit Niall like a kick to the gut. Black fixed him with a piercing look. "With you gone and Wilkinson . . . distracted, she'll benefit from a husband."

A muscle jumped at the corner of his right eye. Why in blazes was he telling him this? "Penelope believes that? Or you?" The question came fast and sharp, before he could call it back. Niall didn't want to know that after he'd gone there'd be a bloody fancy gent about.

"Me." Ryker consulted his timepiece once more. He pocketed it and then held Niall's gaze. "Thank you," he said, with his usual somberness. "I know you hate this world as much as I do." More so. "Thank you for entering it anyway and verifying that Diana was unharmed."

He'd thank him.

An assignment completed.

A job well done.

Niall stared after Ryker's tall retreating figure long after he'd gone, finishing the remainder of his cheroot.

I am going home.

And for the first time since he'd damned Ryker for forcing this assignment on him, he damned him all over again for yanking it so swiftly away.

Chapter 13

For all intents and purposes, the night had been a resounding success. Her father had been smiling, truly smiling, for the first time in a year. Diana had established a tentative friendship with her sister-in-law—a sister-in-law whose wedding Diana hadn't been invited to, but who'd tonight extended an invitation to a small soiree she and Ryker would host at the end of the Season. It was the mark of a new beginning with her family.

Even the *ton* hadn't been wholly disdainful. She'd danced several sets. One with Lord Maxwell. Another with Lady Penelope's brother-in-law, Lord Christian St. Cyr. Of course, both sets had been carefully coordinated by the viscountess so Diana didn't find herself relegated to the wall for the entire evening.

And all Diana could focus on was one singular detail: Niall had not inspected her room.

Unable to sleep, Diana sat with her knees drawn to her chest at the upholstered window seat that overlooked the quiet London streets. The full moon's pale glow periodically peeked out through the heavy hang of cloud cover to bathe the cobblestones in a soft light.

He'd not even accompanied her to her chambers.

For the first time since Niall had been assigned Diana's guard, he'd not done his methodical, detailed search of her rooms and then stalked off with the stealth and silence of a London pickpocket and nothing more than a curt "Night."

Rather, they'd returned from Lord and Lady Milford's with him trailing at a sizable distance and then disappearing down the guest corridors where he kept his rooms.

Setting the forgotten book down on the bench, she dropped her chin atop her knees and rubbed back and forth over the soft fabric of her white nightshift. Niall Marksman was not a man to forsake his duties. It went against the fierce guard who'd taken up position at Lady Milford's ballroom, like he was the head of the King's Army leading his men into battle.

It did not make sense.

Unless he was leaving. Then it made complete sense. She stopped her distracted movements as the niggling possibility that had taken root upon their arrival two hours earlier grew. Mayhap he'd decided after all that he wished his freedom. Mayhap . . .

The softest tread of footsteps from out in the hall cut across the early morn quiet. Her heart skittered a beat as all the terror of those gaping doors and windows and broken axles stirred to life once more. Forgotten terror. Terror she'd not so much as given thought to since Niall had entered this household to oversee her safety.

Biting the inside of her cheek, she quickly reached back and silently loosed the ring that held the curtain. She caught her breath as the heavy satin fluttered into place.

Do not be a dunderhead. You're making monsters out of shadows, just as your father accused.

No doubt it was only a servant snuffing the candles before retiring for the early morn hours.

A floorboard groaned, and she bit the inside of her cheek hard. Scrunching herself against the wall, she sought to meld with it. She trained her ears for a hint of sound. The longcase clock ticked inordinately loudly, emphasizing the thick hum of quiet. Diana concentrated on those marked seconds passing, and with each beat, when no enemy yanked back the curtain and exposed her hiding, some of the tension slowly slipped from her frame.

"You are being silly," she silently mouthed. Niall had been right to his doubts. What harm could anyone wish her? Her connection to Ryker was at best distant and worst nonexistent. As such, she could never be used as a pawn to hurt him, or anyone. Even her own father had ceased to see her. Logic restored, Diana angled her head enough to peek through the crack in the curtain.

She swallowed a cry, suppressing it with her fingertips.

The candle's eerie glow played off the stark white fabric of a gentleman's shirt. She blinked slowly.

A tall gentleman.

A very tall gentleman.

A familiar one with impossibly broad shoulders and corded muscles better fitting a prize fighter.

Niall? she silently mouthed.

There could not, however, be any mistaking that form. At some point he'd abandoned his crimson jacket and stood in nothing more than his burgundy front-fall breeches, white shirtsleeves, and boots. Her fingers twitched with the need for her paintbrush—a need to capture him as he was, unaware, his back to her, focused on one of her many paintings. Diana inched forward, and, holding her breath, she dipped her head daringly around the curtain. Her breath lodged in her lungs. There was something so very intimate about being near a man—nay, near *this* man—with his waistcoat, cravat, and coat sleeves abandoned. The fine fabric of his cotton shirt played off the muscles of his back.

She should announce herself. Should have done so the minute he'd entered the room. And she most certainly shouldn't be spying on him unawares.

He moved, and, her heart climbing into her throat, she ducked back into hiding. Diana pressed her eyes closed and silently prayed that he'd not discovered her here spying like a naughty child. The floorboards creaked, and she shrank against the wall.

Another stretch of silence descended, and, holding her breath, she looked around the edge of the curtain.

She silently cursed.

Niall had moved on to another easel, but he remained unmoving, unwilling to give up his place in her parlor. An aromatic trace of smoke tinged her nostrils. Diana silently whiffed the air. Curiosity pulled her back for another glimpse.

Arms folded at his chest, Niall periodically raised a small cheroot to his lips and took a deep pull.

She cocked her head. When she'd been a girl, she'd often curled in the side of her father's leather button sofa while he attended his ducal business. Oftentimes with a small, carved wood pipe clenched between his teeth. Until mother had discovered them that day. Seething and fuming, she'd delivered a stinging lecture to both Diana and her husband for daring to do something so plebeian as to smoke. Inside their sacred home, no less. It was the last time Diana was allowed to wander without a nursemaid closely following, and the last she'd had a trace of that fragrant tobacco—until now. What would her mother say if she could see this man born of the streets, in her parlor, guarding her daughter, and now leaving a trail of cheroot ashes and smoke about? Given her crimes, it seemed fitting and right that even this aspect of the duchess's world should so collapse.

"Are you intending to sleep on that seat?"

Niall's low baritone rumbled around the parlor. Diana gasped and pitched sideways. She quickly caught the edge, saving herself from tumbling out from behind her hiding place—her less-than-impressive hiding place.

Her skin went hot with humiliation, and she briefly cast her gaze to the window's small hook latch. It couldn't be more than—she peered out into the dark and sighed—thirty feet. Alas, she was many things: impulsive, given to prattling. But she was not a coward.

With another sigh, Diana shoved the curtain wide. "You knew I was here the whole while?" She swung her legs over the side of the bench, and her night skirts settled softly about her ankles. *The blighter.* Though she couldn't determine if she was angrier with him for having found her, or herself for being hopelessly unable to do something as simple as hide.

His lips quirked in one corner, dimpling his scarred cheek, lending a gentleness to him when he was only ever hard and menacing. "It's my job to hear and see everything, love." *Love.* It was nothing more than a casual, toss-away endearment, and yet it was as though a thousand butterflies had been set free in her belly and celebrated that freedom by dancing wildly about. "If a man doesn't hear the person sneaking, he ends up with a slit throat and a blade in his belly."

His stark words tossed an ominous chill over the room. She shivered and huddled deeper inside her wrapper. What must his life have been like? Again, she touched her eyes on those scars. Badges of honor that marred his face. She wondered who'd brought him pain and hated that he'd ever known such suffering. Shame filled her for having been a wholly self-absorbed lady who'd not considered the plight of others. "You know something about that?" she asked needlessly, torn between never wanting to know and needing to.

He took another pull from his cheroot and slowly exhaled. "Oi know a lot about that," he said gruffly, slipping back into that guttural Cockney. And yet, with the vagueness to that reply, he kept her out. Was it to protect himself? Or did he, like everyone else, believe Diana too weak to know the truth of the world around her?

She watched him as he smoked, enthralled by his smooth, damn-the-world ease. Soon he would leave, and who Niall Marksman was or had been, or would one day be when Diana was gone and languishing in Bedlam, did not matter. Or it should not. He was just another transient person moving in and out of her life. Not vastly different from her own parents or the suitors who'd once visited this very room. But in the three weeks they'd spent together, he'd become an inextricable part of her life. The one person who'd spoken plainly to her and not treated her as though she was a duke's daughter who should be pampered for it, but oddly how little she knew about him. "Is that how you came by them?"

He arched an eyebrow.

"Your"—she motioned to his right cheek—"scars."

As if they were chatting over tea and speaking of mundane matters like the weather, he tipped the ashes of his cheroot into a nearby vase. "Sometimes."

In his laconic reply, he could not make clearer his desire for Diana's silence.

Diana pushed slowly to her feet but was unable to force movement into her limbs. "Did that happen often to you?" she persisted, wanting, before Niall Marksman left, to tear down some of the walls and understand who he was. "Did men try to steal from you?" A heartbreaking image slid forth of Niall as a boy with a mop of black curls and fearful blue eyes, fighting for his life as someone tried to lift from him the few possessions he'd then had.

Niall froze, the cheroot halfway to his lips. "Is that what ya believe?" he asked, the jeering quality that had peppered their every earlier exchange now restored with her bold questioning. "That Oi was a poor, scared, innocent boy, sleeping in an alley, marked up by older, tougher men?"

Her throat worked, and she fluttered her hands about her neck. "I . . . yes . . . no . . ."

He took a step toward her, and the alacrity of that movement sent Diana stumbling back. She caught the edge of a mahogany side table to keep her feet planted. Forcing herself to not run off, scared and silent, as he surely expected.

"Oi was the one who stabbed men while they slept."

A dull humming filled her ears. She did not believe it. Refused to accept the lies he fed her. She gave her head a clearing shake, but the buzz of confusion remained.

With a hard, mirthless smirk, Niall continued to smoke his cheroot, eerily calm through her confusion. "Oi wasn't the poor street urchin ya've painted in your mind, Diana. Oi killed on command."

His words rang with a truth that numbed her inside, penetrating the wall of shock. He was a killer by his own admission, and his unapologetic, unyielding stance said he had not a single qualm about it. Yet of all those hideous, horrid words uttered, only two held her gripped.

On command.

Loosening her clutch on the table, she forced her fingers open. "Who would require that?" she asked softly, drifting over to him.

He eyed her warily the way he might a midnight specter come to haunt for the crimes he breathed aloud. "Wot are ya on about?" Those coarse, guttural tones were so thick she had to strain and make them out.

Diana stopped before him and touched the tip of her index finger to the vicious white scar that started at the corner of his nose and arched over his right cheek. He winced but did not draw away from her faint caress. "You said you were made to kill." It was a distinction. A slight one. And yet so very meaningful. Did he even realize that?

He stiffened and then hastily tamped out his cheroot on the rose-inlaid table, tossing aside the small scrap. "Ya 'eard wot ya wanted to."

"I heard what you said," she quietly corrected, her eyes touching on the small white circle just above his eyebrow. How did a person come by that very small, very precise mark?

His jaw worked reflexively, and she saw the war he waged within. The war to keep her out, as he'd no doubt shut everyone else out before. Because for the misery of existing alone in a solitary world, there was something far more dangerous, far more heartbreaking, in dwelling among people who sneered and jeered.

For the station divide between them, Diana and Niall were more alike in the most elemental ways that mattered.

"How old were you?" she softly urged when he still volunteered nothing.

"Seven? Eight? Oi don't know."

She tipped her head.

A harsh, ugly, empty chuckle rumbled in his chest. "Oi don't even know 'ow old Oi am, princess. Me ma sold me to Diggory when Oi was a babe."

Diana let her hand fall to her side and buried it in her skirts to keep him from detecting that faint tremble. He'd see it as weakness and confirmation of every ill opinion he'd ever carried of her. "Diggory," she repeated. Again, that name. A heavy pressure settled in her chest.

Niall nodded.

He spoke of evil—a person selling a child to a brute. It was an ugliness that matched the crimes of Diana's mother. Then, it was the very *same* crime her mother was guilty of. Only the Duchess of Wilkinson had taken no coin for turning first Ryker and then Helena over to that monster. She'd done it with nothing more than her societal status in mind.

"'e schooled me on how to use a blade. Forced me to off rivals and enemies." His eyes grew distant, and in this moment he ceased to see her, or anything beyond the visions inside his head. How she wanted to climb inside and battle back his demons for him. To make his pain her own. "There was a boy," he said, his voice peculiarly absent. "Ryan." His lips twisted as if with bitter remembrance. "Tiny waif. 'e moved quicker than a rat scurrying through piles of refuse. Diggory had seen that speed and sought to use it to pick the pockets of theatregoers outside Drury Lane. Took 'im in. He was a lousy pickpocket," he said, more to himself. "Oi tried to train him, but . . ."

But . . . That word hovered in the air, as real as if it had been spoken.

"But," she gently prodded, capturing his cheek in her hand and forcing his face back to hers.

He blinked. Did he even remember before now that she was here?

"Oi couldn't pick pockets anymore. Oi'd gotten too big. Wanted me to kill for him instead. I wouldn't do it."

She caught her lower lip hard between her teeth, imagining Niall as a boy. He would have been mutinous, with a defiant glimmer in his eyes and a dark curl hanging over his forehead. "What did he do?" she asked, needing him to finish this telling as much for him as for herself.

"Two of Diggory's men 'eld one of his rivals. A miserable bruiser. 'is name was Boyd. A man Satan himself wouldn't 'ave 'ad a use for."

His voice grew hoarse, and she ached to fold her arms around him and hold him close. Knowing, however, to do so would sever the connection and end his telling. So she stood frozen, motionless, waiting for him to continue. And this time she did not prod, but waited, with the longcase clock ticking away the passing moments.

"'e took Ryan," he said, at long last. *Oh, God.* "Put a blade to his throat." *No.* "Told me to choose. Either Oi killed his rival Boyd . . ." His Adam's apple moved with the force of his swallow. "Or he killed Ryan."

A chill worked along her spine, icing her flesh from the inside out. *No. No. No.* It was a silent, useless entreaty inside her head. For a different ending to the one she already knew. *Please do not let him say it. Please . . .*

"Oi couldn't do it. Next time 'e promised it would be me and not Ryan choking on my blood." She swallowed back the bile burning at her throat. "It was the last time Oi faltered," he said quietly. "After that, 'e made me mark my kills in that hovel I called home. Every time Oi took a life, he had me carve it in the wall with black ink." He touched his chest absently, his gaze far away. "Kill or be killed," he said, his voice quiet and distant, living with memories only he could see.

Her stomach lurched, and Diana concentrated on breathing to keep from casting the contents of her stomach up. In this instance she proved very much her mother's daughter, for, God help her, if she had a blade on her person and Mac Diggory lived even still, she would have gladly stuck a knife in his heart for what he'd done to Niall and the boy Ryan.

Tears flooded her eyes, and she blinked them back. He'd only take those as further marks of her frailty. "You were a child," she said softly, when she trusted herself to speak. "Regardless of whether you were eight, nine, or ten. You were forced to do . . ." God help her for a coward, she could not bring those words forward, and yet it would not be fair to this man. "You were f-forced to kill, Niall," she finally managed. *How am I so calm? How am I so calm when inside my heart is splintering apart?* "The things you did, you did because you were forced to," she repeated, willing him to see that. "That cruelty is not in your blood."

Unlike Diana, who was forever bound to the evil coursing in her veins.

———— ❦ ————

He'd not breathed those words aloud to a single person. After Ryker had felled Diggory's henchman and sprung Niall free, Niall had fled his former life and never looked back. And never looking back had included never sharing those dark, evil secrets that had earned him a place in Hell early on.

Until now.

Until this woman. A fragile slip of a lady who wouldn't have lasted a day in the Dials and who innocently believed a heavy curtain enough to hide her presence from someone of his stealth and skill.

And yet, even issuing those dark utterances, Diana stood before him anyway. The faint tremble of her hands and slight quiver of her lower lip the only mark of her upset. He searched for disgust in her expressive blue eyes, but saw nothing more than sadness, regret, and—he recoiled, looking away—pity.

"Oi don't want your pity," he snapped, spoiling for a fight, needing one. What had made him share those words with her? Why now, when he'd kept all thought of Diggory and the dark deeds he'd carried out for that man tightly shut away?

She shook her head, and her perfectly plaited golden braid flopped over her shoulder. "I don't pity you," she whispered. Her full lower lip quivered.

"You're as bad a liar as ya are a sneak, Diana Verney," he muttered.

She erased the space between them, stopping so close the fragrant hint of flowers that kissed her skin wafted about him. He filled his lungs with that purifying hint of innocence. Innocence in a world riddled with nothing but blackness.

"You would take on guilt for things that were done to you as a child," she said softly.

"You're wrong."

If she heard the dangerous warning there, she gave no indication. "Am I?" she countered in her willingness to take him on, braver than most grown men in St. Giles. "When was the last time you killed someone?"

He'd spent his whole life believing fancy ladies like Diana weak and fainting, pathetic excuses for people. Yet, she didn't wilt or bolt from him with horror of his revelations. That grudging respect he'd carried for her for these three weeks now gave way, allowing a deeper, abiding appreciation for her strength and courage.

Niall looked away. "Oi got caught keeping some of the loot from a theft. Stabbed me for it." He rubbed his hand over the place that vicious blade had speared his flesh.

Diana buried a broken gasp in her palm.

The terror of that long-ago day surged forth. Niall's screams as the blade sluiced through his skin. The burning agony. Sweat beaded his forehead, and he briefly closed his eyes, willing back the memories. "Your brother saved me," he managed to squeeze out through his constricted throat. So she might know the depth of the bond between Niall and the man who shared her blood. Drawing in an even breath, he opened his eyes. "After that?" Niall shrugged. "Oi left that hovel and vowed to never kill again and never return to that place." And he hadn't.

The silver flecks in her eyes glimmered with sadness, and she claimed his hands in her own. "And *that* is why you are not the monster you take yourself for."

Niall's gaze went to the disparateness of them. Riveted by that juxtaposition. Diana's skin lily white, soft like satin, and neatly manicured, and his scarred, riddled with marks and jagged nails. He had no place putting his hands, stained forever with the blood of men he'd killed, upon her in any way.

Yet she showed no trace of fear, and it roused a disquiet. It had been easier, safer, to see her as a pampered miss afraid of the world around her. Only to find, with her unflinching through the darkest stories of his past, that she was stronger than most men of his acquaintance.

"Ya'd make me out to be someone Oi'm not," he clipped out, yanking free of her grip. "Oi may not 'ave killed men, but Oi've beaten them. Threatened them." Done other vicious things that even he couldn't breathe aloud to this woman. Not when it would shatter her innocence even more than he had with talk of his black sins.

She rocked on her bare heels. "Yes, well, I expect those men no doubt deserved it."

That was it. Ten words. Trusting ones that proved again her lack of fear . . . and the inherent goodness in her soul.

"What manner of woman are ya, Diana Verney?" he puzzled aloud.

"A practical one," she said automatically. "One wise enough to see that you did what you had to do in order to survive, Niall." She touched her fingertip to the scar above his brow, left by Diggory's cheroots, and he fought the hungering to lean into that butterfly soft caress. "And one who is glad you're alive for it," she murmured softly.

He started. He'd never doubted his siblings' loyalty, but not a single person, not even the woman who'd given him life, had given thanks for his existence. He served a purpose: to keep people safe and to create work for bastards in the street. Beyond the purpose he served as head guard, what need did anyone have of him? Uncomfortable by Diana's raw honesty and the peculiar lightness her admission roused in his chest, Niall disentangled their hands. He stalked over to her portraits, pausing beside one all-too-familiar image.

Even in watercolor she'd captured the dilapidated buildings and layers of grime and muck covering the uneven cobblestones of St. Giles. Not just any part of St. Giles. He peered closer.

"It is from the day H-Helena"—she tripped over her words— "and I were to visit the club."

The day Helena had shot Diggory dead, and Diana Verney had come streaking inside the Hell and Sin and into his arms for help.

He moved on to the next portrait. This scene, of a different end of London. The lush greenery of Hyde Park set amid a backdrop of a turbulent storm, with rain battering down on two figures—a slender, cloaked female . . . and him. He glanced over his shoulder and found Diana, her cheeks blazing red, even in the darkened space.

Niall returned his focus forward.

An utterance she'd breathed in the midst of that rainstorm slid forward.

"They're all places you've been," he said quietly, piecing together the eclectic array of artwork.

Diana cleared her throat, and he felt her approach more than heard her, hovering at his shoulder. "Hardly many," she conceded, confirming his supposition. She moved in a whir of white skirts and gathered a book. "But I hope to." Coming forward with that small leather book, Diana held it out like an offering to him.

Niall hesitated. He was not a man to seek or want entry inside another person's thoughts, hopes, or dreams.

Diana pressed the open sketchbook into his hand, making the decision for him. "I wish to go here," she said, with a restored enthusiasm to her lyrical voice. She jabbed the page, forcing his eyes away from the lively color brightening her cheeks and to the page. The deep blue of the waters captured held him momentarily transfixed. From those green and sapphire waters rose a jagged mountain lined with green shrubs and brush. "It is St. George's," she clarified, and her eagerness was infectious. He studied the page while she spoke. "They call it New London."

He snorted as dry irony slapped at him, and he briefly glanced between her and the sketch. "There isn't a thing about London in that page."

"Well, the cobbles came from Wales," she explained, motioning to the gray road paved on that sheet, "but otherwise, I agree." And this time when she spoke, she did so as a woman who seemed to forget Niall's presence, and damned if he didn't hate that faraway place she dreamt of with such longing. "It was formed by volcanoes, and"—she dusted her fingertips over the water she'd skillfully painted—"they say the sand of St. George's is pink and soft like satin under your bare feet." It was hard, for even him, one of London's most jaded cutthroats, to not be drawn in by the fantastical lands she painted. Her voice took on a far-off, distant quality. "And the water, they say, is a cerulean water." She nibbled at her fingertip, studying her work, and then slowly, meticulously, severed the page from the book. "My attempts appear too dark, and yet no matter how many times I attempt, I can just not get it quite right. Until I see it . . ."

He snorted. The only island he'd ever known was the Queen's England, and their waters were as black as their streets. "Who says that?"

Looking up abruptly, she knocked into his bent head. He grunted, waving off her apology. She opened and closed her mouth several times. "Who says what?" she blurted.

He jerked his chin at the sketch in her hands. "About their fancy waters and sands?"

A little blush dusted her skin. "Uh . . ." He narrowed his eyes, having lived a jaded enough life to detect when an innocent miss was prevaricating. She had her secrets. They all did. But damned if he detested hers. "Helena's cousins by marriage," she said at last, reluctantly. "They are from a seafaring family. The Viscountess Redbrooke's brother is a merchant, and he's told tales of St. George's."

And Niall, who didn't give a jot about anyone or anything, found himself filled with jealousy for the nameless "he" who'd filled Diana with tales of places Niall had never been, nor would ever go.

Through his tumult, she set down that page and spoke casually. "Because of the vast ocean and plentiful cedar trees, the people who lived there turned to privateering and . . ." She dropped her voice to a conspiratorial whisper. "Piracy." A curl popped free of her loose braid and tumbled over her eye.

A wistful smile pulled at his lips, and he brushed back that single golden lock, tucking it behind her ear. She spoke of pirates as though they were romantic characters belonging in the pages of a book and not the bloodthirsty wretches who plundered and pillaged. How different they viewed the world. "Ya find pirates romantic?" Such a detail would have earned his scorn three weeks earlier. Now it was just an endearing part of this innocent lady who'd enthralled him.

"No," she said quietly, unexpectedly. "But it is fun to sometimes imagine a world of excitement where men and women sail the seas and venture into waters different from our own." *Our own.* And when she spoke that way, she created an intimate connection where it was a world they, in fact, shared. An illusion. Nothing more. Diana stepped away from him and took that fragile hint of warmth with her.

Niall watched her every careful movement as she wandered away, settling at last before that St. Giles painting. "You're leaving."

It wasn't a question. "They apprehended the men who attempted to kill Penelope," he said gruffly, giving her more information than he would another soul.

She looked back. "Did they?" she asked cautiously.

Something was expected of him here. He knew it by the glimmer in her cobalt eyes, but he'd never been a man to make any sense of emotion or feelings, so he gave nothing more than a brusque nod.

"I see." What did she see exactly? Mayhap it was the early morn hour and the shock of Ryker's earlier revelations, but Niall couldn't make sense of a goddamned thing. Diana came forward, palm extended once more.

He eyed it a moment and then folded it in his scarred grip.

"Thank you," she said softly. "Thank you for remaining on when you never wished to be here. Even when you didn't believe there was a threat." Diana drew her hand back, and he mourned the loss of that touch. "Goodbye, Niall."

That was it. *Goodbye.* One word that spoke of closure and marked his time here done.

She recovered her rough sketch of St. George's and placed it in his hands. "It is yours," she said softly. "A gift." Her eyes glittered with what might have been sadness. Or was that his own selfish hopes? "To remember me by."

As if he could ever forget her. Unnerved by that realization, he looked to the gift she'd bequeathed.

The soft tread of her footsteps marked her retreat, and panic knocked around his chest. This would be the last he saw her. From then on, there would never be a need for their paths to cross or their lives to intersect.

Niall strode after her.

Diana paused, angling her head back.

"Oi'll see ya to your chambers," he said gruffly. One more time.

She gave him another little smile. "I no longer require help going to my chambers, Niall. I saw to it myself long before you, and I'll continue on the same way after you've gone."

And with that, she left.

Chapter 14

Diana padded silently down the darkened halls. Her breath came in quick, ragged spurts, and she fought to keep from giving in to the torrent of emotion threatening to drag her under. Hating the pain Niall had known. Hating he'd leave on the morrow, and she'd never again see him. The words shared by Niall had rooted themselves inside her brain and remained there, forever to stay, long after he left here.

Pain cleaved at her heart. Away from his intense, all-knowing eyes, she gave in to the onslaught of sadness, fury, and regret for all he'd known. And something worse, something that stole her breath and filled every corner of her being—hatred. Hatred for the men who'd forced such evil upon Niall. And with that hatred, there was a bitter resentment for members of the *ton* who'd been uncaring of the plight of a small boy in the streets—and herself for being guilty of that same charge.

As she walked, she passed her eyes over the town house, a home she'd taken for granted. Now she looked at it as Niall surely had, taking in the elaborate golden frames. The French malachite box no more than an afterthought upon a painted gilt side table—both pieces extravagant testimonies of wealth and privilege. Shame filled her.

Diana had always only ever been given the best. She'd lived a lavish, opulent lifestyle as the Duke of Wilkinson's cherished daughter, free from fear and hunger. Never knowing the evil that dwelled inside a person's soul. Wholly insulated from the darkness that Niall had been forced to endure. At the age she'd been attending painting sessions and learning the fluid moves of a curtsy, a blade had been thrust into Niall's hand. He'd forged an existence from nothing and created an empire that sustained men, women, and children. Triumphing in the face of adversity and coming out a man of strength, convictions, and courage. Admiration swelled for all he'd done and who he was.

Whereas Diana?

She slowed her steps, pausing beside an Italian Rococo–style mirror. The smooth cut glass reflected back the sad, regretful eyes of a woman who'd allowed herself to be shaped into nothing more than an empty-headed, oblivious miss.

Your purpose is to be dutiful and obedient.

That stern lecture delivered countless times by her mother echoed around the chambers of her mind, and with a hard smile, Diana stuck her tongue out, the childlike gesture a small battle against every social lesson.

She may share her mother's blood and eventual path to madness, but along the way she would not sell her soul to rank and privilege. A mantle lifted from her shoulders, a sense of being set free, when in other ways she would remain imprisoned. And she found on the whole of this dark night some solace in that. Forcing her gaze away from the mirror, Diana resumed the long march to her chambers.

Once inside, she closed the door behind her. Then, within the sanctuary of her rooms, she hugged her arms close to her chest and borrowed support from the heavy panel. Found a soothing calm in the cool night air as it caressed her face.

Night air?

She paused, lowering her arms slowly to her sides. Her gaze flew to the open window at the opposite end of the room. A gentle breezed tugged at the floral drapes; it set the fabric dancing noisily.

She wet her lips. It was silly to react so to an open window. There were any number of reasons for it to be open.

But there were also countless reasons it should not . . .

Shivers of apprehension fanned along Diana's spine, and she pushed slowly away from the door. The floorboards groaned, creaking ominously in the quiet. "M-Meredith?" she called, her voice trembling.

"My lady?"

Diana cried out and spun toward the dressing room.

Her maid rushed out. "Forgive me, my lady," she said, her voice heavy with sleep. The girl buried a yawn in her fingers.

The tension slipped from Diana's frame, and she pressed a hand to her racing heart. "No. That is all. I was just . . ." Imagining monsters in the shadows. She grimaced. "That is all. There is no need," she said, embarrassment making her cheeks go hot.

Silly nonsense.

Meredith hurried over to the floor-length crystal doors.

"That is fine," Diana called, staying her. "You may leave it. You are relieved for the night," she said.

"You're certain, my lady?" The girl hesitated, and with Diana's nod, the maid curtsied and took her leave, closing the door softly behind her.

As soon as she'd left, Diana exhaled slowly through her closed lips. "Do not be a dunderhead," she whispered. She was proving herself the cowardly miss she'd been accused of being by too many, imagining monsters out of shadows. Lady Penelope's assailants had been apprehended. Diana stalked over to the window and reached up.

Then paused. She skimmed her gaze over the walled-in garden at the back of the town house. The full moon flitted in and out from behind the heavy night cloud, periodically casting the overgrown gardens into complete darkness. In a soft whisper of cotton night skirts,

Diana sank to her knees and layered her arms to the sill. Dropping her chin atop her folded hands, she stared down.

How many times as a girl had she sat in this precise spot? Eyes closed, she would kneel at the edge and attempt to label the flowers by the scents that wafted into her rooms. Those gardens had been her mother's pride and joy, tended to with the care and love a parent might show a child. Diana turned sad eyes to the now unkempt pink rosebush and boxwoods long in need of pruning. There had never been any such love from Diana's mother—not for her. Not for anyone. The duchess had proven herself incapable of that gentle emotion. Instead, she had filled Diana's childhood with orders and commands and lessons on propriety. There was never affection or warmth or pride. Until Diana had made her Come Out, and her mother had seen in her a prize to be married off to increase their family's rank and holdings.

Her mouth stung with bitterness, and she forcibly brought down the window with a hard, satisfying *thunk*. Shoving to her feet, Diana turned and gasped.

A bald, hulking figure grinned slowly. The scent of garlic and ale slapped at her senses.

She cried out, but he slapped a palm over her mouth, muting the sound. Terror licked at her brain and coursed a path through her. She screamed against the brute stranger's coarse, gloveless palm, her sounds of help stifled and buried. "Ya 'aven't made this easy for me, bitch," he whispered against her ear.

Her dread spiraled, and Diana bucked and thrashed against his punishing grip. He wrenched her arm behind her back, and tears sprang to her eyes. She yanked her head back and forth, glancing desperately to the doorway. *Niall . . .*

"None o' that," he rebuked, giving another tug on her arm that sent tears tumbling down her cheeks. "Moi liege ain't 'appy with 'ow difficult this has been. Wants to do it for 'isself." He licked at his lips. "But nuffin was said about not enjoyin' ya first, princess."

Revulsion snaked around her insides, and Diana renewed her struggles. She tore at the flesh of his palm with her teeth, gagging on the metallic taste of his blood as it flooded her mouth.

He grunted. "You're going to wish ya hadn't done that." The hiss of metal thundered around the room, blending with her strangled, raspy breaths against his hand. A piteous moan seeped from her lips, lost by the weight of his hand. The toothless brute brought his arm back.

Oh, God. She recoiled, curling into herself. He cuffed her against the side of her head. Stars exploded behind her vision, and the earth dipped and swayed under her feet. Diana struggled through the fog, clinging to her senses, dimly registering him dragging her over toward the connecting door inside her chambers. Her fear doubled with every step he took. The moment he wrestled her from her rooms and home, she was as good as dead.

Useless tears stung her eyes, blurring her vision. *I don't want to die like this.* She renewed her efforts at freedom, dragging her feet hard into the thin Aubusson carpet.

The hulking brute cursed under his breath and spun quickly. Then, for a brief, miraculous moment, he removed his hand from her mouth. Diana sucked in a panicky breath to scream down the household. That cry ended on a shuddery hiss as he caught her around the throat and drove her back against the wall. Pain radiated along her spine. "Oi said shut your mouth, bitch." He stuck his face close to hers. "Was Oi not clear?" She struggled to draw in breath, choking and gasping. His unforgiving hold meant to punish and kill. Her lungs burned, as she ineffectually tugged at his corded forearms.

Her frantically roving eyes collided with a nearby Wedgwood lilac vase. She kicked her legs out at the table. The porcelain piece exploded in the nighttime still.

And as her attacker loosened his hold on her neck and resumed dragging her from the room, Diana prayed.

———⚮———

Niall remained amid Diana's paintings long after she'd left.

Yes, as Ryker had pointed out earlier in the evening, Niall should be relieved. Penelope's assailants had been caught, and Niall was now free to return.

"Get a bloody 'old of yourself," he mumbled, yanking another cheroot from inside his jacket. Stalking over to a lit sconce, he struck the wrapper and took a healthy pull from it. He was tired. There was no other accounting for this blasted melancholy.

He should have retired long ago. But Niall had never been a man who'd wanted, needed, or craved sleep. When a person closed his eyes and let down his guard, enemies crept in and rewarded that stolen peace with a knife in the belly—and eternal silence.

In a few hours, his belongings would be packed, and he'd ride away from the fashionable end of London's Mayfair District and on to the underbelly where sinners dwelled until their death. Except as Niall quit Diana's Parlor, as he'd come to think of it, he stole a final look back at that grim capture of St. Giles Street.

I am going home.

Wandering the quiet halls, however, he realized it was not long-ago customs and habits that kept sleep at bay—but rather, her. Diana Verney.

Cheroot in hand, Niall stalked through the Duke of Wilkinson's corridors with the same methodical steps he took when doing a sweep of the Hell and Sin Club. Only there was no late-night drunken revelry or booming laughter filling these halls.

Rather, a soft, peaceful quiet Niall had never before known existed.

And he wasn't going to miss a goddamned thing about it. None of it.

Ya fucking liar.

185

Bloody hell on Sunday, if he wasn't going to miss the exasperating chit. He inhaled another lungful of smoke from his cheroot, allowing it to fill him, and then slowly breathed out a small white ring.

Stalking down the corridor, his footfalls fell silent, muffled by the plush carpet.

Until his siblings of the street, people had proven themselves to be inconstant, fleeting figures drifting in and out of Niall's life. People who ended up locked away at Newgate or in the hull of a ship. And those were the unfortunate ones who didn't find themselves dead for their crimes. As such, he'd not given any thought to the whores or gaming-table workers who'd suddenly quit their posts and moved on to other ventures. People left. People died. Those were the only black and whites of life.

He perused portrait after portrait of bewigged Verney ancestors, powerful men and women memorialized in paint. Men with long, noble noses and high brows. The same artist may as well have masterfully created each painting through the ages. Slowing his steps, Niall moved down the hall, taking in each of Diana's stern-faced relations whose flat lips conveyed a disdain for the men and women who'd dare gaze upon them. These were gents who shared the blood of kings and lords, and who'd passed that pure blue blood down to their equally noble children.

Niall came to a slow stop alongside one gold frame; this painting was at odds with all the others. A regal lady stood frowning and hard-eyed beside a soft-eyed gentleman. His portly form and ruddy cheeks gave him away as the Duke of Wilkinson. He stood in direct juxtaposition to the harsh severity of his wife. It was not, however, that noble couple who held Niall frozen, but rather the widely smiling Diana as she'd been years earlier. The smile on her dimpled cheeks met her twinkling blue eyes, both expertly captured by the artist.

Niall absently snuffed out his cheroot on the mahogany hall table and abandoned the scrap.

When he was a boy, Niall had lain on the dirt-stained floor in Diggory's shanty that had served as a bed. His first thieving partner, Connor, had gone missing, never to return. Not a word, sight, or sound was ever heard from the child, near in age to Niall's own young years. Niall had stared up at the cracks in the threadbare ceiling with terrified eyes, knowing the truth early on—there was no one who'd either note or care if Niall Marksman suddenly, one day, disappeared.

In that, Diana wasn't vastly different from everyone to come before her. She'd required a guard. He'd served in that capacity, and now his tenure here was done. His chest tightened, and Niall forced his gaze away from the painting and resumed the trek abovestairs.

This weakness was why he was better off gone. Weakness saw a man dead in the streets. Niall needed to return to St. Giles and resurrect those thick walls of hatred he'd built years earlier for all the men, women, and children of Diana Verney's station.

He reached the landing. Unbidden, his gaze traveled down the opposite end of the hall to where Diana now slept. Of course, being forced into the lady's company for the better part of a month, it was only natural that he'd formed a relationship with her.

A relationship that had him hungering for both the words on her lips and the taste of that satiny, soft, bow-shaped flesh. "You're a bloody fool," he muttered, giving his head a hard shake. Lusting after a lady of the *haute ton* was folly that a man deserved to have his cork drawn for. Acting on that desire, as he had not once, but twice, and dreaming of it every night thereafter, was a treachery that Ryker should happily gut Niall over. With his bloodstained fingers, the last thing Niall had any right to was putting his hands upon Diana Verney.

Niall started for his rooms—and then froze. The candles sent shadows flitting and dancing on the immaculate ivory carpet. Or rather . . . a largely immaculate carpet. He wheeled slowly around. Not taking his gaze from the faint mark on the floor, Niall stealthily padded over to it.

It was the faintest incongruity. Yet in the streets of St. Giles, ignoring an incongruity resulted in fatal mistakes.

He crouched on his heels and skimmed the back of his knuckles over that fresh stain.

Lifting his hand close to his eyes, Niall inspected the residual on his fingers. His pulse pounded hard as he came slowly to his feet and did a sweep of the hallway. He carefully withdrew the pistol from inside his waistband and, with his gun extended, searched around.

Of its own volition, Niall's gaze slid down the hall to Diana's chambers. It was silly. Now he was seeing monsters, just as she had. The mud belonged to a careless servant. A mark that would surely be tended to any moment by a dutiful maid.

Even so, Niall eyed Diana's arched doorway a long moment.

The distant report of shattered glass spilled from within her chambers, springing him to movement. Blood roaring in his ears, Niall sprinted down the hall. There could be any reason for that mark or the breaking glass. And yet, deep inside, a warrior from the street, he knew the truth long before his logical mind accepted it.

Niall shoved her door open and froze. It was an infinitesimal pause that had cost too many men their lives and Niall too many scars on his body. And yet, until he drew in his last, worthless breath, the horror of this moment would forever remain. An ashen-hued Diana, held in the grips of a hulking bear of a man, looked back at him with the terror that came when a person stared down death and knew that dark fate ultimately prevailed. His heart thudded wildly in his chest.

The bastard muttered a black curse under his breath and placed the edge of his dagger against her throat.

Oh, God.

"Marksman." The man knew him. "Get in here. Shut the goddamned door. And if ya make a single noise, Oi'll slash 'er."

Diana's lower lip trembled, but she gave no other outward show. When any other person, regardless of station or lot in life, would have been quaking and crying, she remained stoically silent. How had he ever thought her weak? Moving slowly so as not to spook the man holding her, Niall drew the door closed quietly behind him.

"Now lock it," the toothless stranger ordered.

Lowering his weapon to his side, Niall held up his spare palm calmingly and sank to his haunches. All the while his gaze remained fixed on the hulking brute.

"That's good. Now stand real slow." As Niall complied, the man's grip slackened on Diana's throat, enough for Niall to detect the muscles of that long, graceful column bob. Fury went through him like a slithering serpent poised to strike, and he fed the dark seed of hatred. Not allowing himself to give in to fear. Fear would only see Diana with her throat slit. His heart thudded hard against his rib cage. "Ya weren't supposed to be 'ere," the man rebuked, dragging Diana close.

She whimpered, and her eyes slid closed.

An unholy bloodlust gripped Niall, strengthening him. The man's moments were limited. Except, with his advantage, he was too cocksure arrogant to see as much. To see that Niall would end him, in this very chamber. Niall forced his lips up into an indifferent grin. "I have excellent timing."

The pockmarked brute grunted. "Shut your goddamned mouth and drop your gun."

"Don't do it, N-Niall," she urged, the tremor in her voice gutting him.

"Shut your mouth, bitch." The knife trembled against Diana's throat, and she bit her lower lip. Dark, beady eyes darted about. So, he saw he was trapped. To use a pistol would bring down the Duke of Wilkinson's household, and the bastard would be found out. To kill Diana would only spare Niall and result in the bounder's death. "Oi said drop it, Marksman," the man hissed.

Desperate men, however, did desperate things.

Niall took a step closer, his dagger pointed at the floor.

"Don't take another step," the bastard said loudly and nicked Diana's flesh. A strangled cry stuck in her throat, and a crimson drop trickled down her neck to the modest décolletage of her nightshift, staining that white fabric.

Diana looked at Niall beseechingly, imploring him with her eyes.

His stomach dipped, and for a dizzying moment he was sucked into the terror—numbed, powerless—of that scared boy forced to choose between Ryan and his own soul's worth. Niall forced his gaze over to the hulking brute. "Who sent you?" he forced himself to ask, inching closer.

The stranger snorted. "Ya think Oi'd tell ya? Ya weren't supposed to be 'ere," the man said again, reiterating that revealing admission.

"Well, I am." He continued coming.

"Oi said stop and drop your weapon," the stranger repeated. The shaky timbre of his gravelly tones hinted at a man on the fringe of losing control. He pressed the blade against Diana's throat, and a little moan spilled past her lips.

"Oi said drop—"

Niall tossed the knife sideways. The assailant's panicked gaze went to the weapon. It was a mistake. In one fluid movement, Niall yanked the pistol up and fired. The loud report was met with an agonized scream as the assailant dropped his weapon and staggered back, clutching at his shoulder. Niall bolted over, but the attacker stole over the balcony and was gone.

Rushing outside, Niall looked over the grounds, finding the stranger just as he hit the ground with a loud groan.

Niall cast a quick look briefly to where Diana stood ashen-faced and then back at the assailant—gone.

Cursing himself for having let the man go, he turned back to where Diana remained so motionless. He swiftly pulled her into his arms. He buried her face against his chest. "Shh," he whispered. His opponent gone, the reality of how close she'd come to death sent blood roaring to his ears, muffling the sounds of her weeping. "You're all right," he said harshly, his reassurances as much for him as they were for her.

Her body convulsed as she sobbed brokenly against his chest. "Niall." Her tears soaked the front of his chest, and here he'd thought himself immune to those crystalline drops, only to be proven a liar by the woman in his arms. "I—I thought . . ." Her voice caught and then broke as she dissolved into another torrent.

Niall layered his cheek to the crown of her hair. "You're all right," he continued, the words a litany. A reminder that she was safe. With him, still.

Footsteps pounded outside the hall. The handle resisted the person attempting to break their way in. "Diana," the duke's frantic cry filtered in. "Open this door." The handle jiggled.

Reluctantly setting her aside, Niall retrieved his gun and opened the door a fraction.

Swiftly taking in the liveried servants and duke, he admitted the small contingency inside.

Several footmen spilled into the room, with the portly duke following close. "M-Marksman, what is the meaning . . ." The duke's blustery demands ended abruptly as he caught sight of the blood on his daughter's floor. All the color leached from his cheeks as he pulled Diana out into the hall. Niall itched to drag her back and hold on to her, reassuring himself that she was safe. Unhurt. "What happened?" the duke whispered.

"Your daughter was right." Niall flexed his jaw. "Someone wants 'er dead."

Chapter 15

A handful of hours after the attack, Diana sat perched on the leather button sofa in her father's office. Sunlight streamed through the floor-length windows, those soft rays at odds with the hell that had unfolded.

The constable having come and gone, the men just shown in by the butler were those Niall called family: Ryker, Adair, and Oswyn. Shoulder to shoulder at the doorway, they had the look of a small army prepared to battle. It was a fierce lot. Towering, powerful figures of men who'd strike fear in the breasts of all, and less than four weeks ago, Diana would have included herself in that number.

From behind his desk, her father came to his feet. "Gentlemen," he greeted. As though it were a social call. As though a man hadn't infil-trated their home and put a blade to Diana's throat, and—her breath coming fast—she shoved the thoughts aside and belatedly stood. "If you will excuse us, Diana," her father said in the gentling tones he'd used when she'd scraped her knees as a small girl.

Five pairs of eyes went to Diana. Five men who'd send her on her way and discuss her fate. For the whole of her life, others had made decisions for and about her. She'd been robbed of a voice by govern-esses, nursemaids, and her own parents. What was worse, however, is that the one truly responsible for that complacency was Diana herself. She'd allowed herself to be silenced. No more. "I'm not leaving," she said quietly.

"Would anyone care for a brandy?" Her father made his way dismissively over to that well-stocked sideboard. He passed his hand over the crystal decanters and then stopped, turning slowly back.

She looked briefly to Niall. Stationed at the edge of her father's desk, his hands clasped at his back, he stood in wait, his expression revealing nothing.

"Diana," her father continued in that patronizing tone that set her teeth on edge, "this isn't the place for you." He slid a wary look over at the terrifying group of men.

Shock slammed into her. Even though Ryker was his son, and Niall had entered the duke's home and saved Diana's life, he still saw the men who'd been more family than anyone else to him as somehow different. Lesser. And with all his failings to come to light this past year, the last myth of her father's greatness tumbled before her eyes. "Where should I be, Papa?" she demanded. "Tucked away, safe in my chambers?" Those same rooms where Niall had been forced to shoot a man again. *For me. Because of me.*

She snagged the inside of her cheek.

"Diana," her father exclaimed. Shock sent his white eyebrows shooting up. He slowly set the decanter down.

Yes, for nineteen years she'd been the dutiful, naive Diana, whom her mother had sought to maneuver through life like a chess piece. That girl she'd once been would have never dared do anything as bold as to question her father's wishes. "I'm not leaving," she said once more, drawing her shoulders back.

Niall moved into position beside her. She started at the unexpectedness of his appearance, and a warmth suffused her heart at that show of support, chasing away the chill that had dogged her since this morn.

"She stays," Niall commanded in a steely tone that brooked no room for argument.

Any other gentleman would have shut her out. It had taken but her first meeting to determine he was unlike any man she'd ever known.

Giving a reluctant nod, the duke motioned to the sofa. "Very well," he said, compressing his lips in a flat line.

As Diana and her father reclaimed their seats, however, the other men present remained tautly coiled.

Ryker broke the silence. "Niall?"

Niall proceeded to methodically recount the events of the early morning. With his detached telling, Diana locked her hands on her lap to still those shaking digits. *You insisted on remaining. The very least you can do is listen to him.*

"Someone wants her dead . . . confirmed the previous attacks . . ."

How could he be so remarkably calm after . . . after . . . ? Her mind shied away from the horror that had unfolded in her bedroom. But in his loud orange wool jacket and fawn-colored pants, he may as well have been any other gentleman discussing mundane matters over port and cigarillos.

"The home was searched for additional assailants?" Adair interrupted Niall's telling.

A scowl marred Niall's rugged features. Yes, he would chafe at having his work here questioned. None would be immune to that displeasure, including his brothers. "I interviewed Diana." Ryker narrowed his eyes on Diana, and her cheeks warmed under his scrutinizing look. If any other gentleman present noted that intimate use of her Christian name, they gave no indication. "I assembled the servants. Questioned those awake during the attack and those who'd been sleeping. Did a search with the constables of every room, window, and door. There was no forced entry."

A pall descended over the room.

The assailant had effortlessly slipped inside, just as easily as he'd gone out. By all rights, she should be dead . . . and would have been if Niall hadn't been returning to his chambers, and she hadn't managed to topple that vase as the stranger dragged her from the room.

Moisture dotted her forehead. The remembered metallic taste of blood in her mouth sent nausea roiling in her belly. *Do not think of it. Do not think of it.* She briefly pressed her eyes closed, willing back the memories. The terror cloying at her breast. The cry as Niall's shot found its mark . . .

That was the last man I killed . . .

And he'd been forced to lift a weapon again . . . because of me.

Her breath hitched painfully in her chest. It was in her blood and could not be divorced from who she was.

"Was it an act of revenge because of that man?" her father put to the group.

That man. He spoke like a child warned of the Awd Goggie and afeard of being made a meal by that evil fairy. Diana looked away from him over to Niall, who with his fearlessness and boldness, was her father's opposite in every way.

The men present stared expectantly at Niall. He rolled his shoulders. "Oi don't believe he's one of Diggory's."

Diana furrowed her brow. Which would mean . . . Diana was the one in possession of an enemy?

Ryker folded his arms at his chest. "On what do you base that?"

"He didn't just kill 'er," Oswyn pointed out, wiping the back of his hand across his bald pate. "'e woulda killed 'er if he wanted 'er dead. Why let her live?"

Niall rubbed his chin with the heel of his hand.

"He was bringing me to someone else," she blurted, the memory forgotten in the panic of the moment rushing forth.

His gaze shot to hers questioningly.

"He said I'd proven too difficult to kill, and the man he worked for wished to do that."

"Why didn't you tell me that?" Niall demanded, coming closer.

She tipped up her chin. "I forgot, Niall."

"Ya cannot forget those details, Diana," he gritted out, bringing her to her feet. "Is there anything else ya forgot?"

"I don't know," she said, hanging on to her sanity by a thread as her mind raced. "If it's forgotten, I wouldn't really remember it, would I?" she retorted, finding a soothing calm in her frustration. It kept her from falling over the precipice of fear and madness that her assailant had shoved her to the edge of.

"Niall," Ryker barked, and Niall and Diana looked as one to the other forgotten guests watching them peculiarly. "Who would wish the girl harm?" Ryker asked the room at large, bringing them back to the matter at hand.

The girl. That was how the world treated her. All except Niall, that was.

Niall frowned. Did he, too, take umbrage with that demeaning address?

"No one," the duke blurted, shaking his head so abruptly his hair tumbled over his brow. "Who *could* wish her harm?"

A little frown worked at the corners of her lips. There was no shortage of gossip and unkind words for Diana by the peerage. But gossiping about her was vastly different from attempting to harm her.

"The lady has at least *one* enemy," Adair pointed out, needlessly.

Oswyn captured his chin between his thumb and forefinger. "Too bad ya only caught 'im in the shoulder. I woulda killed 'im dead." How freely this guard bandied about that word to Niall, who was so haunted by it. Diana pressed her fingertips against her temples.

Niall took a charged step forward. "You're questioning 'ow Oi cared for her?" he shot back.

The older man rushed toe-to-toe with Niall. "Everyone knows ya don't 'ave it in ya to kill again," he groused. "The man needed killing."

Adair hurried to insert himself between them.

"Enough," Ryker snapped.

Diana jumped to her feet, proving herself a coward once more. She could not be with Niall in this moment, knowing the darkness she'd forced on his soul. "If you'll excuse me?" she said, her throat convulsing. For, ultimately, blood would tell, and her mother's would continue to shine through in Diana's every action. Unable to meet Niall's eyes, she skirted around his well-built frame.

"Diana?" Niall called after her, the gruff concern of his baritone so very different from the pitiless figure who'd first entered her household. He shot a hand out, capturing her forearm. "I'll accompany you."

Diana registered the focus of the room trained on that possessive, intimate gesture.

"You've searched the home. I do not require an escort."

Nonetheless, Niall glanced over at Oswyn. A silent look passed between them, and as she started from the room, the older guard followed close at her heels.

And with every step she placed between her and Niall, the heavy cloak of guilt about her shoulders grew.

The meeting with the duke concluded, Niall walked alongside Ryker and Adair, accompanying them to the foyer.

"You look like hell," Ryker observed.

He flexed his jaw as the horror of a few hours ago revisited him. His insides twisted as he was assaulted by the image of Diana, a blade at her throat. One quick flick of the ruthless bastard's wrist and he'd have opened her neck right there. Nausea broiled in his belly. "Shooting an unknown assailant in the dead of night will do that," he got out.

"Yes," Ryker concurred. "Is it only that?"

Mayhap it was the absolute lack of sleep, or mayhap it was the fight to the death, but Ryker's words brought Niall's mouth opening and closing, with no reply forthcoming.

"You called her Diana," Adair pointed out, unhelpfully.

"Several times," Ryker added.

Niall stumbled and then quickly righted himself. Favoring both brothers with a scathing glower, he whipped his head about. This wasn't the goddamned club, where all were loyal to them. "Shut your goddamned mouths," he hissed, shoving open a nearby door and forcing his brothers inside.

He gritted his teeth. Of all the bloody rooms to stumble into.

Diana's sanctuary.

Spoiling for a fight, Niall kicked the door closed with the heel of his boot and folded his arms at his chest. "Well? Say whatever it is you'd say and be done with it." In their world they spoke with absolute bluntness. There were none of these veiled hints and prevarications.

"I believe we did just say it," Adair suggested, the ghost of a grin on his lips. "You're inordinately familiar with the lady."

Inordinately familiar? Niall sputtered. "She's . . . she's . . ."

Ryker arched an eyebrow.

"A lady?" Adair finished for him. Niall frowned. "Ryker's sister? An innocent?"

"Aye, she's all of those things." Or she had been. "Your bloody point is made," Niall gritted out. Somewhere along the way Diana had become so much more than any of those neatly ticked items off Adair's list. He dragged a hand through his hair. "Did ya expect me to be a bloody beast to her?" he snapped.

His brothers spoke in unison. "Yes."

Yes, well, fair point there. Niall had only crafted a smile for the nobles he'd so hated for the benefit of the Hell and Sin, and only to grow their fortunes. Beyond that, he'd been perfectly clear that he'd rather dance with the Devil through the flames of Hell than have any other dealings with the *haute ton*.

A large hand settled on Niall's shoulder, and he looked to the owner of it. Ryker met his eyes squarely. "You prevented it." Niall drew himself tight. What was he on about? "This"—Ryker slashed his palm up and down, gesturing to Niall's frame—"panicky look in your eyes. You need to stop doubting yourself."

Doubting himself? Is that why Ryker believed Niall was out of sorts? Then, why shouldn't he? When he'd sent Niall from the Hell almost four weeks earlier, Niall had been so fixed on his own failings that he'd snapped and hissed at Ryker for the new assignment handed down. He wouldn't know that in the nearly thirty days he'd been with Diana, he'd not missed the club for five minutes that he could string together. No, Niall's sweaty palms and knotted stomach had everything to do with how very close Diana had come to meeting her maker.

"Tell me what you require." Ryker neatly shifted the topic, diverting Niall from his tumultuous thoughts and on to matters he could understand and control.

"Oswyn," he said automatically. There wasn't another outside Ryker, Calum, Adair, and Helena whom Niall trusted more. He'd been the first man in their employ, and he'd proven his loyalty countless times through the years. He silently inventoried the duke's Mayfair residence. A servant's entrance in the kitchens. The front doors. "I'll require four guards, in addition," he said at last, erring on a greater number. He'd doubted Diana before. He'd not be so careless where her life was concerned. Not again.

"It is done," Ryker agreed. He looked to Adair. "Adair will remain behind, as well. Calum stays at the club."

If the other man felt any of the same misgivings and annoyance at being sent to live among the nobility, he didn't show it.

"You'll also want guards on Helena," Niall reminded him, and worry darkened Ryker's eyes. "I've already sent word to Somerset." Having retired to their country estates for the summer, Helena and her husband would be unaware of what had unfolded and be easy prey for it. And yet—Niall moved, restless—Diana hadn't been murdered in her bed. In Diggory's unscrupulous world of "kill or be killed," the only revenge that would matter was ending a person. It wouldn't have mattered who did it, or how, or when. He stopped before that painting of St. George's and stared at those cerulean waters—a mythical paradise with pink sand so at odds with the hellish reality of this world. He captured his chin in his hand. By Diana's remembrance of the morning attack, however, someone not only wished her dead but also wanted the rights to that task.

A shadow fell over the painting.

"I am grateful to you for saving Diana."

Tension brought his shoulders back. "Did ya think Oi wouldn't?" he demanded, directing that harsh query to the canvas.

"I believe you'd lay your life down to save any member of our family, even those not deeply connected to us." Like Diana.

With a blade against her jugular, commanding Niall to not release his weapon, she'd shown more courage than any man in the Dials faced with that same ghastly fate. For her courage and strength, she was more like them than Ryker would ever credit . . . and more than Niall would have liked, too. Still, Ryker treated her as one of the others.

"I know this is not the assignment you wanted." Now, it was. Somewhere along the way everything had shifted and changed, making Niall's once logical world murky. Now, he'd sooner use his own knife and cut himself before turning Diana over to anyone else—his brothers included. "If you—"

"My place is here," he said curtly, turning around. He'd trust implicitly his own life to Adair or Calum. But this wasn't Niall's worthless hide—this was Diana.

Ryker nodded once. His gaze moved to a point past Niall's shoulder. "Interesting painting," he remarked casually, when there never was, nor ever would be, a thing casual about the impassible gaming-hell proprietor.

Stiffening, Niall followed his stare over to another rendering. Diana's form could easily be made out upon that canvas, alongside Niall's scowling self. Heat prickled across his cheeks, and his fingers tugged uncomfortably at his cravat.

"Mayhap we can purchase it for the club?" Adair suggested, in the first mark of levity for the day.

Niall turned up his middle finger at his chuckling brother.

"The next thing you'll tell me is you're taking tea and biscuits with the lady."

Pastries.

"What was that?" Ryker asked, shock set in his features.

Christ, now he was talking aloud? What was life in Mayfair doing to him?

The heat of embarrassment rushed to his neck, and he cleared his throat. "Given what happened here a few hours ago, I think it's hardly the time to be ribbing me or making jests," he said impatiently. Then, that had always been the way of St. Giles. A person killed or an attempt on one's life was just another day in the streets. As such, they'd not see this day as any different. Niall flexed his jaw. Where Penelope's near murder had reduced Ryker to an incoherent, irrational shell of a street tough.

Ryker gave Adair a look. "Of course," Ryker said solemnly. He jerked his chin, making for the front of the room. Then paused. "If you require anything, send word immediately."

Niall nodded. As soon as he'd gone and Adair went off to perform another interview of the servants, Niall started down the opposite hall and headed abovestairs. Needing to see Diana. To confirm she was, in fact, all right. He had seen more dead bodies and killed more men than an undertaker in London. Until he drew his last breath, he'd recall her terror-filled eyes as her assailant had her about the waist. His stomach pitched.

If I'd searched her rooms first . . . If I'd been there, she would have been untouched by that ugly . . .

Niall came to a stop outside her chambers, just as the door opened. Diana's maid rushed into the hall, hurriedly stepping past Oswyn.

"How is Lady Diana?" Niall put to her as soon as she'd closed the door.

The girl paled, averting her eyes from the new fierce guard stationed outside her mistress's rooms. "H-Her Ladyship is resting," the maid said, her voice threadbare. "Asked to be left alone this morning."

Given the excitement of a few hours ago, it was only natural Diana would require sleep. After the battle, when one's heart beat a normal cadence and reality trickled in, it brought a bone-weary exhaustion. And yet . . . Niall slid a frustrated gaze at the doorway. He'd foolishly thought—hoped?—she needed to see him as much as he did her.

The maid shuffled back and forth on her feet.

"That will be all," he said brusquely, and she darted off. Niall promptly set up sentry alongside Oswyn.

"Ya need to rest, Niall." The old guard spoke the way a father might to a son. Might. Niall knew less about father–son bonds than he did the rules of London High Society.

"I'm not leaving," he said, gaze forward.

"Niall. Oi'm here. Go." Oswyn settled a heavy, scarred palm on Niall's shoulder. It was a strong one. A capable one that had saved Niall's arse more times than he'd deserved. "Nothing will happen to the lady the three hours ya're sleeping," he urged, sensing Niall's waver.

With a reluctant glance back at her doorway, Niall started for his chambers.

Chapter 16

All people reacted differently to seeing a man shot.

Some cried. Others fainted. Some trembled, paled, and went silent. Diana had retreated.

Or in this case, presented a false show, humming and painting and carrying on just as she had since the first day Niall entered the Duke of Wilkinson's employ. And avoiding a goddamned word with Niall.

It had been two days since the brute had attacked her in her bedchambers, and despite his efforts to speak with her, she remained largely smiling and terse in her replies.

If he were a man capable of laughter, this ironic moment would certainly be a time for those explosions of mirth. Since he'd entered the duke's home, he'd wanted Diana Verney to cease her prattling, questioning, and interest in him. Now she'd done just that, and he mourned the loss of the person she'd been around him.

Standing guard at the front of the room, Niall boldly studied her movements. She angled her palette occasionally and dashed her brush over the previously blank canvas.

Mayhap it isn't that she's retreated. Mayhap she's seen you for the bloody monster you are. He firmed his jaw. It had been inevitable. For all her efforts to turn him into a friend of sorts, he'd always been Niall, the bastard with a made-up surname who didn't even own a birthday. Unlike those fancy gents with their long names and titles. A kind of gent she deserved. He went still. Not that he *wanted* to be deserving of her. There was no reason. He'd no interest for anyone in his life. He had his club, and she, despite her protestations of the contrary, would one day wed one of those lily-white lords without blood on his hands.

His patience snapped. "Are ya done?"

Diana paused, her brush dipped upon that palette.

She couldn't even bloody look at him. His annoyance spiraled, and he fed that vastly safer emotion.

"I just started—"

He cast a hard glance at the maid who'd also set up sentry whenever Diana and Niall were alone. The girl jerked to her feet, embroidery frame in hand, and beat a hasty exit. Niall yanked the door closed.

A frown on her crimson bow-shaped lips, Diana turned slowly around and glanced about for her maid.

She is afraid of you. It is there in her avoidance of your eyes.

"Mr.—?"

"If you call me Mr. Marksman," he seethed, "I'm going to turn you over my goddamned knee."

Her mouth formed a perfect circle, and with the same hesitancy she'd shown four weeks earlier when he'd found her skulking around his alley, she set her palette down and rested her brush on the edge of it. "Did you just threaten to spank me?"

Except, even with her indignant shock, she'd conjured wicked images, delightful ones of her sprawled naked on his lap, while he caressed the rounded swells of her buttocks with his palm.

"Oi should," he countered, his voice garbled to his own ears. "You're behaving like a child."

Diana's gaze shot to his. Outrage blazed to life, that volatile emotion giving her cheeks color and fully restoring her to the unwavering lady who'd tossed his world upside down. "How dare you?" she demanded.

It did not escape his notice, however, that she made little attempt to move away from that frame canvas. Shrugging out of his jacket, Niall tossed it into a noisy heap atop the blue upholstered sofa.

"Wh-what are you doing?" she squeaked.

Doing what he should have done when he first arrived here. Only, he'd been remiss. He'd failed to believe any real threat existed, and it had nearly cost her. Fear turned over inside. He'd not make that mistake again. Niall dragged the sofa, pulling it alongside the edge of the room.

"Niall?"

So, he was Niall again? The fickle traitor. Not trusting his anger, Niall hefted the table out from the center of the room and deposited it on the opposite side.

"Ya don't have to like me," he informed her, his voice breathless from his exertions as he heaved a King Louis XIV chair from its usual position. "Hell, ya do not even 'ave to talk to me." He paused to dust the back of his shirtsleeves over his perspiring brow. "Oi told ya from my first day here, Oi'm not here to be your friend." She'd insisted otherwise. She'd invited him for goddamned tea and pastries and ordered him to sit. She'd asked him of his past and shared hers. And now she'd simply cut him from her life like he was an inconvenient thread from her gown that needed snipping?

At her silence, he looked up. Did he detect a flash of pain in her innocent doe eyes? Or did he simply imagine that out of his own pathetic musings? For her delicate features were solemnly set, at odds with the smiling miss she'd been moments ago. A muscle ticked away at the corner of his eye. Her guarded expression served as another unnecessary reminder that he was the manner of man who destroyed all around him: life, happiness. Those were illusive dreams that belonged to another.

What he was capable of, however, was unwavering strength—keeping people alive. And by God, he'd keep her alive.

Niall unsheathed his dagger, and at the hiss of metal, Diana gasped.

She stumbled back, knocking into her canvas. The frame tipped sideways and landed on the floor with a loud crack. Her canvas joined it in a sad heap, and the recently painted strokes bled like crimson-and-emerald teardrops, running down the page.

He came forward, not taking his gaze from her. "Wh-what are you doing?" she panted, flicking her gaze over the rearranged furniture.

The truth slammed into him. Why . . . she sought for a place to hide.

Pain exploded in his chest. She knew him so little that she believed him capable of hurting her. Niall pointed the first weapon he'd acquired after he'd joined Ryker's ranks across the room, directly at Diana. "Ya need to learn to protect yourself. Oi won't always be here."

Her face spasmed, briefly reflecting his own inner turmoil to that truth. *Bah, she doesn't feel regret. She feels a goddamned deserved fear of the monster you are. Of the monster you've always been and will always be.*

He stalked over to her in three long strides, and Diana sprinted sideways. Too late. Niall shot a hand out, enfolding her wrist, ending her retreat before she'd made it even a foot. Niall shoved the hilt of his dagger into her hand.

She flexed her fingers, making no attempt to take it. "What is this?"

It was a weapon that mattered as much as his own club, that he'd never let another person touch—including his siblings—until her.

"Take it," he directed.

"I'm not—"

Niall stuck his face in hers. "Oi said take the knife, Diana."

Her breath came in little spurts. It fanned over his lips, mint and chocolate and the taste of fear just as tangible upon them. Diana gave her head a tight shake. "I'll not do it, Niall," she whispered.

He narrowed his eyes. "Take the goddamned knife."

Despite the rapid rise and fall of her chest, she remained resolute. Shoulders back, proud and unflinching like a gang leader marched to the gallows, holding on to her pride until the end. In her bold determination, she was both breathtaking and exasperating, and he didn't know whether to kiss her senseless or give her a damned shake.

She darted her tongue out over her lips, and he swallowed a groan at his weakness for her. With a curse, Niall spun away from her. "Ya won't learn to defend yourself?" He attempted a different approach. A call to her logic and reason. "You, the same woman who came to St. Giles in a hired hack and asked for a guard—"

"I did not ask for a guard," she gritted out. "Ryker supplied one." One. "Me."

Diana tipped her head at an endearing angle.

Niall jabbed the heel of his dagger against his chest. "He supplied *me*, princess. But ya are one of those ladies who doesn't want blood on her hands," he chided with a forced derision that sent the color draining from her cheeks. "Ya want to be coddled and pampered," he continued over her indignant gasp, deliberately needling, "content to paint your damned happy images, while other people protect—"

She shot her palm out. Those long, slender digits trembled slightly, ravaging him. *It is for her good.* Niall had always known the ways to force a man to movement. Diana was no exception. "Give me," she seethed. She was a proud, courageous woman who'd not sacrifice another person's life because of her own weakness.

Niall pressed the jewel-encrusted dagger in her hand. Purchased honorably with the first funds he'd earned at the Hell and Sin, Niall had vowed to reshape his life and never work for anyone but himself.

Diana weighed it experimentally, as though testing its mass, familiarizing herself with the feel of it. This blade that had saved Niall's worthless hide more times than he'd deserved.

"It's a simple tool," he instructed. "A silent one, and dangerous not only to the person being assaulted but also to the person holding it."

He moved into position behind her and captured her hand. "If you'll not do it for yourself, learn for the people you care about."

She tilted her head back. "I can't stab a person, Niall." Through her thick golden lashes, desire poured from her eyes. Of its own volition, his head dipped. He froze. And then, drawn helplessly nearer for another taste of her, Niall lowered his mouth closer still. Diana closed her eyes and leaned up, offering her mouth to him, her meaning clear: she wanted him. Desired him, still. She might view him as a monster, but he was a man she still hungered for. A bitter resentment coursed through him as he hastily stepped out of her arms.

"Fine. Then hit me."

He may as well have stated his intentions to overthrow the king for the befuddlement that glimmered in her hazed eyes. "*Hit* you?" she croaked.

Reining in his lust, Niall plucked the knife from her fingers and tossed it to the floor. The tip lodged in the once immaculate hardwood, and the blade thrummed back and forth with the force of his throw. "You need some way to defend yourself."

Wide-eyed, Diana alternated her stare between Niall and the dagger.

He rolled up his sleeves.

With every inch of his arm flesh exposed, Diana's golden eyebrows shot up so high, they'd disappear into her hairline soon.

Niall stood with arms at his sides. "Well?" he urged.

"You're mad," she whispered.

She remained motionless as he circled her. "You need to keep your chin down." He positioned her head, lingering his fingers on the satiny expanse of her nape. Another wave of desire went through him. "And cover your face," he murmured and, moving directly in front of Diana, brought her arms up into the correct fighting pose.

Letting out a sigh, Diana tossed out an ineffectual jab. It didn't even graze him. "There. Now, are we done?" Without allowing a reply, she stepped around him.

Niall caught her around the waist, ringing a breathless gasp from her as he brought her back before the mirror. "We're not finished," he whispered, his lips a hairbreadth from her mouth. "Until I indicate your lesson is over and you're sufficiently trained. Are we clear?" Such commands came from ordering about the guards who answered to him inside the Hell and Sin.

Diana shook her head. That jerky movement nearly brought their mouths together. "I'll not be ordered about."

He slid his eyes closed. Of course she wouldn't. She could not. She was a slender Spartan warrior woman and a siren at sea rolled into one, and he and any man would be hopeless against her commands.

"Very well. Will you please bring your arms up," he urged, demonstrating the stance.

She complied.

"Now hit me."

He is mad.

And Diana only knew so with the confidence of a woman who was headed for a future of lunacy, but she'd sooner lop off her arm than put her hands upon this man in violence.

She dropped her arms to her sides. "I have already told you," she gritted out, "I don't plan on stabbing anyone or punching you." He had been the only person who'd treated her as his equal in every way. He'd let her inside his world and encouraged her to share hers. Saved her life. She was not striking him no matter how many times he demanded it. Diana again cut a berth around him.

He quickly stepped before her, cutting off her escape. "Let me give you the damned lesson, princess."

This princess nonsense, again. Diana set her jaw. "All right."

Some of the tension went out of his frame.

"As long as it does not involve me striking you," she clarified.

He let loose a stream of expletives. Alas, Diana had ceased to shock long ago. A year to be precise. "One day I'll be gone, and you'll be left with those rakes and rogues who want to steal a kiss and sneak a feel." A savage glimmer lit his nearly obsidian irises.

Her heart jumped a beat. What was to account for that barely restrained fury? Did the possibility of her with another man fill him with some resentment? Why would that be if he didn't care for her in some way? Regardless of what Niall Marksman felt or didn't feel for her, however, there would never be a man after him whom she'd allow to caress her. "There are no worries there, Niall," she said softly, stroking her palms down the front of his chest. It was a mistake.

Her mouth went dry. The heat of his flesh singed her hands even through the fabric of his linen shirt.

His thick, charcoal lashes swept down, concealing the raw power radiating from within those blue orbs. "Because you think gentlemen are honorable?" He peeled back his lip in a derisive sneer.

Pain stabbed at her breast. Did he truly believe she was like her father and the rest of the ruthless *ton*, who viewed those titled lords as superior? "Because they've already demonstrated their lack of interest." Men who'd not give a second thought to committing her the moment she showed signs of madness. As such, she'd no interest in binding her-self to one of those faithless, spineless cowards.

A savage growl better suited a primal beast shook the walls of his chest, breaking that charged awareness. "For Christ's sake, Diana, how can I teach you if you'll not strike me?"

"I'll not hurt you, Niall," she said simply, lifting her shoulders in a little shrug. As long as she was able, she would never put her hands upon another person in violence, and certainly if she did, it would not be Niall.

Like one of those fierce lions she'd stared on with awe at the Royal Circus, he took slow, menacing, predatory steps closer, stalking her. "Hit me," he whispered.

Diana retreated a step. "N-no." She didn't know what to do with Niall when he was this enraged, snarling predator.

"Hit me," he barked, sticking out his chest, and the fabric of his shirt rippled, displaying defined muscles suited to a man who'd fought in the streets and risen up. Diana's eyes went to the midnight tufts of hair that peeked from the top of his fine linen shirt. Her mouth went dry.

"Are you paying attention?" he barked.

Cheeks awash in heat, she whipped her head up. "I'll not do it, Niall."

"You're a coward."

She gasped. He thought so little of her. That thought shouldn't cause this keen ache, and yet it did. "How dare you?"

"Don't like the truth?" A smile, cold like a winter's frost, iced his lips. "That you're nothing more than a pampered princess who expects to be guarded but who's unwilling to stick her nose into the fight."

Agony sluiced away like a dull knife, carving a place in her chest. She fought to move her lips, to bring forth an indignant reply—and came up empty.

He marched forward, unyielding. "Nothing to say?" he taunted with harsh mockery, a shell of the man she'd come to know.

"I'm no coward," she breathed through her fingertips, hating that wispy quality to her rebuttal.

"Prove it," he jeered, closing the space between them, and Diana hastened her retreat, glancing about. Of their own volition, her panicked eyes went to the door. Niall swiftly cut off her path of escape, and she gasped. "Hit me," he urged on a steely whisper. "You know you want to."

She balled her hands into fists. She'd not let him bait her. That is all he sought to do. Squaring her shoulders, she looked through him.

"You're furious right now." He walked a slow path around her. "That's good. It is pumping through your veins, princess—"

She whipped her furious gaze to his. Fire burned in her depths. "Do *not* call me princess."

"Then do not act like one." He spread his arms wide, making himself her target. "Hit me."

"Stop it, Niall," she bit out.

"Hit me," he boomed, pounding his chest. "Come on, surely there is some of your mother's ruthless blood flowing in your—"

Diana shot her fist out, catching him in the jaw. The force of her blow sent his neck flying back. She hissed as pain stung her knuckles and snapped her from the blinding flash of rage that had caused her to lash out. Quickly jerking her arm close to her chest, she stared on with a slow-dawning horror. *I punched him.*

Niall chuckled and caught the wounded flesh in his palm, rubbing, a wry smile on his lips. "Impressive, princess." Pride filled his eyes, and she recoiled. "That—" His words trailed off and he frowned. "Diana?"

Diana's throat bobbed.

Everyone had a breaking point.

It was the moment where sanity snapped and madness crept in, and you were exposed for the lunatic you were.

Just as she had revealed herself to be in this instance.

Oh, my God. What have I done?

Nausea roiled in her belly and sent bile burning up the back of her throat. She choked it back. With an infinite tenderness that threatened to shatter her, Niall drew her into his arms and pressed her ear against his chest. His heart pounded loudly against that powerfully muscled wall; the steady thump matching her own heart's rhythm.

A strangled sob caught in her throat.

He stroked the back of her head. "I wanted you to hit me."

Yes, he had, and she'd not wanted to, but ultimately her fury had spiraled, stealing her control, logic, and reason—and proving her very much her mother's daughter. For of all people to incite her rage, it had been Niall, the man who'd stolen her heart and—

She froze. No. She'd no intention of falling in love or marrying, or trusting her heart, soul, or any other part of herself to a man. And yet—no. *No. No. No.* Except repeating that desperate litany in her head did not make it untrue. She, who'd seen the faithlessness of men but who'd also sought to protect herself from hurt and any others from her lunacy, had fallen hopelessly and helplessly in love with a man who at best liked her a little and at worst abhorred her immensely.

Her eyes slid closed.

"Diana?" Those gravelly, guttural tones that whispered around her dreams in the night when the house slept on penetrated her terror, bringing her eyes open. Gasping, she wrenched away from him. Panic twisted away at her insides, knotting them in a vicious, unyielding vise.

Diana fought to draw air into her constricted lungs. It was the height of folly. A mistake that had nothing to do with the station divide between them and everything to do with who Diana was. For even if Niall, a man who hated everything she represented, wished to share a future with her, there was no future she could give him that would be of any worth. A man tied to her would only end up like her father, the Duke of Wilkinson, with a wife shut away and a household of servants and the occasional guest who stared on and pitied. Diana stumbled out of his arms. "Stay away," she panted, straightening her arms before her and warding him off.

His sapphire eyes darkened, glinting with a fleeting glimpse of hurt. He immediately dropped his arms to his sides. Of course, that was all she was capable of—hurting others. Her gaze fixed on the bright red mark on his square chin with that faint cleft.

Diana tossed her hands up. "Why could you not leave me be?" she cried, the frantic timbre of her voice matching the pealing screams of those souls locked away in Bedlam. She wanted to clamp her hands over her ears to blot out those memories.

A muscle jumped in his jaw, only highlighting that faint bruise forming on his flesh.

"Could you not see I've not wanted to talk to you?" she rasped. She'd attempted to stay away from him. Had, out of a deep-seated guilt and shame, tried to put distance between herself and Niall. But in the end, he'd not let her. "I stayed away from you." He flinched, and she continued ruthless. "But you could not leave me be." There was a darkness in her soul Niall didn't know about, and one that she'd send him on his way before he could ever see. Her throat tightened.

She darted around him.

Niall scrubbed a hand down his face, and this time he let her go.

Diana's breath rasped loudly in her ears as she flew from the room and down the halls with such speed her curls tore free of the pearl peigne at the base of her neck. The locks tumbled into her face, about her shoulders, whipping wildly as she ran.

She took the stairs two at a time, tripping over herself in her bid to escape. A sob stuck in her throat, and she quickened her strides.

She reached her chambers and froze with her fingers on the handle. The guard Oswyn exited her chambers and froze. Diana's own ragged breaths, her assailant's ruthless threats, the sound of his cries as Niall's bullet hit him, all ricocheted around her mind in a great cacophony of sound. Her arm jerked back reflexively. She could not go in there.

"It's safe in there. Oi checked for ya, my lady."

His deep, threatening Cockney forced her fingers to move, and she quickly pressed the handle.

Bypassing the faint stain servants had been unable to scrub from the carpet, now permanently marked, Diana made straightaway for her armoire. Jerking open the doors, she tugged free her cloak.

Her maid entered the rooms just as Diana shrugged into the muslin garment. "My lady?" she asked hesitantly.

"The carriage," she instructed as she gathered her valise and a sack full of coins.

The girl hesitated. "Does Mr. Marksman—?" A hard look from Diana silenced Meredith and sprang her into movement.

Diana stepped out into the hall, not far behind Meredith. As a duke's daughter, neither servants nor lords and ladies dared challenge Diana. Until Niall. He'd not given a jot about her status as ducal daughter. Instead, he'd treated her with raw honesty.

Her bruised knuckles throbbed. *And I put my hands upon him . . .*

Hastening her stride, Diana rushed back along the same path she'd taken moments ago.

A short while later, she was traveling through the streets of London. She stared blankly out as the fashionable cobbles of Mayfair gave way to the darker, less-traveled roads of St. Giles. As the carriage rocked to a stop, Diana stared numbly through the slight crack in the red velvet curtains across the street to Bedlam Hospital.

The muscles in her chest tightened, and she struggled to draw a breath into her lungs.

He'd provoked her. Had been seeking to provoke her, and she'd known as much. Even knowing it, she'd still allowed him to slip under her thin skin and unleash that violent side of her soul.

Tears flooded her eyes, and she blinked back the useless crystalline drops. One fell, followed by another and another.

It had been inevitable. After all, Diana well knew the blood that coursed in her veins and her eventual fate. A fate that could never, and would never, include a life with Niall Marksman.

Chapter 17

Niall had never possessed Adair's or Calum's easy charm around the women and whores at the Hell and Sin. Where his brothers, Ryker excluded, had always demonstrated an innate ease in reading women and placating them, Niall hadn't the patience to either care or sort through just what those complex creatures were thinking. It did not, however, require the skill of a rogue or charmer to gather the very obvious truth about Diana—she wanted nothing to do with him.

Her silence these days stood testament to that. Since she'd seen him shoot her assailant, she'd not looked at him the same. *And did you expect she would?*

At that moment, he'd proven himself the mercenary cutthroat she'd insisted he wasn't. Now she knew. The memory of her horror-stamped features after he'd taught her how to hit and wield a weapon rooted around his brain.

It had been one thing when he was a man standing guard outside her parlor when no threats of danger were about. It was an altogether different thing when Niall demonstrated his effortless ability to kill.

He stared down at the toppled easel and the now-dry painting, making out the early shapes of three figures. Two men. One woman.

A familiar bedroom. Diana's chambers, on the night of the attack. His gut clenched. Was it a wonder that she no longer wanted anything to do with him?

With a curse, he kicked the wood frame and it skidded over the hardwood floor. He hated himself for giving a damn that she viewed him as a monster. In truth, she wasn't off the mark. He'd used her vulnerabilities—her station, her mother, her gentle spirit—to push her over the edge.

As a resourceful man moved by logic rather than emotion, in doling out a much-needed lesson to Diana, he had done what needed to be done. What Ryker had sent him here to do: he'd taught her how to protect and defend herself and given her tools to arm herself against the rakes, rogues, and street thugs of the world.

So why was he filled with this sick, hollow emptiness?

Niall dusted a hand over the back of his face. Because he'd rather cleave off his blade-wielding hand than be the source of her pain. In the gold-framed mirror across the room, his pale visage reflected back at him. The horror and anguish in her pale-blue eyes would stay with him long after he took his leave and never again saw her.

Delicate footsteps echoed outside the room, and, heart hammering, he looked up.

Disappointment filled him.

Diana's maid lingered in the doorway, her frame partially concealed around the edge of the door. The pale-faced girl made a clearing noise in her throat. "M-Mr. Marksman?"

"Yes?" he growled, and the maid ducked outside and then a moment later peeked back in, studiously avoiding his eyes. As did every last man, woman, and child of his damned acquaintance.

Only Diana had ever gone toe-to-toe with him. Even in this room a short while ago, hating him as she did, she'd proudly tipped her chin back and challenged him at every turn. "What is it?" he repeated, borrowing those gentling tones he'd heard Calum adopt with the former prostitutes in the hell. Niall's efforts, however, came out more of a garbled, impatient growl.

The skittish girl darted her eyes around the room, touching on the rearranged furniture and the upended easel. "My lady . . ." She hovered at her doorway.

"She's not here," Niall said gruffly, claiming his jacket from the King Louis chair and shrugging into it.

"Yes, Mr. Marksman." The maid cleared her throat. "That is why I've come. She's gone out."

"Out?" he echoed, turning slowly back to face the servant.

"Ordered the carriage, sir, and rushed off."

His heart froze in his chest as he tried to put the maid's words to right. "Was she accompanied by—"

"No one, sir." The girl spoke quickly, wringing her hands together. A shriek burst from her lips as he flew across the room and gripped her by the shoulders. "P-please, s-sir," she pleaded.

"Where—?" Did that hoarse, panicky query belong to him?

Diana's lady's maid peeked about the room, and he gave her a slight shake, wringing another cry from her. "St. Giles, sir. She ordered the driver to bring her."

He abruptly released the maid, and she stumbled away from him. St. Giles? What in bloody hell would Diana be doing there?

"Bedlam, sir." The servant's whispery soft pronouncement barely reached his ears. "She's made for Bedlam."

What in bloody hell? His panic swelled in time to his pounding heart.

"Sh-she's gone there once before because of her . . . because of her . . ." Her mother.

Unleashing a barrage of curses, Niall raced from the room. He tore down the hall, bellowing for his mount. With each step, terror ran through him. He, Niall Marksman, cutthroat from the Dials, was numbed with fear.

Bypassing the footman waiting with his cloak, Niall charged through the front door opened by the butler and bounded down the steps. His furious movements were met with curious glances from passersby. Ignoring those miserable blighters, Niall grabbed his reins and tossed his leg across his mount.

With a shout, he urged Chance into a gallop. The Mayfair streets, crowded at the fashionable hour, slowed his progress, and with every passing moment, he damned the lords in his way. He focused on that anger, unable to give over to the fear licking at the edge of his senses that threatened to drive him mad.

What was she doing at Bedlam? Was the silly twit visiting her mother, that damned murderer? Diana would risk her life and virtue among those ruthless guards who'd gladly strip her of her virginity.

A half growl, half moan lodged in his throat, strangling him. "Hyah," he barked, leaning over as the fashionable ends of Mayfair gave way to the darker, seedier parts of London. The less-traveled roads that Diana had no place being—by herself. Nearly two days after they'd determined someone was, in fact, attempting to kill her.

By God, he would kill her himself for this and then do it once more for scaring the everlasting shite out of him. He reached the edge of St. Giles Fields and yanked hard on the reins, slowing Chance's strides. The spirited mount whinnied its protest and bucked against the commands. Niall adjusted the reins, bringing him under control. All the while he scraped his gaze frantically over the quiet thoroughfare, searching for the duke's carriage.

Oh, God, what are ya thinking, ya bloody twit? Raising a hand over his eye, he shielded himself from the sun's glare and glanced around. With a single command, Niall halted Chance.

And then he found it. Relief assaulted him, more fortifying than drawing air into his lungs. Niall abruptly shifted direction, making for that gold crest emblazoned upon a familiar black door. Jumping down before Chance had come to a complete stop, Niall motioned over the driver and turned over the reins. The bewigged servant opened his mouth to speak, and Niall held up a silencing hand.

Then, reaching up, he tossed the carriage door open. Squinting at the abrupt shift in lighting, he found her. "By God, Diana Verney, if ya ever—" The cutting diatribe died on his lips. An eerie silence hung over the carriage, the rattle of an occasional passing carriage ominously punctuating that quiet. Huddled in the corner of the coach, Diana remained stock-still, giving no indication she'd heard or cared about his arrival.

"Princess?" Niall implored gruffly, hefting himself inside.

The driver pushed the door closed behind them. Niall opened his mouth to rain down a diatribe when she spoke, softly interrupting him.

"Do you believe it happens quickly?" she asked, her voice peculiarly empty. "Or do you think it happens gradually, over a matter of time, so that no one realizes until it's already happened?" She directed those questions to the windowpane, the clear lead revealing the singular focus of her blank gaze trained ahead.

Niall followed her stare out to the sweeping institution across the street and frowned. His terror and anger dissipated as a new concern swept in. "Love?" he asked slowly, sliding carefully into the bench opposite her.

"The madness." At last she looked to him, and the anguish and terror spilling from her eyes ravaged him. "Will I kn-know?" Her voice broke, and she hastily attended Bedlam Hospital across the way once more.

Niall didn't want anyone's secrets. Not even his siblings'. A person was entitled to those dark fears and silent thoughts without intrusion. One didn't pry, because frankly, other people's demons were their own. No one could slay them, and so there was no point in sharing. He'd operated that way for more than thirty years. Everything had changed. She'd changed him, slowly chipping away at those walls, so that he now sat helpless before her. Desperate to erase the stark pain marring her delicate features and bring back the smile she'd so freely shared since he'd entered her household.

This empty shell of a creature bore no hint of the formidable, spirited woman who thought nothing of challenging him and doing as she damned well pleased. Restless with his inability to sort through her fears and make them his own, Niall edged closer to her seat until their knees brushed. "Will you know what?" When she remained silent, he gently caressed her cheek, bringing her attention back to him.

Her lower lip trembled, and she swiftly caught it between her teeth, stifling that faint quiver. Did she believe he'd judge her as weak? Four weeks ago he would have. Since then, she'd challenged everything he'd previously accepted as fact about the nobility. She'd stared down death and hadn't broken—until now.

"When I go mad."

He cocked his head. What—? His heart wrenched; that damned organ feeling more than it had in the whole of his sorry existence. "Oh, love," he said hoarsely, scooting closer. Niall gathered her gloveless fingers in his. Despite the early summer's warmth, there was a chill to her skin, and he rubbed those long digits between his own, attempting to bring warmth back to them. "Why would you believe . . . ?" Then his gaze wandered over to the window. Of course. It was why she didn't wish to marry. At last it made sense. "Ya aren't going mad, love," he said, wincing at that pathetic attempt. His heart cracked. Niall had always scoffed and sneered at the fancy toffs who visited his club, finding those dandies pathetic, useless scraps of manhood. Only to now find himself wishing he possessed the effortless words of assurance to drive back Diana's grief.

At last she looked to him, a sad smile playing on her lips. "Oh, Niall, you believe you can command something or someone and will it to be, simply with your words alone." Her throat moved. "But even you cannot stop it from happening. A person is an extension of the blood that flows in their veins."

His stomach muscles clenched involuntarily, as those words he'd hurled came slamming back at him. He cursed. "That's not wot Oi meant."

Her fingers plucked at the fabric of her cloak. "It is." She spoke without recrimination. "You see yourself marked by your birthright, Niall, but your mother . . ." He stiffened. He'd not thought of or wondered about the woman who'd given him life in more years than he could remember. "Your mother worked as she did to survive. That did not make her a bad woman. It did not make her evil. She'd no other option." Odd, he'd come to appreciate and accept that a person did anything and everything they could to survive on the streets of St. Giles, only he'd never thought of his mother in that same light. "Giving you away wasn't the evil in her soul. Nor can you know why she did so." She met his gaze squarely, gutting him with the agony in their blue depths. "But my mother. She did not pass to me rank and title alone, those details that don't truly matter to a person's worth." She paused. "She passed on her blood and her madness. As did my father . . ." Her words trailed off to a threadbare whisper.

He'd never have pretty, soothing words for her or anyone. Niall gathered her onto his lap. She held her body taut against his, and he folded her close until the tension left her. "You are not your mother." Nor the cowardly duke.

"I'm more my mother than you are Diggory," she said against his chest, her voice muffled.

He frowned. He'd inextricably linked himself to the bastard who, early on, had shaped Niall into a pitiless killer. He'd never questioned his own evil. Had seen himself only in that dark, ugly light. Diana had thrown all that into upheaval. He tipped her chin up, forcing her eyes to his. "That you even worry of becoming her means you are nothing like her," he said with a gruff somberness, willing her to see that.

Tears flooded her eyes, and those crystalline drops that would have earned his scorn and derision a month prior now suffused his chest with an aching pain. How in this short time had Diana challenged every aspect of whom he'd built himself to be? "But I will become that." Her voice emerged as a faint whisper.

"Ya never treated me as though I was different from you."

She blinked.

"Since I met you," he clarified. "You didn't treat me like a ruthless thug from the streets."

"You're not," she insisted, giving her head an impassioned shake.

Niall brought her bruised knuckles to his lips and pressed a gentle kiss there. "And that, love, is why you're nothing like your mother." Or anyone else he'd ever met.

———❧———

For the past year, Diana had focused on nothing more than her eventual descent into insanity. She'd linked her mother's evil to her own blood and saw in it how easily her father had cracked. As such, she well knew the future awaiting her.

Here, outside that very hospital she'd expected to find her home one day, Niall forced her to look at herself . . . apart from her mother.

Would her mother have ever, regardless of age or point in her life, cast so much as a glance at Niall Marksman, or the men he called brothers? No, the ruthless woman who'd punished Diana for dancing in the rain and sacked a servant who'd become too friendly with her daughter would have sooner burned herself than mingle with people of other stations. That cruelty and unkindness was not a product of insanity . . . but rather the person the Duchess of Wilkinson had always been.

Her breath caught as she was buoyed with a healing lightness.

Niall brushed another kiss over her knuckles. "That is why you don't wish to marry."

She nodded, even as it was a statement more than anything.

Niall could not understand. Not truly. Society saw a woman and believed the only fate awaiting her was that of marriage. Since her birth, Diana's family had had the expectation that she'd make a noble match. When she made her Come Out, Society had had the same expectation. But then, she'd once dreamt of an altogether different life for herself.

"I always longed to fall in love," she said wistfully. A memory slid forward. Two porcelain dolls, elegantly clad, dancing out the future she'd envisioned with her optimistic child's mind. She tugged at the fabric of her cloak, attending the muslin fabric. "When I'd just learned my letters, my nursemaid would force me to write verses over and over. While I did, she'd sip from a small silver flask. She never checked past the first two pages."

Niall shifted on the bench and angled her in his lap so he could more easily reach her gaze. "And what was on the pages she did not check?"

Warmth filled her heart. How well he knew her. Knew her when no one else did. "I kept a list of all the characteristics I desired in a future husband."

"Well?" He jerked up his chin, demanding those items she'd never before shared with anyone.

The man who'd dragged her abovestairs to Ryker's office would have never bothered with questions for her. He wouldn't have cared to because he'd not even liked her. Now, how free he was in speaking with her.

"He'd allow me to ride astride." The one time she'd attempted such a scandal had found her in her rooms for the whole of a day, unable to leave for even her meals.

Niall chuckled and rubbed his hand in small circles over the small of her back, and she closed her eyes, feeling that deep rumble of his mirth. "Ya'd never ask permission, Diana. Ya'd simply do it."

Her heart swelled to bursting. She'd only ever been the duke's dutiful daughter. Except to Niall. Warming to her telling, she continued. "He would enjoy picking flowers and painting."

A strangled, garbled laugh shook his frame, and she joined in, feeling free for it. For him being here with her. She thought back to the girl she'd been, furiously dashing away at her list. "He would, of course, be honorable and caring. He would love me more than anyone," she explained softly, finding a soothing calm in Niall's gentle caress. "We would have a kennel of dogs and a household of laughter." All gifts she'd dreamt of as a child but never truly known. She shuttered her expression. "And then at eighteen, I learned who my father was."

A somber mask fell over his features, chasing off all earlier hint of mirth.

"He was a man disloyal to my mother." Bitterness lanced at her chest. She'd hoisted her father upon this pedestal of greatness. "A man who loved another and had children whom he didn't look after." It hadn't mattered that he'd not known of Ryker and Helena's existence. It mattered that he'd failed to know. "He committed my mother, a woman who deserved to be committed, but a woman he also never loved. I won't be that woman, Niall. A proper societal hostess who sips my tea while my husband visits your clubs, and beds other women, and loses a fortune." Her voice shook with the power of her resolve. "I won't be my mother, Niall." Not in that way. "I'll not bind myself to a husband." Not a societal one. *You would want this man.* That dangerous whisper danced around her mind. She ran her fingertips over a white crescent scar on the top of his hand. How had he come by that wound? Who had held *him* when he was hurt and suffering?

They remained that way for a long while, with seconds passing into minutes, and the minutes losing themselves into some amorphous sense of time. Niall made no attempt to fill that quiet or issue pretty words or assurances the way a gentleman of the *ton* might. And she found a beautiful solace and calming peace in that, something so much deeper and more meaningful than empty platitudes.

When he set her away from his chest, she railed at the barrier erected again, the one that forced reality in. "You shouldn't be here, Diana." He shifted her off his lap, and she settled on the opposite bench. "We don't know who wants you"—dead—"harmed, but unless I'm with you, then you cannot sneak off."

She eyed him curiously. Was she just an assignment to him? Or had she come to matter to him, if even in some small way? Oh, she'd no delusions that Niall Marksman would ever open himself up enough to care, particularly for a lady from the station he rightfully despised. But surely, in his frantic worry coming to her and holding her as he had, there were some feelings there. *And how pathetic I am for craving even those small scraps.*

Niall bent, and a hiss of metal filled the carriage as he fished the dagger from his boot. The oval-shaped sapphires adorning the hilt glimmered and glittered in the sunlight streaming through the curtains. Wordlessly, he held it out. "Here," he said gruffly. When she made no move to take it, he pressed it into her palm. Her fingers curled reflexively around the cool hilt.

"I don't—?"

"It's yours. Every person needs to have a weapon." His voice possessed a gruff quality. "This weapon served me well over the years. It was the first thing Oi purchased with the coin from my club. Oi want you to keep it with you. Always." So, when he wasn't around . . .

His meaning was clear, and she may as well have inadvertently pressed the tip of the blade against her belly for the pain that truth brought.

"You would give me this?" she asked, emotion wadded in her throat. This weapon that meant so much to him. She held it out. "I cannot take this, Niall." This, the second most important item to him outside his club.

He grunted and held up his palms, warding off her attempts. "Take it."

"Niall—"

"Oi said take it."

Her lips twitched, and she reverently caressed the enormous sapphires along the handle of the weapon. She'd come to learn and love so much about him. That gruff exterior he painted for the world, demanded everyone see, she saw clean through—there was a goodness and gentleness that he could not even see in himself. Did not want to see. But it was there and real, and so very beautiful. "Thank you," she said softly, lowering it to the velvet bench.

He gave a brusque nod. "We should return."

Yes, they should. To that town house that had been an empty, lonely cage for nearly a year. Niall reached for the handle and then stopped. "Sometimes people are just bad, Diana. It has nothing to do with blood or insanity, but rather who they are. There's nothing bad about you."

Not looking back, he pushed the door open and jumped out, leaving her alone.

There's nothing bad about you. They were the closest words to a compliment Niall Marksman would ever give a person, and yet they touched her deep inside for the raw realness to them. He'd stripped away the veneer people coated their words with, found her greatest fear, and allayed it with the simplest of praise.

As the carriage made the slow journey from St. Giles to Mayfair, Diana peeled the curtain back, staring out. Niall rode alongside the carriage, a sentry ensuring her safe return home. With his ease in the saddle, he had the look of a warrior bracing for battle, seeking foes from any corner. In him, she searched for the boy he'd once been. Sadness suffused every corner of her person, leaving an aching hole in her heart. A starving, scared child on the streets; how easily he could have become the boy, Ryan, killed as a lesson doled out by a merciless gang leader. And Niall had been the fortunate one. Allowed to live, but beg like a dog and take lives in order to survive. *Sometimes people are just bad . . .* Yet, Niall was not bad or evil.

Diana had lived the past year inextricably linking herself to the woman who'd given her life and the crimes she was guilty of, only to have Niall force her to look at her existence through entirely different eyes. Make her question . . . that mayhap there was not an evil in her blood because of who her parent was. Diana drew in a slow, healing breath, letting it fill her lungs and every corner of her person.

"I am not her." She whispered the truth aloud, saying it—believing it—for the first time since all the crimes had been revealed. Just as Niall was not Diggory and the dark acts forced upon him as a child. Diana released the curtain, and it fluttered whisper-soft back into place.

She looked over to Niall once more. Mayhap before he took his leave, she could help him find peace for himself. Help him see himself as the strong, courageous man who'd thrived when any man would have crumpled under the struggles he'd endured. And that would have to be enough . . . knowing he found his way, free of anger.

Yet, selfishly, she wanted so much more. She wanted him in her life—forever.

Chapter 18

Later that night Diana stared out the floor-length crystal doors over-looking her mother's prized gardens. Those long-overrun grounds in desperate need of care and tending. The moon hung high in the sky, bathing the walled-in area in a pale moonlight.

Were it not for the faint glimmer of his cheroot, Diana would have missed him.

It was the first glimpse she'd had of him since they'd returned that afternoon. For the glimmer of a hopeful moment, she'd believed that mayhap he'd let her in. But as soon as the thought slid in, she recalled his aloof silence as he'd trailed behind her.

No, they may have forged a friendship and a bond these past weeks, but she was never a woman Niall Marksman would or could love. The station divide between them alone would always be too great for one with a deep-seated resentment for the peerage to overcome. His friendship would have to be enough.

She drew open the doors, and the early summer air spilled into the room, wafting in the fragrant hint of those overgrown roses.

Niall glanced up. "Princess." He flicked his ashes.

Once there would have been an acerbic bite to that greeting. She stepped out onto the balcony and layered her arms on the stone rail. "Sir," she called down quietly.

Even with the space between them, the faint glow of the moon played off his grin. How easily he now smiled. Selfishly, she wanted that ease to be a product of her presence in his life. To know she'd brought Niall some of the happiness she'd been missing—until him.

"Can't sleep?" she asked.

"Doing a final search of the grounds."

She rested her cheek along her arm. "You're always working."

"It's all I've known."

That wasn't true. He'd known struggle and strife and death and pain. And how she wished she could ease those memories and replace them with new ones that included them together.

"That tree needs to be chopped down. It should have been long ago," he said, raising a frown on her lips. "The man who invaded your chambers would have never found his way inside."

She briefly studied the object of his fury. The aging oak reached back to the oldest memories she carried of this place. It had been an incongruity stuck inside the metropolis of London, and she'd been in awe of the tree for it. "If he was determined, Niall, the absence of this tree would have never stopped him."

He scowled. "It would have at least deterred him."

"Don't you dare," she chided.

He furrowed his brow.

"Speak to my father."

The ghost of a smile played at his lips. "I didn't say I was going to speak to him."

She snorted. "You didn't have to, Niall." For, somewhere along the way, their thoughts had begun to move in a synchronic harmony at odds with the icy aloofness between them all those weeks ago. "I thought you were avoiding me," she confessed softly.

He hesitated, his cheroot halfway to his mouth. Ah, so he had been. Niall took another pull and slowly exhaled a perfect plume of white smoke. "I couldn't avoid you if I wanted to, princess."

If I wanted to . . . which meant he didn't want to. It was silly to feel this lightness in her chest at that vague noncompliment . . . and yet that was all she'd ever have from him. Diana hitched herself up onto the ledge, and with a curse, Niall dropped his cheroot. "'ave ya lost your bloody—" Those words he'd once hurled before, he now cut off abruptly, leaving unfinished. It was a tender consideration most would never expect of Niall Marksman, the fearless guard from the Hell and Sin. "Get back, Diana," he cautioned.

Mayhap, months prior she would have heeded that warning. Certainly before her mother had been carted off to Bedlam. Dukes' daughters didn't shimmy down trees and certainly never to meet a man alone in the gardens. Mayhap even after her mother's imprisonment, Diana would have honored those same age-old expectations for her. In these months, however, she'd found a much-needed, longed-for control and reveled in it. She shot an arm out and grabbed the long limb jutting toward the balcony. Concentrating on that branch, she pulled herself onto it. Her heart caught and dipped with the sudden drop, and she quickly righted herself.

Rushing to the base of the tree, Niall let loose a barrage of black curses. Her skirts rucked up about her knees, Diana shimmied down the oak. The jagged limb under her grip transported her back to those forgotten days of her childhood.

As soon as her feet touched the ground, Niall was at her side. "Wot—?"

"When I was a girl, my mother would not let me in her gardens." That brought him up short. Rubbing her arms distractedly, Diana wandered along the grass, damp from the late-night dew, the cool soothing on her feet. "I was only permitted with my governess, and only for my lessons on floral arrangements and floral paintings." Diana stepped out onto the graveled path. The stones bit into the soft flesh of her feet. Ignoring it, she made her way determinedly to the *prized* pink roses. "In the dead of night, I would sneak out here. I would jump over that ledge." She turned and pointed back at the balcony. "And climb down that same tree."

She felt Niall more than she heard him. "What did you do when you were out here?" he asked with none of his usual reluctance.

"I would smell the blooms and then steal one single rose each time I did." A little chuckle escaped her. "It was such a small show of rebellion, but I reveled in it. Until . . ." Her gaze grew distant on one bush choked in weeds.

You are not to ever enter these grounds. Ever. Dukes' daughters do not scale trees like a common chimney sweep.

"Until . . . ?" he encouraged.

Niall rested his palms on her shoulders and drew her back against him the way a tender lover might. "She discovered I'd been sneaking out and had the limb closest to my window chopped down." It was the last time she'd snuck outside. She leaned against him and shifted the discourse to now. "Ryker and Penelope's dinner party is tomorrow." Of course he knew that. Niall knew everything where her movements were concerned. She bit her cheek to keep from asking the question on her lips. Would he accompany her? Not as a guard in Ryker's employ, but as a man who wished to simply be with Diana.

His muscles jumped. "Yes." Just that one syllable, a single utterance that gave no hint of what he truly thought, if anything, of her admission.

"I believe they're trying to play matchmaker," she murmured to herself. She cast a glance at him. His tense mouth and hard eyes told her everything she'd believed since that familial invite had been issued. Looking away, she turned her attention to the night stars. Staring up at them, in this overgrown garden, she could almost believe that she and

Niall were elsewhere. In the country, mayhap. Away from London and the harsh expectations that followed them both here.

"Your brother wants you to be safe," Niall said at long last, only confirming her suspicions. "He believes an honorable gentleman will do that . . ." *When I'm gone.* The words lingered as real as if they'd been spoken.

Annoyance swirled in her breast. He'd defend Ryker's machinations? "I have learned firsthand how honorable *gentlemen* are." Unlike Niall and his brothers, who'd shown greater loyalty than the whole of the *ton* combined. "And I'll not marry for it." She paused. "Certainly not a nobleman," she reiterated. Not anyone. Or that had been her resolve of a year earlier. Marriage had been an easy dream to let go of because there had been an absolute absence of goodness about her. And then she'd met Niall. And he'd slipped into her heart and made her feel, and yearn, and want again . . . all those dangers she'd sworn to never succumb to.

"There are some good men," Niall said. That admission came as though dragged from him.

Her stomach twisted. Did he even now seek to foist her off on another so he was no longer responsible for her? "Oh?" She arched an eyebrow.

"Your brother-in-law."

Yes, Helena had been blessed to find that happy union. It did not escape her notice, however, that he didn't put Ryker into that latter category.

"And?" she asked, arching an eyebrow.

He scratched at his brow. "Oi'm sure there's other good gentlemen," he groused.

Diana shifted in his arms and passed her gaze over his face. "Is that what you believe? That I should marry some *honorable* gentleman?"

A muscle pulsed in his jawline, and he instantly veiled his expression. "It doesn't matter what I think."

"To me it does," she swiftly countered. In his time here, he'd become more than a guard. He'd been the only true friend she'd known in her life. And what was more, she needed to know that it would matter to him if she wed another.

Niall reached inside his jacket and withdrew another cheroot. Diana deftly slipped it from his fingers, holding it from his reach. She tossed the unlit cheroot aside. Did he realize he hid his answers and emotions behind those small lit scraps?

Frowning at his discarded cheroot, he folded his arms.

Did he not know there was no man she wanted other than him? That he was the only one to whom she'd trust her future, knowing he'd protect it and allow her the self-control she'd been denied for the course of her life. "Is that what you want?" she repeated.

His jaw worked. "I . . ." Her heart hung suspended in her breast. "I want you to be safe."

Safe.

That empty, meaningless wish. She stepped away from him. Folding her arms in a lonely embrace, Diana looked past his shoulder. Up at the sky. Anywhere but in his eyes, which always saw more.

Before he'd entered her life, her course had been set. She would have the freedom to explore and find happiness away from the suffocating folds of London's Polite Society. With Helena's help, she'd charted a path and found a way . . . and Niall had merely been a fleeting person in her life until she boarded that ship and sailed away.

Everything had changed. Since Niall, she'd given but fleeting thoughts to that impending journey. Her throat tightened. What would it be like when they were separated not only by the streets of London, but by an entire ocean.

He shot a hand out, caressing her cheek. That coarse, callused palm—a warrior's palm that had known toil. Hands that had built one of the greatest gaming empires in London. And hands that had been forced to kill. "I want you to be happy," he said hoarsely.

Of course, even he believed that it was one of those respected noblemen who could bring her that elusive gift.

"I'll not be happy married to *any* nobleman." She continued impatiently, over his sound of protest. "Do you see any honorable men at your clubs?" she countered, with a sardonicism that raised a frown. Why, even her father stood as a testament to the perfidy of those noblemen. "I'll not trust myself to anyone, Niall." Her voice broke, and she swiftly looked away. She'd already laid herself bare before him. She'd not have him see her reduced to this weakness.

"You're afraid, and so you've vowed to never marry, but someday you'll meet a gentleman who isn't loike your da. A man who'll make you happy and can give you all those things you wished for."

I already found him.

A pinprick of pain stabbed at her heart. It was an unnecessary reminder that she'd never be anything more to Niall than an assignment he'd taken on. He might like her, as he'd claimed. He might enjoy talking to her, even share parts of himself. But he'd never give his heart to her. Mayhap he was incapable of trusting that damaged organ to anyone.

Diana drifted closer, lifting her palms. "You make—"

He quickly stepped away in a tangible rejection of the words on her lips. "You should return to your rooms."

She'd not beg him for a scrap of his affection. Nor would she humble herself before him. "I see." She saw all too clearly, more than she wished. With a juddering nod, she started on her heel. She made it no farther than the base of the tree. Niall shot a hand out, capturing her wrist, bringing her back around.

Diana's breath caught on a noisy gasp.

"What do you think you see?" Some unnamed emotion darkened Niall's eyes, turning those sapphire irises nearly black.

Her throat worked. "That it doesn't matter to you whether I marry."

"You're wrong," he whispered, resting a hand on the trunk of the tree and effectively trapping her. "When I think of you married, of a man even courting you, I want to become the vicious street fighter I was raised to be and tear him apart with my hands."

Her lips fell open.

Niall reached his other palm out, and he again stroked her cheek. "I'm not a fancy lord. I'm not capable of chivalry and restraint. I can't have you, but I don't want anyone else to have you, either." Her breath caught, and she tipped her head back, needing his kiss.

He cursed and immediately shoved her behind the tree trunk. "Quiet," he ordered against her ear.

Diana's pulse hammered as he swiftly yanked out his pistol and moved to the center of the gardens.

"A servant claimed he heard someone sneaking outside." Adair's quiet interruption from the front of the gardens contained a healthy dose of surprise.

Niall's brother.

Niall's reply was lost to the distance between them. She peeked around her meager hiding place to where Niall and the other man now spoke.

"You're getting lazy," Adair drawled, accepting the proffered cheroot Niall held out and lighting it on one of the lamps.

"I wasn't sneaking," Niall muttered, and her lips twitched at the boyish annoyance. Seeing him with his brother, that easy banter, presented Niall in this new, unfamiliar-until-now light of sibling.

Adair chuckled. "Mayhap not, but even when you weren't, you were always mindful of your steps."

That sobering reminder of what Niall's existence had been like left her with an aching sadness. What must it have been like to always watch one's words or steps . . . with the greatest worry not being the nasty gossips about you, but rather the need for survival?

"Ryker wants you there," the other man was saying. "He wants us all there."

Niall scoffed. "First Helena put requests to him about her ball, and now Ryker'd do the same thing with his damned dinner party."

She stilled as she realized they now spoke of Lady Penelope's formal dinner party.

"Penelope is hosting it for the purpose of marrying the girl off." Adair took another pull from his cheroot. "The sooner she's wedded, the sooner we'll both be free to return. That should please you."

She gripped the trunk, and the jagged bark bit into her palms, and it wasn't until Niall spoke that she was able to release the breath she'd not realized she was holding. "My concern isn't about when I can return, but Lady Diana's safety."

Adair dropped his cheroot and ground it under his boot. "Of course." His pearl-white teeth flashed bright in the night. "But it would be preferable if she was safe *and* married to a fancy toff so we could return." He shot out an elbow and knocked Niall in the arm.

Her brother, her father, her sister-in-law, Adair—they all spoke so freely of Diana marrying a nobleman like Lord Maxwell. They saw in that gentleman wealth, strength, and influence. How very wrong they were. The Earl of Maxwell with his dogs bore not a glimmer of the might and power that Niall Marksman did.

After learning of her father's betrayal and witnessing the ease with which he'd sent his wife away to Bedlam, Diana had resolved to never wed. She'd failed to know, until Niall, there existed men such as him. Loyal ones who'd battle any demons, real or imagined. Men who could be a partner in life.

And she wanted him.

In her life . . . forever.

There should be a suitable terror at that realization, and yet if he was to leave, she wanted to steal whatever moments she could with him.

Adair started for the doorway, and she held her breath when he paused to look back at Niall.

"I'll be along shortly."

The other man nodded and then stalked off.

Niall remained rooted to the same spot, staring at the doorway, and then, after an interminable stretch, returned to the tree.

"Come. You need to return to your rooms," he said, the way a nursemaid might scuttle off a recalcitrant charge. He heaved himself onto the low-hanging branch and effortlessly pulled her up. They were silent the remaining climb, until he helped her over the edge of the balcony.

He was so determined to push her away.

How to make him see that he wanted her in his life?

Chapter 19

Niall helped Diana over the ledge and followed in behind her. Since he'd arrived, he'd been inside this very room every day and night. Somehow this moment, outside those perfunctory, formal searches, was very different. Tension thrummed in the darkened chambers, emphasized by Diana's audible breath.

Desperate to break that charged awareness, Niall set about the familiar—searching the room again. While he worked, he felt her eyes on him, following his every movement.

His gaze went to the mahogany four-poster bed, taking in that massive wood frame. The white sheets and equally white coverlet drawn back were wicked temptations that had Chance laughing at Niall for the weakness in him. He briefly closed his eyes.

"What is it?" Diana murmured, her husky contralto closer, indicating she'd moved.

He managed to shake his head. "I should go."

She sailed closer, and the fragrant hint of flowers and innocence wafted about his senses. "Stay."

That one word, a single syllable, washed over him. Conjured by his own wicked hunger.

He swallowed hard.

Diana captured his hand, and her delicate touch forced his clenched grip open. She pressed his hand to her chest. Her heart pounded under his palm in a steady, frantic beat. Oh, God. "I said stay, Niall," she repeated in a siren's voice that entreated and commanded all at the same time. There were a thousand and one reasons he should go.

She was Ryker's sister, a fraction below royalty, and forever divided from Niall for that birthright alone.

And there was one reason to stay—her. He was a bastard in every sense of the word, for with all those reasons, he wanted her still.

With a groan of surrender, Niall covered her mouth with his. Diana melted against him, her breasts crushing the wall of his chest as she met his kiss in a desperate exchange. Parting her lips to allow him entry, he touched his tongue to hers, swallowing her breathy moan. Almond tinged her breath—heady, intoxicating, and sweet.

Diana wound her arms around his neck and, with a boldness that sent blood pounding to his veins, angled his head as though she needed to be closer. As though she'd been craving this moment as long as he himself had. Sweeping her in his arms, Niall carried her over to the bed and set her down in the center.

Chest rising hard and fast the way it had when he'd bolted from determined constables, Niall backed away several steps, giving her an opportunity to change her mind. Even though turning around and never knowing all of her would be harder than any battle he'd fought in the streets. He'd never blame her for that decision. He well knew she deserved better than to bed a man with blood on his hands.

Diana shoved herself up onto her elbows and eyed him through heavy golden lashes, a question in her eyes.

"Tell me to leave," he rasped. He'd known since the day he stole his first scrap from another scrawny, desperate urchin that he belonged only to St. Giles. "Remind me Oi don't 'ave any place putting my 'ands on you." For reasons that had to do with more than the social divide between them. It had to do with her birth connection to Ryker and Helena.

"Niall," she whispered, sitting upright in a flutter of skirts. "How do you still not know?"

He gave his head a shake.

Diana held his gaze squarely. "Those noblemen you'd push me toward . . . They do not have a jot of the courage, honor, or strength you have in your smallest finger alone." Her words ran through him. "I don't want a nobleman, or anyone else." She stretched a hand out. "I want *you*."

I am lost. Niall groaned. He shrugged out of his jacket and tossed it aside. It sailed to the floor in a noisy heap. And with every discarded scrap and boot, Diana stared on. He strode over to the bed and climbed atop and hovered his hands about her.

She captured his hand, twining her fingers with his. "You have been the only man who's treated me like more than a fragile piece of china. Don't you dare treat me any differently now." Shoving up on her knees, she sidled over, looped her hands about his neck, and kissed him.

All his reservations melted away.

His pulse thundered loud in his ears as he returned her kiss, stroking his hands over her body, learning the curve of her hips. He drew back and she cried out softly, struggling to pull him close again. "You are so beautiful," he whispered, dragging a path of kisses from the corner of her lips. He suckled at her earlobe, and she made a breathless sound that was half moan, half laugh.

"Shh," he breathed against her ear.

"That tickles."

He gathered her buttocks in his hands and, giving a slight squeeze, dragged her close. Her lips parted on a little gasp. "It isn't my intention to leave you laughing, love," he pledged, and then all amusement faded from her expressive eyes, leaving in its place a desire that matched his own. Reclaiming her mouth, Niall's tongue dueled with hers. Blood rushed to his shaft as she boldly met his embrace. He struggled with the delicate row of buttons along the back of her gown, his hands shaking.

I am shaking.

He, who as a young man had bedded whores in an alley and then had lovers in the Hell and Sin, now found himself humbled and uncertain in ways he'd never been in the whole of his life. Abandoning hope for the tiny grommets, Niall yanked, and the beads flew about, pinging noisily upon the coverlet and wood floor, rolling around. Aching to at last see her bared before his gaze, Niall pushed down her bodice and chemise.

A blush stained Diana's skin, and she hastily folded her arms about herself. "Don't," he ordered, staying her movements.

She let her arms fall to her sides.

"So beautiful," he whispered. Reverently, he cupped one of the plump mounds in his palm and flicked his fingertip over the engorged flesh. "So very beautiful," he rasped, and then closed his mouth around the tip.

Her ragged breaths filled the midnight quiet, and when she twined her hands in his hair, anchoring him close, he reveled in that bold encouragement. He suckled all the harder, drawing that turgid flesh into his mouth, flicking his tongue over it until her wild moans echoed from the rafters. He switched his attention to her neglected breast.

"Niall," she pleaded, her fingers clenching and unclenching in his hair.

"I have wanted to do this from the first moment I saw you," he panted against her chest.

He slid a hand between her legs and brushed his palm over the downy thatch of curls shielding her womanhood. "Th-the first time inside the club?" She whimpered and moaned, splaying her legs wide for him.

Despite the fire burning through him, he grinned. Her probing question even through her desire was so patently Diana Verney. "Not then," he admitted, slipping a finger inside.

Her breath hitched loudly, and she spasmed in his arms. "I-in the a-alley?" With a beautiful abandon, she began to lift her hips in a slow, rhythmic motion, rocking against his caress. Her wet nectar coated his fingers, slicking the way.

Moisture beaded on his forehead, and he squeezed his eyes shut, attempting to focus on her question. "My third day here," he managed to get out, sliding another finger inside.

She cried out, and he swallowed that sound with his kiss. Their tongues tangled in a long meeting.

"You were sashaying down the halls," he whispered against her mouth, continuing to stroke her drenched core. With his other hand, he cupped the generous flesh of her left hip. "You were singing a tune."

"Was—was I?" she asked, eyes clenched tight. Her undulations took on a frantic, increased movement. She was close. Her wetness coated his fingers.

"But it wasn't your hips." He trailed kisses down her neck and found her breast once more. He hovered his mouth over the sensitive flesh.

Diana whimpered and made incoherent pleading noises with him as she tried to guide him to the swollen tip. "Wh-what was it—" Her query ended on a little hiss as he flicked her nubbin.

"Ya invited me to join ya." At the time, he'd been shamed by his own pathetic weakness that he'd been so enthralled by her seeing past the evil scarring his person and soul. Now, he saw, it was the moment she'd stolen his heart. Proved herself unlike even the street toughs of St. Giles who only saw a beast. "And Oi've been yours ever since." That confession emerged on a low groan as he shucked off his breeches and kicked them to the edge of the bed.

She caressed her fingers over his scarred cheek. "Niall," she whispered, searching her eyes over his face. "I—"

Terrified by the words on her lips, he covered her mouth and resumed his stroking. There would be time enough for reality later. Later, he'd face what they'd done here and the emotions battering at his chest. For now, this is what he'd know—her in this primitive, raw way that would bind them. He pressed the heel of his palm into her center, and she bucked into his touch.

She broke their kiss. "I want to feel all of you," she rasped against his lips, even as her determined fingers yanked at the edges of his woolen shirt.

That request, and her purposeful efforts, had the same effect as one of those buckets of shop water that had been hurled at him as a boy stealing sleep on a London stoop.

He gasped and wrenched away. His chest heaved from the force of his desire and panic. "Wot do ya think you're doing?" His voice emerged as a gravelly order that immediately dimmed the hunger in Diana's revealing eyes.

"N-Niall?" She stared at him in abject befuddlement.

Witnessing that hurt and confusion was like taking a blade to the belly. He scratched a frustrated hand over his brow. "Ya don't need to see me," he said gruffly, reaching for her.

She caught his hand. "No." Diana paused, giving him a meaningful look. "I *want* to see you. All of you."

Terror clogged his throat, and he struggled to swallow around it. He'd never revealed his whole scarred body to a single woman he'd taken. Not even his brothers had seen the marks riddling his frame. The words tattooed there. Something in exposing himself to Diana this way would leave him vulnerable in ways he'd never been.

Had she pressed him and made demands, he'd have grabbed his breeches, tugged them on, and walked away, even as it would have killed him. Instead, she lay patient, her body opened before him—her meaning clear. She trusted him and asked for that same gift.

Frantic, Niall glanced around at these chambers befitting a princess. For this wasn't about trust. It was one thing to give her words of the crimes he'd someday pay penance for at the gates of Hell. It was another to lay proof of his evil before her.

He warred with himself. The moments ticked by, and then with numb fingers, he grabbed the edges of his shirt. He'd not claim the gift of her innocence until she witnessed him and all his flaws before her. Still unable to meet her gaze, Niall tossed the garment to the floor and waited.

The mattress gave a slight groan as Diana crawled over to him. She stopped so close that the heat of her body caressed his, and then a soft, broken sigh slipped from her lips. "Oh, Niall," she whispered, her fingertips going to one of the many scars riddling his skin. He flinched as she trailed her index finger almost lovingly over a jagged, lightning-shaped mark at his side. Then she lingered her touch on those four words above his heart. *Kill or be killed.* Minutes may have become hours as, with an infinite tenderness, she stroked those four marks. She lowered her head.

"No," he pleaded, knowing her so well, he knew what she intended.

Ignoring him, she placed her lips against each scar. As though with that tender caress, she could heal the memories and the nightmares and the marks themselves. But then, mayhap that was the power she possessed, because in her arms he didn't think about the demons of his past . . . he only thought of her.

Diana sat up and gave her focus to one single scar, until now neglected by her. This was no mark made by a bullet or blade, but rather a brand. Her lips quivered, and a sheen of tears filled her eyes.

Once, he would have mocked those drops as signs of her weakness and pushed her away. He'd never been, nor would ever allow himself, to be an object of pity. But in this, with agony fairly bleeding from her blue eyes, his heart throbbed and beat harder from the evidence of her caring.

"It doesn't hurt," he forced himself to say, as she at last brushed her fingertips over the "D" emblazoned forever on his chest. The tattoo left by the man who'd made him kill and served as Niall's master for the first horrifying ten or so years of his existence.

"No," she whispered, raising her eyes from that old wound to his. "But it did at one time, and I expect it hurts even more now, in different ways." How accurate she was, this woman, unafraid and unashamed to speak of emotion.

His own screams reverberated around his mind, blending with Diggory's laugh as he'd touched the scorching flame to Niall's chest. He struggled to breathe, fighting past the old horrors—

When Diana placed her mouth on the puckered flesh, that tender caress brought his eyes open.

"He is gone. Let him go," she urged. "He will never hurt you again."

His body jerked taut. And then the truth of her words slammed into him, robbing him of the air in his lungs. He'd lived his life in fear. It had been there long after he'd escaped Diggory's clutches. In the walls of the Hell and Sin, Niall had battled back terror that his empire would end and he'd be the same desperate, starving boy in the streets forced to murder to survive. That same fear had been there each time the club had been infiltrated, and all the suppressed nightmares had surged to the surface after the attempt on Penelope's life. This is why he'd been sent away. It made sense—at last.

Diana traced her index finger over that long-hated "D." "Every time you see this mark, do not think of him, think of me." She raised her eyes to his. "Think of this night in my arms."

Groaning, Niall crushed her mouth with his. His manhood throbbed to life against the small of her belly, and he guided her down beneath him. He again found her moist center and stroked her sleek folds until her moans were reverberating in the silent chambers. Her body grew taut, and her movements took on a frenzied, frantic rhythm.

"Please," she begged, scraping her fingernails down his back. She parted her legs, and on a hiss, he positioned himself at her center. His shaft throbbed and pulsed as he ached to bury himself swift and deep inside her.

"Easy," he whispered, those words for himself as much as they were for her. Then slowly, inch by agonizing inch, he pushed himself through her wet folds, sliding inside her tight sheath. Niall froze, as his manhood pressed against the thin barrier between him and bliss. "Oi don't want to hurt ya," he rasped, dropping his brow to hers.

"You could never hurt me," she breathed.

With a groan, he claimed her mouth and pushed past that wall. Her body stiffened, and he swallowed her cry.

That sound of her pain cut across the maddening blaze of desire clouding his senses, restoring a fleeting control when all he wanted to do was pound hard and fast inside her.

"I—I was wrong," Diana said, her eyes tightly clenched. "That did h-hurt."

At the slight tremble of her bow-shaped lips and a single tear sliding down her cheek, a wave of tenderness washed through him. "Oi'm so sorry, love," he whispered against her ear. He trailed a path of kisses from her tender lobe over to her brow. Her cheek and then her lips.

Their tongues tangled and twisted in a ritual of desire that sent blood rushing to his manhood.

Diana's moans gave way to broken, ragged pleas of desire, and he began to move. He drew himself out and then slid forward over and over again. Slow. Giving her time to adjust to the feel and size of him. She wrapped her arms about him and held tight. Then she began to meet his thrusts until they were moving together, conjointly. Diana lifted her hips frantically, meeting his every stroke.

She stiffened, and her channel clenched about his shaft. Oh, God, he was going to spend.

"Come for me," he pleaded, and reached between them to stroke her slick nubbin.

Diana shattered on a scream, and he followed her over that magnificent precipice, hurtling, hurtling, and then falling as he came inside her in long, rippling waves.

Gasping for breath, Niall collapsed, catching himself on his elbows to keep from crushing her. Their chests rose and fell together, with their hearts pounding a like maddening beat.

His passion slaked, reality intruded. Good God, he'd hurt her. Niall drew back, but the sated smile on her lips called back his words.

"I've never felt anything like that," she murmured, and with her eyes closed, she had the look of the cat who'd swallowed the cream.

And he, Niall Marksman, a man without even a name, felt himself grinning without any of the trappings of guilt, anger, or fear she'd rightly identified in him. Brushing a kiss over her mouth, Niall rolled sideways and took her against his side.

There'd be time enough later for all the folly in what had just unfolded, but he'd not shatter this moment with the reality. He stroked his palm down her flat belly, caressing her satiny soft skin. From her birthright to even her body, she was his opposite in every way. But she'd seen more in him than even he saw in himself.

A faint little snore broke into his gentle musings.

She slept.

Reaching down, he shoved the rumpled coverlet out from under them and brought it up over her naked body. Not before he lingered his gaze on her sweetly rounded frame. His shaft throbbed to life, aching to know her once more.

He swallowed a groan.

It was time to leave. There would be time to sort through all of this after. But he had to leave, before his presence here was discovered. It was one thing for her to trust him with the gift of her virtue. It was an altogether different one to ruin her reputation among the nobles who'd eagerly cut her again from their fickle fold.

Reluctantly, Niall swung his legs over the edge of the bed and climbed to his feet. With a little moan, Diana burrowed deeper into the bed, sliding into the spot he'd previously occupied. As he dressed, Niall kept an eye on her. Her small, bleating snores filled the rooms, endearing in ways that he'd only have seen as dangerous before.

Niall crossed over to her gold vanity and grabbed for his cloak—and froze.

A small, official-looking scrap of vellum stood bright in the otherwise darkened room.

Diana's shuddery snore brought his attention briefly away from that page. Verifying she still slept, he returned his attention to it.

It wasn't his place to delve into her personal belongings, and certainly not forgotten letters left on her vanity.

Nonetheless . . .

Niall grabbed the page and skimmed.

> My lady . . .
> There have been changes to the agreed upon travel terms set out. *His Lady's Honor* will set sail one week earlier, at the original agreed upon time.
> Captain Nathaniel—

Niall crushed the sheet in his hands. "Wot in 'ell is this?" he hissed.

Diana sprang up in her bed. The coverlet dipped to her waist, baring her breasts, and if he weren't filled with a seething fury, the sight of her, a lush siren, would have tempted him from his very thoughts. Squinting, she rubbed at her eyes. "What are you—?" He stalked over, and her words trailed off, guiltily. "Oh, that."

That is what she'd say. Focusing on that anger that healed him from hurt, Niall hurled the document at her, and it noiselessly floated to a heap on the coverlet. "That is why ya needed a guard for six weeks," he charged, as all the pieces at last made sense. She'd come to Ryker with specific terms laid out.

Frowning, Diana grabbed the sheet and pulled it up to her chest. With the other, she recovered her sheet. "You and Ryker assumed it was for the end of the Season. I saw no reason to correct you," she said, so very matter-of-factly that he reeled.

Niall stumbled back a step and glanced around, feeling at sea the way he had as a boy picking his first pocket. "You saw no reason to correct me, along the way?" he demanded, when he trusted himself to speak and not shout. All these weeks, she'd slipped inside his heart, called herself his friend—he cringed—and all along she'd been planning to make off for wherever St. George's was.

At last the lady had the good grace to flush. She fiddled with the scrap in hand, that damned sheet that marked her time here as nearly complete. "I have not given it much thought since you came into my life, Niall," she said softly. Rising, she hurried and gathered a wrapper and drew it on over her naked form.

He dragged a hand through his hair, as her quiet words ripped an empty laugh from him. "Oi'm flattered, love."

She winced at the mocking condescension there, but he refused to feel guilty. She'd entered his damned club, upended his world, forced him to enter hers, slipped inside his heart, and all along she'd never had intentions of being here past the beginning of summer. His stomach lurched, and he spun away, unable to look at her. To look at the one person he'd ever trusted and loved, who'd board a ship and sail from his life. This was a loss different from her marrying and remaining in London. This would be a parting that saw them separated by a sea and world.

The floorboards groaned, and he flushed. He'd failed to hear her approach. She'd robbed him of even his street sense that kept him alive. Diana touched a hesitant hand to his sleeve. "You can come with me?"

He chuckled, the sound as empty as it had been the six weeks prior to her arrival in his life.

Diana stepped in front of him. "That is a question," she said softly. "Come with me?" she repeated.

Come with me.

Leave.

St. Giles and the Hell and Sin and his siblings and all dependent upon him. He made a sound of disgust and stepped quickly away, needing space between them. Needing to protect himself once more. "Ya know Oi can't leave, Diana. Moi life is here."

She flinched, and he may as well have struck her for the pain that glared from within her eyes. The sight of it cleaved him in two. Made him wish he was a better man for her. One deserving of her. Then she righted herself and met him with the same dignified strength she'd shown since their meeting in the alleyway outside his club. "Make a new life, with me."

Her words hung in the air, powerful and potent. They sucked the energy from his limbs and robbed him of words and proper thoughts. What she asked of him . . . to simply set aside his work at the Hell and Sin, and go off with her, begged him to forget those dependent on him and the stability he needed.

She touched her fingertips to his lips. "You don't have to answer now, Niall."

"No. Oi have until your goddamned ship leaves," he hurled like the beast he'd always been.

Not even flinching, Diana continued, "There is no life for me here."

"But there is one here for me, and you'd have me throw it away." She winced, and he forced himself to ignore that evidence of her hurt. "All because I found out your plans." He gestured angrily to that vellum sheet clenched in her white-knuckled grip.

"I would have told you. I . . ." She gasped as he took her by the shoulders and gave her a slight shake.

"When?" he cried softly. "When would you have told me?"

Or had he mattered so little that she'd have departed and never given another thought to the bastard from St. Giles whom she'd given her virginity to? That mocking question whispered around his mind, stinging like vinegar tossed on an open wound. At her guilty silence, he released her suddenly, and she stumbled back, catching herself at the edge of her bed. His gaze unwittingly found that crimson stain, and his stomach heaved. "Or was it that you just wanted to have a baseborn street thug between your legs?" he asked, his tongue making that hated question come out as garbled.

Diana clutched that damned page at her throat. "How could you ask that of me?" she whispered. "I lo—"

"Don't," he barked, and then stole a look back at the panel between them and Oswyn. If he was of his right mind and rationale, he'd care that the old guard had no doubt heard more than was safe, but he'd lost all reason where Diana was concerned. "Don't give me your empty words."

"They are not empty, Niall," she entreated, turning her hands up. "I love you. Surely you know that."

Unable to take his gaze from that page, he gave another empty laugh. "You love me so much you couldn't tell me and would have just left." With a disgusted growl, he stalked away.

Diana let out a cry of frustration and stalked over to him. Brandishing that page the way she might a weapon, Diana placed herself between Niall and the doorway. "How dare you? If I'd told you, you would have never allowed me to leave. You'd have told Ryker or my father."

Despite her worries he'd have told the duke, he'd learned long ago that her father was a broken shell of a man who couldn't be trusted to protect her. "I wouldn't have told your father."

"Fine. Ryker, then."

Niall met that accurate supposition with an unyielding silence. He wouldn't have simply let her go off on her own, set sail aboard a ship with only cads and scoundrels and lusty sailors for company.

Some of the fire went out of her eyes and slipped from her narrow shoulders. "You wouldn't have let me go," she whispered, raising an aching gaze to his. "But you do not want me in your life. Not truly, Niall. You said it before yourself."

The weight of that left him frozen.

A broken, agonized smile turned her lips up. "You know I'm right." She drew in a jagged breath. "But I want to be wrong. Come with me."

And unable to sort through the torrent of emotions and questions swirling inside, he gave his head a slight shake. "I don't . . . I can't . . ." He grabbed for the door handle, when she spoke, freezing him.

"You are a coward, Niall Marksman."

He jerked around. She'd accused him, Niall Marksman, a man who'd slit throats, fired pistols, and filched from among a throng of London's most powerful nobles . . . of being afraid.

And yet, in these very rooms, she'd proven the myth of his infallibility.

"You talk to me about being afraid, but you're no different," she challenged. "You've allowed Diggory and your fears to keep you trapped in your club."

Fury roared to life in his chest. "How dare you?" he seethed. "Oi'm not afraid of anything." Except her. She had single-handedly taken down every barrier he'd erected about himself.

"Saying it does not make it true." She held her ground. "You've lived in your club for so long, you're afraid to step outside that world," she spoke over his interruption. "You can go anywhere, and yet you choose not to."

"You don't know a bloody thing about it, princess," he hissed. There were people who relied on him. An empire that saw men, women, and children from the streets safe, with food in their bellies, and—

"I know you are afraid."

Her quiet charge sucked the air from the room, replacing it with a heavy, thick, palpable tension. A muscle ticked at the corner of his eye, and she touched her fingertips to that slight pulsation. "And for all your thoughts about us being so very different, the truth is we are more alike than you'll ever credit." Diana let her arm fall to her side.

"We are nothing alike, Diana," he said sadly. "Not in the ways that matter to Society."

And with that, Niall left. He closed the oak panel behind him, erecting a tangible barrier while he sorted through the charges she'd leveled.

Oswyn stared at him, his gaze revealing nothing. And Niall, one of the most violent thugs in St. Giles, felt his neck burn hot with a blend of embarrassment and shame.

He made it no farther than a step.

"That shouldn't have happened." Oswyn's reproach may as well have been an echo of his very thoughts.

Niall stiffened. The other man might be correct, but Diana's reputation would be in tatters if word of her lying with a London street tough found its way through Mayfair's hallowed halls. "I don't know what you're talking about," he said in hushed tones.

The guard who'd been the first ever employed by the Hell and Sin demonstrated a daring not a single other man, woman, or child in Niall's employ had dared show. "It can't happen again, and don't say ya don't know what Oi'm talking about, Niall," Oswyn snapped, shattering his characteristic calm. The balding guard stole a quick glance about and then came forward. "If you're discovered in the bed of Black's sister, the club will never recover. Men like us"—he passed a hand between them—"we don't marry dukes' daughters. We marry whores and servants, if we wed."

Bitterness stung Niall's mouth. He knew his friend was right. Hated him for it. Hated himself even more for having lost so much of himself in such a short time to a woman he had no right to. *Mayhap that does not matter. She wants more with you . . . wants a future.* As soon as the thoughts slid forward, he pushed them back. What future could he offer her inside a gaming hell? As long as she was tied to him, she would be forever bound to danger . . . not just this fleeting peril that existed from an unknown predator.

A hand touched his shoulder, and he looked blankly to those scarred, callused digits. "Let that be the only time. Your secret will be your own. We're guilty of far greater crimes than that." Yes. Murder, thievery, and countless other sins. "But it's time to step away from the lady. Unless you intend to marry her." The heavy irony in those coarse tones required no confirmation or denial from Niall.

Come with me.

Involuntarily, he looked once more to her fancy arched door.

Oswyn's curse shattered the quiet in the hall. "Surely ya aren't thinking ya can marry the chit?"

To give his hands something to do, Niall adjusted his purple silk cravat. "I'm thinking it is none of your business what I'm thinking," he said in those cultured tones any lord would be hard-pressed to identify as false. He may have known Oswyn for all of his adult life and trusted the security at the Hell and Sin to his care, but he'd not answer to him. And certainly not here in the middle of Wilkinson's corridors.

An uncharacteristic flash of emotion lit Oswyn's eyes: hurt. "Ya think Oi don't care about ya? Your brothers and ya took me in and gave me work when I had no other future awaiting me but death in the streets."

Another wave of guilt assailed Niall. He grimaced. Good God, he'd spoken more of feelings and emotions and all the uncomfortable sentiments that marked a man as weak more times these four weeks than he had in the whole of his thirty or thirty-one years of existence. "I know, Oswyn," he said quietly. Just as he knew the ornery guard was correct about Diana.

"There is the club," the other man pointed out. Did he sense Niall's wavering? "Even if ya marry the girl, Society will never look kindly to one of our kind touching one of them."

And too many relied on them. That truth rang loud.

"She's Ryker's sister," Oswyn pointed out, needlessly.

"Do ya think Ryker would reject a match between us because of my birthright?" Niall demanded, spoiling for a fight. Desperately wanting it.

"No," Oswyn said calmly, cracking his knuckles. He let his massive arms hang by his sides. "Since his marriage, he'd allow it and not think about all those dependent on him."

Men, women, and children who'd clawed and fought to survive in St. Giles and at last found security at the Hell and Sin. Niall threatened that all—for Diana.

"Regardless," Oswyn said, interrupting his silent thoughts, "ya cannot move between the two worlds. Either ya join Ryker as a guest and make yourself honorable and respectable for the girl"—Niall would have to be deafer than a post to fail to hear the skepticism there— "or . . ." *Or let her go.* "Ya let me accompany the duke and his daughter to Ryker's dinner and begin putting some distance between ya."

Come with me . . .

His heart, that damned organ that had proven itself real and wholly, surprisingly intact, climbed into his throat.

"I'm her guard," he managed to squeeze out.

Oswyn scoffed. "All your brothers will be present. Me. No 'arm would come to her."

Niall hesitated. "I haven't decided what I'll do for tomorrow," he hedged. No harm would ever befall Diana as long as Ryker, Calum, or Adair was present. The greatest threat posed, however, was not to Diana but to Niall, and being forced to sit through a formal dinner party with gentlemen invited solely as prospective husbands for Diana.

The loyal guard gave Niall a long look and then spoke in gruff tones. "Ya don't kill, Niall," he reminded him. "Not anymore." There was no condemnation or judgment there. "Ya know I won't hesitate to end a man for her."

Yes, he knew that. Oswyn and his brothers, even Helena, had been stronger in ways than Niall after Diggory's machinations.

"Just as ya know what ya need to do, Niall," Oswyn murmured, giving his shoulder a squeeze.

Aye, he knew.

I have to let her go.

Chapter 20

The following evening Diana went through the same motions she'd gone through for three years, standing before the same vanity while her maid helped her into her gown.

Seated before the vanity, Diana took in the visage reflected back. Those dark circles under bloodshot eyes. The blankness on her lips. She cocked her head. Did her maid, just like the remainder of the world, see the sadness in her? Or did no one look enough to see anything more than what she was on the surface?

Only, Niall had looked . . . and seen.

"Lift your head just a bit, my lady," Meredith said cheerfully, angling it the way she might fiddle with a small pup. "There." Her maid slid a ruby-encrusted coronet atop her head. It was a piece fit for a queen, or, as Niall had first mockingly then endearingly referred to her, a princess.

"Do you require anything else, my lady?"

"That will be all," she replied automatically, her gaze lingering on the rubies.

Meredith dropped a curtsy. "I'll inform His Grace you'll be down shortly." With that, the girl took her leave. When the door closed and Diana was at last alone, she returned her attention to the bevel mirror.

Since last evening, Niall had been businesslike and perfunctory toward her. He'd not avoided her, but neither had he been the same man who'd become her friend these past weeks—and she mourned the loss of that closeness. For she knew, even without words confirming any truth otherwise, what that distance meant. He would not come with her. His life was here. And what was worse, he didn't see her as part of it because of a social divide that would always matter to him.

A soft tap at the window broke across her thoughts, and she spun in her seat. Her heart sank.

Niall gave a silent tap on the glass and arched an eyebrow in a silent request.

And despite the significance of him being outside those balcony doors, sans formal evening attire, and knowing that meant he'd no plans to attend Ryker's dinner party this evening, she smiled. Coming to her feet, Diana lifted up her chin in acknowledgment.

Noiselessly, he parted those doors and slipped in her rooms. How did a man of his sheer size and strength move with such stealth? He closed those crystal panels behind him and stood there, unmoving.

Diana shattered the silence. "You aren't coming," she observed softly.

He gave his head a slight shake. "You'll be safe with my brothers and Oswyn—"

She moved quickly, his avowal abruptly cut off. "I'm not worried about my safety." Four weeks ago she had been. Four weeks ago she'd thought of ensuring her safety and then boarding her ship for St. George's. Everything had changed. Diana stopped a handful of steps away. "Is that why you've snuck in my chambers?" she asked. "To tell me you'll not attend Ryker's dinner party and to assure me of my well-being?" *Let it be more. Let it be that you've considered my offer and will join me when I sail.*

The sad, regretful glint in his eyes, however, told an altogether different tale. "I have never known another woman like you," he said quietly, and that wistful admission bore more a hint of goodbye than the very word itself. A vise tightened about her heart as he stroked the back of his knuckles along her cheek.

"From the moment I caught you sneaking inside my club, you tossed my world around," he murmured, and she leaned into his distracted caress. "I hated everyone connected to the nobility . . . but you were nothing like those lords and ladies I'd come to hate. I never thought about leaving St. Giles, and I certainly never thought about leaving London." Her heart lifted, and then, with his next quiet admission, promptly sank. "And never before did I regret the responsibilities that come with running my club—until now. I cannot leave, Diana."

The cinch squeezed all the tighter, making it impossible to draw in anything more than a shallow, shuddery breath. "No," she said at last when she could speak through that pain. "You can leave, Niall." As much as it left her aching inside, she backed away from him, and his arm fell uselessly to his side. "You're choosing to stay." Just as he chose not to let her inside his world. Just as he'd chosen his club over a life with her.

His face contorted. "Diana . . ." Except there were no words forthcoming. What could he say then? Short of altering his opinion out of some unwanted, useless guilt she might have instilled with her accusations.

"It is fine, Niall." How did she manage that lie? How did it come out so even and steady when she was breaking inside?

Niall searched her face with his eyes and opened his mouth as though he wished to say something more. Then promptly closed it. With sleek, stealthy steps, he was immediately at the window.

"Niall," she called out when he gripped the handle.

He cast a questioning look back.

She sailed over and positioned herself between him and those glass panels. Coming up on tiptoe, she pressed her lips to his in a fleeting kiss. It was a faint meeting of mouths that sealed the exchange as a goodbye. She sank back on her heels. "Thank you," she said softly.

He shook his head.

"You helped me see that I'm not my mother." Diana touched her fingertips to the place where he'd been branded by that monster, long ago. "Someday, you'll also find that you are not Diggory or any of those acts you were forced to commit to survive." And when he did, only then could he move on and begin again. Mayhap with a woman whom he loved enough to let inside his world and even leave his own. Oh, God. Her heart cracked and broke all over again.

His Adam's apple bobbed. "Diana . . ."

"Go," she urged, favoring him with a smile that threatened to shatter her facial muscles. "Or I'll begin to think you like me."

A pained laugh escaped him, and he briefly dropped his brow to hers. "Oh, Diana."

The door handle jiggled, effectively ending whatever words he would have uttered. They looked to the front of the room.

"My lady?" Meredith called from the other side of the locked panel. "His Grace sent me to ask after you."

It was time.

"Tell him I'll be along in a moment," she called.

The rapid flurry of footsteps indicated the girl had left. Diana turned back to Niall and started.

Her balcony door hung open, with a path just wide enough for a man to fit himself through. She looked outside just as Niall lowered himself to the ground and stared after him until he'd disappeared in the shadows.

Pulling the door closed, she turned the lock and on numbed legs made her way from her rooms, through the halls, and belowstairs to where a footman stood in wait with her cloak.

"Diana," her father greeted with an absent smile, that empty expression directed at the gold timepiece he now consulted.

That was it. Three syllables. Her name. And not a single word more uttered as they filed in the carriage and lurched forward, to Ryker's residence moments later.

Seated on the velvet upholstered bench, Diana stared at her father across from her. As the sprigged coach rattled along the cobblestones past the periodic street posts, the candlelight played off her father's features. His heavily jowled face bore more wrinkles, a mark of the sadness and tragedy of this past year. His once smiling eyes bore a vacancy that had killed all earlier glittering warmth.

"When I was a girl," she began quietly, as the turn of the wheels over the cobblestones filled the carriage. Her father at last looked to her. "I despised all my lessons in mathematics." Unlike Helena, whose mind had been born to decipher numbers, Diana had always been useless where they were concerned. "But I was enthralled by Shakespeare. Did you know that about me?" she wondered aloud, that question as much for him as it was for her.

"I didn't," he said with a melancholy glint in his perpetually sad eyes.

As a girl, she'd placed him in the spheres where mythical kings and magical men of folklore went. As a woman, she now saw she'd lived with a fanciful view that no mere mortal could have dared aspired to. "I often thought of myself as Cordelia and you my beloved papa." But she'd never truly been the principled heroine. Along the way of life, Diana had confused obedience with honor and lost key parts of whom she'd always been—until Niall. "King Lear banished her for being truthful, and she returned years later, when he was nearly mad." Her father stiffened, and pain contorted his wrinkled features. "And at last, he gives her his love. He imagines a life with her in it." Diana's fingers curled reflexively around her reticule. "It was only until just recently that I realized, Papa."

"Realized what?" he asked hoarsely, with more life in that question than he'd shown her since Mother had been carted off.

"I was never the daughter you truly desired . . ."

He made a sound of protest, but she spoke over it.

"I was the daughter you felt obligated to have."

"That is not true," he said, his face crumpling.

Once, the sight of his suffering would have stifled any further words. She was no longer that dutiful girl, however, putting his happiness before her own.

"Isn't it?" she retorted, stripping all inflection from that challenge. "You loved Helena and Ryker's mother. My mother . . ." She bit the inside of her lip and then forced herself to go on. "My mother was the woman you had no place marrying, and yet you wed her anyway. For that devotion you both showed to your rank and status, you both lost everything—your happiness. Your chance at love. The real families you were meant to have." Delia Banbury, the woman who'd been her father's mistress, had known nothing but misery for her relationship with the duke.

Tears filled her father's eyes, glazing those blue irises that were Diana's, Ryker's, and Helena's all as one. "I have many regrets, Diana." The muscles of her stomach knotted as he spoke. "Many times, I thought of that very thing. What if I'd never married your mother? What if I'd married Helena and Ryker's mother instead?" He painted an image of those three together, a bucolic family of four that Diana would have never been part of, or belonged to. "But there would never have been you, Diana, and I would have never given up knowing you or having you in my life, even for the happiness it would have brought me being with Delia." He covered her hand with his own, and she stared at his gloved palm. "I am so very sorry I've not been a father to you this past year."

Tears stung her own eyes. It had been so very long since her father had seen her . . . or spoken to her. "It is fine," she whispered. He'd lost so much and grieved for even more. That had changed him. She could not forgive his absence these past years, but she could understand it. His misery, however, was also of his own making.

"I'm not going to marry any of the gentlemen there," she said quietly, and he furrowed his brow at that abrupt shift in discourse.

"It is just a dinner to see if you'll suit," he assured her, patting her hand.

"I do not want a societal husband." *Like him.* That meaning hung clear as if it had been spoken aloud.

Her father winced.

"I'm leaving, Father," she continued.

His brow creased. "Leaving? Where . . . ? What . . . ?"

"With Helena and Robert's cousin, Captain Stone."

He scratched at his head.

Of course he wouldn't recognize the name. That was the man he'd been for the past year—one who didn't see the world around him. Including his own daughter. Before Niall had entered her life, she'd taken her father's apathy as a mark upon her own character. No longer. She was no more responsible for the actions of her parents than Niall was responsible for those acts committed at force by Diggory. She drew in a breath. "I'm going, Papa." Whether or not he approved.

That jerked him to. "You cannot simply leave. Why . . . why . . . you are a young woman."

Of course, he'd be of that opinion. It was the same one held by every last lord in Society. Only Niall had proven different. Her heart pulled. "There is nothing for me here." Niall would never be hers, and staying in her gilded cage when he returned to London's underbelly would kill Diana's spirit. She didn't want to become that woman. Not again.

"Not even Mr. Marksman?"

Her lips parted. Closeted away in his rooms, she'd believed her father hadn't seen anything past his own misery.

A sad glimmer danced in her father's eyes. "I've been neglectful, but I'm not a fool. You care about him."

Nay, she didn't care about him. She loved him. Her throat moved, and she gave a slight nod. Mayhap before he'd retreated from her, she would have shared everything in her heart . . . including the heartbreak of Niall's unwillingness to let her inside. Too much had come to pass.

"You'll not stay for him?"

"Do you disapprove?" she asked guardedly.

He frowned. "I would rather you find a good, honorable nobleman who'll see you safe and happy."

Diana stared sadly back at him. All the years of happiness he'd lost simply for honoring that commitment to rank. "You've learned nothing," she whispered into the quiet. As a girl, she'd seen him only as a benevolent, always smiling lord. Kindly to both his servants and lesser lords. How empty that kindness, in fact, had been. "You, who married mother instead of the woman you loved, would speak to me of wedding a nobleman?" Anger made her voice shake. Given his own betrayals, he'd dare equate that rank with words like *honor*? All along she'd believed her father blind to her. Only to find he was blind to everything that mattered.

"I'm not passing judgment on the boy," her father explained, with more life in him than he'd shown through any of their limited private discourses. "But no father," he went on, "would ever choose Mr. Marksman for his daughter." He spoke gently, the way he had imparted scraps of information when she'd been a child.

Her mouth soured. "Then those men are fools." Because Niall had more valor in his littlest finger than the whole of the peerage combined.

"I want you to be happy."

Niall makes me happy. Leaving London and this stifling society would make me happy . . .

However, only the latter could belong to her.

"Diana—"

Whatever her father intended to say next came to an abrupt halt, as the carriage jerked to a stop.

Diana caught the edge of the seat to keep from flying forward.

Her father pulled the curtain back. "What—?"

The carriage door opened, and Oswyn stuck his head inside. "Trouble, Your Grace."

"Trouble?" her father squawked.

The old guard stuck a hand inside toward Diana. "Ya need to come with me."

She shot a hand out and then froze, riveted by his callused fingers. Hands not unlike Niall's with the scars upon them. However, it was not the jagged white marks that earned her notice, but rather his red, swollen knuckles. Unease skittered along her spine, and she edged away from him.

"What kind of trouble?" her father demanded, pressing his head against the window again, like a child eager to arrive at his destination. "This isn't Mayfair. Where in blazes?" Diana looked past him out at the streets of St. Giles.

What . . . ?

With a vicious curse, Oswyn clubbed her father on the side of the head, and his mouth formed a small circle before he crumpled in his seat.

Diana's heart stopped.

Run.

Clutching her reticule, she lunged for the other door. Pushing it open, she jumped outside, catching herself quickly. Ignoring the pain radiating up from her feet, she sprinted across the street.

She made it no farther than three paces.

Two figures started across the cobbled road, making their way closer. Tall, coarse, heavily pockmarked strangers—men better suited for nightmares than the streets of London.

Panting, Diana whipped her gaze about. Her panic redoubled as she caught her driver's and footman's prone forms slumped in their seats. She made herself go still.

"That's better," Oswyn grunted. "There's nowhere for ya to go." The tall, burly guard continued over and grabbed her by the forearm. "Ya 'aven't made it easy for me. For any of us. Now come—" His voice soared to a high howl as she yanked out Niall's dagger and thrust it into his hand.

Free of his hold, Diana wheeled around and raced away from the lumbering strangers hurtling toward her.

Letting loose a scream to bring down the night sky, Diana ran . . . right into a massive wall. The air left her on a swift exhale as she sailed back and landed hard on her buttocks. Niall's knife slipped from her hands and clattered noisily as it hit the cobblestones. Tears sprang to her eyes, and she fought through the agony radiating up her spine to push to her feet.

Oswyn was already there, fury burning from his battle-ready eyes. He shot his fist out and clubbed her on the side of the head.

Flecks of silver dotted her vision, and a loud humming filled her ears. Diana dimly registered the collection of strangers talking quickly over one another, and then her legs gave out from under her.

And she remembered nothing else.

Chapter 21

Niall hadn't known a night of quiet in the duke's household since he'd arrived.

Now he lay on his borrowed bed—a bed that, since he was being honest with himself, was damned comfortable—staring up at the colorful mural overhead.

Trying not to think of Diana's barely concealed hurt as he'd rejected her offer.

Trying not to think how he'd snuck off and watched her carriage until it had pulled away with her father and Oswyn.

Trying not to think of her in that damned silk amethyst gown and its damned daring décolletage as she sat alongside some name-less gent, a man her family and all Society would deem a perfect match for the duke's daughter.

Trying . . .

And failing.

Niall covered his face with his hands. "Shouldn't you be gone?" he groused.

Adair's low chuckle rumbled from the front of the room. Having survived by breaking into some of London's wealthiest homes, Adair was unrivaled by many in his soft footing. "You heard me enter."

Then, Niall's very life had depended on detecting even the faintest of sounds, and that skill could never be divorced from whom he was now. "I hear everything," he muttered, and, dropping his arms, he pushed himself up to the edge of the bed.

Clad in a sapphire jacket and brocade waistcoat, Adair couldn't look more uncomfortable in his evening wear than had he donned a chemise and been forced to prance through the duke's town house. "I'm leaving."

As Adair's was a statement more than anything, Niall opted to say nothing on it. Instead, he shrugged out of his jacket and tossed it onto a nearby chair. It fell on the gold satin cushion and rested there.

"And I take that to mean you have no intention of coming," his brother mumbled, yanking at his cravat.

"There's no reason for me to be there," he said, taking care to avoid Adair's gaze. "Oswyn accompanied her there, and Ryker and Calum, and you, will be in attendance." Why would his brother not just go? Niall didn't want to be saddled with any further probings. Except . . . guilt slid in. *I should be there with her.* And this need had nothing to do with a sense of obligation. In his time here, Niall had come to care for her. Love her. *I love her.*

His stomach heaved violently, and he fixed on breathing. But there was no escaping it. He had fallen in love.

Adair glanced around the room, and then, pushing away from the door, strolled over to the carved oak Green Man desk. "You're certain?" Adair prodded, relentless.

Niall hadn't been certain of anything in more than four weeks, since he'd met Diana.

"I'd rather not suffer through an evening with a table full of . . ." Adair's words trailed off as his gaze snagged on the top of Niall's desk. He perused the single item resting there. "Pretty," his brother observed.

Neck hot, Niall strode over to the drink cart and poured himself a glass of brandy. "I'm not coming," he said, sidestepping the questions there.

Adair continued to eye him and then pushed away from the grand piece of furniture. "Then I'll leave you to your own company this evening. I expect you're probably eager for a break from your responsibilities. How else to account for your asking Oswyn to step in for you."

Niall stiffened. "Oi didn't—" *Do not rise to his bait. Do not rise to his bait.* His brothers had always known better than any other precisely how to get under his skin. Misery loved company, and Adair was determined to drag him along to the lion's den of Polite Society.

With a resigned sigh, Adair gave another pull at his rumpled cravat. He lifted his hand in a silent parting and pulled the door open.

Diana's maid stumbled into the room. Red-cheeked, she looked between Niall and Adair. "B-beg p-pardon, Mr. M-Marksman." That pained, nervous timbre to her voice that she'd shown whenever in his presence had not faded with time. The girl went out of her way to avoid him. The only time she'd voluntarily sought him out had been the day Diana had gone off to Bedlam. She swallowed loudly.

He set his glass down hard. "What is it?"

"Th-there is someone here demanding to see you." She dropped her voice to a scandalized whisper. "A child."

Adair gave him a quizzical look. "What child would have need for a meeting with you?"

Niall frowned. "None." Not here. At the Hell and Sin, plenty of desperate lads and girls sought roles inside the club. Those street urchins wouldn't be here.

Meredith fisted her skirts. "Smith." She glanced to Adair. "The butler," she clarified needlessly. "He's been trying to send her away, but she said he'll have to throw her out by her"—her blush deepened—"*arse,*" she said on another whisper. "She said *arse,* and now Smith is gathering the footmen and—"

Niall was across the room in three long strides. He brushed past the girl. Incongruities represented dangers that only a fool would ignore.

They raced through the corridors. With every step, the shouts and curses grew, increasing in volume. Questions spun through Niall's mind. He and Adair reached the top of the stairs. The sight that greeted him brought him to a jerky stop. A small cloaked figure battled a butler nearly four or five decades her senior.

"If you touch me, by God, I'll cut your bollocks off," the girl spat, slashing a vicious blade at the butler. Two crimson-clad footmen streaking forward jerked to an abrupt halt and looked back and forth between each other. They immediately fell back.

"This is the Duke of Verney's residence." That proud reminder from the butler was ruined by the warble of his voice and the speed with which he stumbled away from her.

The girl snorted. "I don't give a rat's arse if it's God himself's kingdom," she said, and there was an air of familiarity to that voice. Mind racing, Niall tried to place it. "I'm not leaving until—" She looked up. The girl shoved the deep hood of her sapphire cloak back, revealing a familiar bespectacled face. Peeling her lip back, she looked him up and down. "It's about damned time," she muttered.

"You're looking for me," he boomed.

"Marksman," she said in greeting. His name came out more as an epithet than anything. "We meet again." The butler grabbed for her arm, and she jerked her chin. "Tell this bastard to get his hands off me, or my brother will gut you both and feed you your guts for supper."

"Her brother?" Adair asked from the side of his mouth.

"Killoran," he muttered, starting down the stairs.

"Killoran?" Adair echoed dumbly, following quickly behind.

If the girl was discovered here, a street war would rage until every last member of Killoran's gang or Niall's family was dead.

"Yes, Killoran," she called up. "The bravest, most powerful lord of the underworld, and certainly the greatest gaming-hell owner in the kingdom. Who are you?" she demanded of Adair when they stopped before her. "Never mind," she muttered. "It doesn't matter. Where can we meet?"

This diminutive member of the Killoran clan would invade the duke's household and demand a meeting. Niall had been stabbed by too many lads smaller than this girl to not know proper wariness.

Smith made another attempt to grab the girl, and she kicked him in the shins. A hiss slipped past the older man's lips as he collapsed on the floor like he'd been shot.

Cleo Killoran rolled her eyes. "This one," she muttered. "Take yourself off," she ordered. "I'm seeing to business here. Can't you see that, you silly rotter?"

To the man's credit, Smith straightened and then looked to Niall for his cue.

Niall jerked his chin at the hovering servants. "What do you want?" he demanded as soon as the duke's footmen and butler had hied themselves off.

Miss Killoran pursed her mouth. "I heard of your foul temper, Marksman. It is indeed as ugly as your face."

Adair went slack-jawed.

"What's wrong with this one?" She motioned her knife in Adair's direction. "Are you a lackwit?"

At any other time, Niall would have been impressed and amused by the show of spirit that could effectively silence Adair. "I'll not ask you again—"

"And I'll not have this meeting in the middle of a foyer." She stole a glance around. "A fancy foyer. But a foyer, nonetheless."

When both men remained silent, she leveled Niall with a glare. "You want to take this meeting. Trust me."

"The word *trust* uttered from the mouth of a Killoran," Adair muttered, earning a vicious kick.

He grunted.

"Ten minutes," Niall conceded. He gestured for Cleo Killoran to precede him.

Suspicion danced in her brown eyes, and she jerked her head. "I'm not allowing you to walk behind me."

"Oi'm certainly not going to let a bad-mannered Killoran with a knife in hand and a gun on her person to walk behind *me*."

They locked in a stalemate. A sound of disgust escaped her. "You both can go to Hell." She jerked her hood back into place, concealing those drab brown curls. "I've not come to posture with one of Black's hotheaded guards. Not even to discuss a certain lady you've done a dismal job of guarding." Miss Killoran beat a quick path to the door.

And just like that, all the energy and air was sucked from the room.

Breath frozen in his lungs, Niall reached for the girl. She easily danced out of his reach and brandished a pistol. "Try that again, Marksman, and I'll kill not only you but your brother." She flicked a derisive glance up and down Adair's frame. "Your equally ugly brother."

"What did you mean by that?" he rasped, as panic swirled around his belly.

Adair caught him by the arm. "She's a Killoran," he reminded him. "Lady Diana is safe."

"Not here," Killoran's sister ordered, blatantly ignoring Adair.

His pulse racing, Niall led the way through the corridors to the duke's office. Adair's reminder warred with the girl's veiled threat.

As soon as he closed the door behind them, Cleo Killoran spoke. "You came into my home and threatened my family."

He brought his shoulders back. "Is that what this is about? A like visit to the one I paid your brother?"

"You're not dealing with a child, Marksman," she snapped. "I'm nearly eighteen and wield more power in my gaming hell than you ever will in yours."

He concealed his surprise. Eighteen? The waiflike creature with a mass of silly ringlets had the look of a lord's pampered child and not a woman who'd been reared and raised inside a seedy establishment. Niall folded his arms at his chest.

"I'm here to strike out new terms between our hells. I help you and yours . . ." She flicked a gaze over at Adair, who stood sentry by the door. "And you pledge to never harm a Killoran."

Niall met that demand with mutinous silence. A man's word was his bond. When one made a pledge, he honored it . . . or his life was forfeit.

"Is that why you're here?" Adair ventured, without inflection. "To do your brother's groveling?"

The young woman stitched her eyebrows into a line. "We don't grovel." Dismissing him, she looked back to Niall. "We do, however, stay true to our word and honor it. I have information about a lady in your care." She scoffed. "Or who's supposed to be. You aren't much of a guard, Niall Marksman."

All Niall's senses thrummed to life, and he snapped erect.

"Ah, I see I have your attention." Taking apparent relish in his disquiet, Cleo Killoran turned the knife over in her hands.

"I'm listening," he said brusquely. All the while he fought the volatile energy running amok inside him.

"Someone wishes the lady dead. It isn't one of ours," she said hurriedly, backing away from him when he surged forward. "And as a testament of our pledge and a promise we seek from you . . . I'll give you names."

Niall's chest rose and fell heavily. "Who?"

"I want your word," she demanded. "And I want a favor."

"Anything." She could have asked for his share of the Hell and Sin and he would have granted it.

"Niall," Adair barked, a veiled warning there.

Yes, any other time, matters of truces and deals with Killoran were ones discussed by the whole of their group. The moment Cleo Killoran had waltzed in and breathed mention of Diana's safety, all those old rules had crumbled.

"I have sisters. We don't have noble connections like your kind." That sneer on her lips conveyed an antipathy that matched Niall's one-time feelings for all those of the peerage. "I want invitations and introductions for my sisters. Are we clear?"

It wasn't a promise he had any place making. It was one that required Helena and Penelope and their families to form a connection with some of London's most ruthless dwellers. But he'd sell the last unblackened sliver of his soul for Diana's well-being. "We're clear."

Cleo Killoran assessed him through jaded eyes and then nodded slowly. She spat into her gloveless palm and held it out.

Niall automatically took it in a firm shake that sealed their agreement. "I want names."

Adair's black curse darkened the office. "How would she even come by that information, Niall?"

"Because I have ears," she rejoined, fire flashing in her eyes. "And there are more men like you"—she jerked her chin at Adair—"who fail to see a woman has a brain in her head and speak around us as though we're invisible." The young woman pulled her hand back and gave him that name. "Diggory."

The beating of the clock thundered around the room. This is the name she'd give. "Diggory's dead," he said, annoyance making his tone sharp.

"Bah." Miss Killoran slashed her blade at the air, and he stepped away from that gleaming dagger. "The problem with Black, and all of his men, is he's only ever seen a man as deserving of power, and those same men as threats."

What was she on about?

"It is Diggory's wife." She spoke as one conversing with the village lackwit.

Diggory's—he froze. Amelie Diggory. She'd been not many years older than Niall himself when he'd lived in that hovel with her. After Diggory had set her aside for Ryker's mother, she'd become a sharp-mouthed shrew. And by the rumors that had circulated in the streets, had found herself imprisoned and shipped to Australia.

"Impossible," Adair said for him. "She's been gone for years."

"Gone and returned." Cleo Killoran pursed her mouth. "And she was as happy to see my brother in control of Diggory's empire as she was to find Diggory dead doing the Duchess of Wilkinson's dirty work."

At last it made sense as this girl neatly slipped all the confused-until-now pieces of a puzzle into their proper place. The person who'd been seeking revenge for Diggory's death was none other than his wife.

"He deserved to die," Adair said, filling the void.

"I never said he didn't," Killoran's sister retorted. "Regardless, the duchess earned a powerful enemy." She held Niall's eye. "An eye for an eye."

Niall rocked back on his heels, feeling as though he'd had a fist plowed into his solar plexus. "Diana," he whispered.

As casually as if they spoke of the weather, the young woman nodded. "She has her."

For a long moment, those three words hung in the air. Niall blinked, trying to make sense of them. A loud buzzing like a swarm of flies on a hot London day filled his ears.

"Impossible."

Did that denial belong to him or Adair?

"You questioned the loyalty of our people," Miss Killoran chided. "You need to look closer at those in your fold. Your man Oswyn is even now escorting her to Lady Diggory."

The earth dipped, swayed, and faltered, and Niall shot his hands out, searching for purchase and finding it at the edge of a sofa. *Oh, God.* "Impossible," he repeated, his tongue heavy in his mouth. It couldn't be. She was at Ryker and Penny's for a formal dinner party.

"Here." Matter-of-factly, Miss Killoran reached inside her cloak and fished out a small scrap. "This contains their whereabouts."

He accepted the piece with numb fingers and frantically scanned the page.

Adair reached past him and tugged the ivory vellum free. "It's a goddamned trap," he bit out, favoring Killoran's sister with a glare. "Oz would never betray us."

The young woman glowered in return. "*Someone's* been betraying you since my brother came to power."

As Adair and Miss Killoran traded insults, Niall's mind raced back to a year prior. To the night Oswyn had abandoned his post. Helena's now husband, the Duke of Somerset, had found his way abovestairs, and their sister and bookkeeper, Helena, had been sent away for it. The note placed inside Penny's rooms informed her of Ryker's previous relationship with Clara. Niall crushed the sheet in his hands and sought to pick his way around what was real and what was false in this remarkably unsteady world.

"Surely you aren't listening to her," Adair snapped.

Cleo Killoran gave a flick of her skirts and then drew her hood into place. "Do with that what you will. It's her life."

Niall's stomach pitched. *Think . . . think . . .*

"Come with me to Ryker's dinner party. We'll find the lady there, and then you can put aside any worry roused by *this* one."

"This one?"

While Cleo Killoran and Adair locked in battle yet again, a memory slid forward.

Too bad ya only caught 'im in the shoulder . . .

His mind slowed, then stalled, and then churned to life in a dizzying motion.

"Oi didn't mention his shoulder," he whispered.

"Niall?" He dimly registered Adair's question.

Lost in his own muddled thoughts, Niall worked back to the morning following Diana's attack to the meeting with his brothers and Oswyn. Oswyn's volatile charge and reminder about his capabilities and Niall's unwillingness to kill. Never once had he mentioned where he'd shot the bastard inside Diana's rooms. Which could only mean . . .

"He knew," he said hoarsely.

The words slipped between his clenched teeth.

Adair gripped his arm. "What are you—?"

Niall spun and grabbed his brother by the forearms. "It is Oswyn," he rasped, as panic swamped him. "He's the insider. The one who has betrayed us." He released Adair and stumbled back, feeling like a small ship tossed out to sea in a turbulent storm. He dragged his hands through his hair. "It was why he advised me against attending." And Niall had sent her off alone. Emitting a piteous moan that belonged more to a wounded beast than himself, Niall bolted from the room, bellowing for his horse . . .

"Surely you aren't taking this girl at her word?" Adair called after him.

"See her safely delivered home," Niall ordered, never looking back.

A short while later, he galloped through the quiet London streets, for the first time in his life praying that he'd indeed been duped and that even now he rode into a trap.

For if he wasn't, and Killoran's sister proved correct, then tonight Niall had sent Diana off to the slaughter.

And for the first time in the whole of his thirty-odd years on earth, Niall prayed.

Chapter 22

A sharp kick to the stomach brought Diana awake.

Sucking in a painful breath, she struggled upright. It was as though she'd waded into a thick haze of fog, and she blinked slowly, trying to sort out where she was. And why her arms were wrenched painfully behind her and bound at the wrists.

And then it all came rushing forward. Oswyn's betrayal. And now it would seem—her abduction.

"You're awake." Another kick followed that announcement, and Diana hissed, curling into herself. She fought through the haze of pain and desperately sought to bring into focus the tormentor with those boots of steel. But her head throbbed with a vicious pain from where she'd taken a blow to the head. "Ya 'aven't made this easy for me, girl," the woman went on in her coarse cockney. "Oi've 'ad an easier time fighting my way back from a penal colony than killing ya."

"Thank you," she croaked. Hating that hoarseness that spoke of fear. Wanting to be strong when Niall would only have ever been intrepid and commanding.

A startled laugh escaped the older woman. "You're a mouthy one." She followed that with a kick to Diana's side, tearing a gasp from her lips.

Agony exploded at the point of contact, and she pressed her eyes tightly, not wanting this woman to have the pleasure of her tears or terror.

When the pain abated, Diana forced her eyes open and winced. She promptly caught her head in her bound hands and cradled it. All the while she skimmed her gaze quickly over her makeshift prison. About half the size of her studio, the room was filled with stained mattresses, a handful of broken chairs. A table. She narrowed her eyes. Two men. One of those guards a faithless cur. Rage filled her for the man who'd betrayed Niall and all his siblings.

"Ya don't approve of the accommodations," the woman taunted, calling Diana's attention away from the traitor Oswyn, who stood with his back to her, gaze trained forward on the door.

Forcing her eyes away from his hated form, she looked to the stranger. The woman was gaunt, with dirt-stained cheeks and unkempt, greasy black hair, and yet there was an astonishing elegance to her classically beautiful features. "You're mistaken. It isn't the accommodations but rather the host."

The stranger laughed, that sound clear and bell-like and very much at odds with the evil burning in her emerald-green eyes. "You're not what Oi imagined for a duke's daughter."

Pulling her bound wrists close, she ever so slightly shifted back and forth, trying to work herself free. "I'm afraid you have me at a disadvantage." She paused and raised her bindings up. "Several disadvantages, if one wished to be truly precise."

In one fluid movement, the woman whipped a knife out from the front of her apron and brought the blade back.

Diana wilted away, but her captor slashed those bonds, freeing her. She bit her lip as the blood rushed painfully back to her wrists.

"Amelie Diggory," the emaciated woman supplied, ringing a gasp from Diana. The woman smirked. "Even ya, a duke's daughter, knows his name."

Given Diana's abduction, today was likely the day she'd meet her maker. Such a realization should bring with it a staggering, debilitating terror. But, God help her, she'd be damned before she allowed her captor to believe it was anything less than antipathy for Diggory that pulled forth her response. Even if it expedited her own death. "It would be hard not to," she answered between tight lips. "Your father brought suffering to many of those I love."

Amelie Diggory jammed the hilt of her dagger against her opposite palm. "My father?" she scoffed. "Mac wasn't my father. 'e was my husband."

Her husband? Why, the woman couldn't be many years past thirty.

"'e married me when Oi was fourteen."

Diana's stomach lurched. She had been only a child. Despite the fact that this woman had abducted her and intended her harm, a wave of pity assailed her.

She cried out as Amelie Diggory twined her fingers in her hair and wrenched her to her feet. Tears sprang to her eyes as Diggory's wife dragged her close. Their noses touched. "Your bitch of a mother brought him that woman," she snapped.

"Delia Banbury," she whispered, the name automatically leaving her. Ryker and Helena's mother. Again, the Duchess of Wilkinson's crimes reared themselves. They would always be there, remaining on in the pained existences of Diana and her siblings.

Her captor released her suddenly, shoving her hard. Diana caught herself against the wall. "Diggory didn't 'ave the need for a street whore when he could have the taste of a lady. Oi eventually got rid of her," she added, with a casual shrug. "Fed her enough poison until she turned her toes up."

Gooseflesh dotted her arms. She'd killed Helena and Ryker's mother. Oh, God. This was the evil Niall had spoken of. It moved far beyond the glimpse Diana had witnessed with her own mother's atrocities and extended into a depth of the Devil's darkness. She inched away from the madwoman and then abruptly stopped.

The handful of lit candles played off her prison, illuminating one wall. Drawn to the cracked plaster, Diana wandered over and touched one of the many peculiar inked marks. And knew.

Diana layered her forehead to one of those marks made long ago and struggled to breathe.

This is the place Niall had called *home* as a boy. This had been the wall he'd been forced to nick off an inventory of all the men and children he'd killed. Biting her lower lip, she let her quavering arm fall to her side. The thought of him and his strength through all life's darkness spilled into every corner of her person, giving her strength. Steeling her spine, she turned back to Diggory's wife and met her gaze squarely. "Why don't we move beyond the history lesson, and you explain what I'm doing here?"

Amelie Diggory grunted. "Oi could end ya for your insolence."

She forced a smile. "Come," she scoffed. "You intend to kill me, anyway." But why?

"An eye for an eye," her captor repeated, brandishing that serrated blade. "Mayhap Oi should carve an eye out first. Hmm?"

Diana's courage flagged. *Do not look at it. Do not look at it.* The ruthless madwoman wanted to reduce her to a blubbering mess.

"Oi returned from Austrail to find your mother could not stay away from my husband. Enlisted his 'elp a second time to off Helena. Was to pay 'im good coin for that job."

That job. Helena's murder. Bile stung the back of her throat, and she choked it down. How easily this woman spoke of her sister's death. "You are a monster," she whispered.

"Oi'm the monster? Your ma is the one who paid for the murder." She stitched her eyebrows into a menacing line. "Only she didn't pay. Wouldn't do so until the job had been done. And my Diggory paid the price. Must pay . . ."

Must pay. Must pay. Must pay . . . A debt paid.

Those inane ramblings spilling past her mother's lips echoed around her memory. Diana sucked in a sharp breath through her clenched teeth.

Her mother hadn't been speaking of Helena's death, but rather the debt she owed this woman before her.

Her life was forfeit. It had been since the moment her mother had forged a partnership with Diggory, all those years ago.

Amelie Diggory smirked. "Oi see ya understand now."

Diana dug deep for a brave retort, but her teeth chattered noisily, and she hugged her arms close to her waist.

There was a difference between knowing someone wished you dead and confronting it head-on. Knowing at any moment a blade would be pushed into your person and twisted until you drew your last painful breath.

She bit the inside of her cheek until the metallic hint of blood tinged her senses.

I do not want to die . . . Not here. Not like this. With this woman.

On the heel of that was the aching truth that she'd never again see Niall. His visage flashed behind her mind's eye. Niall, who with his deep sense of responsibility would hold himself to blame for letting her go off with Oswyn. She squared her shoulders, as resolve fueled her determination. She'd not have her death on his conscience. "Why bring me here?" she challenged. "Was it because your lackeys failed so many times before?"

Both guards snapped to attention, leveling her with glacial stares.

Diggory's wife chuckled. "Ya 'ave an overinflated sense of your power. If Oi'd intended to kill ya before, it would have been done.

There woulda been no satisfaction if Oi'd killed ya quick. Oi wanted ya to know it was coming. And then wanted to watch your face as I gutted ya like a fish."

Her stomach muscles knotted involuntarily, and she went motionless when Amelie Diggory touched her knife to Diana's belly. The sharp sting of the metal bit through the fabric of her gown and dug painfully into the soft flesh of her stomach.

"And Oi wanted your ma to know it was coming and that there was nothing she could do to stop it. She took everything from me, and tonight I'll do the same."

The trick is waiting for a person to falter and jumping at that weakness.

Diana lifted her chin mutinously and stared past her shoulder to the guards at the front of the room.

"This is how you repaid my brother and Niall's loyalty, Oswyn?" Diana said derisively. He stiffened. "After everything they've done for you?"

"Everything they've done?" he boomed, wheeling about to face her. "Is that wot ya think? Oi been with them from the beginning and was never more than a guard."

Diana balled her hand into a tight, proper fist. "They gave you security and stability," she countered, boldly challenging him.

"Shut your goddamned mouth," he thundered, taking several lunging steps toward her.

Amelie Diggory whipped around. "Enough. Ya don't speak unless you're spoken to by me. It doesn't matter what this bitch says. Are we clear?"

Diana sprang. She swung her fist at her captor's temple. The woman cried out as the knife slipped from her fingers, then stumbled and fell to her knees. Blood roaring in her ears, Diana took advantage of the confusion and dove at the knife, just as Oswyn reached for his gun.

But he was old and distracted and slow.

Diana caught Diggory by the hair and yanked her up. "Put it down," she panted, pressing her knife against the woman's throat.

"Ya can't kill me," her captor turned prisoner taunted.

A faint click sounded from the front of the room. Diana darted her gaze briefly over to the other thug. "Drop your weapon and leave," she ordered, infusing an edge of steel into her command. "Or I'll cut her throat. I swear I will." To prove her intent, Diana sliced the flesh, opening up a small wound.

For the woman's bravado, the rhythmic working of her throat muscles told a tale of fear. She gave an infinitesimal nod, and the pockmarked thug tossed his gun to the side and took his leave.

"Now, you, Oswyn."

"Oz isn't going anywhere," Amelie Diggory vowed.

Panicked, Diana's voice pitched higher. "I said get out."

The door flew open with such force it bounced noisily against the wall.

Her heart lifted as Niall filled the doorway, like a dark, avenging warrior of old.

Amelie Diggory grabbed Diana's wrist and wrenched it behind her back, knocking the weapon loose.

Pistol trained on Niall, Oswyn immediately recovered the knife and handed it over to Diggory's wife.

"Well, if it ain't Niall Marksman, the Lord of the Underbelly. Ya arrived just in time to watch me gut Wilkinson's daughter."

Niall had witnessed so many horrors he'd believed himself immune to them.

He'd been wrong.

Standing there, witness to Diggory's wife with a blade at Diana's throat, was a horror that would haunt him until he drew his last merciful breath.

His gaze briefly touched on hers. Oh, God. The terror spilling from her revealing eyes gutted him in ways that no blade ever could.

"Amelie," he greeted this woman, not many years older than himself. After he'd escaped Diggory's clutches, he'd not thought of the people left behind. He'd done everything in his power to bury the darkest memories and begin again. Only to now be confronted by this place of his childhood. And a person of his past.

"Put your gun down, Marksman," Amelie directed.

He fought for a semblance of calm, drawing on every last lesson learned with Ryker, Calum, and Adair. Lessons that had kept them alive when they'd confronted this same evil in the streets. "If you're determined to kill her, why should I set aside my weapon?"

Diana paled.

"That's a lie," Oswyn barked. "'e loves her."

Niall flashed a hard, empty smile. "I don't love anybody." It was a lie. His heart beat only for the woman who even now had a knife at her throat, and if she died here, they may as well end him, too, for he'd cease to be.

"Ya bedded 'er," Oswyn shot back, taking a hasty step closer, away from Diana.

Keep coming . . .

It was a litany inside Niall's mind.

"I've bedded lots of women, Oswyn." *You fucking traitor.* Niall tamped down the savage hunger to beat the other man dead with his bare fists. Oswyn's death was coming. It was a certainty.

The older woman pursed her mouth. "You're a fool, Oswyn. If ya think him bedding a bored lady with a thirst for a street tough meant anything." She laughed, that sound harsh and empty as his had once been. With her every shaking movement, that blade wobbled at

Diana's throat. "Ya never did care much about anyone. Ya had the best of Diggory in that way." *You are not Diggory.* "But you are here," she said in a contemplative manner.

Unable to meet Diana's eyes and lose the thin grasp on his control, Niall gave a slight nod. "She's Black's sister, and if I leave this place with her dead, my future inside the Hell and Sin is done." He forced out that lie. *Why did I resist her for so long? Why did I not take the gift she offered?* A vise cinched at his heart. They should, even now, be at Ryker's damned dinner party together, suffering through a *ton* event together . . . and in a handful of days boarding a ship for a place of pink sand and cerulean waters, leaving all this behind.

"She needs to die. A debt must be paid." That other familiar lecture Diggory had beat into all the boys and girls who'd done his work.

"Surely you aren't fool enough to believe you can simply kill a duke's daughter and walk away from it?" he scoffed.

Amelie's arm tensed, and panic kicked his heart's rhythm several beats. Desperate people did desperate things. He was proof of that.

"Doesn't matter if Oi walk away." There was a panicky thread to her pronouncement. "Oi'm not afraid of death."

"Everyone is afraid of death," Diana said softly, and he silently cursed.

"Shut your goddamned mouth, ya bitch," Amelie cried out, pressing the blade harder into Diana's flesh.

She clamped her lower lip between her teeth.

"It seems we are at an impasse," Niall conceded. "I'll have to kill Oswyn first so we're free to focus on resolving the matter between us."

The guard guffawed as though he'd heard the wittiest of jests. "Ya can't kill me, or anyone, Marksman. Ya haven't killed a man since you left this hovel."

There was truth to that claim. Niall's hands clenched reflexively around his pistol. The metal cool against his palm. *Do not take that bait . . .*

Tired of the cat-and-mouse game with Diggory's wife, Niall cocked the hammer of his pistol. "Tell me what you want."

"Oi want her dead. Oi want 'er to pay for Diggory's death."

"Diggory took his payment from the duchess. It was his decision that ultimately saw him dead."

Amelie snarled and then flared her eyes. "Oswyn!" she screeched, jabbing her knife at the door. The loud report of a pistol blared around the room.

Heart racing, he looked to the entrance of the room to where Adair stood with his arm outstretched, the head of his gun still smoking. Taking advantage of the other woman's distraction, Diana wrenched free and grabbed her by the wrist.

The knife fell, and then as one, they both dove for it. With Diana emerging triumphant. Niall and Adair raced forward and then stopped, as Amelie fished a pistol out of her pocket.

The faint click of her hammer sounded as she leveled her gun at Diana's back.

"Diana," Niall cried out. Arm shaking, Niall leveled his gun and fired.

Amelie's lips formed a round moue, and the pistol clattered to the floor, then she crumpled to the floor, dead.

It was over.

Chapter 23

In the two days following Diana's abduction, there had been a steady stream of guests and visitors to the Duke of Wilkinson's town house. There had been constables who'd come, to speak not with her but rather with her father about their abduction. When a duke and his daughter were touched by unpleasantness, Society paid attention. Whereas Niall and Adair's heroic acts that day? Well, that had been met with a good deal less of the king's praise than Ryker . . . the illegitimate son of a duke.

It was a reminder of why Niall hated this world. And why she herself did. It was also a more poignant reminder of the impregnable divide that mattered more to Niall than it ever had or would to Diana.

Seated at the window overlooking her mother's gardens, Diana involuntarily dropped her cheek atop her knees, the satin cool against her skin. Her gaze went to her attempted sketches and paintings that littered the room.

That place she, regardless of her father's disapproval or dissent, planned on journeying to, anyway.

Alone.

For with all the visitors, of which her brother, Ryker, had been a frequent one, there had been one person who'd not come.

Niall.

The morning following the *Grand Evénement*, as the gossip columns had written, Diana had told herself that Niall would be inundated with meetings and questions about her abduction. By the afternoon, when he'd still not come, she'd acknowledged that there was the matter of the security of those at the Hell and Sin. The people dependent upon his quick thinking and abilities. After all, he and his siblings had been betrayed by a friend from within. As such, Niall couldn't simply leave and pay Diana a visit.

By the second morning, she'd come to the gradual, painful realization—he wasn't coming. And it wasn't because she didn't matter to him, as he'd insisted to Amelie Diggory. Because she wasn't one of those empty-headed misses who couldn't see what was before her. He'd risked his life and returned to a place of his darkest nightmares, to save her. No, it wasn't that he didn't care.

It was that he didn't care *enough.*

Tears pricked her lashes, and she blinked them back. Hating those useless drops.

Footsteps sounded in the hall, and her heart lifted. Jerking her head up, Diana whipped her gaze to the front of the room. And that silly, hopeful organ promptly slid down to her toes.

The butler stood at the entrance with Lady Penelope at his side. She was a woman with kind eyes. Keen ones. "The Viscountess Chatham," he murmured, and backed out, leaving them alone.

Diana immediately sat up and swung her legs over the edge of the bench. Planting her feet on the floor, she stood. "My—"

"I do so hope you don't intend to 'my lady' me," Penelope said with a gentle smile. "I'm not one of those proper, dull creatures who stands on ceremony."

"No," Diana murmured. A young woman who'd wed a stranger to save her reputation and then taken residence inside a gaming hell, she'd likely been born with courage Diana herself was only just searching for and discovering inside herself.

Her guest lingered in the doorway.

"Would you please sit?" Diana issued belatedly.

"Indeed. Thank you."

Diana braced for the worried looks and concerned eyes . . . that did not come. And something in that . . . in not being tiptoed about the way Ryker, the servants, and her father had, lifted a weight from her shoulders. "I hope you do not mind. My husband is visiting with your father, and I thought I was long overdue for a visit," she explained, as she came forward. Penelope's path toward the indicated ivory sofa was interrupted, and she stopped.

Diana followed her stare to the objects commanding her attention.

"May I?" Penelope asked, motioning to the collection of canvases.

Diana gave a hesitant nod. Other than Niall and the servants who saw to the cleaning of this room, no one but former art instructors had been privy to her work. There was something humbling in having those paintings exposed. Work that served as a window into Diana's limited experiences and her future dreams.

"You're quite good," Penelope said, studying the sketch of St. Giles. At Diana's murmured thanks, her sister-in-law cast a brief look over her shoulder back at Diana and then returned her focus to that painting. "I'm not merely being polite," she said with a bluntness that raised Diana's first smile in two days. "My sister-in-law, the Countess of Sinclair, is quite a gifted artist. She was my former governess and instilled an appreciation for art. Though my sisters and I were dreadful studies and hardly comparable to Juliet's work. After her influence, I've always *enjoyed* sketching, but I do not have anywhere near your talent."

Diana had stolen but a handful of nonconsecutive hours of sleep. Even if she hadn't, however, she strongly suspected Penelope Black's chattering would have had this same, dizzying effect.

Lady Penelope continued strolling deeper into the room and lingered before a rainy day captured in an empty Hyde Park. With unabashed curiosity, she leaned forward and peered at the painting.

"Would you care for refreshments?" Diana squeaked, desperate to divert her attention from Niall and Diana together, frozen in that image.

Whipping around, Penelope shook her head. "No. Thank you."

Diana was assailed with relief as the other woman joined her in the previously indicated chairs.

They sat in protracted silence, and Diana considered the lovely woman her brother had married. There was an inherent goodness in her, absent in so many of the peerage. And yet, Diana must have a black mark on her soul for staring at her in secret envy for knowing how Niall had been these two days. For knowing just how Niall had spent these past two days when Diana herself could only hazard a guess.

"How is he?" she asked softly. As soon as the question left her, Diana's cheeks flamed hot. "They," she hurried to correct. "How are Mr. Marksman and Mr. Thorne?"

Penelope cast a look over at that painting of Hyde Park, and this time when she returned her focus to Diana's eyes, there was a woman's knowing. "He is well," she offered with an uncharacteristic solemnity. "He was briefly questioned by the constable over the events, and he's since been—" Busy with his club.

Pain lanced her heart, as real as if Penelope had spoken those words aloud.

She welcomed the diversion as a maid entered, bearing a tray of pastries and a pot of tea. The girl set it down, dipped a curtsy, and then took her leave. "Would you care for a cup?" she offered, studiously avoiding the young viscountess's eyes.

"Please." As Penelope accepted the proffered cup, she continued speaking. "My mother often said a cup of English tea would cure any of the world's woes." A hint of mischievousness underscored her next conspiratorial whisper. "Of course, she failed to credit that the tea, in fact, comes from India."

Pouring a second cup for herself, Diana stared down into its tepid contents. How singularly odd. To go from being abducted from a carriage and held with a knife to her throat, and then eventually rescued by Niall and Adair—to sitting here conversing about tea, over tea.

"Some months back," the other woman said suddenly, "when I married Ryker, I moved into the Hell and Sin. Niall could not have been angrier at my presence there."

Thoughts slid in of Niall as he'd first been. Hot-headed. Derisive. Filled with loathing. Yes, knowing him as she did, Niall would have been anything but pleased in having his empire invaded. By a lady of the peerage, no less.

"I was determined that he would like me," Penelope went on. "After I'd been stabbed, he bound me, carried me through the streets of London and back home. From then on, he saw me as a sister." Her eyes twinkled. "Albeit, one he still kept his guard up around."

"Having saved his life, you would only ever have Niall's respect and loyalty," Diana said quietly. He would honor that brave act with his allegiance and friendship.

"Yes," Penelope concurred. She scooted to the edge of the chair and leaned forward. "He has asked about you." That admission brought Diana's eyebrows shooting up.

"D-did he?" What had he said? Had his merely been polite inquiries?

"He did," Penelope confirmed with a nod. "Both times my husband returned from meeting with your father. Niall rushed him with questions. 'And, Diana?'"

Diana lifted her head in silent question.

"Niall doesn't ask about anyone. Not even his own siblings. But you . . ." She smiled gently. "He has. Numerous times."

Her fingers curled involuntarily in the fabric of her skirts, and to give those digits something to do, she picked up her cup. "You make more of it than it is," she said softly, not pretending to misunderstand the other woman's meaning.

"Perhaps," Penelope acknowledged. "But I do not believe so."

Heavy footsteps from outside the parlor saved Diana from replying.

Her father cleared his throat, and the two ladies both stood. "Lady Chatham," he greeted with the formality befitting two strangers meeting, and not a young woman and her father-in-law.

Except, this was what Diana's father had become. Because of his inability to see past that ancient title, he'd lost so much with Ryker, Helena, and their families. It was whom he'd been thirty-two years ago, when he'd chosen another over his true love. And it was whom he still was now, with his daughter.

"Lord Wilkinson," Penelope greeted. "I expect my husband is waiting for me." She gathered Diana's hands in her own and gave a light squeeze. With that, she was gone, leaving Diana and her father alone.

All her life she'd believed her father so very different from her mother. He'd been smiling where she'd been severe. He'd been kindly toward his servants, where the duchess couldn't even be bothered to look at them. But in so many ways, they were the same. In ways that could never be good.

Her father looped his thumbs inside the front of his breeches and rocked on his heels. "Your brother came to speak with me."

"He has been devoted," she acknowledged. When he'd every reason to hate Diana. When he could have blamed her for her mother's role in his and Helena's disappearance, he hadn't. He'd offered her help, taking her at nothing more than her word.

"He is a good boy," he said, his blue eyes glassing over with a sheen of tears. Then, seeming to remember himself, he pulled the door closed and came over. Gesturing for her to sit, he settled his rotund frame in the chair previously occupied by the viscountess. "We spoke at length about your . . . desire to leave." Her father paused. "Given everything that has happened, it would be, he believes . . ." The muscles of his face contorted in a paroxysm of pain. "We believe it would be in your best interest to put London behind you. For now, at least."

Her lips parted, and she tried to get words out. What was he saying?

"I am saying I'll turn over your funds as you requested. If going will make you happy and free you from . . ." He waved his hand. "From everything that has happened with your mother and my neglect and what transpired these past weeks, then I want you to go. For you."

He'd offered her everything she'd wanted for more than a year. The opportunity to control her funds and explore those worlds she'd only read about in pages. To go off and paint and discover if St. George's was, in fact, a land of pink sand and cerulean waters. "Thank you, Papa," she said softly.

He gave a juddering nod. "In the carriage, I was . . . wrong about Mr. Marksman. It was unpardonable to suggest he was less worthy of you because of his birthright." Her father heaved a great sigh. "After you were abducted and I came to, I raced not to any of those proper gents I've called friends over the years." Men who'd failed to come around after his wife's scandal. Diana let that go unspoken. He'd been hurt enough. Even with his failings, she'd not have him suffer. "The only people I trusted to help see you returned were Ryker and his brothers." Her father gave her a long, agonized look. "As I was racing to them, I thought about you as you'd been as a girl. You were always so *happy*, Diana." His voice broke, and tears filled her eyes. "Your smile, it dimpled your cheeks and lit your eyes." It had been his smile. "And I haven't seen it for nearly a year. I was too selfish to think about that until you were gone. Then all I could think about was how if you were safe, I'd want nothing more in life than your own happiness," he said, on a sob that shook his shoulders. "And I didn't care if it was Mr. Marksman or your journey to St. Georges. But I would give it to you."

Tears fell freely down Diana's cheeks, and she let them roll unchecked. "Oh, Papa," she whispered, going to him. She wrapped her arms around him as he wept. His arms automatically came up about her.

"I am so s-sorry," he said between his great gasping tears. "I am so sorry for not having been there. For failing you and your mother before. For—"

"Shh," she whispered, holding him tight, the way she had as a young girl who'd scraped her knees and sought comfort in this same embrace. "I forgive you."

And at long last, a calming peace stole through her.

He'd given her nearly everything she'd wished for.

But even her father could not give her what she yearned for most—Niall Marksman's heart.

Arms clasped at his back, Niall assessed the crowded floors of the Hell and Sin.

The tables were overflowing with guests, tossing down fat purses. The clink of crystal touching crystal as spirits flowed freely.

He'd been gone five weeks and back but one day, and yet nothing had changed. It had all continued on as though he'd never left.

Niall's gaze touched on the Earl of Maxwell, sipping brandy at his private table. And Niall recalled the damned ball when the young lord had his hand on Diana's waist as they'd danced. Would he be the man to court her? Woo her? Win her? He briefly closed his eyes.

Everything had changed.

"It feels good, doesn't it?"

Distracted from his musings, he looked over at Adair. He had the easy look of a man relieved to be out of Mayfair and inserted in St. Giles once more.

"Being back," the other man clarified, gesturing to the floor. Adair rolled his shoulders. "The sounds of this place. The smell of it. It's home."

Home. Niall rolled that word through his mind. Odd. This place had over the years represented security and stability, but never had he looked at it as a home. *Home* was a word better suited for a fiction book, for a place where families dwelled and laughed and built memories. Whereas the Hell and Sin had never truly been that. Not to Niall.

Shouts went up at the center of the club, and they looked as one to the roulette table, both poised and versed on the peril in any unexpected sounds. Several gentlemen slapped a lucky winner on the back and motioned over a serving girl for celebratory drinks.

Some of the tension went out of Niall.

Yes, all here was the same as it had always been. Day over day, minute to minute, the same in every way. That sameness had provided his security . . . but prevented him from truly living.

You've lived in your club for so long, you're afraid to step outside that world. You can go anywhere, and yet you choose not to.

Niall looked out once more at his club. Calum stood conversing with a dealer at the faro table. Young women moved between tables, poured drinks, and continued on. It was familiar. It was safe. Just like he preferred his life, after breaking free of Diggory's hold. He passed a wistful once-more gaze over this great club, built with the blood, sweat, and turmoil of a London street tough. "No problems here," he murmured to himself.

"There hasn't been in the two days since *her* visit," Adair acknowledged.

Cleo Killoran. That small slip of a woman who'd single-handedly led Niall to Diana and unraveled the sinister plot against her and Niall's own club. For that, Cleo Killoran and every last person she called kin would have Niall's unswerving loyalty. Killoran's younger sister had also managed the seemingly impossible—orchestrating a peace between the rival establishments.

Lord Maxwell shoved to his feet and, glass in hand, strolled through the club. From his elegant dress and unscarred visage down to the rank bequeathed him by some king of old, he was everything Niall would never be. Once that had grated. No longer. "There won't be any more problems," Niall predicted, following the earl's lazy movements and then dismissing him. "Not ones brought by Killoran." It didn't mean Killoran wouldn't continue to curry the favors and memberships of their patrons. But Niall would wager his life that the sabotage had been effectively ended with the deal struck between their families.

Adair grunted. "Time will tell."

Niall had once been that same jaded cynic. Until Diana. His heart lurched, aching with the need to again see her. "Ya'll excuse me?" he said quietly.

Adair flared his blond eyebrows. "Of course."

Yes, because in their well-ordered world, Niall never did something as outrageous as turn his shift over to anyone . . . Calum, Ryker, or Adair included. With a final look about the club, Niall nodded his thanks. He wound his way through the crowded club. Patrons scurried out of his path, avoiding his eyes and presence altogether.

That fear shown around him had only been exacerbated since word of Diana's abduction, and Niall's murder of the brute who'd held her had circulated in every last gossip column.

It was one kill, however—God willing, a final one—he'd never regret. Niall reached the back of the club and nearly collided with Calum. "Ryker wants a meeting."

No one ever wished to be summoned to Ryker Black's office. It inevitably resulted in demotions and vanquished posts. Once that call would have sent Niall's hackles up. No longer. Niall nodded and made to step around him, but Calum shot a hand out. He clasped his forearm and gave a slight squeeze. "It is good having you back."

His throat squeezed, making words impossible. He mustered a smile that felt more of a mangled grimace than anything. Then Calum marched off. Niall stood there for a long moment with the club's near-deafening din filling his ears. He cast another glance back, lingering his gaze on where Adair and Calum now spoke. With a small smile, he took his leave of the floors and made the familiar climb abovestairs to the private suites.

He reached Ryker's office and stopped. There was an odd air of finality that hung in the space. *You do not have to do this.* Niall thumped his fist hard on the door panel.

"Enter." Ryker's booming response carried through the heavy oak.

Niall pressed the handle and stepped inside to another familiar sight: Ryker behind his desk, poring through one of many leather ledgers. He picked up his head. "Niall," he greeted, shoving the book aside. It was their first real meeting since Niall had returned from Mayfair.

Niall closed the door behind him and entered. As he strode over to the wingback chair positioned before Ryker's tidy mahogany desk, he took in the touches made to this sacred space by Ryker's wife. Prior to his banishment from the club, he'd viewed the material changes with derision. A mark of Ryker's weakness for not only his wife but of the structure of this establishment itself. Now he saw the vases brimming with flowers as a mark of the happiness Penelope had brought.

Ryker motioned to the chair. "I understand you are through with your end of the investigation." This is why he'd been summoned.

"Yes," Niall confirmed. The questions put to him and Adair about the fate of two London street roughs had been few, and the investigation quick. "Our reports were sufficient." Then, to Society, the deaths of men such as Niall and those who'd dwelled in Diggory's hovel at some point in their lives didn't much signify. He'd believed that was how all the world viewed him and his family. Diana had proven the error there.

Ryker rolled his shoulders. "I spoke to them, as did the duke. They'll not bother you." He flashed a grin. "Wilkinson and I have ensured you're free to work, without further distractions."

Wilkinson. Niall had never given much thought to the strained, nonexistent relationship Ryker had with his father. Had Niall been born to such a man, would he have clung to that hatred and resentment? Now, having his eyes opened to the shades of gray in life, he was not so sure.

His brother folded his arms at his chest and stared at him with assessing eyes. "Are you . . ." He grimaced. Yes, regardless of how Niall and Ryker may have been altered by the influence of good women, they'd never be men at ease talking about one's feelings or emotions. "Troubled by your role—"

"No," he interjected swiftly and truthfully. "I've no regrets." And he didn't. Not when the result had been Diana's survival.

Ryker drummed his fingertips along his black coat sleeves. "According to the investigators, they hauled off five men who did Amelie's work." He paused midtap. "We were all wrong about Oswyn."

Niall gave another distracted nod.

Standing, Ryker stalked over to the sideboard and poured a brandy. He turned and held up the glass, but Niall waved it off.

"I did not properly thank you," Ryker said when he'd returned to his seat, "for saving my sister." He leaned back in his chair and cradled the crystal snifter between his fingers.

"I don't want your damned thanks," Niall snapped, and his neck instantly heated. Diana had initially been an obligation. An unwanted assignment.

Hooding his lashes, Ryker eyed him. "You are adjusting to being back?" he asked, the meaning clear—something was not right with him.

Niall gave a slight nod, and then, restless, he continued to skim his gaze around the room. *You've lived in your club for so long, you're afraid to step outside that world. You can go anywhere, and yet you choose not to.*

Diana's whisper-soft words echoed around his memory as real as when she'd spoken them. Days ago. A lifetime?

Clearing his throat, he reached inside the front of his jacket and pulled out several folded sheets. He handed them over to Ryker, who took them.

"You need a new vetting process for the guards we've hired," he began, as Ryker opened and skimmed the first page. "Simply hiring men who lived on the streets because we ourselves came from there is no longer enough. You need to be discriminatory in the process."

Ryker slowly worked his eyes over the first page, lingering his stare on the words.

"That's a new schedule for the guards," he said as Ryker moved on to the next sheet. "We've expected them to go without rest. It was cost-effective but also wrong to the men here. You'll also need to question those closest with Oswyn. Find out what they knew. If anything." Most men would have been staggered by that betrayal. Niall and Ryker, however, had been born to the streets. "Men from the Dials can withhold from a constable. We can read them differently."

His brother folded those pages and laid them in a neat stack before him.

You've lived in your club for so long, you're afraid to step outside that world.

Niall drew in a breath and let it out slowly. "Adair needs to oversee security."

Ryker's shoulders went taut, and he leveled his gaze on Niall's face. "Surely you don't still doubt yourself? My sister is alive because of you. You thwarted two attempts, and there is no one I trust more, Niall." He held his stare. "No one." Given that Calum had been Ryker's right-hand man since they'd all found one another, Ryker's words were a testament to his faith.

Niall layered his palms along the side of his chair. "I know that." Again, he studiously avoided Ryker's eyes. In the weeks he'd been away, he'd divorced himself from Ryker's connection to Diana. Thrust back into the club and into his presence, he was forced to confront what he'd done—he'd not only bedded his sister but had also fallen in love with her.

"You're avoiding my eyes, Niall." Ryker spoke in his probing, gravelly tones. "You never avoid anyone's."

A man did when he was in the wrong, and there could be no mistaking. Niall was in the wrong. "I am in love with your sister," he spoke so quickly.

Flummoxed, Ryker fell back in his chair. And had this been any other exchange and the topic someone or something other than Diana Verney, Niall would have hooted with a newly discovered laughter at the shocked-silent Ryker Black.

"You don't like the nobility," his brother finally said into the silence.

"No. I don't. I didn't," he swiftly amended. "Thought they were all the same." He drew in a ragged breath and, glancing about, raked a hand through his tousled hair. "Diana, she's different, though." She'd shown him that station and birthright didn't define a person's worth or character.

Ryker's midnight brows dipped. Did he disapprove? He should. Any worthy, decent brother worth his salt on earth would take umbrage with a man like Niall falling in love with his sister. Niall fished another page from inside his jacket and slid it across the desk. "This is why I'm here," he confirmed in solemn tones.

Ryker briefly dipped his gaze to the handful of lines, and given what they signified and represented, Niall should feel something. Regret. Sadness. Fear. And yet . . . he felt none of that. Instead he felt this great, hopeful lightness in his chest. "What is this?"

He jerked his chin at it. "It's my resignation."

His brother's frown deepened, and he shoved the page back. "I'm not accepting your resignation." It was the hard-edged tone that had earned him rank of leader among his small gang in the streets.

"I'm not asking for permission. I need to do this." He shook his head. "I want to," he corrected. And again, there was no fear. "If she'll have me." *If I didn't bungle it so badly three days ago when I put this club before a life together.* "I'm marrying her." Niall jutted out his chin.

Ryker froze with the drink halfway to his mouth.

"I'm marrying her," Niall repeated. If she'd have him. "I love her."

The other man, this friend who'd rescued him from inevitable death and further darkness, set aside his glass, saying nothing. Meeting him with a heavy silence.

Then: "You love her."

Filled with a restive energy, Niall jumped up and began to pace. "I wasn't supposed to want, need, or love anyone." Even with his brothers and sister, he'd built up walls to keep them out. Diana had kicked every single flimsy defense down. "She makes me laugh and makes me want to be a better man."

"You are a good man, Niall," Ryker somberly put in. "Only you failed to see it."

He jerked to a stop and looked at his brother with keen eyes. "You knew."

The ghost of a smile hovered on Ryker's lips. "Initially I believed you were too damned stubborn to concede the post to Calum, but after Maxwell's visit?" He chuckled. "Yes, well, I gathered you cared." His smile faded. "I just didn't know if you would be able to see that in time."

In time? Niall furrowed his brow.

"Her ship departs today." Ryker picked up a folded missive stamped with the duke's seal and tossed it across the desk. It landed noiselessly on the edge. "This arrived from Wilkinson. Apparently Stone was forced to sail this afternoon."

All the air lodged in Niall's lungs, and he grabbed that offending note. *No.* That ship she'd been planning on boarding wasn't to leave until—

"The duke thought you should know and sent around word. Asked me to see that you know. Should it matter."

The earth resumed spiraling in a frantic whir. "Should it matter?" he bellowed. He stalked over to the desk and, leaning over it, dragged his brother to his feet. "Why did you wait to tell me?" he rasped, panic knocking away in his chest. *Why did you wait to go to her?*

"Would you rather remain and argue me on my timing of sharing the important information?" Ryker glanced over at the longcase clock. "Or would you rather get to the docks before she boards her ship?"

Letting loose a volley of curses, Niall abruptly released him. What in blazes did a man need to travel? He'd never stepped foot outside the London city limits. One hour. He had sixty minutes before her ship sailed off. Nothing. He'd no time to gather anything. Not if he wanted to board that ship with her. His pulse racing, Niall sprinted over to the door and wrenched it open.

He crashed into his sister-in-law, who grunted and stumbled back, catching herself against the wall. The burden in her hands toppled to the floor. "Niall," she said with her effervescent, always-present smile.

"Penny," he mumbled and raced around her.

"I believe you'll need this," she called when he reached the end of the hall.

He spun back.

Penelope held a valise aloft. "Most people travel with trunks and valises, but this will have to do." She beamed.

Emotion balled in his throat, momentarily choking him as he rushed back to collect the—he squinted—*floral* valise?

"It is floral," she confirmed. "But no one other than me has traveled," she prattled. Calum and Adair stood at the opposite end of the hall behind Penny. Niall took in this ragtag group of people he called family. People who'd apparently known him better than he knew himself. "Thank you," he said hoarsely. "I—"

Penelope leaned up on tiptoe and kissed his cheek. "This isn't forever. After your grand travels, you'll of course return with Diana." He blinked, as befuddled as he'd always been by her ramblings. "I don't expect to be the only lady inside this club, forever."

"Penelope," Ryker said firmly.

She widened her eyes. "Yes, right. Right." Gathering his spare hand between her palms, she squeezed. "Go to her. Quite unromantic if you miss her and she sails off without you."

Oh, God. The reality of time reared its head.

"Your mount is readied," Calum called. "I'll follow and collect Chance. You haven't much time if you intend to board the same ship as the lady."

Board the ship with his lady.

If she'd have him.

Grinning, Niall bolted down the hall.

"Marry her," Penelope yelled after him. "You have to marry her first."

He intended to.

Moments later Niall was guiding Chance through the busy streets of St. Giles, with Calum riding close behind. What if he was late? Why in blazes had they waited to tell him?

It's your damned fault, you fool. He'd been busy putting everything to rights, when he should have gone to her first and given her the words of love she deserved.

He steeled his jaw. Nothing would stop him from getting to her now. Nothing—

Chance let loose a violent whinny and came up hard on his right hoof.

Christ.

The loyal beast snorted, and, heart sinking, Niall swung his leg over and dismounted. He led the stallion over to the edge of the busied roads. This horse had been with him from the moment he'd purchased the Hell and Sin. Sinking to his haunches, he ran his palm over the leg.

Chance tossed his head violently, and Niall stood. "Shh," Niall urged. He took Chance's midnight-black face between his hands and stroked his palm down the middle of his eyes, scratching that place he loved.

"I'll take care of him," Calum promised, trading the reins of his mount for Niall's. "I'll have someone come and collect him," he promised. "Find someone at the wharf, but you need to go," he said quietly. "Now."

That curt reminder snapped Niall into movement. Climbing astride Calum's horse, he leaned over his shoulders and raced on. He wound his way through the throngs of carriages and people. Ignoring the furious calls he left in his wake. The summer wind slapped at his face, a soothing balm against the terror in his chest. *Be there . . . be there . . .*

After an interminable ride, Niall jerked on the reins of his mount, bringing him to an abrupt stop. The creature pawed and scratched at the air and then settled its hooves on the ground. He searched frantically and found a small street urchin. "You," he called, as he jumped down. The boy rushed forward. "There is a man coming to claim this mount. See that you care for him." He handed him a sack of coin that rounded out the boy's eyes.

Abandoning his valise, Niall sprinted through the wharves, searching his gaze about at the ships. With their white sails whipping in the summer wind, they stood out majestic. Frantic, he continued running. He grabbed the arm of a nearby sailor, startling a gasp from the man. "*His Lady's Honor*," he demanded, panting from his exertions.

The man shook his head and wrenched free.

Niall continued his frantic search, grabbing the arms of other passing strangers.

"*His Lady's Honor?*" a young, golden-curled street tough repeated. "She's there . . ." Niall followed his gesture, and his heart sank. *No.*

Relinquishing the other man so quickly he fell back, yelling. Panting from his exertions, Niall bolted to the end of the dock. "Diana," he bellowed. "Diana." It was all he could manage. One word. Her name. He reached the end as her ship continued its slow pull away from the Thames. "Diana," he cried, and merchants and sailors bustling about took a wide berth around him.

Breathless, he collapsed with his hands atop his knees. He sucked in great, heaving gasps of air, drawing it into his burning lungs. He welcomed the agony, embraced it. She was gone. He'd been too late. *You fool. You goddamned fool . . .*

"Diana," he cried out once more.

"Yes, Niall."

He spun around as all the sounds of the wharves faded to a distant hum in his ears. He'd imagined those two words and yet . . . he stared unblinking at the small cloaked figure ten paces away. "Diana," he whispered.

She drifted over, her soft green cloak catching in the breeze as she walked. She stopped before him.

"You didn't go," he whispered.

"No," she said softly, as another gentle gust yanked several curls from her neat chignon.

With fingers that shook, he brushed those strands back. "What I said . . . it wasn't . . ." He tried again. "What I said to Amelie, I didn't mean . . . ," he said hoarsely. "It was . . . I was trying—"

Diana pressed her fingertips to his lips, silencing him. "I know, Niall."

"Oi was putting things in order so Oi could come with you." His words spilled over one another. "And then your damned ship changed its departure date and my horse came up lame and . . ." His throat worked spasmodically. "Oi thought ya left," he said raggedly, pressing his eyes closed, still not sure he'd not merely conjured her of his own yearnings. He tossed a look back at that ship, sailing off into the distance, becoming a smaller and smaller fleck upon the horizon. "Oi thought Oi'd missed ya."

Diana palmed his cheek, forcing his eyes to hers. "I was going," she said softly. "But then I realized."

Emotion balled in his throat. "Realized?"

"I wanted to see the cerulean blue water and the pink sand and the world outside London." She lifted an aching gaze to his. So much love poured from their depths, his chest tightened. "But I want you at my side when I do. I was coming back for you. To try and convince you. To try and—" He covered her mouth with his, claiming her lips in a tender meeting, willing her to feel all the love he had for her.

"I want to be with you," he said hoarsely, dropping his brow to hers. "I want to go and travel and not be afraid anymore. And when I'm with you, you make me not afraid." Once he would have been ashamed and horrified to think those words, let alone breathe them aloud. "You showed me that love is stronger than hate and . . . I love you, Diana. My heart is and always will belong to you."

Her lips quivered in a smile. "I love you, Niall Marksman." She threaded her fingers through his. "Let us go explore the world together."

A lightness suffused his chest and spread slowly through his being. *I am home.*

Acknowledgments

Back when I wrote my first book, *Forever Betrothed, Never the Bride*, the Hell and Sin Club spoke to me. I imagined heroes and heroines living on the fringe of society and their lives colliding with the nobility. Over the years, the Sinful Brides series continued to speak to me.

Last March, Alison Dasho and the entire team at Montlake Romance allowed me to bring that series to life. To my editors, cover designer, and marketing team, thank you for making the Sinful Brides possible. And more, thank you for all your wonderful support! I'm so very honored to be part of the Montlake family!

About the Author

USA Today bestselling author Christi Caldwell blames Julie Garwood and Judith McNaught for luring her into the world of historical romance. When Christi was sitting in her graduate school apartment at the University of Connecticut, she began writing her own tales of love. Christi believes even the most perfect heroes and heroines have imperfections. Besides, she rather enjoys torturing them—before the couple earn their well-deserved happily ever after. Christi makes her home in southern Connecticut, where she spends her time writing, chasing after her courageous son, and caring for her twin princesses-in-training. For free bonus material and the latest information about Christi's releases and future books, sign up for her newsletter at www.ChristiCaldwell.com.